WAIT FOR IT

SHANNON MYERS

First Printing: 2020

Paperback ISBN- 978-1-7332748-7-6

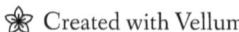 Created with Vellum

ALSO BY SHANNON MYERS

From This Day Forward Duet

(David & Elizabeth's Story)

From This Day Forward

Forsaking All Others

Standalone Novels

(*Travis & Katya's Story*)

You Save Me

Operation Series

(*Dakota & Zane's Story*)

Operation Fit-ish

(*Kate and Nate's Story*)

Operation Annulment

Silent Phoenix MC Series

(*Grey & Celia's Story*)

Deserter (Book One)

Protector (Book Two)

(*Mike & Lauren's Story*)

Renegade (Book Three)

Traitor (Book Four)

(*Full Cast*)

Savior (Book Five)

Fairest Series (Can be read as standalones)

(Charm & Neve's Story)

Through The Woods

(Killian and Ari's Story)

Wait For It

Fictioned Series

(Hayden & Jake's Story)

Protagonized

For those who broke above the surface—the ones who sucked in grateful breaths of air through newly formed lungs, all the while knowing that there is truly nothing sweeter than freedom.

We survived.

AUTHOR'S NOTE

On Saturday, March 16, 2019, I received a phone call that rocked my entire world. When I saw my brother-in-law's name flashing across the screen, I initially assumed that he'd pocket-dialed me. It was four-fifteen in the morning, after all.

I would later learn that when a person calls enough times within a short period of time, it will override the 'Do Not Disturb' feature on the phone.

"Shannon..."

His voice broke, and I immediately asked, "What happened?"

It took him several tries to get his breathing under control enough for me to understand that my sister had been involved in an ATV accident and was being life-flighted to Denver.

Even now, if I close my eyes, I can still hear the fear in his words.

Tremors overtook my body, quickly followed by uncontrollable sobbing as I tried to process the news. I had this naïve hope that she'd sit up in the helicopter and demand to be taken home, adamant that there'd been some mistake.

You see, never in a million years did I think anything could shake us. We'd already overcome so much in the eighteen months prior to the accident, forcing ourselves to confront and work through the messy parts of our relationship.

I'd gotten comfortable.

Complacent.

Convinced that we'd become invincible.

I didn't know it then, but she'd be in a coma for two weeks. It seems like such a short period of time now, but those fourteen days felt like months. I would sit in my office at night, unable to sleep because I was convinced I might miss an update from my brother-in-law.

My stomach was in knots from the first phone call until she woke up. The nurses would call her a medical anomaly because someone whose brain had shifted fifteen millimeters off the midline typically didn't wake up. They lay in surgical ICU until eventually, they ceased to exist.

The first time I saw her, she'd been off the ventilator for about a week, but had undergone a tracheostomy to help with her breathing. As I looked past the various tubes and wires, I struggled to find traces of the woman who'd been my best friend since I was two and a half.

She was awake, but not.

Physically she was right in front of me, but it felt as if she was a million miles away.

We were encouraged to write in a notebook and to offer her the pen to communicate. It was rare that we called each other by our actual names. Some days, she was *Meza* and I was *Uza*, Russian sisters who enjoyed a good bottle of vodka. Other times, we'd simplify things and just refer to one another as *Seester.*

And don't even get me started on the conversations where we poorly attempted to nail a British accent while quoting from our favorite movie, *Bridget Jones's Diary.*

Keeping with tradition, I took the pen, and wrote:

Seester, I love you!

I didn't expect much, if anything. She shocked me when she took the pen and immediately replied:

I've loved you as well :)

It was the sign I'd waited for, the proof I'd needed that she was still in there.

As she became more alert, the hospital said they were going to be releasing her to *Craig Hospital*, the absolute best place for brain and spinal cord injuries.

My brother-in-law showed me the brochures and I jokingly said it reminded me of a book I'd tried to write in 2018 but had never completed.

He asked me about it, and I explained the premise as a twist on *The Little Mermaid*, with a woman recovering from a multitude of injuries she sustained in a car accident and a baseball player with a blown-out knee. They meet in a rehab facility and—well, I don't want to spoil anything for you.

I told him how I'd gotten stuck and had left it unfinished to work on other projects. We went on to other things, but when he was taking me to the airport later that afternoon, he brought it up again.

"What if the reason you couldn't finish the story before was because you were supposed to tell your sister's story? What if that story and hers are one and the same?"

With his blessing, I agreed to tell a fictionalized version of my sister's accident and during my second trip up, I was able to see first-hand what an average day is like for those recovering from a brain injury.

I consulted informally with the nurses and therapists and took copious amounts of notes, building the world you're about to enter.

In November, I was able to visit with the author, Laura Kaye after hearing her speak. As she'd also survived a brain injury, I was eager to get her thoughts on recovery. Instead, I was given something even better—a reminder to give grace. Just as I'm not the same woman I was a year ago, I hadn't realized how unfair it was to expect my sister to be the same as she was before the accident.

Thank you, Laura.

As for *Through The Water,* the details are written as I remember them occurring, with the exception of a few artistic liberties I took here and there to better fit the story.

For example, *Craig* is strictly a rehabilitation hospital for those with brain or spinal cord injuries. You wouldn't find an attractive baseball player recovering from knee surgery there, but you just might at *True North.* Although, I will add that "Restaurant Night" is an actual event, meant to help patients practice ordering food, self-feeding, and socializing with one another.

In the book, Ariana is unable to speak when she arrives at the rehab facility. In reality, Shayla was speaking by the time she left the hospital to transfer to *Craig.* Just like Ariana, it was very soft at first and you had to strain to make out what she was trying to communicate. By the time I arrived three weeks later, the raspiness had faded and her voice was growing stronger.

This is a deeply personal story to me and my family. There were days I questioned even telling it at all; but in the end, I felt that it was important to give these characters a voice.

I've tried to approach this subject with the utmost respect and reverence for everyone involved. Please know that any mistakes are mine, and mine alone.

My sister's progress to date is nothing short of a miracle. She's home with her family and is gradually rediscovering her passions, as well as picking up a few new ones. Just like Ari, she clawed her way to the surface and fought to make it back to shore.

Because that is what she is.

A fighter.

———

For more information on *Craig Hospital*, or to make a donation, click here.

"*Kill the prince and come back; hasten: do you not see the first red streaks in the sky? In a few minutes the sun will rise, and you must die.*"

The Little Mermaid
-Hans Christian Andersen

PROLOGUE
ARIANA, AGE 9

"Burdens are for shoulders strong enough to carry them."

-Margaret Mitchell, *Gone with the Wind*

THE SCREEN DOOR slammed shut behind me with a reverberating bang, but I kept running. I couldn't take another second inside that house.

It had been my turn to sit and read to Mama.

Usually, she stared blankly at the wall with a thin line of drool running down her cheek. Every now and then, her eyes would seemingly dance around the room, focusing on my face for a brief second before bouncing off to something else. Grandmother once told me that they were just filled with the joy of God's love, but Mama never seemed happy when her eyes were like that.

She would cry out and speak to people who weren't there. It used to frighten me until I discovered she was sick.

I wasn't supposed to have heard, but I was really good at hiding and just as quiet as a little church mouse. Most of the time, people didn't even realize I was in the room.

Papa had told Mama she was sick with sin and begged her to

repent, but she'd just laid there, moaning loudly. I wasn't sure how the sin had gotten to her when she never left her bed, but if Papa saw it in her, then it must have been true.

Once he left, she'd cried until the pillowcase beneath her head was soaked with tears before calling out for me and my sisters. Her voice was soft like mine, though, so no one ever came.

The July air was thick with humidity, and without even a hint of a breeze to cool things down, it was like running straight into an oven. My gray linen dress clung to my skin, and each inhale felt like I was trying to breathe underwater.

I ran until I reached the hedges lining the perimeter of our small gated community before dropping to my knees with a wince. Sharp leaves and twigs scraped along the exposed skin on my arms and legs, compressing the old and new bruises lining my sides. Still, I took a deep breath and pushed forward until I was completely hidden from view.

It was the only place I knew I wouldn't be found. At times, the house felt like a living, breathing thing peering over my shoulder. Like it was studying my every move in anticipation.

Out here, it was silent.

A sanctuary.

And right now, I wanted to stay hidden forever.

Mama hadn't stayed quiet today.

I hadn't even gotten through the first chapter before she reached out and grabbed my arm, knocking the book to the hardwood floor. Her grip had been surprisingly firm as she'd yanked me off the chair and into the bed beside her. The sheets were damp with sweat and stunk of sick. Mama's room always smelled different than the others in the house.

She tucked my back to her chest and wrapped her heated body around mine. While I lay stiffly in her arms, I tried to recall whether she'd ever held me before.

Perhaps when I was a baby, but if so, those memories had faded long ago. As far as I could remember, she'd always been like this.

Sick.

"Ari, my little dove," she'd whispered, her breath warm against my ear. "I've been so naïve...about all of it."

I'd tilted my head up and watched as she licked her chapped lips, surprised to find that her eyes were bright and focused for the first time in ages. "M-m-mama?"

"Shhhh... I've got you now. You're safe." The soft cadence of her voice had a mesmerizing effect, lulling my body into a relaxed state.

I'd settled against her with a sigh, feeling her mouth curve up into what might have been a smile against my cheek. That was what had made her next words all the more shocking.

I hadn't been prepared for them.

"He's going to kill me," she'd stated simply. "I'm getting in the way of his dreams. I think... I think that maybe I've always been in the way because I know the truth. There's nothing beyond the wall that doesn't exist here."

I'd sucked in a breath but hadn't said a word. My heart had thumped steadily while my curiosity wrestled with Papa's teachings.

"And I love him... maybe that's my biggest sin," Mama had said, her voice remaining steady and calm. "I'll always love him, Ari. He was so charismatic—I thought we were gonna change the world together."

"Y-y-you—you s-still c-can—"

I hadn't meant to say the words aloud.

"Do you remember when that man came to the gate seeking help? I think you were five—maybe six? He came right in the middle of a tropical storm. The streets were starting to flood, and then, there he was, under one of the lights. You could smell the booze on him from a mile away as he hollered to see Pastor James..." Mama's words had tapered off, and I'd rolled over, expecting to find her asleep again.

Instead, she was mashing her trembling lips together as if to keep from crying. "The man needed help—at the very least, he needed a place to dry out and sober up. Your daddy turned him away and went back inside.

"I waited until everyone disappeared before slipping out to find him. I handed him an old coat and a sack of—goodness, I don't even remember what was in it. I just grabbed whatever I could from the fridge and pantry. Do you know what he said to me?"

"W-w-what?" I'd whispered, far too invested to not hear every last detail. Thoughts of life outside our community made the hair on my arms and neck stand tall, yet sparked my curiosity in ways that no other topic could.

Mama's lips had stretched into a thin smile as she'd brushed the hair back off my forehead. "Told me about how all he wanted to do was get back home to his boy and be a good man. Said he must have prayed the right way to be sent an angel. Do you see what's wrong with that?"

I'd shaken my head, completely puzzled.

"I'm no angel, Ari. But that man mistook my kindness for something otherworldly. And that was when I knew that your daddy didn't want to help people... not really. He wants to lock himself away behind the walls, turning a blind eye to their suffering. No matter what he tells you, we're no better than they are, little dove. We're all the same."

I'd scooted toward the edge of the bed when Mama closed her eyes, only to be tugged right back. She'd crushed my small body to her chest, making it hard to draw a breath. As I didn't know the next time she'd be lucid, I let her hold me just as tightly as she wanted.

"Need you to promise me something, Ari," Mama had whispered urgently before cupping my cheek with her palm. "Promise me that when you're old enough, you'll get out. You and your sisters will run and never come back here."

Whatever hold she had on reality loosened, and she began mumbling nonsense about the house listening in on our conversation before slipping back into a state of silence. Her mouth had gone slack, and the tears she'd cried clung to her lashes as she stared unseeingly toward the wall.

It was as if she were dead. I knew better, but my mind dredged up a ghost story my sister, Ashlynn, had once told me. Behaving like the entirely rational child I was, I'd scooped up my book and bolted from the room faster than a prairie fire with a tailwind.

Perhaps it wasn't how Mama had wanted, but I'd run... right to my hiding spot in the hedges where I was determined to stay until her desperate warning made a lick of sense.

My skin was hot and sticky, and my bladder had suddenly become uncomfortably full. Still, I wasn't stepping one foot inside that house until Papa and my sisters got back.

As the youngest of six girls, I had a tendency to get stuck with the most tedious of tasks. Sister Sarai oversaw the community library but had fallen ill over the past year. When I wasn't reading to Mama, I helped out, sorting through the book donations for appropriate additions.

Papa preferred that we only keep books that reinforced our faith in some way. Otherwise, it was as if we were giving our brains junk food.

Trash in, trash out.

Instead of burning the rejects, as was customary, I hid them in the folds of my dress and smuggled them back to my room. I'd always been a voracious reader, and these books were no exception. I kept them hidden in the wooden slats of the box spring beneath my mattress, devouring the words by the soft glow of my nightlight while the rest of the house slept.

I fell in love with Mr. Darcy alongside Elizabeth, wept with Jane over Mr. Rochester's deceitfulness, and learned about courage and compassion through the eyes of Scout Finch. The one constant in every book was that the world was a flawed, but ultimately beautiful place in which to live.

There's nothing beyond the wall that doesn't exist here.

I freed a particularly worn copy from the bodice of my dress and lay back against the earth with a shake of my head. Grandmother had warned us that we weren't to trust anything Mama said while she was sick, yet here I was, doing just that.

Mama also thinks the house is alive... just like you.

"J-j-just a c-c-coincidence," I said under my breath. "A s-silly little c-c-coincidence."

"Ariana!"

At the sound of Brother Bradley's voice, my shoulders rolled forward, and I dropped my book before tucking myself into a tight ball. Beads of sweat ran down my arms, stinging the cuts left behind from the thick bushes, but I didn't dare move.

For the most part, the church followers left me alone. Not Brother Bradley. It was as though the man had a radar that alerted him to my presence. He always needed me to hug him or sit on his lap, things I'd grown too big for years ago.

I would have preferred to sit with Mama while she stared blankly over being alone in the house with Brother Bradley. He made my skin feel prickly, but he and Papa had been friends since they were children, so I was forced to be polite.

"Come on, sweetheart. Your mama is wondering where you ran off to."

I hurriedly tucked the book back into my dress. Keeping my body close to the wall, I crawled away from the sound of his voice. Had I stayed put, I would never have known the hole existed.

It had clearly been used by animals as they made their way in and out of the neighborhood, yet had somehow remained undiscovered by the security guards.

Grandmother liked to tease me because I was small, but it just meant the hole was the perfect size for me. As I squeezed through, the sleeve of my dress got caught, tearing a small hole in the fabric I'd be forced to explain later.

I stared down at it, my stomach already churning in anticipation. I belched softly, fighting to keep my lunch from coming up onto the sidewalk. "I-I-it was just a l-l-little accident."

My hands began to tremble as Brother Bradley called for me again. I tucked them across my chest and took in my surroundings.

There were several cars parked along the sides of the street, but otherwise, it was deserted. Brother Caleb sat in the guard booth, reading a magazine. His head was down and his feet propped up against the glass, completely unaware I was nearby.

"I-I-it's not as if you're r-run—running away," I muttered. "Y-you're j-just looking, so c-c-c—calm down."

I managed to get the shaking under control after several deep breaths, enough for me to venture away from the wall. Doing my best not to trample across the flower beds, I slipped around the corner.

There was laughter coming from behind a nearby copse of trees. After checking for people, I jogged across a grassy field and crouched beside a chaste tree.

This was a test, plain and simple.

Papa believed it wasn't safe for us to be out in the world. It was the entire reason he'd developed our little gated community.

The walls are in place to keep us safe.

Either he was lying, or Mama and the books were, and I was not going back in until I knew the truth.

I made it to the tree line, confident in my decision, only to freeze in my tracks at the sharp snap of a twig.

Coming out here had been a mistake.

A heat-induced madness.

Papa had warned us the world was full of evil people— people who wouldn't think twice about hurting us to get to him.

And I'd stupidly left behind the safety of the wall to run right into their waiting arms.

I jerked my head wildly to the left and right, hoping to spot the danger before it managed to find me. I could explain away a torn dress, but not a kidnapping. My eyes came to rest on the broken twig beneath my shoe, and I exhaled a shaky breath.

"S-s-see—see? It was you the whole t-t-time. Now, don't you f-feel s-s-silly?"

"N-no... n-not really," I responded with a snort before clapping a hand over my mouth.

Well, if my loud stomping hadn't frightened the evildoers away, the fact I was carrying on a conversation with myself should do the trick.

Another giggle broke free, and I mashed the heel of my hand against my lips, thoroughly amused at the thought of anyone being scared of me.

This time, before taking my next step, I carefully checked for stray twigs and branches. And perhaps I kept a firm grip on the silver cross around my neck until it left indentions on the palm of my hand.

Just in case...

Sweat trailed down my spine, leaving me irritated I couldn't wear loose-fitting clothing like the boys did during the summer months. Each damp trickle set my teeth on edge. Still, I'd come too far to turn back, so I pushed through the low-hanging branches until a large body of water came into view.

Karankawas Lake.

It wasn't as if I hadn't known it was there. The library in the main house overlooked the water, and I'd spent many an afternoon idly watching the colorful blur of boats as they zipped past. Seeing the rippling waves left in their wake wasn't the same as hearing the whir from the motors or breathing in the faint smell of fuel.

Sunlight reflected off the surface of the lake at just the right angle, making it appear as if the water was glowing. Along the shore, young children ran back and forth, shrieking as they splashed lake water at one another. I smiled and resisted the urge to join them before settling back against a large tree trunk with my book. It was the perfect spot.

I could see everything, but no one could see me.

The sun moved across the sky as the hours passed, but I was lost in a world of cotton plantations and southern belles, completely oblivious. Perhaps if I'd been paying more attention, I would have remained ignorant to the ugliness lurking just out of sight.

I initially mistook the sounds of raised voices as my own imagination. Most of the boats were now nothing more than tiny dots of color on the horizon, and the beach—almost deserted.

Almost.

Even from where I sat, it was clear the three boys hadn't come to enjoy the water.

"She was my girlfriend, you son-of-a-bitch!"

I sucked in a breath and flattened my spine against the bark of the tree. The boy who'd spoken turned and glared in my direction. I brought my hand over my mouth, pleading with my body to be silent. An eternity later, he returned his attention to his companions.

A boy with dark hair, who I assumed was the target, stepped forward until his toes were almost even with the angry boy's. He let out a rough bark of laughter as if seeing someone upset amused him. "You want me to believe that Blair was your girlfriend? How much crack did you smoke before you called me down here?"

My nostrils flared from the exertion of keeping my breathing steady, but no one spared a second glance in my direction.

Then, without so much as a warning, the angry boy clenched his hands into fists and punched the smug one square in the jaw. The two began to pummel each other while the third boy stood off to the side, clearly not willing to get involved. He was obviously the intelligent one of the group.

Those who spare the rod of discipline hate their children...

I'd heard Papa say the words more times than I cared to admit, but it was apparent that no one had ever told the dark-haired boy. Rather than making a scene, he needed to take his correction and choose to do better in the future.

Then again, it seemed they enjoyed being hurt.

After landing a particularly rough hit, the dark-haired boy stepped back and ran a hand through his dark hair. He flashed a triumphant grin, seemingly ignoring the river of blood running from his own nose.

The mistake was in not checking behind him. His heel got caught up in a pile of rope someone had left behind, propelling him backward. As he fell, his head caught the edge of an abandoned metal cooler, and he landed against the dock with a sickening thud.

My lips parted in a silent scream when the boy didn't get back up. He lay motionless, arms splayed out at his sides. The other two looked at each other in question, but it was clear the fight was over.

"H-help him," I urged with a whisper, sighing in relief when the angry boy bent to lift his body. Instead of going for help, he dragged him farther onto the dock before unceremoniously dropping him into the water when he reached the end.

My book fell from my lap, forgotten, as I mashed my fist against my lips to keep from screaming.

The smart boy seemed to share my horror. "What the hell, Chris? I said I'd help you fight him, not kill him. Shit, I can't be a part of this!"

Get him out of the water.

It was now close to dusk, and the sunset cast an eerie orange glow over everything, but there was no longer beauty in this place. The two boys took off across the beach in a dead sprint while I watched the end of the dock, hoping the boy would resurface.

"H-h-he's not y-your problem," I reminded myself, the words bitter on my tongue. The theology I'd cut my teeth on had collided with a new reality. If I held fast to my beliefs, I was condemning someone to death. But if I acted on his behalf, then I was betraying my family and my church.

Fear paralyzed my limbs, keeping me pinned up against the tree. I stayed there until the two disappeared from view before making my decision.

"Y-you are S-Scar—Scarlett O'Hara," I hissed. "B-br-bravely f-facing down the Y-Yankees on your way home to T-T-Tara."

And then, with no regard to the teachings or even my own safety, I ran toward the danger. The water cooled my sweat-drenched skin, yet pushed my small body back to shore. I fought my way past the waves before diving under with a growl. The water was murky, and every blue-green shadow looked like a body until I was right on top of it.

Just as I began to lose hope, I saw him, caught under the dock. I looped an arm around his chest and tried tugging him toward the shallows. Instead, his dead weight pushed us toward the bottom, and it took all of my strength to propel us in the right direction. My lungs burned something fierce, urging me to let him go and swim for the surface.

Black spots began to move among the blue-green shadows, but I kept swimming, willing my body to relax. I'd been around water my entire life. There was a pool in the community, as well as a small fishing hole. My sister and I had snuck out more than once to visit them when the heat was unbearable, and sleep refused to come quickly.

Sneaking out of the house after curfew hadn't been easy, but time and time again, Ashlynn and I had gotten past the guards without being seen. She was the one who'd taught me to swim and, later, how to hold my breath for increasingly extended periods.

It was training that had paid off not two weeks ago.

A guard had discovered my nightdress near the fishing hole and begun searching the grounds. Ashlynn had pulled me under as his flashlight skimmed over the water. The minutes had ticked by, and my vision began to blur, but the guard eventually moved on. When the water went dark, we'd kicked our way to the surface, desperately sucking air into our lungs. I'd been forced to sneak back into the house naked as my nightdress had been confiscated, but we'd never been caught.

You can do this.

I relaxed and let the waves I'd fought against moments before carry us lazily toward the shore. Then, using my legs and the last of my energy, I pushed us forward until the sandbar rose up beneath my feet. It was enough for me to propel the upper half of my body above the water with a strangled gasp. After several attempts, I managed to lift the boy's head too.

Exhaustion set in, but I kept pushing forward, dragging the boy onto the beach before collapsing across his chest with a groan. Waves lapped against the shore, punctuated only by the sounds of my ragged breathing.

I'd done everything I could. The rest was up to him.

Just as I began to fear I'd been too late, the boy jerked violently beneath me, coughing up mouthfuls of lake water. I gripped his shirt with both hands and weakly pulled him onto his side just as I'd seen Sister Sarai do once for Mama when she got sick in the bed.

"I've got you now," I panted. "You're safe."

His eyes remained closed, and I hesitated before pressing my fingers to his jaw. A jolt of something electric arced through my body like an errant lightning bolt had been cast down from the heavens.

I'd often felt a heat quietly simmering away within me, but with one touch, it had built to something like a wildfire. The blood left my limbs, redirecting all of its focus to the muscular organ galloping against my breastbone.

Feeling emboldened, I shifted closer, brushing the water droplets from his long dark lashes. He was, without a doubt, the most beautiful thing I'd ever seen. Up close, I realized he wasn't a boy, but something closer to a man. His jawline was dotted with stubble, and my fingers moved down, reverently tracing the outline of it.

"It's time to wake up now," I whispered softly.

As much as I wanted to stay with him, I had to go back. They were bound to be looking for me by now. But first, I needed to ensure he was going to be okay.

His eyelids fluttered at the sound of my voice before he managed to open them, peering up at me in confusion. Against the darkening sky, his blue eyes appeared almost gray. I continued stroking his cheek, enjoying the roughness against my palm.

Like sandpaper against satin.

"Are you good?" I blurted, immediately regretting the question. He was obviously a good person, or God wouldn't have placed me in his path. He would have been left to die under the dock.

Down the beach, a couple of teenage girls were laughing loudly as they jogged across the sand while their dog splashed through the water beside them.

He blinked several times before focusing on my eyes once again. I brushed the damp hair from his forehead, committing his every detail to mind before forcing out a stammered cry for help. Something brushed against the back of my hand, and I looked down, surprised to see his fingers moving delicately over my skin. His brows pulled together, and he frowned as if he hadn't expected me to be real.

Remembering Mama's story, I felt the need to confess, "I'm no angel."

He swallowed and opened his mouth just as the girls made it over. I allowed myself one final look before pulling my hand free and darting back into the trees to grab my book.

My shoes were like damp kitchen sponges beneath my feet, squishing loudly every time they came in contact with the earth. By the time I made it back into the clearing, the sun had dipped below the horizon. Not only had I missed dinner, but storytime as well.

It wasn't until I was squeezing through the hole again that I realized I hadn't gotten my answer as to whether Mama or Papa was right.

And it would be the next day before it dawned on me I hadn't stuttered once when talking to the boy.

CHAPTER ONE
KILLIAN

"You see, you spend a good piece of your life gripping a baseball, and in the end it turns out that it was the other way around all the time."

Jim Bouton, *Ball Four*

IF THERE WAS one thing in life I was sure about, it was baseball. Unlike most everything else, there was no overthinking the fundamentals. It was as simple as throw the ball, hit the ball, and catch the ball.

Had it ended with that, there probably would've been more people walking around with a glove on the one hand and a ball in the other. The game required strategy and skill, though, and that was what made it interesting.

Not everybody could do it.

Sure, they might've known right-handed batters were more successful against left-handed pitchers and vice-versa. Still, the majority of the general population couldn't hit the broad side of a barn.

My mama liked to joke that I was born with a baseball in my hand. My father had played ball in college and spent a few years in the minors before a knee injury ended his career. When I came along, his dreams were revived and placed squarely on my shoulders.

Luckily for him, I had a knack for it.

I was picked up by Houston right out of high school and spent a year with Quad Cities in the Class A league. I'd been cocky even back then. I knew I was better than half the guys in the majors. Unfortunately, it had taken the team a lot longer to catch on, and even then, they'd only moved me to Double-A in Corpus Christi.

When I was twenty, I was brought up to play for the Hurricanes thanks to center fielder, Austin Pineda's injured wrist. I made my debut and snagged my first career Major League hit in the bottom of the fourth. After that infield single, I was convinced they were going to bring me up permanently.

Instead, they sent me back down—not to Double-A. No, I was promoted to Triple-A. It was frustrating—*ESPN* had ranked me number one in the top one hundred prospects. Everyone knew Pineda was done, but Houston hadn't budged. Christ, I'd even been named Minor League Player of the Year but was stuck earning peanuts until my rookie contract ran out.

I'd started the next season in Fresno until, once again, Houston brought me up; this time to replace Tony Mack. He'd been slumping badly at the plate, and it was a huge opportunity for me. From there, I'd recorded my first career four-hit game and was named American League co-player of the week. I began breaking, not only the *Hurricanes'* franchise records, but American League rookie records as well. I even managed to snag the AL Rookie of the Year award.

After that, I was in.

And when this season ended, I fully expected to be smashing some records off-field. With all the free-agent chatter, the Hurricanes were going to have to step up their offer if they wanted to keep me in cobalt blue and white. I was looking forward to watching the bidding war unfold.

"You ready, Red? It's all you, baby!" Chavez slapped my back, and I fought back a grimace before nodding.

He'd been calling me Red since the day we met, said my name reminded him of the Irish beer. I'd almost slipped up and called him *Limp Dick* a couple of times, a lovely term of endearment I'd overheard his wife use when she thought no one was listening.

"Tie it up, and get us into the playoffs, man," Chavez pleaded as he looked up into the stands, no doubt searching for Gabrielle. To my extreme regret, I followed his gaze and found her almost immediately.

I tried looking away, but not before she caught me staring. She winked and ran a hand down her chest as if brushing away invisible crumbs. I rubbed at the back of my neck and avoided making eye contact with Chavez, hoping he hadn't noticed.

As her husband's teammate, I shouldn't have known her tits were as fake as a Nigerian prince offering up half his fortune via email. I should have been ignorant about the sounds she made when she was coming.

And the award for Biggest Douchebag of the Year goes to...

Killian Reed, ladies and gentlemen.

In my defense, I never set out to sleep with my teammate's wife. At the time, I hadn't even known she was married. Gabrielle approached me at a team after-party a year ago, and we fucked in a bathroom.

End of story.

When she'd shown up at the next practice, I'd chalked it up to another cleat chaser gone stage 5 clinger. I'd known exactly what she thought as I watched her saunter across the field house. It had been written all over her face. She'd convinced herself that out of all the women in the world, she'd be the one to tame me.

Convinced I'd known where things were headed, I actually opened my mouth, prepared to rattle off a speech I'd perfected over the years: *"It's not who I am... I thought you understood... don't cry."*

Instead, she'd stalked past me, without so much as a *fuck you very much*, leaving a cloud of Chanel in her wake. I'd watched in utter confusion as she embraced Chavez before putting two and two together.

Only then did I realize just how badly I'd screwed up. If it had been the first time, I would have chalked it up to a minor mistake and moved on.

But it wasn't the first time.

Before Gabrielle, there was Elliana, Carlos Cabrera's wife. I hadn't escaped that one unscathed either. I got a broken nose, and Cabrera got traded to Seattle.

Coming up to the majors was like being invited to an all-you-can-eat buffet. I had access to all the willing women I could ever want. Still, it had become increasingly evident my dick was only interested in the unavailable ones.

It was around that same time that I got the wake-up call I needed. *Sports Illustrated* had rated me number one in baseball. I could've waxed poetic about the subtle differences between a screwball and a circle changeup, but when it came to women, I was utterly lost. As I wasn't willing to throw away my entire career on another instance of bad judgment, I was left with one option.

Self-imposed celibacy.

It was only supposed to be for a month, something that had initially seemed impossible. If I wasn't dodging rabid female fans after the game, I was forced to endure heated looks from women almost everywhere else. I couldn't even remember the last time I'd gotten a cup of coffee that didn't have a phone number hastily scrawled on the side of it.

In my infinite wisdom, I'd let it slip that my dick was on hiatus. Something Bailey, my teammate and best friend, found equal parts amusing and disappointing.

"Delayed gratification is for the poor schmucks who can't do any better. Not us."

He was right, of course. With the kind of money we made, the world was at our fingertips. But, instead of giving up my vow and going back to business as usual, his words had the opposite effect. I began to consider the possibility women weren't throwing themselves at Killian Reed.

They wanted the player.

The money.

The fame.

Late one night, after a few too many beers, I made the decision not to take another woman to bed unless:

A) I could testify under oath that she wasn't married, engaged, or otherwise spoken for.

B) I clearly saw a future with her.

Twenty-one-year-old me would have promptly choked on his beer and told me I didn't deserve to own a penis.

Still, I held steady as one month stretched into two, taking matters into my own hands when the going got tough. That was over a year ago, and I'd still yet to meet a woman who didn't see dollar signs or a tabloid story when she looked at me.

But, I was still on top where it counted.

My first love had always been the game, and we had a long life ahead of us. The rest was just details.

The ancient PA system crackled to life as the announcer informed the stadium I was up. The Hurricanes' playoff chances rested in my hands. Completely in my element, I swaggered up to the plate with "Walk on Water" by Thirty Seconds to Mars blasting through the ballpark speakers.

This was it.

We were down by a run with Jimenez on second, and, thanks to Chris Harms chasing three straight pitches into the dirt, we now had two outs.

This was game seven against the *Kansas City Bears*—at home, for crying out loud. We'd dragged it out long enough. It was time to give the fans what they wanted.

Me.

I cut my eyes over to the dugout and got the sign from the manager to take the first pitch.

Dammit.

The Bears' pitcher, Adam Coley, wound up and sent a fastball in on the inside corner. It was a good pitch, but I knew I could've turned on it and at least pulled it into the outfield.

Behind in the count, I had to watch for his curve. He had a good fastball with a bit of movement on it, but his curve was downright nasty.

Coley knew I could hit and, just as I expected after the first pitch, threw a curve way outside. The catcher kept it in front of him, preventing Jimenez from advancing to third. His next one was more garbage outside.

Another ball.

I was given another sign to take the pitch but decided to disregard anything other than a sign to swing away. My hunch paid off when Coley threw a hanging slider. I was already moving when I realized my error.

That's no hanging slider, it's a goddamn breaking ball.

The momentum from my swing pushed me forward, and I ended up chopping it. Out of options, I began hauling ass to first, knowing the ball was fair without even looking.

It was identical to my first Major League hit, with the minor exception being I now had six additional years on my legs. My cleats pounded against the dirt, each steady thump matching my heart rate.

The crowd's roar became deafening as the announcer shouted, "And he's hit a chopper down to third. Sanchez bare hands it—"

Fucking Sanchez. For a rookie, he'd been killing it all season.

I could leg it out.

I'd almost hit it right off the damn plate.

If Jimenez made it to third, we still had a shot.

The wind whistled in my ears as I sprinted, drowning out the crowd. With each inhale, the scents of childhood flooded my nostrils.

Dirt.

Pine-tar.

Cotton candy.

I breathed them in, all while knowing that most people would kill to be in my cleats. Inside this chalk baseline, I was king, and there was no better feeling in the world.

It was going to come down to a bang-bang play at first. I just had to pray the ump ruled in my favor. I heard the smack of the ball on leather just as I hit the bag, but instead of being called out, it hit the heel of the first baseman's glove and rolled back toward the dugout.

I risked a glance to my left and watched as Jimenez rounded third, heading for home. The first base coach threw up the sign and told me to stay, but I knew I could make it to second. One more base hit, and then I'd score the winning run—no extra innings needed.

I was the hero.

With adrenaline coursing through my veins, I planted my left leg to cut toward second base. For a fraction of a second, I thought I had it.

Then, I felt the pop.

The pain was like a freight train, stealing the breath from lungs and taking my legs out from under me. I exhaled a low groan, coming down hard on my left side.

"And Reed is down as he turns to second," the announcer helpfully reiterated, on the off chance the fans had their eyes closed during the play. "It looks like they're going to tag him, but he's hurt."

I tossed my helmet, gritting my teeth as I writhed in the dirt, worthless as a sidesaddle on a sow. The Bears' first baseman, Kelly, somberly walked over and dropped down to tag me.

"Your knee?" He nodded toward where I held my leg in a death grip.

I squeezed my eyes shut and nodded, knowing I'd be making today's edition of *ESPN's Not Top Ten*. Thoughts of my father filtered through the haze of agony as the team closed in, rapidly firing questions I had no way of answering.

Not in my current state.

Unable to handle the sudden silence that had descended over the ballpark, the announcer continued his long-winded rambling.

"There's certainly some confusion over on first base. I think Reed thought he had an opportunity to make it to second—and it appears they're calling for the stretcher. After reviewing the replay, it looks as if his knee goes inward. Killian Reed is down just after making the turn at first base, and it looks bad, folks."

Asshole.

One of the trainers helped me into a sitting position, but the movement sent shockwaves of white-hot pain radiating throughout my leg, damn near forcing me back down.

I was just getting started—what if this was it?

CHAPTER TWO
ARIANA

"I'm jus' pain covered with skin."

-John Steinbeck, *The Grapes of Wrath*

I WAS DREAMING of the boy again.

Over the years, the details had faded to little more than a shadowy figure with blue-gray eyes and sun-kissed skin, but I knew it was him.

The moment I went into the water, I broke the rules and found goodness where none should have existed. Coincidentally, it was also when I discovered there was truth in the old adage, *'no good deed goes unpunished.'*

My father hadn't believed for one second I'd simply fallen into the fishing hole. Especially not after Brother Bradley—or Brad, as he'd insisted I call him—had informed him I'd been missing for hours. In the end, I accepted defeat and took my punishment in stoic silence.

I'd saved a life, and though the boy had never answered me, I wholeheartedly believed he was good. Perhaps if he hadn't been, things might have played out differently.

Maybe then I would have been able to do as my father commanded and set my mind on things above, and not the things of earth.

But even ten years later, the boy with blue-gray eyes was still the one fantasy that hadn't been tempered with a harsh dose of reality. Night after night, he haunted my dreams, leaving me aching for a life I could never have.

I was dreaming of him again, only this time we didn't reach the shore. Angry waves battered our bodies and dragged us down into icy depths. The pressure was like a band around my chest, increasing until I was sure my ribs were going to snap. I inhaled the frigid water, desperate for relief from the ever-increasing pain.

Relief that was just out of my reach.

Instead of waking with a pounding heart and sheets soaked in sweat, I found myself in a living nightmare where my body remained suspended in a dream-like state.

Consciousness came to me in waves, piercing the surrounding darkness with flashes of color and the soft sounds of whispered conversations before dragging me back into the abyss.

I'd resigned myself to a life spent caught between two worlds when I discovered I could make my eyelids flutter by directing all of my attention to them. It took every ounce of focus, but I did it over and over again until, at last, my eyes opened. The sensation of drowning didn't disappear entirely, but it was more bearable now that I was awake.

"Ariana, squeeze my hand if you can hear me," a disembodied voice encouraged from somewhere above. "You're okay, you're safe. Right now, you're at St. Michael's Hospital in Houston."

Fatigue weighed on me like a heavy wool blanket, but I managed to squeeze the hand wrapped around mine in response. The rest was harder to process, and I blinked slowly as if doing so might bring the words and the room into focus. A doctor was paged from somewhere nearby, but in here, it was quiet, allowing me to think.

Hospital.

I stiffened when the word permeated the fog surrounding my brain. Only sick people went to the hospital.

Was I sick?

The pounding in my skull gave a resounding yes, as did the persistent waves of dizziness and nausea. Even the scent of illness hung over the room like an unwelcome house guest, dragging long-forgotten memories of Mama to the forefront of my mind.

From somewhere nearby, machines began to beep loudly, each high-pitched tone a solemn reminder of how life could change in an instant.

During the holidays, the church held a toy drive for the local children's hospitals. Minus a routine tonsillectomy, I couldn't recall ever being a patient in one.

"Ariana, you are safe." Each word was slowly enunciated as if I were hard of hearing. I wondered if they were trained to repeat things like that.

Were there patients who actually believed it was perfectly normal to wake up in a hospital?

Maybe I was the only one who rationalized that if I was bound to a hospital bed with a splitting headache, then the odds were probably pretty good I was about as far from safe as one could be.

The woman's face finally came into view. I parted my lips to say something, only to be overtaken by a sudden coughing fit. The hoarse, soupy cough rattled my aching ribs and triggered my gag reflex. I blinked away the tears and swallowed until the urge to vomit passed, wondering where they kept the trashcans.

Just in case.

Incidentally, I also began to wonder why I'd fought against unconsciousness.

In the chaos of my hacking, something popped off my throat, flying across the room before landing with a solid *ping*.

"Whoops, we've lost your speech valve. Let me grab another one."

I waited until the woman turned her back before reaching for my face, feeling a thin tube protruding from my nose. Thinking it might relieve the excruciating pressure in my skull, I had the bright idea of tugging on it, which led right into another coughing fit.

"Oh—no, no, no," the nurse chastised as she pried my fingers away, forcing my hand back down to my side. "We don't want to use the restraints again."

Restraints?

What kind of hospital were they running?

And how had I ended up in it?

I remembered eating one of Sister Rebekah's famous lemon pies, my lips puckering at the tartness. Maybe she'd poisoned it, intending to kill her grumpy husband, Brother Benjamin, but had mistakenly sold it to me. My temple throbbed like a drumbeat in response, and I scratched poison off the list.

Headache due to reading by the nightlight for years?

It didn't seem severe enough to warrant a trip to the hospital. Maybe my horse, Pepper, had finally gotten her revenge after years of being forced to compete in equestrian sports. I couldn't rule it out entirely. She had gotten rather sassy in her old age.

I shifted against the pillow beneath my head, needing to alleviate the ache at the back of my nose.

No, I couldn't think about that now.

Having run out of clever ideas, I began to search the room for clues. A white piece of paper hung from an IV pole beside my bed, and I squinted at the blurred words until they shifted into something resembling a sentence.

Right bone flap out.

Which meant... absolutely nothing to me.

Moving on.

Wait, I had it. It was like that children's song.

How'd that one go again?

Right bone connected to the—*nope... still means nothing.*

Obviously, my sense of humor had remained intact, or what passed for humor when it came to me. But I was still missing essential information explaining how I'd landed myself in the hospital.

I tried but couldn't recall a catalyst any more than I could solve an algebraic equation off the top of my head. Although, it soon occurred to me that perhaps my mathematical difficulties weren't due to any injury or illness, but a lifelong aversion to putting the alphabet into number problems. Maybe not the earth-shattering revelation I'd been hoping for, but it was a step in the right direction, nonetheless.

My nose twitched again, begging me to reach up and yank the tube out.

Just one tiny pull, and the headache would be gone.

Having fallen for the exact same thing once already, I tucked my hands under my thighs and prepared to wait it out. The date was written on a marker board hanging on the wall closest to the bed. As I read it, the chirping from the machines intensified, along with the fluttering in my chest.

The severity of my condition was spelled out in large black numbers. I'd been trapped in a void of nothingness for three weeks.

Three weeks.

Twenty-one days.

Billions of minutes—just gone.

Again, math hadn't exactly been my best subject.

When I lost something, I typically found it by going back to the last place I remembered having it. As crazy as it seemed, maybe I could do the same thing with my fractured memory, retracing my steps until I pieced everything together.

While the nurse busied herself with something across the room, I closed my eyes and began sifting through the rubble. Steering clear of any detours involving lemon pies and fussy horses, I concentrated solely on what I knew to be true. If I listed enough concrete facts, the answer was bound to come to me.

My name was Ariana James. I was nineteen years old. I lived in Houston, Texas, with Tristan and my mama—*no, that wasn't right.*

Mama was gone.

I ended up in the hospital because...

What I needed was right there, but it was as if the film in my head had suddenly hit a brick wall, leaving behind a fragmented mess of memories. Everything else lay just out of reach on the other side.

It only hurts if you let it...

Those seven words hadn't failed me yet. I was just going to give my brain a little break and try again later. Indifference replaced irritation, and I reopened my eyes, pulling my hands free as footsteps approached my bed.

"Here we are," the nurse said, attaching something to my neck. "Good as new."

I could ask her. It was just a simple matter of writing the question out in my head and reciting each word slowly and clearly. My stomach churned in apparent disagreement, but it was better than not knowing. Taking a deep breath, I drew myself up tall and opened my mouth.

Make yourself heard.

"I got here as soon as I heard."

I withered instantly at the sound of his voice, my rehearsed words fleeing back into the recesses of my mind. A shudder worked its way down from the base of my skull before settling in the area between my shoulder blades.

He's going to kill me.

Mama's warning had chosen a most inopportune time to pop in, but there was no stopping it now.

"I'm here—I'm here now." His fingers brushed against my hair and my back involuntarily arched off the bed. Searing pain moved powered through the center of my chest, sparking and pulsing like a downed power line.

When I was a child, I'd experienced periodic episodes where I would wake, only to find myself unable to move or speak. I was forced to lie against my pillow, completely helpless, until my brain and body were no longer opposing forces.

That in and of itself wasn't terribly frightening. It was what occurred during those moments of paralysis that left me quaking in fear. But this wasn't a hallucination or the trick of an overactive imagination.

This monster was real.

"Did you hear that, Ariana? Your father is right here with you." The woman's mouth stretched into a wide grin I couldn't quite return.

Once people realized who my father was, I became someone worth knowing. The disinterest in their eyes morphed into expressions of star-struck wonder. Despite what the world believed, growing up the daughter of a megachurch pastor hadn't exactly been smooth sailing.

I'd known Tristan James was a household name by the time I could walk. He'd written instant bestsellers, appeared every Sunday morning on televisions across the country, and had an entourage of celebrity followers.

Tristan loved being in the spotlight, and with his gravity-defying dark hair and piercing aquamarine eyes, the media just loved him right back.

Tristan James: America's sexiest pastor.

Seriously.

As if that was even a real thing.

When people claimed he looked much younger than forty-six, he'd attribute it to doing the Lord's work, conveniently leaving out that his eldest daughter was twenty-four.

I pushed my trembling fingers beneath the white sheet, hoping no one had noticed. I'd been doing so well, reading my Bible and praying more... just like he wanted.

After thousands of mistakes over the years, I had it down to an almost exact science and could sense when the world was close to slipping off-axis. If I stepped in at the right moment, I could keep him happy, and the façade was preserved.

As far as anyone knew, we were one happy family.

It was only when the world slept that I found myself wanting something I couldn't put into words—this desire to be seen as more than Tristan James's daughter.

I wanted freedom.

"Do you know how long I've been waiting for that call?" He asked, his mouth tipping up in a smile that conveyed nothing.

Was he angry?

Did he know how I'd ended up here?

Tristan gave an almost imperceptible shake of his head as if he'd been granted a direct line into my thoughts. The nurse continued beaming, unaware of our silent conversation.

No to what—both? One?

Tell me! I wanted to scream.

"Melanie," Tristan stated, turning his attention back to the nurse and signaling the end of our little discussion. "Would you mind if I prayed?"

Melanie readily agreed, jarring the side of the bed with her hip in her hurry to reach Tristan's outstretched hand. I winced as the pain in my head expanded like an overfilled balloon, but instead of fading to black, the room seemed to grow brighter.

Or maybe it was just Tristan's unnaturally white teeth.

"Heavenly Father—"

I added my own silent prayer. Obviously, it had been too much to ask for freedom. At this point, I was willing to settle for unconsciousness.

The rhythmic beeping from the machines made tuning out his words easier than I imagined. The nurse might have believed differently, but if he was here, then I was not safe.

And all the prayers in the world wouldn't take away from the genuine possibility that this time, he'd gone too far.

He reached for my hand as he spoke, letting his beady eyes search my face. I'd seen this look more than once, an unspoken reminder to stick to the script. Suddenly afraid of what he might see reflected in my own eyes, I turned away from his probing gaze.

Knowing I hadn't said a word was one thing. Convincing him of the fact was a completely different animal.

I glanced up when Tristan's voice cracked in the middle of his impassioned monologue, surprised to find he wasn't glaring at me in suspicion. Not even close. I watched in a sort of horrified fascination as moisture pooled in his blue eyes before spilling over onto his lashes.

Tristan James did not cry.

Ever.

On the morning Mama passed, his eyes had remained completely dry. He'd seemed almost relieved to be free of the invalid wife and her accusations.

The memories cropped up sporadically, but my thoughts were still very much jumbled together like skeins of yarn in a wicker basket. Tugging on the string of one fact didn't lead to the next. It only seemed to further entangle the threads of the others. Mama had been gone for years, but the memory of her death was as fresh in my mind as if it had happened yesterday.

I fought against the sudden surge of panic and looked down to where my hand rested in Tristan's, studying every line until I became convinced that I was, in fact, still an adult. For reasons I couldn't explain, the past had taken a firm hold over my mind, distorting reality.

"And Father, we—we just need—" Tristan tried covering his mouth, but he was too late.

What happened? I knew my lips were moving, but I couldn't hear the sound of my voice.

"Ariana." He squeezed my fingers with a hiccuped breath. "You were driving the convertible and lost—you lost control, sweetheart."

It didn't make any sense. If I went anywhere, I would have taken the Audi. I shook my head, mouthing, *No, I wouldn't have—*

It only hurts if you let it...

The heat in my chest moved up to my esophagus, yet I remained silent. I freed my hand from his and rubbed frantically at the base of my throat.

Tristan's face crumpled again, and he dropped his eyes down to the sheet. "You... you didn't have a seatbelt on and your head—" His words trailed off in a sob of fragmented sentences before Melanie intervened.

"Ariana, you hit your head. The doctors had to remove a piece of your skull to help with the swelling. If the pressure on your brain remains low, I expect they'll look at scheduling a surgery soon to replace it."

Why can't I talk? I mouthed, resorting to hand gestures when she didn't seem to understand the question.

"Well, you were on mechanical ventilation for a little over a week before the doctors were able to perform a tracheostomy. So, right here..."

Taking my hand, she gently guided my fingers up my throat. "You've got a little hole. Now, with that speech valve on, you can talk. It'll just take some getting used to."

I touched the circular valve again, waiting for some sudden burst of clarity. She'd handed me the missing puzzle pieces, yet I couldn't seem to make them fit together.

As the rough sounds of Tristan's sobbing filled the room, I was forced to confront an alternative truth. Maybe the reason he wasn't telepathically urging me to stick to a narrative was that this time, there wasn't one.

It only hurts if you let it...

Without a doubt, I knew my name and basic information. If I focused, I could even recall the live worship night we'd hosted at the church back in May, down to what I'd been wearing.

Simple black wrap dress. No shoes.

The filing cabinet of my mind had kept a diligent record of every significant event in my life, save one. As I glanced back at Tristan, I saw the truth of Melanie's words in his wounded expression.

He wasn't responsible for my accident.

That meant only one thing.

I'd done it.

I'd finally done it.

I'd taken my mother's advice and run, only to prove that Tristan had been right all along. The world was full of evil people, and, given where I was now, it was clear they'd wasted no time in bleeding the last bit of hope from my veins.

CHAPTER THREE
ARIANA

"Sometimes the Bible in the hand of one man is worse than a whisky bottle in the hand of (another)... There are just some kind of men who're so busy worrying about the next world they've never learned to live in this one, and you can look down the street and see the results."

-Harper Lee, *To Kill A Mockingbird*

ONCE UPON A TIME, I believed Tristan James had hung the moon. Although he'd been a mostly absentee parent while Mama was alive—leaving us to care for her while he jetted off to promote his latest book or fill in as a guest pastor at another church—I'd adored him.

While he was away, I would sit with my nose almost touching the television screen, mesmerized by the sound of his voice and the way he always seemed to know just what to say.

I guess I thought if I studied his mannerisms and the way he spoke, I might see something to help me defuse the bomb before it exploded. Knowing how to read his moods was a skill I became convinced would prove useful in the long run.

Disillusionment didn't happen overnight. It was a gradual shift, occurring when I realized Tristan's views didn't necessarily line up with my own. He preached year after year about the flawed and sinful nature of the world, and the pedestal I'd placed him on tipped forward a little more, eventually toppling completely.

I knew there was evil in the world.

I'd seen it with my own two eyes, after all.

Nothing—not even a car wreck—could take away the image of a boy being dumped off a dock like a piece of garbage. But as I confronted the details of my experience, I was forced to admit that had I not witnessed it, I likely would have missed what followed.

People had a tendency to overlook the little, everyday miracles when their lives were going well. It was only in moments of absolute darkness that they looked around long enough to appreciate the positive. Maybe it wasn't right out in the open, but I was a firm believer in seeking out goodness wherever it happened to exist.

That was the fundamental difference between the two of us.

In Tristan's mind, a person fell into one of two categories. You were either a sinner, or you were a saint. He couldn't seem to separate himself from his rigid and unyielding beliefs long enough to consider that a person, or world, might be both and still worthy of saving.

He ruled over his kingdom like a dictator, where differing opinions were seen as credible threats to his ministry. The world was always watching, so there was no room for error.

To me, the pursuit of perfection was draining.

It hadn't always been like that, though.

There was a time when each girl within the church community was allowed to spend three days in the city upon turning eighteen.

Urban Mission had been established as a safe way of giving us a snapshot of the world. My grandmother was certain once we'd seen the sinful way in which people lived, we would better appreciate what my father had built for us.

There were twelve months between us, and year after year, I

watched as each of my sisters headed into the city, accompanied by one of the church elders and his wife. Each returned home looking more than a little shell-shocked, seemingly confirming my grandmother's suspicions.

My eldest sister, Aubrey, had worked in the kitchen at the mission, serving food to a homeless population clothed in little more than rags. A few begged her for money, and one woman had gone as far as offering up her body. Before the trip, Aubrey had planned on enrolling at a nearby Protestant university for the fall semester. Instead, she'd stayed and married Brother Caleb's son, Lucas, in a lavish October ceremony.

Anastasia was next, followed by Avery and Autumn the following years. Each one readily gave up their plans for a college education in favor of a wedding and home within the community.

I'd devoured their stories, ravenous for even the smallest crumb from their travels. Without fail, I eagerly prayed night after night that they might bring back news of the boy with blue-gray eyes.

When Ashlynn turned eighteen, everything changed. She was the sister I was closest to, and the only one to give an honest account of her experience. The night she returned, I'd waited until everyone was asleep before sneaking into her room.

My older sisters had arrived home and slowly drifted up the stairs like balloons in need of helium before collapsing onto their beds in exhaustion.

Not Ashlynn.

She'd feigned disappointment as she told our father of the trip during Sunday dinner. Still, I'd seen the excitement reflected in her eyes. Brother Jakob and his wife, Sister Hana, hadn't been as pleased with their time in the city and had retired to their hotel room early one evening.

"I met someone, Ari," she'd whispered as I slipped beneath her bedcovers, no longer hiding her pleased grin. "I snuck out and walked to an all-night diner. He bought me a cup of coffee before sitting down, and we just—we just talked for hours. His name is Matt, and he just enlisted with the Army, but gave me his unit's information so I can write him letters."

She'd paused before admitting, "So Matt walked me back to the hotel, and then he—he kissed me. He kissed as if we were the only two people in the world. And instead of stopping it, I kissed him right back. I felt like maybe I could have kissed him forever."

Her confession had sent an arc of unfamiliar longing coursing through my veins before it set up camp between my legs. It was similar to the sensation I got when Pepper jumped over obstacles, but I was never left with the urge to nuzzle her neck afterward.

We'd stayed up half the night as she told me of the other things she'd experienced, but her first kiss was what I remembered most. As wrong as it had been, I'd wanted to be held by a man just as she'd described it.

But not just any man.

A pleasant shiver had moved down my spine as I crept back to my own bedroom, and I made a promise to myself that when my turn came, I was going to find the blue-eyed boy and kiss him.

What I wanted hadn't mattered in the end.

Like the old saying, *'The best-laid plans of mice and men often go awry,'* some things are just doomed to fail.

I didn't know it at the time, but within a matter of weeks, Ashlynn would be gone forever. The church would vote to end the *Urban Mission* project, and my eighteenth birthday would pass just like every other day before it. I would stay within the same four walls I'd known my entire life, fantasizing about what it would be like to live somewhere else, to be free to make my own choices.

Something must have happened to turn my fantasy into reality. Some catalyst that left me with no other choice.

Why else would I have tried to escape?

I knew as well as anyone how it had ended for my sister.

———

I snapped out of my thoughts and frowned down at the notebook filled with scribbles. I'd written *hospital* five times with the year sketched out to the side in block letters. Beneath that were strange symbols and obscure words that appeared to be a newly discovered form of cursive. My brain must have decided to solve a mystery without my help because decoding the jargon proved impossible.

"Ariana, do you understand what I'm telling you?" Dr. McEvans moved into my line of sight.

I traced what appeared to be an arrow on the page with my index finger before nodding. While I preferred her brusque assessment over the sugarcoated version I'd gotten from other doctors, I didn't think it was necessary to detail my injuries every time she made her rounds.

I knew.

My head and chest gave not so subtle reminders every time I was forced to get out of bed. There was a cruel sense of irony in spending your entire life wanting to escape only to succeed with no memory of how you'd done it.

Somehow mistaking my nod as a sign of confusion, she elaborated. "With your trach gone, you should find it easier to produce sounds. And now that the bone flap has been replaced, we believe that you're medically stable enough to transfer to a rehab facility."

No.

I preferred to stay right here, with the nurses I knew and trusted until I remembered everything.

Thank you very much.

Dr. McEvans pressed her lips together, clearly fighting a smile. "I understand with everything you've been through, change can be hard, but we talked about *True North*. It's one of the best places for you to be. They can provide a level of rehabilitative care we can't."

But the nurses here knew me and took the time to style my long hair. Each braid was different, but all managed to disguise the scar that ran down the middle of my scalp and around to my right ear. Even the slight depression in my temple area wasn't as noticeable.

I'd been ignored most of my life, and I wasn't exactly comfortable with being noticed now just because my scars were finally visible. I didn't want it to be the only thing people saw when they looked at me.

I was not an object to be pitied.

"Hey, I got here just as fast as I could," Tristan panted from the doorway. "Thought y'all were gonna kick her out before I made it."

Dr. McEvans stood up and offered her chair to him with wide eyes. "Pastor James, I am so honored. Truly. I was just explaining again to Ariana that we're going to be transferring her..." She paused and blinked a couple of times as if trying to recall where it was they were sending me.

It's True North, I mouthed.

Now who has the brain injury?

He crossed the room to where she stood and placed a hand on her shoulder before flashing his megawatt smile. "Belinda McEvans, the honor is all mine. I cannot thank you enough for all that you've done for my little girl."

I fought a cringe at the term of endearment, wondering why he seemed so giddy.

"You—you know who I am?"

His eyes sparkled with amusement as he dropped onto the newly vacated chair. "A shepherd would recognize a member of his flock anywhere. Has Don recovered from his shoulder surgery?"

He was just laying it on thick today.

Instead of considering that someone within the church had played detective, Dr. McEvans was clearly fighting the urge to drop to her knees in exaltation. They conversed for several minutes before she reluctantly excused herself to check on another patient, and Tristan began packing my things.

"Like I was saying, I would have been here sooner, but the phone has been ringing off the hook this morning. First, CNN and then Fox News—everybody wants to hear how you're doing. I told them once we got you settled in at *True North*, I'd be willing to fly out for interviews."

And there it was... proof that there was just no limit to the things he would do to remain relevant. Although, if he'd found a way to capitalize on my misfortune, maybe he wouldn't look too hard into why I'd taken off in the first place. Even without the tightening in my gut, I knew the idea was little more than wishful thinking.

"I'm going to reach out to Justin Thomas again and see if he'd be willing to join me. It'd be good press for his facility. You remember him, don't you?"

Forcing my lips into what felt like a smile, I nodded. Everyone at church knew and liked Justin. The former wide receiver for the *Houston Thunder* and founder of *True North* never missed a service. He'd even spoken one Sunday not long after his facility opened about the game that changed his life.

Justin made a miraculous catch during the 2004 Super Bowl, leading the Thunder to a last-second victory. In his own words, the resulting brain injury cost him his career but led to him discovering his purpose.

Initially, he'd founded *True North* for individuals with brain and spinal cord injuries like him. In the last five years, it had become a sort of mecca for sports injuries as well. As difficult as it was for me to admit, if I wanted my memory back, then Justin's facility was my best chance at recovery.

I could also use my time there to my advantage. While Tristan was busy pandering to the press, I planned on discovering exactly what I'd been running from the night of my accident.

Once my things were packed, Tristan held court for the small crowd who'd gathered near the back of the private van he'd hired. Meanwhile, I scanned the hospital parking lot for something of inter-est, almost disappointed by how ordinary everything seemed.

Where was this land of lawlessness I had always heard about?

"Folks," Tristan drawled. "You've done so much for my baby girl."

His southern accent was almost as strong as when he was preaching a sermon, supposedly it made him more relatable to the blue-collar demographic. Apparently, they were a widely underrepresented group within the church.

Pastor James, he's just like us... only with a private jet and a net worth of fifty million dollars.

"I can't ever thank y'all enough for taking care of her while I was trying to get back home from Haiti." His eyes held mine as he said it as if I needed to be reminded I was the reason his trip had been cut short. Then, he blinked, and the mask slipped back into place. Blinking was one more thing Tristan believed conveyed trustworthiness.

"*Won't you just fill the offerin' plate this mornin'?*"

Blink. Blink.

"*God is just waitin' to bless you if you're willin' to step out in faith.*"

Blink. Blink.

Dr. McEvans made a choked sound, and I looked up just in time to watch a tear make its slow descent down her cheek. "Of course, I forgot that your foundation is based there. Just know it was our pleasure caring for her, and we'll be praying for her recovery."

She didn't look at me once as she said it.

It only hurts if you let it...

Tristan grinned. "Belinda, I would love to pray over you and the rest of the medical team right now. Would that be alright?"

Soft murmurs of eager acceptance rippled through the crowd. In their minds, being prayed over by the Tristan James was probably equal to receiving a blessing directly from above.

The nurse joined the driver up front, leaving Tristan alone in the back with me when the van doors were slammed shut. I wanted to believe it was the frigid air being blasted throughout the cabin that had the sweat-dampened hairs on my arms raised.

It was a warning.

An urge to flee.

When he reached into his pocket, the breath caught in my throat.

He's going to kill me...

I forced the thought away, unable to dwell on anything other than the silent way I was being assessed. Keeping my face blank, I focused on the area of skin between his eyebrows. It was a trick I'd learned from Ashlynn growing up—a way of making it appear as though I was looking him in the eyes while keeping myself safe.

Ashlynn.

My eyes stung, but I refused to break. Not while Tristan was on a mission to slow-blink his way into my head.

It only hurts if you let it...

His eyes flashed with amusement as he pulled his cell phone out. "Thought you'd like a preview of next Sunday's message. It'll be my first time back on stage since your accident."

It wasn't a weapon—it was a phone. I released the breath I'd been holding and nodded,

I'd been granted a reprieve.

This time.

"Now, you know I usually like to start with something light-hearted and funny, but this time I'm going to lead in with the story of your accident," he declared while reading through the notes on the phone screen.

"There comes the point where medicine runs out and faith steps in. Now, I believe we serve a Mighty Healer, and we're about to come into a season of miracles. It works as a segue, right?"

When I didn't respond, Tristan cleared his throat and continued. "We all go through things that aren't fair, and it can leave us with bitter hearts. Maybe someone got the promotion at work you felt like you deserved, or you've had to watch a loved one suffer through illness. Church, I have to confess something. I've been bitter. When I learned the severity of my daughter's condition, I felt despair like I hadn't felt since losing my beloved wife, Colleen."

Mama.

My vision blurred, and I shifted my attention toward the window, aimlessly watching the palm trees zip by alongside I-45. He never mentioned her—no one did. As the years passed, it began to feel as though maybe she'd only ever existed in my mind.

"That despair left me angry, and I cried out to God. I demanded to know if he was testing me like Job. Was I meant to lose everything to prove my faith? Folks, how many of y'all have been there? How many of you have been knocked down by life, time and time again?

"Maybe God isn't punishing you but bringing you into the light. Maybe you got passed over for that promotion because God is opening up bigger doors. Maybe your loved one is battling an illness to strengthen your faith in miracles."

Like a moth to a flame, Tristan's charisma pulled me in, and I found myself nodding along to his every word.

He beamed at my reaction, no doubt already basking in the congregation's shouts of praise. "Once we've raised our Bibles, I'll read from Genesis 22:9. That's the passage that came to me as I knelt in grief. You remember it, don't you little dove?"

My mouth went dry as his 'message' became crystal clear.

"When they arrived at the place where God had told him to go, Abraham built an altar and arranged the wood on it. Then he tied his son, Isaac, and laid him on the altar on top of the wood.

And Abraham picked up the knife to kill his son as a sacrifice. At that moment, the angel of the Lords called to him from heaven, 'Abraham! Abraham!'

'Yes,' Abraham replied. 'Here I am!'

'Don't lay a hand on the boy!' the angel said. 'Do not hurt him in any way, for now, I know that you truly fear God. You have not withheld from me, even your son, your only son.'"

"I was so consumed with the thought of losing my little girl I didn't see it for what it was," he preached from memory, never once taking his eyes off mine. "Now, the world will tell you bad things happen to good people and go on about their lives. A man of God will look inward, though, and see where he's failed. And folks, it's not sunshine and roses when you're trying to turn your tragedy into a testimony."

I wondered if anyone who heard it later would notice that, while he was discussing my injury, the focus was solely on how it had impacted him.

Tristan shifted forward until his head was almost touching mine before lowering his voice. "I put my family above my faith. I stood up in front of my church and demanded they step out in faith while my own heart was tied up in the familiar. I've held on to you because it was comfortable. But if I want to come into the fullness and glory of God, I have to be willing to sacrifice what I love the most."

He's going to kill me...

Maybe not, but he had made it clear he was willing to hold a knife to my throat. The sermon was a cautionary tale meant solely for my ears—a reminder of what Tristan was ready to do to prove himself worthy.

Was love really sacrifice?

If so, then I was beginning to question whether or not I even knew what love was. I'd never seen Tristan put his family above anything. We were nothing more than scullery maids in his vast kingdom.

As I sifted through the rubble of my memories, searching for details about the accident, something Tristan had said began to gnaw at my mind.

If he'd been in Haiti, then who had I been running from?

The click of the turn signal pulled me from my thoughts, and I looked up just as we turned into what appeared to be a residential area.

Live oaks stretched up on either side of the street, providing a canopy of shade for homes far larger than most of the ones within our gated community. The mansion I'd grown up in still dwarfed most of these, a tribute to my father's unfailing faith and the church's deep pockets.

I'd lived my entire life under the assumption the world outside our community lived in poverty. Based on the stories, I'd imagined their restless souls wandering the globe like a band of gypsies, never finding a place to put down roots.

But this was not scarcity.

This was abundance. These were people who were making it without the church, or God's, help. My brows drew together, and I turned back to Tristan, only to find him intently studying the warning label affixed to the transport bed.

When we pulled up in front of a large glass building, he released a breath that sounded suspiciously like a sigh of relief. I never imagined I'd live to see the day Tristan James was as eager to get away from me as I was him.

Directly behind the granite *True North Rehabilitation Center* sign stood a statue of Justin Thomas. His arms were stretched high above his head, making his career-ending catch. I studied it as the nurses transferred me from the bed to a wheelchair, finding it odd Justin would want to commemorate the very thing that had almost cost him his life.

I certainly couldn't imagine commissioning a statue of me next to a wrecked convertible giving the thumbs up.

Tristan kept his distance as we moved inside the facility where a woman stood expectantly. Her long black hair captured the lights from above, shimmering iridescently. While I was mesmerized by her hair, she was captivated by my father in a way that indicated she needed no introduction.

Through her gushing, I determined she was the facility director for *True North*—my home for the next eight to twelve weeks. Then, it'd be back to prison for the remainder of therapy and possibly my life. I fought against the insistent tug of my lips, not willing to risk arousing suspicion.

Tristan handed over a white plastic bag of my belongings but didn't stay once I was shown to my room. He didn't need to—I'd been given my warning back in the van. It was confusing, wondering if he planned on sacrificing me to gain media attention, or if something darker was at play.

It only hurts if you let it...

As a little girl, I would have done anything to please him. As an adult, I knew where that path led. I'd learned to numb myself to the pain in order to survive.

Twelve weeks was a long time.

More than enough opportunity to discover why I'd run away. And once I knew that, I could tackle what to do to keep Tristan's plans of sacrifice from ever coming to fruition.

I dumped the contents of the bag out onto the bed, slightly disappointed when nothing sparked a memory. Not that there was much to go on—just my purse, a pair of sneakers with socks stuffed inside, and my underwear. Whatever I'd been wearing the night of the accident must have been ruined.

A quick check of the purse turned up nothing, other than the realization that my driver's license and credit cards had been confiscated and were now probably residing in the safe back home. I blew out my cheeks and began returning the items to the bag one by one. As I pulled the sock from one of the sneakers, a necklace fell onto the bed, one I'd never seen before.

I threaded my fingers through the delicate silver chain and lifted it up. The rectangular pendant reminded me a little of the doors on an armoire. Each side had delicately carved swirls that, upon closer inspection, resembled octopus tentacles amid waves. It was gorgeous, but definitely not mine. I would have remembered something like this.

Tristan.

My fingers tightened around the gift meant to buy my silence. I didn't know why he'd bothered this time.

I'd traded my voice for one night of freedom.

———

Once I was settled, the assigned tech pushed my wheelchair out into the hall for a tour of the facility, only to remember she'd left her radio behind in the room. "Wait right here."

I waited until she was gone before sliding my left foot from the footrest, planting it firmly on the floor. When putting weight on my toes didn't cause pain, I did the same with my right foot. In the hospital, I hadn't been able to manage more than a few steps before needing a break to rest.

My entire plan hinged on pushing myself to the limit.

Step one—learn to walk without getting dizzy or tired.

I reached for the belt across my lap, only to find I couldn't disengage the lock without a key. Panicked thoughts of being trapped briefly pierced through my armor of numbness before I could rein them in.

It only hurts if you let it...

I just needed a key. My eyes scanned the walls before landing on a cart across the hallway. It was resting in a small vase, like a long-forgotten treasure, and I eagerly wheeled over to snatch it up. After several fumbled attempts, I realized I wasn't holding a key.

A flower, I mouthed, cracking a smile at my own expense. In my haste, I could have sworn I had the right thing. My mind had been playing tricks on me since the accident, leaving me unable to recall familiar words and now, apparently unable to remember what a key looked like.

"The staff is bound by HIPAA laws, as well as the NDA they signed on your arrival. You're good," a well-dressed man stated as he opened a door directly to the left of where I was sitting.

I held up my hand as he approached, but instead of recognizing it as a way of asking for help, he high-fived my palm and continued on down the hall.

No problem.

Expecting someone to help me without the use of my voice hadn't been my best plan. I would just keep looking until the key turned up, though. Something dangled from a corkboard on the door the man had just exited, and I wondered how I'd missed it before. I pulled the object into my hands just as the door swung inward, and a man on crutches hobbled out.

With a triumphant grin, I waved the key before offering it to him. It should have been inherently obvious what I was asking him to do, but instead of taking it and freeing me from my prison cell on wheels, the man looked down with disgust.

"Oh, you've got to be fucking kidding me," he said with a bitter laugh, the rubber soles of his crutches squeaking loudly against the linoleum floor as he turned away.

It wasn't until he disappeared from view that I realized I'd been duped once again. I wasn't holding a key. Just a piece of paper with the words *K. Reed* typewritten across the top.

Oblivious to my escape attempt, the aide reappeared and pushed my chair in the opposite direction the man had gone.

I was trapped.

Maybe it wasn't the injury. Perhaps to an animal locked inside a cage, eventually, everything began to resemble a key.

CHAPTER FOUR
KILLIAN

"It breaks your heart. It is designed to break your heart. The game begins in spring, when everything else begins again, and it blossoms in the summer, filling the afternoons and evenings, and then as soon as the chill rains come, it stops and leaves you to face the fall alone."

-A. Bartlett Giamatti

The Snap Heard 'Round the World: Is MLB's Golden Boy Finished?

The Houston Hurricanes have acknowledged that center-fielder, Killian Reed was forced to undergo emergency surgery after suffering a torn ACL, MCL, and meniscus during a one-game playoff to advance to the ALDS.

Reed, 26, was hurt as he rounded toward second base after a fiasco of a play against the Kansas City Bears. This injury is considered career-threatening for Reed, despite this being his best year yet.

He set career highs with 37 homers, 32 stolen bases, and 103

RBIs for the Hurricanes and has been invaluable as a clubhouse leader for manager Burt Morosi.

Morosi still believes that Reed will be back next season, regardless of the injury. "You don't want to see any of your players hurt, but if anyone can come back from this, it's Killian. He's a smart kid, and I truly believe he'll make an impact in someone's life while he's recovering."

Garrett Sanchez, the Bears' third baseman who snagged Reed's chopper, has other thoughts. "Look, he's a fantastic player, and if he comes back, my guess is that he'll be even better than he was before. But, if he doesn't—and, I'm not saying he's done—he might make an even bigger impact in his second career."

Sanchez seems to believe that Reed could have his pick of jobs.

"He's a guy with an amazing skill set. If he came back as manager or batting coach, I imagine he'd be very successful. He'll land on his feet wherever he ends up."

With Reed at the helm, the Hurricanes were favored to clinch the ALCS after making their first post-season appearance in eight years.

If Reed manages to return to the lineup next season, the Hurricanes can't predict how productive he'll be right away.

As you may remember, Los Angeles Rangers shortstop, Mike Cole suffered a torn ACL and meniscus two seasons ago. After undergoing surgery in July, he missed the remainder of the season. He returned the following year to one of his worst seasons yet—his .717 OPS was nearly 200 points lower than his performance a year before. After struggling through a rocky season, Cole hung up the cleats.

Reed is undoubtedly a more accomplished hitter than Cole—and nearly every other player in MLB history. And while no two injuries are alike, one cannot help but view Cole as a cautionary tale for the Hurricanes because, for the first time in years, uncertainty surrounds one of MLB's most preeminent players.

GODDAMN SANCHEZ.

I threw the magazine aside with a growl and dropped back against the pillows. Hinting I was done—as soon as I was out of this hellhole, maybe I'd pay him a little visit.

Let's see if he backs up his statement when I'm in front of his smug little face.

"It seems bad," my agent began, "But like I always say, any press is good press."

I resisted the urge to tell him where to shove his press, and instead massaged the area between my eyebrows as if doing so might ward off the sudden headache.

"In what world would the end of my career be considered 'good press,' Theo?"

He tipped back in the plastic chair, balancing all of his weight on two legs before fixing me with one of his trademark grins. "Killian, you and I both know you're not even close to the end of your career. So, you had a setback with the knee. There's not a doubt in my mind you'll be back next season, stronger than ever."

"Are we just glossing over the fact that Sanchez happens to be your client, then?" I took a deep breath and lowered my voice. "Look, it is what it is, but the one thing we can't ignore is where I go from here."

His smile didn't slip as he responded in an annoyingly even tone, "Look, we both know you weren't happy with what the team was offering."

In my infinite stupidity, I'd held off on signing a six-year contract with the Hurricanes—convinced another team would swoop in and offer more than three hundred sixty million.

Three hundred sixty million.

Clearly, I was a moron.

My mother had said as much when she saw me after my surgery. In fact, her exact words had been, *"If brains were leather, you wouldn't have enough to saddle a June bug."*

As far as southern niceties went, it ranked just slightly above a well-timed *bless your heart.*

I ground my molars together and released a breath through my nose. "All I'm asking, Theo, is what our plan is. The team wanted me here for rehab, which I took as a good sign, but after reading this? Fuck, I don't know anymore."

He might have faith it was all going to work out like a fairy tale, but I'd seen careers end over less. This industry changed on a dime, and if they saw me as damaged goods, I'd be hanging up the cleats permanently.

Theo brought the chair back down and leaned forward, resting his forearms on his thighs. "I'm not going to lie, Killian. You've got a long hard road ahead of you. In my opinion, your best bet is to ignore the press and focus your energy on getting back on the field. The team has your back for now. The rest is just details."

For now.

I glared first at him, and then, the magazine on the floor. Despite the ominous words, he was right. I couldn't speed up my recovery process any more than I could make the sun rise.

"According to the doctor, I'm looking at six to twelve months of recovery time. Are they going to wait around until next spring or fill the roster?"

Theo's phone vibrated from the inside pocket of his suit jacket. He retrieved it and glanced down at the screen before returning his gaze to mine.

"You've shattered almost every Hurricane record. A blown-out knee isn't the career-ending injury it used to be, and the team isn't short-sighted enough to walk away now..." His phone buzzed again, and he paused to check the screen. "It just takes time to recover," he mumbled distractedly.

"Am I keeping you from something, Theo? Maybe you and Sanchez have a nice picnic planned?" I hadn't intended to raise my voice. I wasn't a yeller by nature—well, outside of the dugout, anyway.

Theo glanced at his watch before standing up and buttoning his jacket. It was apparent I was treading on what little patience he still had reserved for me.

With a sigh, I pulled the ice pack from my knee and carefully shifted my weight toward the edge of the bed. "Now, just wait a second—"

He paused with an arched brow. "You finished with your little temper tantrum, Killian? Ready to discuss things like an adult again?"

I swallowed down the sharp retort and nodded before reaching for my crutches. "I just want to know I have a place on the field—any field at this point."

"It's about time for you to head down for therapy, but can I give you some advice?" Without waiting for a response, he continued. "You need to keep your head down and make healing your number one priority. No outbursts or arguing. Nothing that might cause a scene. And for the love of God, keep your dick in your pants."

Unable to help myself, I chuckled. "That's it? Done. What else?"

"You're agreeing? Did you hear a damn word I just said? No making trouble... no women. We all remember how the Cabrera thing went down. Your career is riding on this, Killian. If you want that contract, you'll cross your *i*'s and dot your *t*'s."

"I believe it's cross your *t*'s and dot your *i*'s, but noted. I'll be on my best behavior, Dad. Besides, I'm pretty sure there isn't a woman in the joint under the age of sixty. I mean, the silver-haired look is in and all—"

"Christ, Killian," he muttered as he turned toward the door. "You manage to keep your dick and your temper locked away, I expect the team will make another offer within the month."

I was so hung up on the latter half of his sentence that I let the man whore insinuation slide. He could think whatever he wanted, as long as he got me a contract. Plus, after the way Bailey had reacted, I wasn't keen on the idea of anyone else knowing my business.

Or lack of business.

"Theo," I said, putting my full weight on the crutches and only wincing twice as the movement jarred my knee. "We're still keeping my location under wraps, right? The last thing I need is the press breathing down my neck if my focus is on getting better, you know?"

"They've been told you're rehabbing, but not where. The staff is bound by HIPAA laws, as well as the NDA they signed on your arrival. You're good."

Once he left, I began the long and arduous trek toward the door, lost in my own thoughts. With rigorous physical therapy, there was a chance I could be on the field within six months. I might miss most of spring training, but at least I'd be back for the regular season.

Clearly, I was living in a fairy tale world. One where happy endings existed outside of the massage parlors and the Hurricanes made me another offer. It didn't stop me from briefly closing my eyes and envisioning myself signing the contract, though.

If you can visualize it, you can make it happen.

The exercise was one of my father's more 'out-there' coaching strategies, but something I'd held onto over the years.

Unlike our relationship.

I briefly registered the flash of red hair and looked down at the woman in a wheelchair, frantically waving a placard with my name on it up at me. The smile on her face told me everything I needed to know.

Here we go again.

"Oh, you've got to be fucking kidding me," I snapped with a forced chuckle, before taking off for the elevators as fast as my crutches would allow.

Theo and I were going to have words.

Strong ones.

———

"You're phoning it in, Killian," my trainer, Rocky, noted from his crouched position beside me. "Do it again, but this time, hold for five seconds, okay? That brace is locked in position, it's not going anywhere."

I stared daggers at the ceiling above me before raising my injured leg off the mat a couple of inches. This trainer didn't know a ball from a strike, yet was somehow my best bet for getting back onto the field.

Just keep your mouth shut, Killian, Theo's voice warned from inside my head. *Do as you're told.*

Two weeks in and I was starting to realize my goal of being back on the field next season was nothing more than a pipe dream. Non-weight bearing for six weeks meant I was stuck performing basic range of motion exercises for Rocky until cleared by a doctor.

I would have preferred any one of the team's athletic trainers to him. Even grumpy old Takahashi, whose idea of rehab involved copious amounts of pain, and strangely enough, acupuncture needles. At least he knew me. He would have understood what was at stake and pushed my body to its limits.

He damn sure wouldn't have me lying on a mat, raising my leg up and down like a trained monkey in the circus.

"That's great! Now, hit it back to me!"

I lifted my head to watch the spectacle. Two of the other physical therapists were taking turns batting a balloon to the woman who'd accosted me for an autograph a week ago. As no one had approached me since, I could only assume Theo had done his job.

Rocky looked down to enter something on his tablet, and I took the opportunity to scrutinize the girl. For rehab—or classes, as we were instructed to call them, most everyone wore t-shirts and shorts.

Not her.

She always looked like she was heading off to Sunday service, and the green floral dress she wore today was no exception. The fabric fell to her knees with long sleeves that ended just above her wrists.

As if sensing someone watching her, she looked up and met my gaze. An intense blush stained her cheeks red and she immediately turned away as if she knew she'd been caught.

I'd seen all I needed to when she showed up outside my door. She was like so many women before her—on the hunt for a knight in shining armor to swoop in and rescue them from the monotony of their everyday lives.

Why else would she dress up for therapy?

Poor thing had probably been told she was a princess her entire life, to the point she actually believed it. She wasn't looking for a husband—not really. No, this girl was after the large bank account and children who could be carted around like the latest accessory, while she mindlessly wandered the aisles at the local grocery store.

Unfortunately for her and every other Stepford wife in the making, I was nobody's knight. And it was going to take more than a dress to distract me from my goal.

That wasn't to say I hadn't noticed her. With her auburn hair, she was a little hard to miss, as was the way her eyes seemed to follow me when I entered a room.

Like she was a puppy in a pet store window.

Not that it mattered.

I had more important things to focus on.

The girl nodded when the physical therapist leaned in to say something but kept her eyes trained on the floor. I couldn't pinpoint what it was about the gesture that bothered me, but something in it left me wishing I could take it all back—the words spoken in frustration... every mean thought.

Guilt.

The feeling was almost foreign. Reed men didn't spend time focusing on their list of regrets.

Why dwell on the past when you're on top?

Every mistake had led me to where I wanted to be. Only now, my future wasn't quite as certain, forcing me to consider that maybe I wasn't the man I thought I was.

Are you good?

The mantra had come into existence after a particularly nasty concussion I'd suffered when I was sixteen. After getting into a fight with a kid from school over something I could no longer recall, I'd slipped and fallen off the dock. From there, the details had become a bit hazy. I came to on the beach and remembered seeing a girl hovering over me.

My mama, in her undying faith, firmly believed I'd been saved by an angel. Whether she was an angel or just a hallucination brought on by the head injury, those three words had been enough to keep me in line until the Hurricanes called me up. But by then, I'd given up the idea of being a *good* person in favor of being the *best* athlete.

Maybe that was where my guilt stemmed from, poking away at my consciousness until I paid attention. When I looked across the room, I no longer saw a crazed fan who'd hunted me down for an autograph. I saw a woman whose own future might have been as murky as my own.

The idea came to me as I was on my way down to the cafeteria for lunch after class. I'd apologize to the girl, maybe even offer to sign some things, and then get back to what I was here to do.

Heal.

I ordered a grilled chicken sandwich and balanced on my right leg long enough to grab a salad from the salad bar. As I did, I envisioned one of the woman's many nurses leaking the details of my good deed to the general public.

Killian Reed Befriends Woman in Wheelchair.

God, the press had been starving for details of my personal life for so long they'd lap it up like a cat with cream.

Maybe Theo hadn't been wrong, after all. The Hurricanes weren't going to drop their star because of one little injury, especially not when they got wind of his charitable behavior off-field.

A staff member took my tray and gestured toward the crowded cafeteria. "Where to, Mr. Reed?"

Naturally, my crutches led me right to her table, already preparing for the good karma headed my way.

"Is this seat taken?" I asked with mock ignorance, only to find myself rendered stupid when she glanced up. My mouth hung slack, and whatever I'd planned to say next fell to the floor, completely forgotten.

The last time I'd been this close, I hadn't been paying attention to her features. No, I'd been more than a little preoccupied with kicking Theo's ass for lying to me about NDAs and HIPAA laws.

But it was her eyes...

Bright green eyes that felt familiar to me in a way that I couldn't explain.

CHAPTER FIVE
ARIANA

"Trouble with mice is you always kill 'em."

-John Steinbeck, *Of Mice and Men*

"SO, what's he like? Does he just captivate you with his every word? Like, when I read *This is the Life of Promise*, I didn't leave my apartment for three days. *Three days*. I was just like so lost in his words, you know?"

I nodded while poking at the peas on my plate. My assigned tech, Tiffani, was twenty-five, had grown up in Galveston, and never missed a single Sunday service at *Eagle Lake Church*.

I'd come to learn all of this because the woman hadn't stopped talking since she discovered who I was. My silence went unnoticed as she filled our days with everything from her thoughts on battling Houston traffic, to the best sermons Tristan had ever preached.

"Pastor James is just like such a light, you know?"

Agreeing to come to True North had just like obviously been a stupid, horrible decision, you know?

She paused long enough to suck in a breath of air before launching right back into it. "At the time, I was waiting tables and just like, saw myself going nowhere. Once I read your father's words, though, I realized, my vision wasn't big enough. Now, here I am. He is a true prophet. I mean, like how blessed are we to have him right here in Houston?"

I scrunched my face up. *Like, just so lucky, I can't even stand it.*

"Oh, listen to me! Rambling on and expecting you to answer. I'll let you eat, and then we'll get you back to your room for a little rest."

My weekly schedule was really just different variations of the same thing. I'd spend thirty minutes with my physical therapist, Natalie, in the gym before meeting Fynn for an hour of speech. Then, it was occupational therapy with Andi, followed by lunch.

I couldn't decide if the lingering exhaustion was due to the rigorous classes or just an inability to hear one more person drone on about how great Tristan James was.

On top of that, I was growing increasingly frustrated because I was no closer to discovering the truth. Trying to force my brain back to where it was before the accident was a monumental task, leaving me in constant need of a nap.

Not that those helped any.

I would doze for what seemed like minutes before Tiffani, or another tech would flip on the lights, announcing it was time for a second physical therapy session with Natalie. I took another nap before dinner at five and was back in bed by eight. The medicine the nurses gave was supposed to help me sleep, but it only seemed to make the nightmares more real.

The mesh tent surrounding my bed didn't help—becoming a prison once it was zipped closed and locked—trapping me inside until the morning tech arrived. The staff insisted it was a safety precaution for brain-injured patients, but I knew the truth.

It was just another way for Tristan to exert his power over me.

A cage was a cage, no matter how shiny the metal.

"Your father is just like," Tiffani sighed almost dreamily. "He's just—"

Bigoted? I offered. *Chauvinistic? A murderer?*

Well, if Mama was to be believed. As we'd been told she'd passed from a brain aneurism, it seemed a little far-fetched. Those first two were spot on, though.

"I really hope Fynn can help you get your voice back." Her eyes softened. "I'd really like to know what you're trying to say. I literally cannot imagine how hard that must be."

I immediately pressed my lips together and nodded. Pitching a fit and thinking ugly thoughts would get me nowhere. It wasn't fair. No one knew what Tristan was really like, and being irritated at someone's ignorance over the matter was just plain mean-spirited.

My injury had given me the chance to observe the goodness and generosity that people outside the church had to offer. And Tiffani, despite her misguided devotion, only wanted to help.

On the rare occasions I asked for assistance at home, I was expected to give something in return—very quid pro quo. *True North* was almost a foreign land, by comparison. The staff seemed not only willing, but eager to serve, expecting nothing in return. I longed for the days before the accident, when I could go to the bathroom alone and shower without an audience, but I was also grateful.

Grateful I'd been given the privilege of witnessing beauty in my brokenness.

Tiffani's only real flaw was placing her faith in the wrong hands, just one of many who'd fallen under Tristan's spell over the years. They dropped every dime in the offering plate, imagining they'd somehow stand out in a sea of forty-five thousand attendees, but it was never enough to gain favor with their idol. Tiffani blamed herself for not being enlightened enough spiritually—*If, like, only she'd prayed harder...*

In reality, her income alone would never be enough to set her apart from the politicians and celebrities vying for a coveted spot among Tristan's flock. And if it were, she'd be forced to give up any ideas of gender equality, fully embracing her divine purpose to serve.

There was a distinct difference between church members and

church followers. Church members were welcome to every Sunday service and heavily encouraged to *'step out in faith and tithe.'*

With the exception of Brad, the followers who lived within the community were connected to our family through either marriage or blood. They were also ridiculously wealthy and pledged more per year than most people probably made in twenty.

No, Tiffani was better off outside the walls.

"So, like, I think I keep missing him. When exactly does Pastor James drop by to check on you?"

Never, I mouthed. *It seems I was sacrificed on the altar of a BMW Z4.*

"I'm sorry," Tiffani apologized. "I'm trying to read your lips but can't quite—did you say Sunday at four?"

For only the second time in my life, I found I could speak without stammering, but no one could hear me.

How's that for a paradox?

I shrugged noncommittally and went back to picking at my lunch. Tristan had returned to his stage, preaching the very sermon I'd heard in the van and giving interviews to any network that would have him.

"Is this seat taken?"

I paused in my pursuit of chasing an English pea across the plate and slowly raised my head. Except for the staff, no one spoke to me.

Ever.

My heart skipped and stumbled when our eyes met, temporarily forgetting the very crux of its existence.

Him.

I wasn't sure who I'd been expecting, but it wasn't the crutch-wielding jerk from across the hall. I'd hoped our encounter in the hall was one we'd never repeat—yet, here he was again—proving that God must have had quite a sense of humor.

I'd spent a good chunk of my life wanting nothing more than to be seen, only to have my request granted at the most inopportune of times.

Be careful what you pray for, am I right?

"What's that?" He leaned down as far as the crutches would allow, still towering over me in a way that felt intimidating. "Did you say something?"

Tiffani cleared her throat. "Well, she can't—"

"Okay, great. Yeah, just place it right there," he muttered distractedly. An aide placed his tray next to mine and returned to the kitchen before anyone could voice their objections.

Our new table mate flashed us a smile before glancing down to my wheelchair. "Oh, uh, you dropped something."

A quick check of my lap confirmed the napkin lying near his feet was indeed mine. This was no paper napkin, either. Oh no, *True North* only used the best of everything. Linen napkins, starched tablecloths—even vases with fresh cut flowers.

It was such a stark change from the hospital—where everything was disposable and easily discarded. If I didn't like the night nurse, it was just a matter of waiting for a shift change. Here, though, there was consistency with the staff and the well-decorated tables.

I pushed back from the table, only to be stopped by the sound of his voice.

"Stay there, I've got it." He adjusted his weight and tried bending over, succeeding in rattling his crutches, but not much else. I bit down on the inside of my cheek, ridiculously satisfied in watching him make a scene over a scrap of linen.

"You know what? We'll just do this," he snagged a napkin off the table next to mine and handed it over with a flourish.

I placed it on my tray, searching his face through narrowed eyes. What was it he wanted? There had to be a hidden motive.

There always was.

He shifted uncomfortably under the weight of my stare before carefully lowering himself onto the empty chair beside me. A strand of jet-black hair flopped onto his forehead, and he casually brushed it back without once breaking eye contact. Gruff exterior notwithstanding, the man was ridiculously good-looking.

I should know.

I'd been watching him all week. It would have been impossible to miss how attractive he was, and while, I approved of his features immensely, it wasn't what had drawn me to him.

"It's like geriatric hell around here, right?" he asked before taking a bite of his sandwich.

In the hallway, he'd noticed me in the fleeting way one would a fly buzzing around their head, but I'd studied him for days, learning about the kind of man he was.

And the more I observed, the less I wanted to see.

Unfortunately, this time, my blatant gawking hadn't gone unnoticed. Tiffani scrutinized the two of us, her eyes sparkling with sudden interest. It was a form of communication that needed no translation.

I jerked my head in response, the back of my neck prickling with heated embarrassment. Knowing my face was likely the color of a strawberry, I turned away and began carefully rearranging the peas into a straight line again.

Good, Ariana. Really good. Completely normal behavior for someone who isn't guilty of anything.

Even the slightest suspicion of wrongdoing on my part would no doubt lead to a visit from Tristan. And, as I still didn't know what had led to the car wreck, I was eager to stay under his radar for as long as possible.

Cutlery rattled amid the low buzz of voices from other patients enjoying their lunches, all seemingly unaware of the disastrous situation unfolding just feet from their tables.

"You know, this facility is supposed to be the best in the country, but it's nothing but old oil and gas tycoons who want to spend their time reminiscing about the glory days," the man rambled in between bites. "They've all got one foot on a banana peel—and has anyone here actually seen the football player? What's his name?"

Justin Thomas, I mouthed to the untouched mashed potatoes in front of me.

"He does all the charity work? God, it's on the tip of my tongue. Watch, it'll come to me in the middle of the night." He hunched down into my line of vision. "Hey, you're awfully quiet over there."

I kept my head down and fidgeted with my new necklace, using my thumbnail to trace the miniature suction cups etched into each tentacle. I knew if I looked up, I'd want to dive into the icy blue waters of his eyes and never resurface. Just like a character from one of the books I kept hidden beneath my bed, the man could only be described as *devastatingly handsome*.

Handsome, for the obvious reasons.

Instead of moving toward my face, this wave of heat surged south, making my stomach flutter like a nest of birds ready to take flight. Clearly, the car wreck hadn't destroyed everything, but I was beginning to question my body's discernment.

Growing up, we'd been taught that sin was like a snake, lurking in dark corners, poised and ready to strike.

I disagreed.

Men like him, with their blue-gray eyes and beaming smiles, were the culmination of my every sinful thought—the reason my hand had found its way beneath my nightgown more than once over the last five years.

Maybe it was just me, but I'd always pictured sin as having full lips, a shadowed jawline, and dark eyebrows.

Yes, I'd noticed his eyebrows.

Some of the older men within the church had remarkably thick eyebrows, like bushy caterpillars sprawled lazily above each eye. His were nothing like that. They didn't detract from his eyes. If anything, they only seemed to enhance his features.

My actions might have looked like interest to Tiffani, but nothing could be farther from the truth. I was simply observing him, the same way one might a bear in the woods.

Warily, and with extreme caution.

Because he was *devastatingly* handsome. Devastating, in that, once he opened his mouth, all of that beauty fell away, revealing the ugly underneath. It was any wonder his foot wasn't permanently wedged in between his full lips.

And he wasn't even aware of it.

To be honest, before today, I hadn't been entirely sure he was aware I existed. Sure, he'd looked right at me in the hallway, but he hadn't seen me.

Not really.

I'd seen him, though.

In class, he refused to put in the work and complained about almost everything, leaving his physical therapist looking defeated. When his friend with the nice suits visited, his angry words drifted across the hall into my room.

I wouldn't turn my back on a man like that any more than I would the errant bear. I'd mistakenly assumed he'd take a hint and leave when I refused to acknowledge him. Instead, he dropped the half-eaten sandwich to his plate and leaned in, searching my face.

"Look, I came over here for a reason," he admitted softly as if trying to recall what exactly that was. "Can we start over and you forget everything I said? Hi, my name is Killian."

Killian.

I stared at his extended hand and clenched my jaw before forcing my eyes up to meet his inquisitive stare. The corner of his mouth turned up when I made no attempt to take his hand. Meanwhile, I was busy dispassionately labeling his facial features to keep my resolve from slipping.

There was a slight bend in the bridge of his nose, probably from a break that hadn't been set correctly. Unlike his left ear, the top of the right one curved ever so slightly away from the side of his head. And, even with the heavy stubble, it was obvious he had a cleft chin. I was nothing more than an impartial observer, completely unaffected by the beautiful man in front of her.

Seconds passed, and he slowly lowered his hand back to the table with a forced laugh. "Christ, is this because of the autograph? Look, you caught me at a bad time, but that's actually what—"

I don't even know you, I mouthed, surprised by the low growl that accompanied my words. I looked past Killian to Tiffani before realizing the sound had come from me.

"Yeah, well, you sure could have fooled me. It seems like I'm intruding on your lunch, so I'll leave you ladies in peace." The rubber tip of his crutches gave a slight squeak against the tile as he stood, but this time, I didn't bother looking up. I needed a minute to fully appreciate what had just occurred.

I'd done it.

Tiffani's expression remained blank, which surprised me. I might have welcomed her sudden vow of silence a half-hour ago, but now it felt strange. If anyone should have had something to say right now, it was her.

Well? I mouthed, slightly disappointed when there was no sound. *Baby steps.*

She released an unsteady breath and leaned back in her chair. "I can't believe that just happened. Like, I'm literally speechless right now."

I nodded in agreement—although technically, I'd been speechless for about a month now.

"Ariana, do you realize what this means?"

I can make sounds? I asked, the side of my mouth lifting in amusement.

"He knew what you were saying," Tiffani said, bringing her eyes back to mine. "Fynn can't even understand you, but Killian did! Twice!"

I stared at her, certain I was gaping.

Had she been at the same table I had? I'd growled—not loudly, but obviously, the next step was speaking. What did Killian have to do with any of it? Not only was the man a jerk, but a conceited one at that.

An autograph?

Please.

Tiffani pushed her chair back from the table, laughing softly to herself. "I think we've had enough fun for one afternoon. Let's get back to your room for a little rest."

I agreed, still stewing over the man's odd behavior. Who did he think he was—the president? I'd simply needed help. Help that he'd refused to give. No wonder his physical therapist looked haggard—Killian was probably convinced the poor guy was in love with him.

What a lunatic...

"Watch out, this one would just as soon run you over as look at you."

I tensed and squared my shoulders, my breaths quickening at the sound of his voice. Saliva flooded my mouth, leaving me wishing—not for the first time—for the power of invisibility.

And there it was, folks.

Blink. Blink.

Devastatingly handsome—the absolute worst kind of handsome a man could be.

It wasn't as if Killian was the first man to taunt me—heck, he wasn't even the tenth. I'd learned it was best to just keep my head down, letting the ugly words roll off me like water on a duck's back. But something in his tone had me clenching my fists and jerking my chin up in defiance, daring him to continue.

Maybe I would run him over with my wheelchair.

Those crutches were going to slow him down considerably.

Killian flashed me a confident smirk, one of his eyebrows cocking up in amusement. The older man at his side seemed less impressed as he dissected me with a thoughtful frown.

I was busy debating the pros and cons of attempting another growl while snapping my teeth when Killian's gaze swept across my face. The scrutiny left me feeling out of sorts, like a specimen in a lab. I lowered my fists, tucking my trembling fingers into the fold of my dress, suddenly eager to be dismissed.

Had I been born anyone else, I imagined I would have found the quirk of his mouth mesmerizing, his words little more than playful teasing. If I hadn't known any better, I would have given Killian second and third chances, hoping he'd prove himself to be different. I would have wasted precious time trying to understand what made him tick while he hid his true nature behind pretty smiles.

I was wrong before.

Killian wasn't devastatingly handsome.

He was charming—which might have been worse. A bear in the woods was a blatant threat, but charming men weren't bears. They were the foxes appearing in folklore—tricksters who cleverly camouflaged their true nature to outsmart prey.

By the time their victims sensed danger, it was too late.

Unfortunately for him, I'd had my fill of charming men and seeing my own terror-filled face reflected in the glow of their sharp-toothed grins.

CHAPTER SIX
KILLIAN

"Baseball is the only place in life where a sacrifice is really appreciated."

-Author Unknown

"WHAT IN THE hell are you doing?"

I made a show of adjusting the pillow beneath my calf and getting comfortable before grudgingly acknowledging the two-hundred-pound gorilla in the room. My father had taken his sweet time in showing up, leading me to almost believe I was exempt from dealing with his bullshit.

"Killian Joseph, I'm speaking to you. You wanna tell me what that was back there? I come here, expecting to find you focused on healing, but instead, it's the same dog and pony show as before. Everything's a game to you."

"Hey, Dad. Nice of you to show up." I shifted my jaw from side to side. "I'm doing great, all things considered. How are things at home?"

If he was expecting a hug and a smile, he'd caught me on the wrong day.

This was all her fault.

I'd tried to do something nice, only to have it blow up in my hand like a faulty firecracker. No matter the circumstances, I'd long prided myself on my ability to stay in control. But it seemed ol' Joe Reed suddenly had some competition in pushing me to my breaking point.

It was supposed to have been a simple apology.

"Don't get disrespectful with me, son. I cleared my schedule to be here."

Christ, had the world suddenly gone mad?

Leave it to Joe to have brought along the guilt trip. The man had been mostly retired from real estate for the past year. And even then, it wasn't as if the firm he'd built was going to run itself into the ground in a single day.

"Really wish you would have called before you came down this way. I would have rearranged my schedule to miss you, and we could have avoided—whatever the hell this is."

His eyes narrowed, but he stayed near the door. "I don't get it, Killian. The team sent you here because they wanted to give you another chance—how many players get that? Huh? And you're pissing it away, screwing around with other patients."

I didn't have time for his shit.

I was tired, and my knee needed icing—and thanks to a recent streak of shitty karma, I no longer had a plan for garnering some positive publicity.

Joe had a real knack for showing up unannounced just as everything seemed to be falling apart. He'd swoop in with his tough love speech before disappearing back to the suburbs until the next time I fucked up.

My life would forever revolve around continual drilling to be the best. Growing up, there were no neighborhood pick-up games in the dirt lot at the end of the block. Instead, I was shuttled from one facility to the next, spending my summers with the multitude of coaches my father had hired to hone my skills.

Reed men didn't settle for anything less than perfect, even if it meant staying out well past dark, mastering the skill. Homework... friends... sleep—they all came second to the game.

To him, I was never *Killian, the kid.*

I was Killian, the commodity.

I'd learned to thrive under pressure, knowing he'd sunk a fortune into building my career. Bitching about my lack of a childhood now seemed petty when I considered where the rigorous training had gotten me.

"Are you committed to putting in the necessary work—"

"Or are you going to settle for being second best?" I finished with an over-the-top sigh. The phrase was just as much a backdrop of my life as a baseball diamond.

"Killian, if the Hurricanes get word you're jacking around on their dime, you're as good as gone," he stated flatly, delivering the spike into my coffin with as much enthusiasm as someone giving a traffic report.

When guilt failed to yield the results he wanted, I could always count on my father to go for the jugular by casting doubt on my abilities. The seeds he planted blossomed into a colorful array of full-blown panic that kept me awake at night, convinced I was finished.

And then what?

I might have inherited his ball skills, but the similarities between us ended there. He'd easily taken to an off-field career after his injury, but the thought of trading my uniform for a suit and tie was nothing short of depressing.

I didn't want to do anything else.

Wasn't built for it.

"You know, Mama brought me a brand-new pair of sheepskin house shoes when she stopped by yesterday. They're real nice too, with memory foam and shearling. But you—you show up with the same song and dance I heard last season after we lost to Toronto. And I really could have used a nice thick pair of socks to go with those shoes too."

"Are you even listening to me?" he snapped. "What do you want me to say, knowing my only child's career is on the brink of collapse?"

Brink of collapse?

Well, it was clear he wasn't getting his PR talking points from Theo.

"Have you ever thought about..." I paused, taking several deep breaths until I trusted I wasn't going to launch a barrage of insults in his direction. "Have you ever thought about not saying anything? Maybe just dropping by to see how I'm doing?"

His grim smile was all the answer I needed. "I'm here now, aren't I? Look, I just think you've worked too hard to lose it all at the age of twenty-six."

I rolled my eyes. "Lose it all? Gee, thanks, Dad. It's nice knowing I can always count on you to not blow things out of proportion."

The truth was staring me right in the face. My father was an old dog whose only trick seemed to be reciting some variation of the same tired schtick.

He didn't give a damn about me. It all boiled down to the player and whether he was toeing the team's line or not. This wound between us had been festering for going on fourteen years.

I imagined things would continue on like they always had with ol' Joe stuck on his soapbox, holding up a tattered cardboard sign, proclaiming that the end was near.

Shape up or risk losing everything.

Not only did Reed men demand perfection, but we weren't really big on apologies either—which brought me full circle. Since when did I care so much about what a stranger thought of me?

I'd dealt with critics my whole life—from the press who hadn't understood the hype surrounding my name, to the rabid fans I'd had to dodge after a loss.

Never once had I felt the need to go back and apologize.

What made her any different?

Maybe it was just a temporary lapse in judgment—a combination of boredom and too much time on my hands. We were, after all, the youngest residents here by a good fifty years.

I let my father's stern warning sink in, wondering if maybe he had it right. My future rested solely on my ability to perform—that was it. If I wanted a contract, then I had to stop fixating on anything other than coming back better than before.

Failure was only an option when it came to my relationship with him.

———

"How's that feeling?" Rocky asked after adjusting the ice packs surrounding my knee. "I think with as hard as we're pushing your body during the day, you're going to notice more swelling in the evenings. The best thing to do is—"

"Fine." I didn't react to the crushed expression on his face before turning my attention back to *SportsCenter*. I actually hadn't minded the nighttime therapy and icing session—even if it meant missing most of game seven of the ALCS. Nevertheless, I needed him to take the hint and get lost.

I'd been in a sour mood since my father's visit and wanted to hear Rocky's thoughts on cryotherapy about as much as I wanted to see Kansas City in the World Series. Judging by the highlights from tonight's game, I was going to be out of luck on both accounts.

"Can you turn this up?" I craned my neck, struggling to read the closed captioning blocks from across the room.

His posture tightened. "Sure, man. Anything else you need? Bottled water? Warm blankets? Extra pillows?"

I caught myself before I snapped and instead leveled a glare at the television. Acknowledging the jab would only make things worse.

"Alright, my bad." Rocky cleared his throat. "I thought because you enjoyed dishing it out, you'd have no trouble taking it. Guess I was wrong, so I'll just leave you to it."

It appeared as if my failed apology had reached the *True North* rumor mill.

"Sure wish you would." I gave him an exaggerated grin. "I'm pretty sure the team isn't paying for your biting wit there, Rock."

I didn't usually mind laughing at my own expense. With Conor Bailey as a teammate, I'd learned not to take myself so seriously. That jackass was continually trying to rile me up over something.

Rocky wasn't Bailey, though.

My teammate and best friend would have seen what I saw—another bitter fan, pissed because I hadn't dropped everything for a goddamn autograph. To gossipmongers like Rocky, though, I was cast as the prick who'd been mean to the nice girl in the wheelchair.

Truthfully, I'd spent most of the afternoon musing over the proverbial bee in the girl's butt. As the only available data had already proven to be inconclusive, I simply wandered aimlessly through my thoughts, confusing myself further.

She hadn't just derailed any attempt at an apology—the girl had refused to even acknowledge I was speaking until I called her out on it.

I don't even know you!

The anger that had been simmering most of the afternoon came to a boil again. Still, it wasn't entirely justified, as I definitely could have handled the situation better.

In hindsight, I probably would have skipped the teasing as it hadn't warmed her to me. If anything, it had only made things worse. There were several moments where I'd actually been convinced she was planning to run me over with the damn chair.

Something I was probably long overdue for.

Whatever. I'd tried and failed—overthinking it wouldn't change a damn thing.

Time to focus on the team.

"Now Sanchez will walk in—"

I jerked at the sudden blast of sound coming from the television speakers before waving a middle finger at Rocky.

"Oh, sorry! Let me fix that for ya!" he shouted over the dull roar of the game highlights before lowering the volume and walking away with a satisfied smirk.

Time to charge the mound, motherfucker.

If he wanted to play, we'd play. I just hoped he knew who he was going up against.

"*—and it's driven deep to left-centerfield!*" the announcer screamed. "*Crawford is going for it... but it's gone! It's over! With Garrett Sanchez's walk-off home run, the Bears are returning to the World Series for the second year in a row!*"

A half-second later, the rectangular closed-captioning box flashed across the screen, confirming the news. Each black and white letter a stark reminder of how I'd let my team down.

The screen cut back to the studio, and I dropped onto the treatment table with a muffled growl. Rage clouded my vision, and I pressed my fingers against my eyelids, stemming the urge to destroy something.

It should have been us.

The Hurricanes were supposed to make history. Instead, a subpar team would be taking our place all because I'd thought I could make it to second base.

Fucking Sanchez.

"The rib fractures don't seem to slow her down. Have you looked at incorporating more walking into her plan?"

Rib fractures?

My pulse slowed, and I lowered my hands before cutting my eyes over to the corner of the room. Rocky was deep in discussion with the dark-haired therapist, Natalie.

They were discussing the girl—I'd bet my paycheck on it. And hearing another person's take was just too good of an opportunity to pass up. Ol' emerald eyes couldn't have fooled everyone, which meant vindication was about to be mine.

Again, it didn't matter.

I'd said my piece and was moving on.

Yes, sir.

I was one hundred percent done with distractions, even if they did have the most beautiful eyes I'd ever seen. She looked familiar —*so, what?* It was probably because I'd met millions of women just like her throughout my career.

And I was only interested in knowing how she'd ended up with broken ribs because she couldn't have been much older than twenty.

Awfully young for the old, *'I've fallen, and I can't get up'* routine.

Wanting to be informed of someone's injury didn't mean I was suddenly going against my plan. This was nothing more than a fact-finding mission because we were going to be sharing space for the foreseeable future.

Made perfect sense to me.

"The persistent dizziness transitioning from wheelchair to standing has really limited what we can do—although, hand-eye coordination is where I expect it to be given the circumstances—"

"What the hell does that mean?" I blurted without thinking.

Obviously, I'd meant to say that in my head.

The conversation ceased, and I quickly jerked my head back toward the television, sensing two pairs of eyes studying me intently. Their glares seemed to contain equal parts frustration and suspicion, which gave me about a snowball's chance in hell of them continuing to talk openly in front of me.

Well, it certainly wasn't the worst odds I'd ever faced...

Of course, there was nothing but celebratory coverage of the Bears on the screen, because apparently, every other sports league had decided to take the night off.

"You can't—" I fumbled with the words before sputtering, "You can't call Sanchez a legend-in-the-making! He's a rookie!"

I doubted the word *legend* had ever been uttered in any sentence on Sanchez—but they didn't know that.

Hopefully.

The silence seemed to stretch on for minutes, and I briefly considered shaking my fist at the screen to really drive home my point before deciding it would only give me away. Out of the corner of my eye, I could just make out Rocky's intent stare. He was debating with himself, looking for a way to prove I'd been eavesdropping.

Like he had any room to judge.

When he finally turned back to Natalie, I released the breath I'd been holding, ready to get some answers.

What happened to you, girl?

Not that it was any of my business. I'd made my mind up and hearing some sob story wasn't likely to change it.

Didn't mean I wasn't going to listen to every word, though.

People loved a sad story, something that really tugged on their heartstrings. Anyone who said otherwise was a liar. In a cynical world, humans craved being made to feel something other than apathy.

It was why those commercials with the abandoned and abused animals were so effective in getting people to hand over their wallets. Although, instead of sitting in a cage looking forlorn, the girl was more likely to be frothing at the mouth while she gnawed on the metal bars.

"What about speech? Has Fynn noticed any improvement?"

At the mention of talking, I forgot about feigning disinterest and turned my head to where I could see both of them.

Natalie sighed. "He said she tries—she even moves her lips a lot, but he's still only able to make out a word or two. It could be residual effects from being on the vent and then having the trach.

"Although, when we were talking, he mentioned something about the location of language areas in the brain. I guess they typically work independently of right or left-handedness, but in a small number of cases, it's the right hemisphere that's dominant for language. With the patient being left-handed, we can't necessarily rule it out."

Rocky circled something on Natalie's tablet with his finger. "It would make sense given that her brain injury occurred on the right side, but I think the fact she's trying to communicate is a good sign, Nat."

"How can we know so much about these injuries, and yet, still so little?"

Oddly enough, I'd just been asking myself something similar. In fact, the revelations had me questioning damn near everything but the color of the sky. I tried circling back to what I knew as the truth, scrambling for answers.

The girl was rude.

Fact.

What little she did say I'd understood just fine, disproving the idea she couldn't speak.

Also, a fact... mostly.

I suddenly couldn't seem to recall if she'd actually spoken the words or if I'd just read her lips. If it was the former, then she was putting on an act.

If it was the latter, then... *Jesus.*

Are you good?

The words landed like a line drive to the face, and my jaw went slack. Rocky mistook my sudden need to leave as frustration over the game and urged me to sleep it off before meeting him in the morning for class.

As I made my way down the hall, accompanied by the lonely squeak of my crutches against the tile, I didn't see how I'd ever manage to sleep again. No, I'd be up for days, reliving every second of our encounter.

I paused when I reached my door and looked back. Her room was right there, but those six feet between us may as well have been an ocean. Even if I could somehow cut the distance and knock on her door, I was now painfully aware of the fact that she couldn't tell me to come in. And, as she used a wheelchair, she wasn't likely to jump up and let me in either.

I wasn't good.

And if I was honest with myself, I hadn't been in quite some time. I'd become a clone of my father, too proud to apologize. Hell, most of the time, I couldn't even admit to being wrong.

I had to fix this.

First thing tomorrow, I'd sacrifice my pride and go over there. I wouldn't get distracted or start rambling, either. This time, I wouldn't leave until I'd made things right.

I settled into bed, coming back to the same unanswered question that had been brewing in my head for the better part of the day.

Why was earning her forgiveness so important?

CHAPTER SEVEN
ARIANA

"There are many Beths in the world, shy and quiet, sitting in corners till needed, and living for others so cheerfully that no one sees the sacrifices till the little cricket on the hearth stops chirping, and the sweet, sunshiny presence vanishes, leaving silence and shadow behind."

-Louisa May Alcott, *Little Women*

The scent of burning rubber clung to my nostrils, along with something else I couldn't quite identify.

Gasoline maybe?

Thick smoke billowed out from under the hood of the convertible, obliterating the last remaining rays of light from the sunset along with any chance of me being found before morning.

I managed to lift my head just enough to determine Tristan's car was nothing more than a twisted heap of metal before collapsing against the earth again with a muffled moan.

Something sharp dug into my palm, but I couldn't move. Drawing even the smallest of breaths sent shooting pain throughout my entire body.

I wouldn't survive long—not like this. My limbs grew heavy in response, tugging me toward oblivion. But instead of bright light or a heavenly voice calling me home, there was nothing but darkness.

I didn't mind.

The void felt familiar—safe.

Like I'd dreamt of it before.

Maybe I had. Perhaps deep down, I'd always known it was going to end like this. I halfheartedly fought against my slipping consciousness before closing my eyes in relief.

It didn't hurt anymore.

This wasn't giving up... it was merely giving in to the inevitable.

"The car's down here!"

I parted my lips to cry out before it struck me that I knew the voice.

And suddenly, I didn't want to be found.

MY LEG JERKED INVOLUNTARILY, rescuing me from yet another nightmare. I peeled my cheek from the damp pillow, ears still ringing from the whine of an engine that miraculously hadn't stalled out upon impact.

It was happening again—fact and fiction bleeding together and leaving me in a strange state of surrealness.

One of the hospital psychologists had recommended moving around to shorten the episode and rouse my mind back to the present. I slowly sat up and blinked, hoping to clear my vision, but the dense fog of smoke remained—the crumpled black frame of the convertible still so close I could almost touch it.

Reality told me it wasn't there and that I was safe in my bed at *True North*, but the nightmare crudely spliced in by my brain begged to differ. I squeezed my eyes shut and fought against the rising tide of panic with each suffocating moment that passed.

The dreams were different every time too. In one, I was still behind the wheel, repeatedly stomping on a brake pedal that no longer worked. In another, the radio stations were changing on their own. It made it virtually impossible to know how much, if any, of what I saw was rooted in reality.

I craved answers but delving into my subconscious for clues only left my mind feeling chaotic, imagining people who weren't there.

People who couldn't possibly have been there.

A brief knock at the door saved me from speculating on the matter further, and I cracked one eye open, relieved to find my hospital room had returned to its normal state. It took several seconds more to rid my mind of the haunting images and slow my racing heart.

It only hurts if you let it...

"Good morning, Ariana," Tsega called as she entered the room, her lips curving up in a wide smile.

I returned the gesture with a small wave, the closest I could get to actual communication for the time being.

Tsega was the weekend aide and, according to Tiffani, a devout Buddhist. She'd felt it was of the utmost importance I know every detail, lest I '*like convert*' before she returned on Monday.

Given the sheer number of whispered warnings I'd received for the past two Fridays, it was evident Tiffani hadn't spent her free time studying other religions. If she had, she would have known that Buddhists typically respected different religious views and weren't exactly known for proselytizing.

She was confusing them with Tristan.

Tsega went over to the large marker board and filled in the daily details, along with who was on-duty. Once that was complete, she helped me out of my mesh prison and into the bathroom for a shower.

Weekends at *True North* were quiet. There were no classes to attend or schedules to keep. Most patients spent their time watching movies or doing crafts down in the common areas with their families.

In an ironic twist of fate, I found the sudden abundance of freedom unsettling. It was a bit like watching sand drain into the bottom of an hourglass—a reminder my time here was running out. I didn't want to sit and paint a teacup or roam the halls in my wheelchair before being carted back behind the walls of a cage I was all too familiar with.

It was a frustrating thing, knowing that what you needed and what you were destined for were miles apart.

Like a well-trained zebra finch, I'd spent my life mimicking the rhythm of my father's song while poking my head through the bars for even the smallest taste of freedom.

"Today's a special day," Tsega explained as she braided my damp hair. "You have a visitor."

I wasn't ready.

I managed a small nod and rubbed my sweaty palms against the skirt of my dress while staring longingly at the bright red exit sign above the door.

If only it were that easy.

Tsega paused her gentle movements and, keeping one hand on my braid, crouched in front of my chair. She studied my trembling fingers, clenched tightly together, before lifting her eyes to my face.

My pulse thundered as she surveyed me, forcing my heart up into my throat with each furious beat. Tiffani might have been nice, but Tsega was perceptive, picking up on the little things that had gone unnoticed my entire life.

Just last Sunday morning, an overzealous nurse had come in. After turning my television to the live broadcast from *Eagle Lake Church*, she'd found it necessary to tell me how Pastor James had saved her marriage. When the first few bars of the opening song had begun to play, she'd placed a hand on her chest with a sigh and asked, "Doesn't hearing this just fill you with hope?"

I'd stared blankly at her, sure she was messing with me.

I was the one singing.

Our worship band had released four albums—the latest of which had been nominated for Pop/Contemporary Album of the Year at last year's Dove Awards—not that I'd been allowed to attend the award ceremony in Nashville.

Brad had once boasted that they'd use my songs until the earth turned to dust because there was something eerie in my voice—something that made people sink to their knees in repentance.

As I'd listened, I couldn't help but agree. The sound was hauntingly beautiful, causing my flesh to break out in goosebumps by the time I reached the chorus. My every word was clear and resolute, leaving me to wonder where the strength went when I wasn't singing.

Tsega had watched me intently during the song, and in the minutes following the nurse's departure when my father came onstage. Then, without saying a word, she'd gotten up and turned it off.

She was doing it again now, studying me like I was a code in need of cracking. I gathered a deep breath, slightly curious to know what she saw when she looked at me—a meek creature who startled at the slightest sound? A fragile woman with no voice?

Perhaps Tsega's view was just as misguided as Killian's. That somehow felt worse than being seen as weak. I turned away as emotion clogged my throat, threatening to spill over in the form of tears.

It only hurts if you let it...

She inhaled sharply before placing her free hand over both of mine. "It's not your father, okay? It's not him. It's a woman—Morgan. If you don't want to see her—"

Morgan? Yes.

To drive my point home, I began bobbing my head up and down in an exaggerated manner, loosening my braid with each eager nod.

Tsega nodded, her eyes glinting with amusement. "Okay. But first, we have to fix your hair again."

With the feelings of relief came a sudden influx of memories and a sharp flare of guilt—*I hadn't thought of Morgan once since my accident.*

How had I forgotten my only confidante? Her family had begun attending *Eagle Lake* when she was fourteen, but it had taken me a lot longer just to work up the courage to say hello.

At youth gatherings, I sat in the back, silently admiring the streaks of white blonde in her dark hair. Later, once we'd been properly introduced, she'd informed me they were highlights and not something she'd been born with—yet I'd never even been allowed to cut my hair, much less alter the color.

Looking back, I couldn't help but feel that by befriending her, I was at least partially responsible for what happened next. If I'd never overcome my fear of speaking to her, Morgan would have been just another nameless face in the crowd.

Safe.

Instead, I'd led her into the monster's lair, never imagining Tristan would take an interest in a sixteen year-old girl.

Clearly, I'd underestimated him.

Her family eagerly accepted Tristan's proposal and moved into the gated community during their two-year courtship, oblivious to the trap that had been set. On her eighteenth birthday, Tristan put a ring on Morgan's finger and an end to her traveling anywhere without an escort.

The white highlights gradually faded away, but Morgan had never lost her spark, which had only made me admire her more. Yet, as much as I'd tried over the last three years, I couldn't bring myself to call her my stepmother. She was, after all, only a couple of years older than me.

My best friend.

The one person who knew me better than anyone else.

An idea began to take root. I'd been going about this all wrong—putting enormous amounts of pressure on my body to speed up the healing process. But the answer had been right in front of me all along. If there was one person who could tell me with certainty what I'd been doing before the accident, it was Morgan.

We never kept secrets from each other.

After Tsega radioed down to the front desk, I kept my eyes on the door, restlessly bouncing the soles of my house shoes against the wheelchair footrests. Somehow, despite the current of nervous energy flooding my body, she managed to tame my braid.

I was so caught up in witnessing Morgan's arrival that when

Tsega offered me a notebook and pen, I handed it back to her in confusion.

"No," she chuckled. "For you... to write down what you want to say."

Oh. Right.

In my excitement, I'd forgotten I was terrible at Charades. Although, in my defense, trying to act out the phrase "Noah's Ark" in front of sixty hyperactive youth members would have been daunting for anyone.

The breath caught in my throat when the door opened and Morgan appeared. She pulled me into her arms, squeezing to the point of pain, but I didn't care.

I'd missed her.

I hadn't realized just how much until I was enveloped in the comforting scent of her raspberry and vanilla body spray.

"I'm sorry, Ari," she rasped before abruptly pulling back. "Am I hurting you?"

I shook my head, unable to wipe the grin from my face.

"Good. I've—" Morgan awkwardly cleared her throat and took a step back, letting her hands drop to her sides. "We've been praying so hard for your recovery. The church, I mean. We—"

Tsega offered her a chair, and she fell silent again, dropping onto it with a frustrated exhale. "Your father—he's just been sick over this. Well, we all have... really."

The thoughtful look returned to Tsega's face. "Did Ginny have you do the family training when you got here?"

"I watched the video, and we discussed the basics. Is that what you're asking?"

Sensing where Tsega was leading with her questioning, I began nodding, pleased that she and I were on the same page.

"Yep, and since you've been informed of the protocol, I can actually step out and let you two catch up in private," she said with another strange expression that made deciphering her thoughts virtually impossible.

The woman was quite the enigma.

Morgan's smile slipped as soon as Tsega left the room. She grasped the arms of the wheelchair, yanking me until our knees butted together.

"What happened to you?" she hissed, her mouth twisting into a brief grimace as she leaned forward.

I pulled the pen from the binding of the notebook and scrawled,

You don't know?

It didn't make sense.

"No," Morgan admitted, sadness clouding her features. "He said you were in a car accident. I needed you to help me understand, but you can't even talk."

We told each other everything—if I ran away, she would have known the reason, unless...

Unless I no longer trusted her.

I released the notebook and dropped my hands down to the wheels on my wheelchair, pulling back until I was satisfied with the distance I'd placed between us.

Was this Tristan's plan—using Morgan as a spy?

It seemed ridiculous—even to me—but there was no other explanation.

"Ari, it's just that Tristan—"

No, I mouthed at the mention of his name, holding my hand up. *Stop.*

The same woman who'd once stood in the middle of Sunday school and proclaimed that the church's teachings were archaic and slanted toward men had seemingly changed her stance without a second thought. Meanwhile, I'd been questioning the accuracy of my memories because I appeared to be the only person in the world who saw Tristan James for what he was.

At night, I'd laid awake, wondering if everyone else had it right. I'd even gone as far as considering the possibility that his treatment of me was nothing more than a direct response to my alleged rebelliousness.

The thought made my stomach churn, but deep down, I knew I wasn't the problem. It didn't matter what other people believed because they didn't know him like I did. They'd never experienced his rage.

But Morgan had.

Maybe to an even greater extent than me.

In what could only be described as unfortunate timing on my part, I'd overheard the sounds of Morgan's quiet sobs while Tristan groaned loudly in what I presumed to be ecstasy. Even with my minimal experience, I wasn't completely naïve when it came to sex. I just struggled to come to terms with the details of the arrangement.

When Sister Helene lectured us in health class on the importance of bearing Eve's sin with submissive hearts, I'd almost believed she was joking. The lesson was just one of many in the church-funded private school curriculum, or, as I'd affectionately come to call it: *A Study in Women's Suffering.*

There'd never been any real education in health class, just a consistent reminder that sex was a necessary punishment for women. We'd once spent an entire semester discussing how faithful and obedient Adam had been until his wife had used her sex to turn him away from the truth.

Because heaven forbid, we take a step back and examine the talking snake and his roadside fruit stand.

Despite our cursed souls, the church inexplicably believed our bodies were sacred vessels, meant to remain untouched and pure until our wedding night. It was a man's divine right to join his body with his wife's, bringing her sins to light. Because nine months of pregnancy and the agony of labor weren't enough.

Unsurprisingly, I'd never been in much of a hurry to marry.

I might have assumed what I'd overheard was nothing more than the physical act of marriage, had I not seen the marks on Morgan's body the following day. No lesson could explain the spectrum of old and new bruises coating her torso.

Nothing could explain that level of brutality.

Which was why I was having a hard time believing she'd see eye to eye with Tristan on anything. There had never been any problems between us. If anything, our shared wounds had only brought us closer together.

"If you would just listen to me—please," she begged, hugging herself.

I shook my head, wanting to vomit as I remembered the things I'd shared with her over the years. Had she been sent to give me a lecture on remaining obedient, or to simply discuss the importance of not crashing Tristan's luxury cars when running away from home?

Suddenly, she jolted upright, staggering toward me. I jerked the wheels again, but only managed a few inches before connecting with the side of the bed.

Morgan blocked my next escape attempt, locking her hand around my cheeks to pin me in place. "Listen to me, goddammit! I'm not here to hurt you."

I tensed my shoulders as her fingers dug into the tender flesh above my jaw but didn't move again. Morgan's chest rose and fell with several rapid breaths before she loosened her hold on me.

"You cannot come back," she forced out, her nostrils flaring. "Do you understand me?"

I nodded, not understanding at all. *True North* could only let me stay for up to twelve weeks. Regardless of what I wanted, eventually, I was going to have to go back. It wasn't as if I was in any shape to do much else. Even if there'd been a solid plan behind my escape, the details of it were rotting along with the mangled remains of the convertible.

Morgan shook her head, one corner of her mouth lifting slightly. "You're looking at me like you think I'm crazy. But I'm not. Ari, you know as well as I do that if you're out here, you're safe."

There was a chance she was telling the truth, but my mind

lingered in doubt. Tristan had never been one to let Morgan off her leash, especially not after what had happened to me. I froze; the hair on my neck lifting at the thought of him crouched just outside the door, patiently waiting for his cue to come in and absolve me of my many, many sins.

I pushed Morgan's hand away from my face and grabbed my notebook.

Where is he? Is he putting you up to this?

She huffed a mirthless laugh and lowered her head. "C'mon, Ari. You're smarter than that. Do you really think so little of me? Tristan's in New York. Dean's working."

My father contracted an outside security firm two years ago, after claiming the church had been receiving threats. Overnight, Brother Caleb and his magazines were replaced by stone-faced men and Dobermans.

Dean must have been working the night of my accident. It made the most sense as he was the only one who ever spoke to us. Well, that and his willingness to look the other way for the right price.

How can I believe you?

Morgan's lips moved silently as she read, mouthing each word like a curse. "I'm a little surprised you haven't figured it out by now. I mean, haven't you been even the slightest bit curious as to why he's not here, watching your every move?"

If Tristan wanted to push for a plea of guilt, he would have sent Brad or another church elder to monitor me until I cracked. The fact I'd been left alone spoke volumes because it meant someone had taken my place. I tightened my hands into fists, squeezing until my fingernails dug into the flesh of my palms.

"That night, Tristan called. He'd wanted me to go down to the church to meet a guest pastor who'd flown in to speak. I guess he wanted to get a feel for the space. The details are kind of a blur now, but when I went outside, the convertible was missing.

"I told him I sent you, Ari," Morgan sighed, confirming my fears. "Said I wasn't feeling well and asked you to fill in for me. What was I supposed to do? Tell him you'd snuck out and taken my car? You know what they would have done to you—"

But what did they do to you?

She lifted her shoulder in a half shrug, eyes glistening with tears. "Nothing I can't live through. Believe me, it's better this way."

Morgan wasn't acting as an emissary to Tristan but as a martyr... for me. She tucked a strand of hair behind her ear, my mother's ring glimmering from her left hand. Everything she possessed had once belonged to someone else—the ring... the clothes... the children.

Had she ever wanted more than a hand-me-down life?

I shook my head at the unfairness of it all. The decision to run away and the consequences of being caught should have rested firmly on my shoulders.

My jaw tightened as a piece of my nightmare came back to me. Morgan's BMW had gone off the road and down a steep embankment. The nurses had confirmed that much. With the tree cover and lack of light, I should have remained lost for days.

She hadn't known my plans or even where I was headed, but someone else had.

How did they find me?

"I wondered the exact same thing and did a little digging. It took some time, but I finally found what I was looking for. Tristan has trackers... on every single vehicle." She shifted from one foot to the other before lowering herself onto the chair. "I haven't told anyone, but I think—I think maybe that's how they found Ashlynn."

I closed my eyes for a long moment, feeling the blood as it

drained from my face, no doubt headed down to stir up my stomach some more.

Ashlynn.

It had been almost two years, but my heart ached just as fiercely as it had the afternoon I learned my sister's fate. Loss was the one wound impervious to time.

Unfortunately, Morgan wasn't finished.

"This is why you can't come back." She hesitated, fished a small teddy bear from her bag, and then gently placed it in my hands. "When we moved away, my granny gave me this stuffed animal. She said it was a way for me to always feel close to her. I kinda thought she was crazy but squeeze it."

I did, surprised to feel a solid mass in the middle of its stomach. *What is it?* I mouthed.

"Well, it turns out Granny was a little skeptical about the nice preacher man inviting us to live in his gated community. So, she hid a cell phone and some cash inside the bear and sewed it up."

Morgan gnawed on her bottom lip. "I know it's not much, but it'll get you out of the city once you're healed. I'd send you to Granny's place, but she—she passed not long after we left."

I didn't understand. She'd had the means to disappear but was willing to give it away without a second thought? It didn't make a lick of sense. The back of my eyes stung with unshed tears, but I wouldn't show weakness now, not in light of what she was offering.

Why?

Her forehead creased. "What do you mean, why? Don't you see? Those trackers are proof Tristan knows where everybody is at all times. Ashlynn didn't die out here—" Morgan lowered her voice. "I think he killed her, Ari. And if you go back, he'll kill you too. No one walks away from him."

There was no time to process the full implication of her words because I was too busy freaking out at the sudden and unexpectedly loud knock. Morgan flinched, tearing her eyes away from mine and back toward the door.

The trackers.

"No," she whispered as if reading my thoughts. "I took the bus. Tristan doesn't know—he couldn't."

A moment passed, and then another, but Morgan stayed rooted to her chair in fright. I would have loved nothing more than to mentally check out for a while, but there was no time. She'd sacrificed herself for me once already. Now, it was my turn to be brave. I scribbled in the notebook before pressing it and the bear into her hands.

When she remained seated, I gave her a gentle nudge with my foot and gestured toward the bathroom.

Go.

Finally, she got up. I waited until the bathroom door closed behind her before moving toward the sounds of incessant rapping. My stomach gave another stern warning, but I ignored it and gently lifted the handle.

As his tall form and hopeful grin came into view, my hand fell uselessly back to the chair. I gaped at him; suddenly grateful I was sitting as the hallway appeared to be tilting. Nothing would have been more horrifying than stumbling into a man on crutches.

The edges of my vision swam in black, and I struggled to keep his face in focus as everything began spiraling out of control.

I was wrong.

Merely losing my balance would be nothing compared to swooning into his arms like a hapless southern belle at the least sign of excitement.

Not that it really mattered.

By that point, my body was already pitching forward into darkness without so much as a please or thank you.

CHAPTER EIGHT
KILLIAN

"Yet far and away- far, far and away- the most critical number in all of baseball is 3: the three outs that define an inning. Until the third out, anything is possible; after it, nothing is."

-Michael Lewis, *Moneyball*

"HEY GIRL, I'm real sorry about your brain." I winced at my reflection in the mirror. "Obviously, don't lead with that. Who says that? Sorry about your brain? Jesus, you suck at this."

I'd been practicing the damn apology for the last hour. Well, twenty minutes of it had been spent working on making my smile appear remorseful, instead of menacing.

My speech needed to be perfect. I'd made the mistake of going off-script once before, but not again. This time there would be no talk of weather or food—nothing that could be construed as rambling.

"Hey girl, I owe you an apology. Yeah, I'm talking to you." I put a hand on my hip and waggled my eyebrows suggestively, before sighing. "Fuck, Killian. Get ahold of yourself. Just apologize to the lady and get the hell out of her room before you mess it all up again."

Now that was a solid plan.

It would have been even better had I gotten her name, but that could come later. Not that I was expecting there to be a later. No, I was just going to apologize and stay as far away from her as possible for the remainder of my time here.

Then again, there was always a remote chance of her name coming up in someone's conversation and me just happening to overhear it.

What was I thinking?

Obviously, I wasn't going to be calling her anything because this was a one-time thing. One apology. Nothing else.

Get in, get out, and move on.

"I think you're ready," I told the mirror with a wink, instantly realizing how off-putting and sexual the gesture seemed. I looked like the perverted uncle at a family gathering—not what I was going for when trying to apologize. "Maybe don't do that. Ever."

The hallway was deserted. Most of the residents were spending their Saturday with visiting family members or playing games down in the common area. Not that I minded. In fact, I almost preferred it. The last thing I needed was an audience of baby boomers, giving me suggestions in the middle of my apology.

After shifting my weight onto my right leg, I released my crutch and knocked firmly. It was a decision I'd gone back and forth on—knowing she couldn't speak or walk—but barging in unannounced seemed like an excellent way to end up on the six o'clock news.

I perused the corkboard affixed to the girl's door while waiting for a response, straining to hear something indicating she was inside. I couldn't be sure, but it sounded like the television might have been on, so I'd give her a minute.

A. James

Abigail? Anna? A—girl who won't come to the door?

After a full minute of silence, I rolled my shoulders and brought my fist down against the wood again, wondering if it might have been better to catch her on the way to lunch.

I continued scowling at the door until, at last, it opened. The color drained from the girl's face as she looked up at me, her hand dropping back to the arm of her chair. I gave her what I hoped was a disarming grin when she began to tremble, while everything inside of me screamed to abort the mission.

Shit. Shit. Shit.

The girl blinked up at me through droopy eyes but made no move to invite me in. There was a slight chance I was giving off the pervy uncle vibe again, but without a mirror in front of me, I had no way of knowing for sure.

"So—"

She tipped forward before I could finish the thought, her eyes rolling back in her skull.

Okay—not exactly the reaction I'd been hoping for.

My crutches fell to the ground with a clatter. I swooped in, managing to catch the girl by the shoulder before her forehead hit her knees.

"Wait!" I groaned, balancing on my right leg. "Wait—non-weight bearing! Non-weight bearing!"

The belt across her lap might have kept her from falling out completely, but the momentum had sent the chair precariously close to ending my career permanently.

"Alright, girl." Keeping one hand on her, I side-stepped the chair and let out a harsh breath. "Need you to wake up now, preferably before someone comes out of their room and calls security."

Doing my best to keep my weight on my good leg, I tucked my finger under her chin and lifted her head, thinking it might bring her around faster. Several strands of red hair had come loose from her braid, and I tucked them back behind her ear, close enough to see the scar she'd been trying to hide.

Her lashes fluttered briefly before opening fully to reveal her gorgeous green eyes. And I was once again struck by the strangest feeling I'd seen her before. Not in here, but years ago.

Maybe another life entirely.

I closed my eyes and conjured up the woman's face before snapping out of it. The feeling of familiarity was nothing more than a wicked case of déjà vu, or hell—maybe just the leftover remnants from a lonely man's wet dream. A man who had not been with a woman in over a year.

Anything else would require a CT scan and a visit to the psych ward.

I studied the reddish-brown freckles scattered across her nose and cheekbones, before following a line of sweat as it moved from her forehead down to her jaw.

A small line appeared between her brows as she returned her eyes to mine, clearly as confused by my gawking as I was. I scanned the hallway for a nurse, deciding apologies could wait for another day.

I'd probably give the poor girl a week or two to completely recover before trying again. Or, if I wanted to avoid her fainting on me again, I could just write a letter and slip it under her door.

All plans of escape went right out the window when she lifted a hand to the side of her neck, covering mine. Her wide eyes were even more remarkable up close, with flecks of gold dotted throughout.

I'd come here to say something, but for the life of me, I couldn't remember what it was.

The bathroom door inside her room suddenly popped open, and the blood surged back up to my brain. I jerked away, grimacing when my brace caught on the side of her chair. The subsequent flash of pain sent me stumbling into the door frame with a muffled curse.

Fully aware of how it looked, I ignored the vibrant pulsing in my knee, loudly explaining to anyone within earshot, "You just fainted, but I think you're alright now. I'm just going—"

"Wait," a voice called.

My knee was throbbing, and I was entirely out of my element.

Even the girl had shifted in her chair and was glaring back toward the room with a deep frown. I couldn't necessarily say I blamed her. Things between us hadn't exactly gone according to plan.

Again.

She might have hated me with every fiber of her being, and I would have understood. However, I really didn't need the woman emerging from the bathroom to think I was some sort of predator. Theo had overlooked a lot in the past, but I was pretty sure this would be viewed as a scandal—which I'd been expressly forbidden from taking part in.

At the time, it'd seemed like an easy agreement to make.

I opened my mouth, prepared to argue my innocence. Thinking about stroking someone's face was not the same as actually doing it and, therefore, not a crime. The courts would back me up on that.

Probably.

The woman rushed out into the hall; her mouth set in a hard line. "You said she fainted?"

I rubbed my forehead, wishing I'd gone for that cup of coffee instead of trying to be a decent person. "Uh... yeah. Seems to be doing okay now, though, so I'll just leave her—"

She glanced at me. "Can you help me get her into bed?"

I flinched at the question, convinced I'd misunderstood. Judging by her saucer eyes and open mouth, the girl hadn't been expecting it either.

The woman continued staring up at me expectantly, and I shot a pleading glance down the deserted hallway before lifting my shoulder in a half shrug. "You know, I think they have people—I'm— you see, my knee's messed up—"

The corner of her mouth quirked up as she looked at the two of us, before snagging my crutches for me. "Well, do you have a second to come in and wait with us until the nurse can get down here? They might want to talk to you about what happened before she fainted."

A long moment of torturous silence passed, during which the girl lowered her head, giving no indication as to her thoughts on the matter.

"But—" I sighed. I couldn't say no, even if I wanted to, not unless I wanted to draw a lot of unwanted attention. I'd have to check the manual, but I was reasonably confident unwanted attention was also covered under the no scandals umbrella.

I scrutinized the woman's features, searching for signs of weakness. Instead of looking away, she tipped her chin up to meet my stare, her brown eyes sharpening in challenge.

Great—where was Bailey when I needed him?

He would have had the dark-haired beauty eating out of the palm of his hand, allowing me enough time to escape. And the woman was beautiful—well, what I could see of her. The baggy dress she wore fell to her ankles and was just shapeless enough to keep her body type a mystery. Inexplicably, there were also what appeared to be sewn-in shoulder pads, something I hadn't seen in women's clothes since I was a kid.

I imagined if I grinned and used the right tone, I could still sweet talk my way out of this, even without my wingman. "Look, as much as I'd love—"

"Oh no, you're not getting out of this." She smirked and raised her voice. "I went to the bathroom and came out to find that my beloved sister had fainted. I'd say you have some explaining to do."

Alright, I was good, but she was better.

"Is there a problem?"

I flinched again, turning to find a very tiny, yet very fierce-looking woman glaring up at me.

"Not at all," the dark-haired woman interjected. "Mr... I'm sorry, I don't think I caught your name."

"It's Killian," I bit out with a tight smile. "Just Killian."

"You see, Killian here was just helping me get my sister back into the room. She seems to have fainted on us—probably low blood sugar or something like that. Would you mind helping us, Tsega?"

The pint-sized aide agreed and, after firing a million questions in my direction, wheeled the woman back inside. The door closed with a soft click, leaving me alone in the hall with the conniving sister.

I inclined my head toward my room, clicking my tongue against my teeth. "Well, it looks like everything is settled here. So, I'm just going to—"

"Did they make you do the training? Like they do with the families?" She blurted out suddenly, running a hand through her dark hair.

"Uh, excuse me?"

"The seizure training—did you have to watch the video?" She drew closer. "If not, you need to get on that. Today! Yes, do it today."

Once she stopped tossing fragmented sentences my way, I asked the utterly logical question, "And why exactly would I need to do that?"

"So, you can sit with her—my sister, I mean. I don't know when I'll be able to get back, and—I'm Morgan, by the way." She thrust her hand toward me with a lopsided grin.

"And there aren't nurses who can do this?" I asked before reluctantly taking it.

Morgan's expression didn't waver. "She likes you."

"What gave it away?" I chuckled. "The fact that she won't even look at me—or wait, it was the intense glaring, wasn't it?"

"She's a little shy," Morgan said with a shrug. "Do you know it took her a year to work up the courage just to wave and say hello to me?"

I raised a brow. "But she's your sister..."

Morgan twisted the diamond ring on her finger before bobbing her head in a nod. "Um, right. So, you can imagine how hard it is for her to talk to strangers. But if you took the class, you could get to know her. Then you wouldn't be a stranger anymore."

"And what's in it for you?" I asked, waiting for the catch.

"Nothing." She swallowed. "I just assumed with the way you were banging on the door, you must have had something awfully important to say. Maybe something you'd like to say to discuss without a bunch of nurses around."

I released my crutch just long enough to scratch my jaw and consider her proposal. Anything more than an apology was liable to draw the wrong kind of attention.

In and out.

Decision made, I squared my shoulders and moved toward the girl's room, ignoring the stinging pain in my knee with every step. "You know, if it's all the same to you, I think I'll just go talk to her now. Let everyone get back to their day."

Her mouth settled in a hard line. "But—"

I pushed the handle down and let the door swing open. "Yeah, might as well get this out of the way. I've got a lot to do."

At the sound of my voice, the girl hurriedly looked away, but not before I noted the bright spots of color on her cheeks. The mesh enclosure surrounding her bed snagged my attention, and I frowned, wondering why I hadn't been given the option of a fort bed.

"Tsega, could you give us a minute?" Morgan asked with a tight-lipped smile. The aide abandoned her post beside the bed, sizing me up as she strolled toward the door.

"I'll just grab her a breakfast tray from the cafeteria. It's just at the end of the hall, but if you need me, my extension is on the board. I can be here within seconds."

My mouth twitched at the implied threat. I slowly hobbled toward the bed, taking care to keep my voice soft. "Hi."

The girl blew out her cheeks, lifting several strands of hair, but kept her eyes on the window. If I wanted to gain any ground, I'd have to take a page right out of Joe Reed's playbook and guilt her into forgiving me.

I grimaced and raised my left foot off the ground. "Can I sit? My knee is killing me. That'll teach me not to throw my crutches down the next time someone faints on me, won't it?"

The girl snuck a quick glance down at the brace before pressing her lips together. She'd effectively managed to avoid looking directly at me since the incident in the hall.

Just as I began to lose hope, she lifted her shoulder. It wasn't much, but I'd take what I could get. I leaned my crutches up against the plastic footboard and checked to make sure her feet weren't in the way before ducking under the netting.

I reached up to touch the mesh. "Hey, this is pretty cool. It's like we're camping."

She bit her lip and fidgeted with her necklace, twisting the pendant in slow circles with trembling fingers. In her defense, I hadn't exactly done anything to warrant her acknowledgment, which was why I'd come over here in the first place.

I plastered what I hoped was an encouraging smile on my face and began. "So, I know you can't talk—"

She jerked her chin up, eyes flashing with anger. *Is that right?*

The words were silent, but the hard set of her jaw as she delivered each one was more than enough to convey her feelings on my little drop-in.

I rubbed my palms against my thighs. "I just wanted to apologize if I offended you yesterday... and also the time before in the hallway. Look, I think we maybe got off on the wrong foot, and I'd like to make things right."

While I talked, the two sisters seemed to be carrying on a silent conversation of their very own.

Great.

Just swell.

I was officially never apologizing to anyone ever again. The entire morning had played out like a bizarre dream. At least in my world, things made sense. And that was including the time I'd woken up buck naked on an inflatable flamingo in the middle of Bailey's pool after curling up with a cask of Macallan the night before.

My shoulders slumped when the girl snatched a notebook from the table beside the bed and began writing. I imagined I was about to get quite the send-off.

She held it up, her chest rising and falling with rapid breaths.

You can go now.

The muscle in my jaw twitched as I read the words. It wasn't as if I'd come into this expecting a warm reception, but I had assumed the girl would at least acknowledge my attempt to fix things.

I massaged the back of my neck. "You want me to leave?"

She swallowed and jerked her head toward Morgan, a flush creeping up her face.

"You want Killian to stay, don't you?" Morgan encouraged, giving her the thumbs up.

I refrained from pumping a fist in the air, keeping my face blank as I turned back to the girl. "If you want me to leave, I will. But I am sorry—seriously, I feel like a complete ass. Can I get your name?"

Wait—where had that come from?

Her jaw went slack, and she began shaking her head. *I don't think—I can't...*

I chewed on my bottom lip while her eyes bored into Morgan, still trying to place where I'd seen her before. As if sensing my stare, the girl tensed and slowly turned back to me. And, this time, I was the one who had to look away.

Her green eyes held more than just specks of gold. There was a brief flash of something else lurking just beneath the surface—something I'd missed before.

Strength.

The girl had grit, but I doubted if she even knew it. It reminded me a little of my mama, just another one of many women who'd given up her backbone to become someone's doormat. Maybe my sudden need to make her smile was nothing more than a knee-jerk reaction left over from childhood.

"Oh, I see. I gotta work for it," I teased, tapping my finger against my lips. "Alright, I know it starts with an A—Alice?"

She wrinkled her nose and immediately shook her head, looking like she'd just sucked on a lemon.

I chuckled. "Give me a second—wait, I got it! It's Adelaide. Can I call you Addy, for short?"

Her brows drew together as she rejected the name with another head shake, but the corner of her mouth turned up ever so slightly. It was all the encouragement I needed.

"Alright, now I know this doesn't start with an A, but before you reject it, you should know I've actually grown kind of fond of this one. How about Girl?"

Okay. She exhaled softly, letting her mouth curve into a smile. It was small, even by the most generous of measures, but it was there.

"Yeah?" I beamed. "Well, alright then, Girl. I'm gonna run and let you get back to your morning. How's that sound?"

The smile faded, and she pulled her lower lip between her teeth with a jerky nod.

"I'll, uh, I'll see you tomorrow, though," I hastily added as I made my way to the door. Apparently, the filter between my brain and my mouth was on the fritz, letting just about anything through.

She lifted an eyebrow, back to clasping the necklace like a shield.

"What do you say we get you some food, Ariana?" Morgan asked as she led me out, fooling no one with her exaggerated wink.

"Ariana," I repeated with a smile.

"Oh, whoops!" Morgan smacked her palm against her forehead. "Silly me, I sure messed up."

I shook my head and was just turning toward my room when Morgan poked her head out into the hall.

"Hey," she hissed. "Don't forget to take the class. Okay—bye!"

There was something really not right about that woman.

After propping my knee up, I sprawled out on my bed with a relaxed sigh, feeling like I'd just sent one sailing over the fence. However, I imagined anyone else who'd witnessed my fumbled apology would have assumed I was now on strike two.

Still in the game.

I pinched the bridge of my nose with a low growl. There was no game—no reason for me to interact with her again beyond the usual pleasantries. My slate had been wiped clean. I could once again focus on my recovery and possible contract with the Hurricanes.

Case closed.

So, why did I want to see her again?

"Because you've temporarily lost your goddamned mind," I grumbled. "And your judgment is shit. That's why."

I'd been down this road before. Women who didn't give their names were typically married or otherwise spoken for. Pursuing Ariana would only end in one of us getting hurt, and my money was on it being me.

"Let's not forget you assumed she was crazy right up until you found out about the brain injury either, chump."

Exactly.

Regardless of what her sister wanted; I had no business being in a room alone with her—not with my track record. I'd said what I'd needed to, and now it was time to move on.

End of story.

Okay, maybe I'd let my imagination roam free when she'd covered my hand with hers, but it was just because she was an insanely gorgeous woman.

She was, I could admit it.

It didn't mean I was going to throw away my career and what remained of my morals for a night with her, though. I didn't negotiate on the field, and I wasn't willing to give up my celibacy for anything less than forever.

Forever? My throat tightened painfully. *Jesus, Reed. Get ahold of yourself.*

Beautiful or not, I needed to rehab and get back to my team before they went looking for a replacement. I was here for one reason and one reason only—to get back on top.

Maybe if I said it enough, I'd start to believe it.

CHAPTER NINE
ARIANA

"If I could but know his heart, everything would become easy."

—Jane Austen, *Sense and Sensibility*

"OKAY. GO." Natalie clicked her stopwatch.

I carefully raised my right foot and tapped the toe of my shoe against the blue rectangular block before switching to the other leg. It was another balance exercise meant to be done as quickly as possible, but my thoughts were elsewhere.

It was all Killian's fault, really. If he hadn't shown up at my door a little over a week ago, then Morgan's ludicrous escape plan never would've seen the light of day.

Killian is the key.

She'd sprung it on me while I was still trying to come to terms with the genuine possibility Tristan was a murderer. Maybe I'd also allowed myself a few minutes to relive Killian's heartfelt apology and the feel of his intense blue eyes moving over my face, but the majority of my time had been spent unpacking Morgan's allegations.

Ashlynn's death had always been shrouded in mystery. One morning she was there, and the next, she wasn't. Tristan told us she'd been killed while crossing a busy street. He'd refused to give any other details before barricading himself in his office. When he'd finally emerged days later, it was only to call off the small memorial service Aubrey had been planning. Then, it was like she'd never even existed.

I'd chalked it up to grief at the time, but maybe it had never been anything more than guilt.

Unfortunately, Morgan's latest scheme prevented me from giving the matter my full attention. It seemed my salvation was no longer sewn into a teddy bear but resting with the man across the hall.

She expected me to seduce Killian—never mind that I had no voice or even the slightest clue how to flirt with a man. I also couldn't look at him without my face turning crimson—*how in the heck was I supposed to trick him into sleeping with me?*

As usual, my thoughts and feelings on the matter weren't taken into consideration.

While I'd never bought into the church's views on love and sex, I wasn't necessarily keen on the idea of throwing myself at someone just because he happened to be the closest available man under sixty.

Killian had a way of leaving me disoriented and abnormally short of breath when he entered a room, which was clearly my body's way of rejecting the idea. I'd always pictured myself ending up with a man who didn't make me feel anything.

Okay, that wasn't necessarily true.

In my mind, I imagined being with someone who didn't make me feel as though I was suffering from an unidentified medical condition. A man who was gentle and funny.

Morgan had been quick to point out that I'd smiled at Killian, but there were times I managed to find Tristan amusing. It didn't mean I wanted to spend the rest of my life living under the same roof, though.

I didn't even particularly care about love, having seen too much to believe in fairy tale endings. I just didn't want to be afraid of a man I was supposed to trust. And Killian, with his sometimes prickly exterior, didn't instill a lot of confidence as a partner.

Not that it mattered as I hadn't interacted with him in over a week, although I'd seen him almost daily. For example, right now, he was icing his knee over on one of the therapy tables—not that I was looking for him, per se.

I noticed things and people. They just never seemed to notice me back.

He raked his fingers through his dark hair while looking down at his phone, and I inhaled a sharp breath, catching my shin on the edge of the block.

Natalie stopped the watch and high-fived my palm. "You seem pleased with yourself, as you should be. That was really good. This time, though, let's try to move just a little faster."

I was doing it again, gazing at Killian and grinning. Getting lost in my head had always been a favorite pastime of mine. The Killian part was a relatively new addition, though.

He lifted his eyes to meet mine, and my heart gave an unsteady thump of approval, urging me to reconsider my stance on seduction.

Patients and therapists moved seamlessly around me, in and out of the gym, like the rushing waters of a river. There was constant motion as people fought to regain their independence, but the world came to a standstill when the corners of Killian's mouth turned up in a grin.

It was complete madness, but I didn't want to stay close to shore, not when he looked at me like that. I wanted to abandon my moral obligations and swim into the current, letting it drag me into deeper waters.

A hand landed on my shoulder from behind, and I whirled around, losing my balance and breaking the spell. Natalie righted me; her brows knitted in concern. "Whoa—I didn't mean to startle you. You okay?"

When I nodded, she began explaining what we were going to be working on next, but I couldn't hear her over the rush of blood in my ears. I tucked a couple of loose strands of hair behind my ear and snuck another discreet glance over to Killian.

He'd gone back to his phone, frowning at something on the rectangular screen. Yesterday, he'd spent most of his time watching the baseball game being broadcast on one of the televisions, his mouth set in a hard line. I'd recognized the longing in his gaze, and my resolve had weakened a little more.

I wondered how he'd react if I went over to him. If I cupped his jaw in my palm, would we even need words? Or would his strong hands instinctively move up to grip my waist, fully aware of what I was after? Would he kiss me slowly, or with a desperate hunger like the men in movies? I chewed on my bottom lip, caught between my doctrine and my desire—and not for the first time, either.

The side of Killian's mouth tugged to one side, and he slowly lifted his head, meeting my gaze. I suspected he'd known I was watching all along, but he didn't seem annoyed... or in any hurry to look away.

Maybe he felt the pull of the current just as much as I did.

———

I was restless as Tiffani wheeled me back to my room after class, reconsidering Morgan's plan in one breath, only to pick it apart with the next. It probably would have been helpful if I'd had some experience with dating over the years, but no one had ever made a lasting impression.

Well, besides the boy at the lake. But, unless Killian ended up unconscious in the pool, I didn't see how the encounter would help me now.

"Oh," Tiffani breathed out. "You, um—just—"

I tensed my shoulders when I saw what she was pointing at—or, more specifically, whom.

Brad leaned against the wall beside my door, tapping out something on his phone. When he saw us approaching, he tucked it back inside his suit jacket and directed his attention to me.

I'd never particularly enjoyed being under the man's watchful eye, especially when I couldn't run and hide afterward. Something about it left me feeling dirty.

"There you are. I was just about to send out a search party." His gaze roamed over my dress, the smile on his face slipping when I crossed my arms over my chest.

"Hello, we weren't informed that Ariana had a visitor, or I would have brought her right away," Tiffani explained as a flush crept up her neck.

He had that effect on women.

Tristan attracted attention due to a combination of good looks and fame. Brad managed just fine without the celebrity endorsements, although I imagined the expensive suits didn't hurt.

He spent no less than three hours in the gym every day and never touched a carb during church dinners. His jet-black hair had gone gray around the temples about ten years ago, only making him more desirable to the women in the church. Many had tried, but no one had managed to land the church's most eligible bachelor.

Personally, I'd never seen the appeal. Being in the same room with the man only made my skin crawl.

"That's no problem." He paused to give her a once-over, his eyes flashing with disinterest. "I was wondering if I might have a minute alone with her, though."

I jerked my head toward him, feeling the color drain from my face. Brad noted the reaction with a barely concealed smirk. He liked it when I was scared.

"Yes, absolutely. You've had the training, I assume?" Tiffani gazed into his eyes, ignoring my silent pleas to send him away.

A blank look skirted across his face before he recovered, this time grinning like a cat who'd just cornered a mouse. "Of course, I did all the training. Now, let's get her out of this chair. She's got to be uncomfortable."

I squeezed my hands into fists and looked away, determined to remain strong even though I had a sneaking suspicion I knew why he'd come.

As soon as Tiffani unlocked the belt, he moved in, his hand dropping down to cup my bottom as he guided me toward the bed. I flinched and tried pulling away, but his grip tightened to the point of pain.

It only hurts if you let it...

I crossed my arms over my stomach as the door closed, sealing my fate with an audible click. A sour taste lingered on my tongue, and it was becoming increasingly difficult to swallow. I forced myself to rehearse Morgan's version of the events leading up to my accident. I was relatively confident I could write every detail just as she'd said it.

Brad slipped off his jacket and placed it on a chair before pulling a small velvet box from his pocket. I shrank back when he loomed closer, mashing my lips together to keep from whimpering.

He wasn't here to interrogate me.

The corner of his mouth lifted as he ducked under the canopy, his thigh touching mine as he sank down onto the mattress. "Now that we're alone, we can talk. I mean, I'll talk, and you'll listen. How's that sound?"

I swallowed again and nodded, my lower lip quivering uncontrollably.

"Good girl. I wanna start by telling you a little story." He undid the top three buttons on his dress shirt before reaching out to touch my necklace, letting his fingers graze along the tops of my breasts. My shoulders rounded at the contact, but I didn't try to pull away again.

I just glanced toward the window, imagining I was small enough to disappear and never be found. My body quivered with dread, but I would not let Brad break me.

"Now, this was supposed to have happened when you turned eighteen, but that whole Ashlynn debacle really threw a wrench in things."

I kept my face blank and continued staring through the glass. It wasn't real. As long as I didn't look at him, I was safe.

Brad pushed the skirt of my dress up, his fingers trailing lightly across my bare thigh as he whispered, "I didn't mind waiting, though. It gave you a chance to get all that rebellion out and me a chance to make myself a little more indispensable to the church. I sold off two of my companies—the deals were finalized this morning. Do you know what that means?"

My breaths quickened, but I held perfectly still, refusing to acknowledge any part of it. With a muttered curse, Brad jerked my face up toward his, the muscle in his jaw twitching.

"You're looking at a billionaire, sweetheart," he growled, digging his fingers into my flesh. "And with that kind of money, I can suddenly get anything I want."

Me.

He wanted me.

It only hurts if you let it...

My stomach was in upheaval, the contents caught in a roiling sea of nausea. There must have been something in my expression because he had a small trashcan in front of me within seconds.

I retched until there was nothing but saliva. Uncontrollable tremors wracked my body, making my teeth chatter together noisily. Stupidly, I'd believed with Tristan reaping the benefits of my injury, he'd forget his talk of sacrifice.

Morgan had been wrong.

He wasn't going to kill me—that would have been too easy. No, my punishment was being auctioned off to the highest bidder. A man who was thirty years older than me and now the church's largest donor.

Brad let the trashcan fall to the tile with a dull thud before pulling my left hand into his, forcing the ring onto my finger. His lip curled in disgust. "I think that was a bit of an overreaction. Do you know how many women would kill to be in your position right now?"

The diamond caught the light from the windows, scattering a

multitude of sparkles throughout the room. It would have been magical had it been coming from anywhere but the brilliant cage around my finger.

Just another reminder, my life would always belong to someone else.

His eyes searched mine once more before he leaned closer. I turned my face away at the last second, and his lips connected with the flesh beside my ear. I couldn't stomach the thought of that man's mouth ever touching mine.

"'And by the law, almost all things are purged with blood, and without the shedding of blood there is no remission,'" he whispered, walking his fingers up my thigh.

If I closed my eyes, I was back in my dark bedroom, feeling the heat of his breath against the back of my neck as he slowly recited the very verse I'd come to hate as an adult.

He was practically panting as he reached the junction between my thighs. "You've always been mine, sweetheart. And I think I'm going to enjoy every second of breaking you."

There was no misinterpreting the words, leaving me to wonder how much of my blood it was going to take to satisfy his lust.

It only hurts if you let it...

I thought back to Morgan's confession a week ago, seeing it in an entirely new light. Upon discovering she'd been promised to a man twenty-five years her senior, Morgan admitted she'd reacted as any sixteen-year-old would have and cried for an entire night. Then, she'd decided to lose her virginity on her own terms—with the college-aged boy who lived next door. To her, it wasn't an act of defiance, as much as a way of taking back her power.

At the time, I'd believed our situations were nothing alike. Killian wasn't some neighbor I'd secretly been in love with for years, and I hadn't been sold to the man who'd made my childhood a living hell.

Things were different now, and I had to make a decision—give up and follow a path that would only lead to more misery, or venture out into the unknown, without a safety net to break my fall. Killian was an uncertainty, but one I'd gradually found myself looking forward to. Brad, however, was a sadist.

Both were chaos, but if it was between giving myself to a stranger or living out my days as Brad's abused hostage, I'd choose Killian.

Now, I just needed to figure out how.

———

"So, I said to Georgia, 'No, you cannot join us for cards.' She seemed pretty upset, but she knew that Margaret was sweet on Arthur." The older woman stuffed a spoon full of food into her mouth before starting up again.

When Helen had initially asked to sit with me at lunch, I'd accepted, grateful for the company. I'd imagined we'd enjoy a quiet meal before retiring to our rooms for the requisite afternoon nap.

It was a decision I'd come to regret.

Mashed potatoes clung to the side of her mouth, but she carried on as if it didn't bother her. "You remember Arthur, don't you? I pointed him out earlier. Such a looker. So, as I was saying, there we were..."

For someone who'd only been at *True North* for a week, Helen had wasted no time in making enemies. There was Georgia, the boyfriend stealer, Ida, the card shark, and Sue, the sister she'd never seen eye to eye with. I could have filled the pages of my notebook with the names of people who'd wronged her.

A pat on the hand brought me back to the conversation. "You are such a good listener. Youths today are just the worst. Noses stuck to glass screens—never interacting with anyone around them. They've become obsessed with capturing the perfect moment that they end up missing it. My granddaughter, April, doesn't even know how to have an actual conversation. You ask her a question, and she just grunts in response. It's like visiting with a damn caveman."

I raised a brow, but Helen was already off to the next topic. "There's no hope for the future. It's just going to be a bunch of precious snowflakes, glued to their buzzing boxes while the world goes to hell. You know what we need? More churches. The youths need to be involved in planting churches all over. That's how you fix the world—"

"Hello ladies, is this seat taken?"

My mouth curved into a relieved smile as I lifted my eyes to Killian's, secretly pleased when his icy blue stare warmed as it moved across my face.

He was wearing a gray t-shirt with two bats crossed into an x. A baseball was superimposed over them, along with the logo for the *Houston Hurricanes.*

I only knew about the baseball team because it had been Ashlynn's dream to see a sporting event when she turned eighteen. She hadn't attended a game, but thanks to Matt, she'd come home with a small Hurricanes towel hidden among her belongings.

After her death, I'd smuggled it into my room to join the other secret treasures beneath my bed. Everything else was either sold off or burned, making it the only piece of her I had left.

"Oh, my—h-hello," Helen stammered, before lifting her hand. "It's you!"

Her reaction was... unexpected, to say the least.

Given her dislike of almost everything, I'd been positive she was going to find fault with him.

His expression dimmed somewhat as he extended a hand. "Killian. It's a pleasure to meet you."

She snatched it with both of hers like it was the last drumstick at a cookout, tilting her head toward the empty chair between us. "Helen. Please, sit down."

He lowered himself onto the chair before turning to me with a smirk. "Hi, I'm Killian. I don't believe I ever got your name."

I slipped my hand into his, struck by the same weird, floaty feeling I got when I rode an elevator. My body might have been sitting perfectly still, but my stomach was in free fall.

"Ari," I breathed, clinging to him like a lifeline. His palms were rough and callused against mine. I considered what he did for a living to have earned them. Was it physical labor, the kind that left him sweaty at the end of every day? My cheeks warmed as I imagined how he'd look without a shirt on.

He cocked his head, and I inhaled sharply, before realizing it wasn't because he'd read my mind.

I'd whispered my name.

Just as I was beginning to think it was lost to me forever, my voice had returned.

"Ari," Killian repeated softly, his voice filled with reverence. There was something right in hearing my name on his lips, like ending a prayer with amen.

"I think she might be deaf and dumb. I've been sitting here doing most of the talking, and she hasn't had the decency to chime in even once," Helen interjected with a shake of her head.

My nose crinkled at her brittle assessment of my character. Perhaps I was a little quieter than most, but it should have been apparent to everyone at the table I was neither deaf nor dumb.

"So, Killian," she simpered, dismissing me from the conversation. "That's a unique name. What does it mean?"

I lowered my head, jolting when his fingertips brushed over my knuckles. When I lifted my eyes, he gave me an encouraging nod and mouthed, *chin up*, before reaching for his fork.

My skin blazed from the heat of his touch. I folded my hands in my lap, confident I was never going to recover from the loss.

"It means church," he answered, keeping his gaze on me like the answer was solely mine. Helen waited for him to elaborate further before moving on to the drama surrounding *True North*.

Church.

My heart hammered against my ribs, sending more than just blood rushing through my veins as I studied his face. The nest of birds residing in my lower belly stirred, awakening something fierce within me. It was accompanied by the oddest feeling that I knew him from somewhere.

"What do you think?" he asked, inclining his head toward me. I had no way of answering, as I'd been quite busy surveying his gorgeous mouth. Every one of his teeth was a healthy shade of white and perfectly aligned with the next. I wondered whether it was the byproduct of good genes or just fantastic dentistry.

Killian's lips twitched as he fought a smile, and I realized he was still waiting on a response. I shrugged helplessly, having spent a good chunk of the conversation staring at him. His eyes sparked with something that indicated I hadn't necessarily been discreet in my perusal.

"Young lady!" Helen snapped her fingers. "What do you think about the aquatic therapy here? I told Killian here it wasn't as good as the center over in Oak Lake. See, that's how you get her attention—just snap."

I gaped at the woman, my face flooding with heat. I was no stranger to condescending people and being ignored, but it didn't mean I was unfeeling. My shoulders sagged and bowed my head, trying to hide my mortification.

It only hurts if you let it...

Killian made a low sound in the back of his throat and pushed back from the table, the fork clanging as it connected with the edge of his plate. Helen continued rattling off the advantages of Oak Lake's facility over *True North's*, seemingly unaware anything was amiss.

"I'm sorry to interrupt, but I just remembered I have somewhere to be." The humor was gone from his voice, and the hairs on my arms lifted at the sudden chill in the air.

He was leaving.

I rubbed my damp palms against my skirt and forced myself to pick up my fork. Once the lump in my throat settled, I stabbed a roasted carrot and brought it to my lips with a huff.

Helen launched into yet another complaint, but I busied myself with the task of chewing and swallowing, tuning her out. It was best not to dwell on what Killian must have thought of me until I was safely back in my room.

"You coming, girl?"

I jerked my head toward Killian, freezing at the sight of his squared shoulders and furrowed brow. The last traces of warmth fell away as he glared down at me, leaving glaciers where his eyes had once been.

"But I'm not finished yet," Helen protested with a sniff. "Awfully rude and disrespectful to just leave someone in the middle of a meal."

He glanced down at me, his icy expression thawing slightly. "What do you say?"

I lowered my fork to the plate, completely ready to leave with Killian until I considered the implications of it. Only two weeks in and I'd just come dangerously close to slipping up. Morgan might have bought me some time, but Tristan had little birds lurking everywhere.

If he got word that I'd gone off alone with a man, I'd be back behind those walls before they opened the cafeteria for dinner. I fidgeted with the pendant around my neck and slowly shook my head before slouching back against the wheelchair with a frustrated sigh.

It was too risky for us to be seen together.

What could I say? *Hi Killian, I'd love to leave with you, but I'm a grown woman who is still terrified of her father. Who's my father, you ask? Oh, just Tristan James, the pastor on television every other day of the week. There's also a strong possibility he killed my sister, but don't worry, you're probably safe.*

The truth was sad, and would no doubt scare the man off permanently. Or worse, cause him to look down on me in pity.

The sullen look returned to his face, and he stood silent, absently gnawing on his bottom lip. I squirmed under the weight of his unhappy stare before forcing my mouth into a smile.

My dress felt itchy against my skin, but I didn't dare scratch. Instead, I returned my attention to the plate in front of me, my fingernails leaving crescent-shaped indentations in my palms.

"You're staying?" Killian tilted his head back toward Helen. "Here?"

I doubted there was an ounce of conviction in my nod, but it didn't matter. Killian was already turning away, the rubber tip of his crutches swiping angrily against the floor as he stormed out. I kept my head down and waited a full minute before pushing back from the table. Tiffani saw and began making her way over to me, and I released a harsh breath, ready for the day to be over already.

Helen tapped her fork against the side of her plate until I reluctantly inclined my head in her direction. "You like him," she said in a singsong voice, giving me a conspiratorial wink.

My eyes went round. I vigorously shook my head, praying no one else in the crowded cafeteria had heard the accusation.

Her smile faded. "Well, do you think about him when he's not here?"

I nodded with a half shrug. So, I thought about Killian. It didn't mean anything.

"And when you think about him, do you feel that flutter in your chest?" She took my heated face as confirmation and smirked. "Then, you like him. Trust me, I've been married four times. I know these things."

I rubbed at the back of my neck and looked away, more uncomfortable now than I'd been only moments before. Killian was just the lesser of two evils. Maybe I was attracted to him on a physical level, but it had only been two weeks. Way too soon to form any sort of attachment.

Helen's eyes bored into my skull as she idly drummed her fingers on the table. "You know, I'm somewhat inclined to help you get his attention. It's fairly obvious you're ignorant in the ways of men and someone like Killian expects to be wowed."

She didn't strike me as the type to help someone out of the sheer goodness of her heart. There was something in it for her, I just didn't know what that was yet.

Before I could dismiss her ludicrous offer completely, I considered the diamond ring hidden back in my room, a bitter reminder of what was at stake if I failed.

CHAPTER TEN
KILLIAN

"Branch Rickey once said of me that I was a man with an infinite capacity for immediately making a bad thing worse."

-Leo Durocher, *Nice Guys Finish Last*

"KILLIAN REED, as I live and breathe," Bailey announced in a falsetto from the doorway to the cafeteria. "Nurses said I might find you here. I let you out of my sight for what—three weeks—and this is what you've become? Eating dinner at five-thirty on a Friday night like some commoner?"

I returned the water pitcher to the counter and gave him the finger. "Why, Mr. Bailey, I didn't have you down on the schedule for today. If you'd told me you were planning a visit, I would have asked the hookers to join us for dinner."

He clapped me on the shoulder affectionately and reached for the glass in my hand. "Allow me. Now, be honest, Grandpa. Are you taking advantage of the early bird special? Because Viagra ain't cheap!"

Several patients scowled in his direction, but as usual, Bailey was utterly oblivious to them. I set aside my annoyance and mustered a small smile. It wasn't his fault I'd spent the better part of the afternoon wanting to put a fist-sized hole through the wall for... *well, I had my reasons.*

I shrugged. "Cafeteria closes at seven, so it's not like I have a choice."

"Christ, seems a bit barbaric. Isn't what's-his-face running this?" He asked as he followed me over to an empty table, snapping his fingers repetitively. "The football player? Fuck, I can't remember his name, but you know who I'm talking about. He signed off on this early dinner bullshit?"

I nodded and leaned my crutches against the wall before joining him. "Look around you, man. I think it's safe to assume most of these patients are probably in bed by six."

"Now, tell your Uncle Conor..." He fluttered his lashes. "Are the nurses at least treating you nicely—rolling out the red carpet for the most coveted free agent the sport has ever seen?"

Bailey surveyed the cafeteria, simultaneously fidgeting with a saltshaker and bouncing up and down in his seat. There were times I found his inability to sit still exhausting—but right now, I welcomed the reminder I had a life outside of this place, even if it no longer felt like it.

I knew the '*most coveted*' bit was little more than candy-coated bullshit, but let it bolster my confidence anyway.

Unfortunately, the moment was ruined when he flashed a manic grin and began making a jerking-off motion with his hand as if I hadn't known exactly what he was implying when he'd mentioned the nurses.

"Everything's fine," I quickly answered, putting a stop to his obscene gesture. "What brought you out this way?"

"Figured I had nothing better to do—" He slammed his hand on the table and boomed, "I'm kidding! Maybe I missed your ugly mug and wanted to catch up. And it's a damn good thing I did. What's this —what's going on with you?"

I returned the saltshaker to the center of the table, avoiding his gaze. "Nothing. Just trying to get out of here—"

"Bullshit." He leaned back in the chair, scratching his beard with his thumb. "Your energy is shit right now. What have they done to you, man?"

Not them—her.

My attempts to help Ari had only succeeded in dredging up long-buried memories from my past. It seemed she had more in common with my mama than I'd initially realized—a mistake I swore I wouldn't make again.

Can't save a woman who doesn't want to be rescued.

I massaged the back of my neck with a tight smile. "I'm just ready to be back. Listen, has the team—I mean, have you heard anything—"

Proving it just wasn't my year, the lights suddenly dimmed, and my train of thought zipped on out of the station, leaving me behind on the platform.

Staff members moved about the room, depositing electric candles in the center of the tables while the soft strains of a violin filtered through the speakers.

Bailey rubbed his hands together with another low chuckle, no doubt imagining all the ways the situation could be used against me in the near future. "You didn't tell me about the romantic dinners, you bastard," he beamed, lowering the chair legs back to the floor.

As for me—well, I'd suddenly remembered why I'd gotten into the habit of eating in my room on Friday nights.

"Welcome to Restaurant Night," the director called from the front of the room. "You'll find your menus in the center of the table. Take a minute to look them over, and someone will be by shortly to get your order."

"See, it's just Restaurant Nigh—"

He roughly smacked my shoulder with the back of his hand, eyes lighting up. I followed his stare and exhaled an agitated breath.

Christ.

Ari mirrored a newborn calf as she traipsed into the cafeteria, arms thrust out in front of her and clutching that damned notebook. She was wearing heels at least two sizes too big and seemed dangerously close to tipping over with every wobbled step. A scowling nurse followed closely behind, gripping the gait belt around Ari's waist like a leash.

I slowly shook my head as I eyed her ensemble, unable to look away from the gravity-defying red hair piled on top of her head in a series of elaborate loops and twists.

It was like staring at a grotesque caricature of a 1950s housewife, complete with the harvest gold apron tied at the waist of her checkered house dress.

"What in the actual hell?" Bailey snorted, before slapping a hand over his mouth.

Ari lifted her chin to scan the room, her mouth curving into a wide smile when she spotted me. The expression dimmed slightly when she realized I wasn't alone but, instead of turning around, she lifted her hand and began staggering in our direction.

Lips, now stained a garish shade of red that hadn't entirely remained within the lines, pursed in concentration as she shuffled the last remaining feet to the table.

"Ari," I asked gently, carefully keeping my face blank. "What are you doing?"

She parted her lips, but there was no sound, and her heavily rouged cheeks grew darker with a blush that would have been visible in any light.

I gave her an understanding nod and slowly slid my hand across the table like she was a wild animal in need of calming, not a woman who was clearly afraid.

Not that I knew the first thing about handling either.

She hugged the notebook to her chest like a shield, ruling out any possibility of a written explanation for the costume. I pressed my lips together and swallowed, trying to ease the sudden need to fix things.

C'mon, Reed. Help her.

"Did you—"

"Want to join us? I think that's a great idea," Bailey interjected as he jumped to his feet. "Here, allow me to get your chair for you."

I'd been about to ask if she needed something—in no realm had I planned on subjecting the poor woman to a man who hadn't matured past the age of twelve.

She cast him a veiled glance and mouthed, *thank you.*

He waited until she was seated before extending his hand. "Ari, is it? Since Reed here is an uncultured buffoon, allow me to introduce myself. I'm Conor Bailey, but if you're more comfortable, you can refer to me as Barnum. Get it? Like the Ringling Brothers?"

"Sit down," I growled irritably. A hot poker of rage tore through my flesh like butter, jabbing the area behind my eyes until all I saw was red. I should have known it was beyond Bailey to keep his mouth shut.

And, I suddenly wanted to put fist-sized holes in more than just the drywall...

However, as Ari was clearly out of sorts and prone to fainting, I avoided launching myself at my teammate and pulled back to take a deep breath.

Whoa there, Reed. No need to make things worse than they already were.

Bailey held his palms up in surrender, before stretching his long legs out in front of him. "Sorry, sorry. Just trying to get to know your friend here. Although, if you'd introduced us like a proper gentleman, none of this would've happened."

"Fine," I conceded.

The side of his mouth lifted in a grin as he redirected his focus back to Ari. "So, tell me," he said, completely poker-faced. "Is this your first circus?"

I dropped my fist to the table with a dull thud, muttering, "That's enough."

His smile slipped, and he jerked his chin in a stiff nod. "Okay, point taken. No need to bite my damn head off just because you've got your panties in a bunch."

Perhaps my reaction was a tad on the defensive side. There was no denying Ari's makeup made her look a bit like a clown in the circus. So, maybe she'd gotten into some psychedelic drugs before getting dressed for dinner. She was still a nice girl who'd already dealt with one asshole today—*two if I was including myself.*

She blew out her cheeks and scribbled something in the notebook before meeting my gaze.

You look very nice.

For reasons I couldn't explain, my pulse slowed considerably as I read it, restoring my vision to its factory settings. "Thank you. You look—well, you look different."

Her soft smile fell into a wince, and I belatedly realized what I'd said hadn't come out sounding like much of a compliment.

She pressed a hand to her chest.

Is this not okay? Would you prefer I wear something else?

My mouth went dry. I lowered my gaze to where Ari's fingers had settled along the swell of her breasts. The dress was as modest as it was hideous, giving absolutely no indication to the woman underneath. Was this the real her, or was she buried somewhere underneath the layers of polyester?

I squeezed my eyes shut as images of Ari flooded my brain, the byproduct of years of visualization exercises. I'd start by swiping the lipstick off using my thumb before planting a soft kiss to the dimple beside her mouth.

It wasn't enough.

I needed her naked and sprawled out before me like a feast. My fingers threading through every strand of her long hair until fanned out around her face like an auburn halo. I wanted to see those green eyes blaze with need as I tasted the salt on her skin, bringing her to pleasure again... and again... and—*Goddammit.*

She had me all over the place.

"Wear whatever you want," I snapped, ignoring Bailey's amused stare as I ran a hand over my face and tried clearing my head.

I bet she'd taste like the ocean.

Great, and with that, my dick was scrambling to get out of the dugout and into the on-deck circle.

Who was the bigger asshole now?

Ari suddenly exhaled several short bursts of air, sounding as though she was trying to fog up a window.

Good one. You are so funny.

My mind went ninety to nothing as I studied the words and her seemingly fake smile, trying to figure out what it was I'd missed. Nothing about any of this seemed humorous.

Bailey leaned in, shockingly unaffected by the fact that we'd gone back in time. "It's pretty clear you went to a lot of trouble for tonight. I hope you didn't do this for him. Trust me, he's not worth this level of —" He gestured toward her face. "Whatever you're calling this."

A woman should always look her best for a man.

O-o-o-okay...

So, Ari had gone a bit cuckoo since lunch. But, on the bright side, I could scratch the cold shower off my to-do list.

Bailey tried stepping in as a pinch hitter, but when his hand moved to cover Ari's possessively, I was no longer considering how to make it up to him. No, in a completely irrational turn of events, I began imagining how I could ruin his pretty-boy face.

"Got a minute, pal?" I clipped out, the muscle in my jaw twitching.

"Nope, sorry," he responded easily as he raised the menu, not sounding the slightest bit remorseful. "I haven't decided what to order yet. I could do the chopped steak, but then again, there's chicken parm. Decisions, decisions. Do you know—can we speak to the chef beforehand?"

I tensed, feeling my pulse in my eyelids. "You aren't staying for dinner."

Before things could devolve into further chaos, a woman I didn't recognize leaned over from the table beside ours, gesturing to Ari. "I'm sorry to interrupt, but I was wondering if I might have a quick word with you, dear?"

Ari nodded and pushed back from the table, clearly just as eager as I was to call it a night. Maybe it was for the best we end this before things got any worse.

"Now, you two boys make yourselves comfortable. We'll be right back." Even though she had to be pushing seventy, the woman tapped her index finger against my nose, a smile dancing on her lips.

I watched Ari teeter out of the cafeteria, resembling a drunk trying to pass a field sobriety test before turning my attention back to Bailey.

He absently chewed on his bottom lip while frowning down at the menu. "I don't see the drinks listed. We'll have to ask for that menu. Right now, I'm leaning toward the chicken parm, but I really want to ensure they have something that'll pair nicely with it, you know—like a golden lager, maybe?"

"What the hell is wrong with you?" I snarled.

"You're absolutely right." He nodded, the corner of his mouth quirking up. "Who passes up the chopped steak? Meat and potatoes, Reed. Meat and potatoes."

"No—she has a brain injury," I snapped, slapping my palm against the table to punctuate each word, hoping to permeate his thick skull. "And you just—you were just an asshole—"

"I was," he readily agreed, lowering the menu. "That's definitely my bad. But, in my defense, you didn't exactly speak up. Kinda like—

oh, I don't know—how you failed to mention the fact that you were into her?"

"What?" I choked. "I'm not anything with her. Christ, what kind of an asshole—you know what, don't answer that."

Bailey reached for my water glass and drained it with an indifferent shrug. "What's the big deal? You're both consenting adults. Wait—" He paused, his brows snapping together in suspicion. "Just wait a fucking minute—you're not still on that whole purity kick, are you? Oh, you are, it's written all over your face!"

I lowered my voice in warning. "That's not what we're discussing here. You're proposing I sleep with a woman who is recovering from a brain injury."

"Well, clearly she's got a brain injury if she's interested in you," he deadpanned.

"Which she is not," I added, scanning the room for any unwanted eavesdroppers.

Bailey cocked his head to the side, the smirk on his face fading instantly. "You don't see it? Who do you think she got all dolled up for, Reed? Wasn't me or anyone of these geezers, I'll tell you that much."

"Just drop it," I pleaded, massaging the back of my neck. My watch vibrated. I lowered my arm, exhaling a bitter laugh as I read the text.

Dad-
Tried calling and got no answer. You around?

Right on cue.

I was more likely to skip dinner in favor of a grueling session with Rocky than I was to text my father back. Hell, I would have taken being interrogated by Bailey in a locked room over another lecture on how I wasn't living up to my potential.

"Look, I'm just saying—as your friend and teammate—it's my job to call it like I see it." Bailey crossed his legs and clasped his hands behind his head, almost resembling a therapist, were it not for the incessant jiggling of his foot. "It's a responsibility I don't take lightly. And I'm telling you now, that girl imagined you naked at least once since she sat down. Trust me, a man knows these things."

The man knew jack shit.

"You picked up on that without her having to say a single word? That's—well, that must have taken some skill. Although, if imagining me in my birthday suit is our only criterion, I reckon we could fill the whole damn ballpark with 'love-struck' women."

His lips twitched. "We're gonna need a bigger stadium."

"Seriously? This is no different than the time you gave my room key to that hotel bartender because you felt a vibe between us. Just let it die, Bailey," I said tightly, pushing the hair off my forehead. My heart lurched in my chest, clearly siding with my teammate on the matter.

"That's where you're wrong." He tipped the chair back again, smirking like he had all the answers.

At least one of us did.

"Now, I'm willing to overlook the makeup—"

I tensed. "She doesn't normally wear any—"

His eyes flickered with amusement. "Ah. That's probably a good thing as her current look is a bit *Bozo-esque*. Regardless, she obviously wants you to notice her, but that's not why you're wrong. Go ahead, ask me why."

"I don't want to," I grumbled while picking at my fingernails.

"Alright, alright," Bailey sighed dramatically. "Stop begging already. I'll tell you. You ready for the bombs of truth Uncle Conor's about to drop?"

"Not really. I lost interest about ten minutes ago."

"Here goes—" He brought the chair back down with a loud scrape and leaned in to rest his forearms on the table. "I don't think that woman has the slightest clue who you are. And that, my surly little friend, is why she's not like the others."

A smirk tugged at my lips as I prepared to blow Bailey's theory out of the water. In fact, I was somewhat looking forward to watching his face crumple as I told him of Ari's little autograph attempt.

I don't even know you.

My shoulders sagged, and I released a harsh breath.

"Knew it!" Bailey punched the air with a victorious growl.

I put my head in my hands and stared blankly at the table while my brain played a riveting game of emotional pinball. Ari didn't know who I was, which should have been good news, but it only made her even more off-limits.

Like red tape and orange cones off-limits.

The girl was trying to recover from an injury. The last thing she needed was the press ripping her to shreds for dating a celebrity. That wasn't even getting into her innocent nature, something other women would no doubt exploit as a way of getting closer to me.

I cut my eyes over to the empty doorway before turning back to Bailey.

"Dude, she's not coming back," he remarked as he unfolded himself from the chair. "I say we go ahead and order hers to-go. And, unless you want to eat alone, you should consider doing the same. I'd love to stay and watch you mope, but I just remembered I have a prior engagement."

———

"This is just to be polite," I noted as I limped along just behind Bailey, nearly colliding with the tray in his hands when he came to a sudden stop.

He jerked his head toward me with a patronizing nod. "Yep. You mentioned that already. It must be such a hardship, taking food to a gorgeous woman. Now, which room is hers?"

"Just up here," I conceded in a gruff tone. "Across the hall from mine."

"Just across the hall from you," he repeated, his eyebrows rising. "Okay, I believe you now."

I straightened. "What the hell does that mean? Why would I lie about where her room is?"

"Oh no," he chuckled, shaking his head. "I believe you about that. I was actually referring to your denial over wanting to bone your mute lady friend. You've been in the desert for so long that you can't see the forest for the trees."

"Wait—what? Was that supposed to be an analogy? It makes no fucking sense." I clenched my jaw and hobbled around the roadblock he'd created before looking back over my shoulder. "By the way, I thought we agreed you were going to drop it."

"I just want to live long enough to see my baby boy find happiness," Bailey explained as he speed-walked past me. "C'mon, old chap. Keep up—wait, maybe you should sit this one out. Can't have you falling off your crutches and breaking a hip, can we? Nope, best to leave it to the professionals. And with her mouth full, I doubt your girl will even know you're not there."

"You son-of-a-bitch," I growled, the rubber tips on my crutches all but squealing against the linoleum in my attempt to overtake him.

He snorted. "What? I'm obviously talking about the delicious food I'm bringing her. Get your mind out of the gutter. Seriously, you kiss your mother with that mouth, Reed?

"Nah," I panted as I broke even with him. "Just yours."

We weren't exactly approaching in stealth-mode, so it was no surprise when Ari's door opened. In fact, I was almost shocked we hadn't drawn an entire crowd with our antics.

"Oh, good." The old woman clapped her hands, beaming from ear to ear. "The cavalry has come to the rescue. You boys read my mind. Come on in."

I stopped just outside the door. "Actually, we were just going to drop this and go—"

She pointed up at the tray with a frown. "But there are two boxes of food on that tray, are there not? No sense in either of you eating alone."

"Yeah," Bailey said under his breath, nudging me with his elbow.

"No sense in either of you eating alone. Seems like someone else said that—oh, I remember now. It was me. You're welcome."

I caught a glimpse of Ari through the open door and stilled. Her long hair was down, trailing in loose, uneven waves down her back. My heart slammed against my ribs, causing the smart-assed reply on my tongue to come out sounding more like a rough exhale.

The outdated dress and apron were gone, along with the clownish makeup. Someone had done a hell of a job scrubbing it off her face too, her cheeks were still tinged pink.

My eyes flickered over the black sweatpants and oversized pink t-shirt featuring two cats fighting over a ball of yarn. It was by far the most normal thing I'd ever seen her wear.

Maybe I'd been a bit too hasty in my decision to write off a romance between the two of us. I could tuck Ari away, somewhere no one could get to her. It wasn't like before with my mama. This time, I wouldn't fail.

Ari lifted an eyebrow, scrutinizing me with a small frown.

We could have been in a stadium filled with women, and I wouldn't have been able to take my eyes off her.

I cleared my throat against a sudden rush of emotion and gestured dumbly toward the tray in Bailey's hands. "You hungry?"

You hungry?

The woman looked like a goddess, and the best I could come up with was 'you hungry?' Clearly, I'd been in the desert too long to converse with the trees—*or whatever the hell it was Bailey had said.*

She nodded, shifting against the pillows and twisting her neck-lace between her fingers in the ensuing silence. I was gawking. I knew it, but it was like I was seeing her for the first time.

And it seemed I wasn't the only one who'd been rendered stupid by the sight of her. Bailey caught his shin on the leg of a chair as he moved forward, sending it into the wall with a jarring thud and nearly losing his grip on the tray.

"Hey—" He cleared his throat, his voice suddenly much deeper than before. "Hi. You got yourself a tent bed. K, did you get one of these?"

"Um—" I fumbled for the next word, suddenly drawing a blank.

What was the question?

The nurse from before sat in a small chair in the corner. The slight smile on her lips indicated that she wasn't reading the book in her hands. She was listening to every word. "It's a Posey bed. It keeps her safe at night."

Bailey nodded. "I just use a nightlight, but that's cool. Ari, you look like you need a drink—uh, a chair." He shook his head and tried again. "You should have a chair. All of them. I don't know why they didn't put a table in here. Do you think there's room for one? I could run out—"

The older woman stopped his rambling with a small pat on the back. "Ariana looks pretty comfortable right where she is. Listen, I imagine my dinner companions have given up on me by now, so I suppose you and I will just have to make do, won't we?"

"I—" He shot me a panicked look as the woman latched onto his side like a leech, protesting, "But I have somewhere I need to be!"

She chuckled in response, keeping a firm grip on his waist. "Oh, I think we both know that's not true, dear. Just humor this old woman, will you?"

Heat curled down my spine. I pushed my shirt sleeves up over my forearms, trying to recall if Ari's room had felt this warm the last time, or if someone had been messing around with the thermostat.

One corner of her mouth lifted as she watched me chew on my bottom lip, searching for an icebreaker. Compliments were always a good start—or maybe I'd mix things up by opening with a joke.

"Hi," I croaked, sounding like a pubescent boy.

Clearly, I was a bit rusty.

Ari's eyes sparkled with amusement, and she reached for her notebook and pen.

That was Georgia.

Like a dummy, I actually glanced back toward the closed door. "Oh, she seems... nice."

She patted the mattress with her fingers and scooted over, inviting me to sit. I left the crutches near the foot of the bed and sat facing her, letting my knee dangle over the edge. The feel of her thigh brushing against mine reawakened my dick and threatened my self-control.

It was probably just because I hadn't eaten, and it was almost—I glanced at my watch—six-thirty. Okay, Bailey might have been right. I'd fallen into a few bad habits—nothing I couldn't break once I was out in the real world again.

Ari briefly covered her face with both hands before returning her attention to the notebook. I watched her gnaw at the corner of her lip as she wrote, wondering if she was considering throwing me out again.

Turns out, there was no Halloween party tonight.

"So, all of that was because you thought there was a costume party?" I shook my head with a relieved laugh. Ari hadn't lost her mind; she'd just been playing a part. "And here I thought it was your everyday outfit."

She winced.

Do you think we could start over and you forget everything I said? Hi, my name is Ariana.

It was the same thing I'd said to her during our first lunch together, and a request I was more than willing to accept. She wasn't the only one in need of a do-over. I'd spent the better part of our time together in the cafeteria imagining her naked, something that now left me feeling like an ass.

Clearly, I was a mess. One second, I was giving up on there being anything romantic between us, and the next, I was convinced I could have my cake and eat it too. I needed to take a step back to consider the situation from every possible angle.

It was the right thing to do.

"Ari," I began, trailing off when her face scrunched up in a completely adorable way.

Adorable?

I scratched my jaw and tried again. "I don't know what you're referring to, but as we've got two meals and nowhere else to be, what do you say we eat?"

My watch vibrated as I was balancing on my right leg to reach our food. I pulled the table toward the bed before glancing down and shaking my head.

Dad-
You going to be up for a bit? I thought we could go over your strategy together.

Ol' Joe was just persistent as hell tonight. I must have fucked up epically if he was calling and texting on a weeknight.

Well, he'd just have to wait because I wasn't dealing with it tonight. I sat back down and watched as Ari idly played with a strand of hair, twirling the curl around her index finger. Sensing my stare, she looked up, her mouth curving into a genuine smile that transformed her entire face.

"You've got a sexy smile," I said hoarsely, wanting to reach out to touch her. "Not that the rest of you isn't—it's just really noticeable without all the crap on your face."

Well, I'd fumbled that spectacularly. The nurse cleared her throat, and I briefly considered telling her to read her damn book. She hadn't turned the page once in the last five minutes.

I made it as far as parting my lips when several things occurred. The mattress dipped, and then the table between us was gone, careening into the wall. Ari leaned forward and placed her hand flat against my chest, her emerald eyes dazed.

The room seemed to grow smaller under her palm, the temperature rising with each passing second. My throat bobbed in a swallow at the feel of her warm breath against the shell of my ear.

"Thank you," she whispered, raising every hair on my neck.

I didn't know what I'd done to deserve her gratitude, but it seemed important that I do my damnedest to find out. By the time I registered the feel of her lips against my jawline, she was settling back against the pillows with a satisfied grin.

It was over in seconds.

I exhaled and stared at her mouth, wondering how, in one move, Ari had managed to break through the bars of my ribcage to wrap herself around my heart.

We couldn't stop there. I hadn't fully appreciated what she'd been offering.

"Let me get some towels to mop that up," the nurse said, pulling me away from my mental self-flagellation and reminding me that we weren't alone.

In the heat of the moment, a glass had been knocked over, sending a steady stream of water running over the edges of the table.

The almost kiss had left even my good knee a little unsteady. I wobbled as I moved off the bed. After cracking my knuckles and rolling up my sleeves, I turned back to Ari with a gruff, "I'm going in. If I don't make it out alive, tell the world I died a hero."

She scrunched her nose and gave me a lopsided grin in response.

After shaking the water off, I passed the containers over to Ari, before emptying the flooded tray into a nearby trashcan.

A scrap of paper filled with cursive handwriting clung to the bottom, and I pried it off to drop in when something caught my eye.

Tell him how handsome he looks. Men need to hear it.

Let him order for you.

Ask for his opinion on what you should wear. He knows what looks best on you.

Laugh at his jokes, even if you don't find them funny.

Let him lead the conversation. Don't bore him with girl talk.

Hold a cigarette between your lips, making him lean in to light it.
Modesty is the best policy.

If he doesn't notice you right away, stand in the corner and cry softly. Chances are, he'll come over to find out what's wrong.

My jaw went slack. What the hell was this—a submissive's guide to mid-century time travel? The fog of lust dissipated, and I let the paper fall from my fingers into the trash, taking the remains of my appetite with it.

There was no costume party.

Ari studied my expression before patting the bed, but I shook my head and forced a smile, choking on my disappointment. "I can't— I've, uh, I've got to return a call."

I'd thought she was different; someone I'd be willing to break my rules for.

But what would I know?

Clearly, I was just the fool who kept finding myself in the same traps.

CHAPTER ELEVEN
ARIANA

"Prejudices, it is well known, are most difficult to eradicate from the heart whose soil has never been loosened or fertilised by education: they grow there, firm as weeds among stones."

-Charlotte Brontë, *Jane Eyre*

A MAN like Killian expects to be wowed.

My nostrils flared as I added more soil to the clay pot on the table in front of me. The humidity dampened my skin, but I welcomed the fresh air. It was a nice change from the fluorescent lights and medicinal stench of the facility.

And pretty much everything that occurred last night.

I closed my eyes and breathed in the salty air, bathing my face in the warmth of the fall sunlight. But it wasn't enough to wash away the memories of him.

Fainted?

Check.

Let a bitter old woman turn me into a sexed-up version of Lucy Ricardo?

Double check.

Temporarily lost my mind and made out with some facial stubble after being told I was sexy?

Check, check, and—maybe there was a vacancy at a rehab facility in another country.

I'd given up any hope of salvaging the evening when Georgia kindly informed me that my look was about seventy years out of style.

Mission failed.

Time to change my name and move away.

But then Killian had shown up with dinner and a forgiving smile, and I'd thrown myself at him, thinking it meant something.

I'll tell you what it means when a man all but runs from your room screaming. It means you're an idiot.

His rejection had left me feeling hollow and dangerously close to tears, but that wasn't why I'd tossed and turned most of the night.

It was because when I'd looked in the mirror yesterday, I hadn't recognized the woman staring back. And it wasn't just the makeup and hair. I'd lost myself, trying to become someone I wasn't—someone who would use another person to gain freedom.

Just like Helen's old clothes, the behavior didn't fit me.

"Are you okay—do you need a jacket?" Tsega fussed with the blanket draped across my legs.

I shook my head. *No, just reliving every mistake I've made since arriving.*

The small morning shower had moved out, leaving behind blue skies and temperatures in the high sixties. In other words, it was perfect gardening weather.

Although, I supposed it could have been forty degrees and I wouldn't have complained. I loved working in the dirt, it gave me a chance to sort through my thoughts.

Satisfied with my response, she sat back to watch me. I picked up the trowel again, surrounding the burnt orange mums with more potting soil.

It was solitary work, but I preferred it to the constant noise inside *True North*. When my thoughts circled back to Killian, I switched out the trowel for my hands, taking my frustration out on the black soil.

Because I was a liar.

I'd been running since day one—from Tristan, the wreck, ghosts from the past—all of it. I didn't know why I'd gotten into the convertible, but with my palm pressed to Killian's chest, I finally felt safe. With each frantic beat of his heart, my steps slowed, allowing me to turn and face the truth.

I was scared.

Not of having my heart broken or spending the rest of my life locked inside a cage. No, I was petrified that the real me would never be enough for anyone. So, I let Brad put his hands on my body and took Helen's horrible advice because their voices would always drown out the sound of my own.

Seeing the dirt caked beneath my fingernails gave me an idea, and I toed off my house shoes, digging my toes into the damp blades of grass.

It was grounding.

And, surprisingly, it reminded me of home. I'd often volunteered to work in the community greenhouse, preparing items to take to the local farmer's market.

No one ever bothered me there. I could work in peace, only leaving when the palms of my hands were good and callused. I think Tristan was under the impression I was deep in prayer, and there were indeed days where that was true, but it wasn't why I'd volunteered for the lonely task.

When I was elbow deep in dirt, I wasn't the daughter of a prophet or a pawn in another one of his games.

I was whoever I chose to be in that moment.

Sometimes, I was a lowly governess, awaiting my beloved Rochester in the garden. I'd snip the dead off of vines and water the massive beds of flowers, all while imagining what it would be like to have someone to call my own. Other times, I was Elizabeth Bennet, walking the grounds with a racing heart as Mr. Darcy professed his love.

"My affections and wishes are unchanged, but one word from you will silence me on this subject forever."

I could have read the line a million times and never tired of it because back then, I believed that someday, a man might express how ardently he loved and admired me.

It was naïve.

Deep down, I envied and admired these fictional women because they possessed something I lacked—free will. Despite the period, they weren't easily swayed by the opinions of men. Love was a decision they made, not something thrust upon them by a voice louder than their own.

Maybe it had never been about running away or finding love, but in being brave enough to live life on my own terms. Everyone had a plan, convinced they knew what was best for me. The constant tug of war had turned me into a powder keg of tension, ready to ignite.

Tristan wanted to use me as an asset to line his pockets.

Brad wanted me broken and in chains.

Morgan wanted me to use my flesh to secure my freedom.

Helen wanted to use me for her own amusement.

But what about me—what did I want?

I squeezed my eyes shut, clenching my fist around the gardening trowel as I fought to hear my own voice over all the noise in my head. The volume reached a brief fever pitch, and when silence descended like a stage curtain, I found myself staring into a pair of glacial blue eyes.

Him.

I wanted Killian—a man who didn't want me to be someone I wasn't. A protector. I'd spent my life surrounded by fakes, starving for something real. Something deep.

Unfortunately, he was probably under the assumption I was a complete loon by now.

"There you are, young lady," Helen crowed as she approached

WAIT FOR IT   147

the table. "I was just thinking to myself that I hadn't seen your face around today. How did your little thing go last night?"

Her upper lip curled, and it took everything in me not to launch the trowel at her face. Whatever doubts I might have had were gone now. The woman had intentionally set me up to fail.

I set my jaw against the wave of heat spreading up my throat and clutched the pendant around my neck, struggling to quash the familiar flare of humiliation. Touching the engraved tentacles had become something of a nervous habit lately, but I liked to imagine it was my talisman.

So far, it wasn't that great at warding off evil.

Fury scorched my chest and rained ash down on my tongue, but I was a girl with no voice. I opened my mouth, only to sigh in exasperation.

Even if I could have told Helen exactly what I thought of her actions, it would have been pointless. The blame rested on my shoulders. I should have known better than to take advice from a woman who dyed the back of her hair jet black while leaving the front white.

She was a skunk, both in looks and behavior.

"You ready?" Tsega asked, her forehead creasing. I couldn't decide whether it was in concern or disappointment. I imagined everyone in the building was aware of my failed attempt at dress-up.

She squeezed my hand when I nodded and began returning the gardening tools to a small wagon nearby. I handed her a shovel, spotting the headline on one of the old newspapers lining the table.

MVP Candidate Killian Reed's Future Questionable.

Killian.

At first, I was convinced I imagined his name. After reading the headline twice, I began to realize what a fool I'd been to think that he and I could have worked. It was almost laughable.

The baseball star and the martyr.

We may as well have resided on different planets.

In my haste to learn as much as I could of his injury and what it meant for the Hurricanes, I'd temporarily forgotten I wasn't alone.

"Not such a catch now, is he?" Helen taunted, clicking her tongue against her teeth. "You know, in my day, we had a no-nonsense approach to dating that you young girls seem to be missing. We accepted nothing less than everything, while your lot is hung up on money and status. It's pathetic."

In twenty-four hours, I'd gone from being clueless to completely indiscriminate when it came to the opposite sex. This, from a woman who'd been married four times.

"She didn't know who he was," Tsega contended, branding a gardening fork like a weapon.

Her smirk faded. "Wait—you didn't know who he was?"

I touched the inked words again and shook my head.

"Oh, I bet you thought you were special," she cackled, her face twisting into a hideous sneer. "You know, I called it the day you arrived. I told Margaret and the girls that you were going to latch onto the baseball player and bring trouble. You're just lucky you went after him and not Arthur, or things would have been much worse for you, missy."

The rules might have been a little different, but this world was no different than my own. It seemed ugly people existed just about anywhere. The Helens of the world were always going to be there, judging and finding me lacking.

It only hurts if you let it...

I released a breath through my nostrils, my molars cracking audibly as they came together. For a moment, I forgot to be Ariana James. Instead, I imagined myself as Anne Shirley in *Anne of Green Gables*, fully capable of breaking a slate over Gilbert Blythe's head to stop his teasing.

While I didn't have a slate lying around, I did have a pot of mums that would do nicely for what I had in mind. Because, for the first time ever, the adrenaline coursing through my body and tightening my muscles wasn't in response to fear.

It was because I was pissed off and not in the mood to be bullied.

Not by Helen.

Not by Brad.

Not anymore.

"That's enough," Tsega said coldly. "You oughta be ashamed of yourself"—

Helen shook her head in disgust. "For what? I did her a favor, really. Men like Killian only want one thing. Sex. He's surrounded by gorgeous women all the time and a weak little thing like her—you know as well as I do, she'd be eaten alive. I doubt he'd even have to pay her off to keep quiet after, because who would ever believe her?"

Who would believe me?

It was a question that had kept me in chains most of my life. What this woman thought of me should have been none of my concern, but I was struck with an overwhelming urge to defend myself. I wanted to watch her choke on the hateful words as I told her the things I'd endured at the hands of Tristan and Brad.

Because I was not a weak person.

And she wouldn't have lasted a day in my shoes.

"We're leaving." Tsega tossed the remainder of the tools in the wagon before turning back to Helen with a scowl. "Ariana is one of the sweetest people you'll ever meet, but instead of taking the time to get to know her, you tricked—"

The old woman rolled her eyes. "Blah, blah, blah. Shouldn't you be off, I don't know, worshiping a cow or something? Isn't that what you people—" Her words cut off in a sudden shriek as the clod of dirt connected with her cheek.

I calmly wiped the soil from my hand and straightened before nodding to Tsega. *Let's go.*

Helen sat in openmouthed silence for several seconds before roaring, "I will sue you, young lady! Help, I've been assaulted! Somebody help me!"

We left her squawking at the table, scurrying back toward my room like a pair of criminals. Tsega took the flowerpot from my hands and placed it on the counter before doubling over.

"The look on her face," she wheezed, her eyes streaming with tears. "I can't believe you did that! Are you okay? You won't get in trouble. I'll tell them the things she said."

It wasn't that.

What happened with Helen had been a long time coming.

My mind was still reeling over the news that Killian was a baseball player. I'd wanted to flee the church, only to run right to another spotlight. The t-shirts and thinking I wanted an autograph—and suddenly, the weird jaw kiss was not the most mortifying thing I'd ever done.

The breath caught in my throat, and I swallowed.

I wanted—

God help me, I wanted Killian.

In a spectacularly stupid move, I'd developed feelings for a man known all over the world. Overwhelmingly chaotic emotions that had chosen to reveal themselves at the worst possible time.

I'd fallen for a baseball player with pretty eyes and a kind heart, thinking we could live happily-ever-after in a place Tristan would never find us.

How was that for naïveté?

———

"You want to tell me again what we're doing here?" Tsega asked as she knocked on the door.

I shook my head, bouncing my legs lightly in anticipation.

"No," she repeated with a strange smile. "Okay. What if we talk about, I don't know, maybe Killian being in your room last night? Or perhaps, your sexy smile?"

In hindsight, trusting the night aide, Sierra, to keep a secret hadn't been my best idea. I didn't know what to do—*feign ignorance and hope she didn't tell anyone, or come clean and hope she didn't tell anyone?*

I licked my lips and took a deep breath just as Georgia called, "Come in!"

Tsega turned her hand against her lips before dropping the imaginary key into the pocket of her scrubs. "Your secret is safe with me."

I nodded, grateful that I had at least one thing working in my favor.

Georgia's room was the only place I knew to go where I didn't run the risk of another awkward run-in. My suspicion that Killian was avoiding me was confirmed when he saw me in the hallway, frowned, and then made a hobbled beeline in the opposite direction.

Clearly, I'd made a mess of everything.

Georgia was reclining in an oversized chair near the television, flipping through a magazine. Her hand lifted in a brief wave when we entered before she sat up to jot something down in a small notebook. "Oh, hello, girls. What brings you here?"

I peered down at the colorful pages spread across her lap before grabbing my notebook. The scenery changed from one photo to the next, but there were smiling faces in every one.

What are you doing?

Georgia reached out for me, and I wheeled myself closer. "Still haven't found your voice, dear? I was just certain last night would have been a turning point for you."

I shook my head, my face heating in shame.

As if she was the embodiment of happiness, the sides of Georgia's mouth stretched wide. "This is for my trip. My hip injury set me back a few months—word of advice, don't let anyone tell you that skiing is something that just comes back to you, because it's not. Had to learn that the hard way, dear. Anywho, now that you're here, would you like to help?"

I hesitated as she passed a magazine over.

But I don't know where you want to go.

"Oh, everywhere, dear," she answered readily. "I want to see the northern lights from a glass igloo in Finland... feast on Danish pastries on the island of Aero in Denmark... discuss the principles of Buddhism at a monastery in Thailand. I am not going to miss a single thing this world has to offer."

I imagined my mouth was hanging open in shock. Everything Georgia had just described sounded too good to be true.

"What about you? What is it you want to see?" She tapped the magazine. "Go on, take a look."

After flipping through several pages, I finally settled on a picturesque village surrounded by mountains and water.

This.

She looked it over. "Ah, The Lofoten Islands in Norway. Can you imagine—staying in a little cottage near the water and eating fresh fish for dinner every night?"

Georgia added something to her notebook with a dreamy expression, as if she could clearly envision herself doing just that. Meanwhile, I couldn't see myself anywhere but inside the church, and that frustrated me.

I swallowed and cleared my throat to get her attention.

Last night you said that Helen focused too much on the rules.

"I also said she was quite a piece of work, but it's true. She's hung up on the way things used to be done, while people your age live in an age of instant gratification."

Which way is right?

Georgia patted my knee. "No one can decide that but you, Ariana. I imagine you could drive yourself mad, trying to compare the two. The best thing to do is just to be yourself and let the rest sort itself out."

My pen dug into the paper.

That's just it. You saw me last night. I think it's pretty clear that being myself doesn't work. He's a baseball player, and I'm—

A hostage of my faith.

A nobody. As much as I want to be myself, it's not that simple. I'm not good enough as-is."

Georgia nodded to herself. "You think that just because he's famous that he wouldn't look twice at a girl like you. See, that tells me we have quite a bit of work to do."

I blew out a frustrated breath.

Makeup? Hair? I tried it already.

Her eyes flashed with amusement. "No, no. Nothing silly like that. Last night wasn't you—that was Helen. Now, it seems to me that you've gotten comfortable being what everyone else wants. But if you knew who you were, my dear, you'd see that it's young Killian who should be questioning if he's good enough for you."

I let the notion sink in before shaking my head, unable to imagine Killian second-guessing himself on anything, especially not where I was concerned.

He's avoiding me.

"And?" Georgia waved a hand dismissively. "Find out why."

My vision blurred. I already knew why.

He doesn't want anything to do with me.

Her eyes squinted as she read the words before chuckling to herself. "You're just willing to give up then? Throw in the towel now that you know who he really is?"

Yes.

No. As much as I wanted Killian to mean something for me, I had to consider the ramifications of pursuing my feelings. I would be giving up any chance of hiding, any chance of never being found.

And yet, I still wanted him.

More than I'd ever wanted anything.

"Imagine if Nickie had given up on Terry when she didn't show up at the Empire State Building," Georgia said with a thoughtful frown. "If the movie had ended with him assuming she was avoiding him or had changed her mind."

I don't know Terry or Nickie, for that matter.

At least, I didn't think I did. Maybe they were the people she'd been sitting with at dinner before rescuing me from myself.

The woman scoffed. "*An Affair to Remember*, Ariana! Surely you know one of the most romantic movies of all time?"

I shook my head, skeptical that a movie fitting my circumstances even existed. It didn't exactly seem like a standard plotline.

"Oh, dear. Well, we are going to remedy that right now. I know they've got it in the video library downstairs. Tsega, dear, please tell me you've seen it."

She looked almost guilty as she shook her head. "I don't really watch a lot of television."

"Girls!" Georgia all but roared with a grin. "How do you expect to find love if you aren't brushing up on the classics? They're practically how-to guides. Just maybe don't rely on them for fashion advice, right Ariana?"

I cringed. It seemed I wouldn't be living that down anytime soon.

———

One trip to the library, and two hours later, the three of us sat sniffling our way through the end credits.

"You see—" Georgia tried before hiccuping. "I just—"

I clenched her hand in mine and nodded, knowing exactly what she meant. While the only similarity between Killian and Nickie was the fact that they were both well-known—one for baseball, the other for his love of women—the story resonated, nonetheless.

"Isn't it just magical? '*If you can paint, I can walk.*'" She clutched her chest and fell back dramatically in the chair. "In case either of you were wondering, that was a swoon and not some medical emergency."

Tsega brushed away the tears on her cheeks with a grin. "I think we caught on to that, Georgia."

"Good. Good. Now, Ariana. Instead of fixating on how you don't feel as if you belong in Killian's world, have you considered things from his perspective? He's surrounded by actors every day. How refreshing would it be to spend time with someone who didn't want something from him? Someone who wasn't using him?"

I fiddled with my necklace before giving her a reluctant nod. Inside, I was being eaten up with guilt. I'd wanted to use Killian as a means of escape. At least I had in the beginning.

She yawned and stretched her arms overhead. "Now that I've had a nice cry, I require a nap. And you—you're going to be yourself, and then you're going to go get your Nickie!"

Be myself.

Tsega wheeled me down the hall, slowing as she neared Killian's door. "You want to knock, or should I?"

I pointed to my temple and winced, my eyes flooding with fresh tears.

"Oh, Ari," she sighed. "Today has just been too much. Let's get back to the room and rest."

God help me, it was a lie.

The real Ariana was a fraud—no better than the other actors. Just because I'd changed my mind before I could go through with it didn't give me an automatic second chance. Maybe my penance would be feeling this ache in my chest every time I saw him.

As I looked at Killian's door, I thought of Terry, trying to explain to Nickie how she'd gotten into an accident as she rushed to meet him at the Empire State Building.

'Oh, it's nobody's fault but my own! I was looking up... it was the nearest thing to heaven! You were there...'

The nearest thing to heaven...

He was—but just as out of reach.

CHAPTER TWELVE
KILLIAN

"Progress always involves risks. You can't steal second base and keep your foot on first."

-Frederick B. Wilcox

THE FOOD at *True North* was supposed to be top of the line, yet I hadn't tasted a single bite of my grilled chicken sandwich as I read over the text message my father had sent just before dawn.

Until recently, Saturdays had always been designated parent days in his book. Now, it felt like he was calling me almost daily. I wondered if he had reminders set in his phone, or if the inclination to reach out to his wayward son just came naturally. Even my mama had been pleading with me to hear him out.

Dad-
Have you heard from the team? I think you need to put the pressure on Theo to handle this before the press forms their own opinions. Love you, but this can't wait.

Love you, but...

There it was. The caveat—because, apparently, I wasn't worthy of something without a catch. My dad loved me, *but* I could do better. On the verge of being offered a slew of contracts, *but* I blew out my knee. I finally met a nice girl, *but* there was a catch.

Maybe it was asking a lot, but just once, I wanted the universe to give me something without that damn conjunction attached to it.

Although, if experience had taught me anything, it was that there was always going to be an angle.

Moving up to the majors was like winning the lottery. Ex-girl-friends... long-lost relatives... there was always someone popping up out of the woodwork, looking to capitalize on my success.

I'd had women claim they were friends of my sister's in an attempt to get close to me—failing to bother with even the most basic of *Google* searches. If they had, they would have discovered I was an only child.

Then there were the particularly vicious few who'd claimed to be pregnant with my 'love child,' only to balk when my lawyers insisted on a paternity test. Those cases had only solidified my decision to remain celibate for the remainder of my natural life.

There had been so many over the years. I'd learned to spot a con from a mile away. The women were all the same, blinded by their own expectations of who I was. When the girl-next-door persona failed to get my attention, they seemed to have no issue with browsing the supermarket tabloid covers for new ideas.

But Ari—I could honestly say she was the one I never saw coming. I hadn't wanted to believe someone like her could ever have a motive.

News had spread throughout *True North* in a matter of hours. All anyone wanted to talk about was Ari's ridiculous outfit. As much as it irritated me that people had nothing better to do, I had to remind myself it wasn't my problem anymore.

It was over before it even really began, but my sex-starved brain hadn't gotten the memo. I'd had dreams of Ari all night, none of which ended with a kiss on the jaw.

Oh no—I'd mentally exhausted all the ways in which a woman could be claimed. It was best just to get it all out of my system. No more waking up to damp sheets and the lingering image of us in the shower, Ari's green eyes trained on mine as she lowered herself to the tiles before taking me in her mouth.

Why hadn't I just asked her where she'd gotten her old-fashioned advice, or why she'd used it on me? While I was at it, why hadn't I gone for the kiss?

I balled my hands into fists and counted to ten until my heart slowed its galloping into a more respectable trot. Only a masochist would look for ways to turn the fantasy into reality—*which I clearly wasn't.*

Nope. I had my eyes on the prize.

Maybe after lunch, I'd take ol' Joe's advice and reach out to Theo, see where we stood on things.

I ignored the first dramatic sigh, hoping my unwanted visitor would take the hint and leave. My teeth came together at the second, and by the third, my patience was shot all to hell.

I jerked my head up with a gruff, "What?"

"Oh, Killian. I didn't see you there," Helen said, dabbing at her dry face with a tissue. "Might I have a word with you?"

I shrugged and gestured toward an empty chair across the table. She shuffled over before fixing me with a pointed stare, clearly expecting me to jump up and pull it back for her.

She had the wrong guy.

Bailey was the gentleman. I was—well, right now, I was the brooding asshole. A role I surprisingly found quite enjoyable.

With a small grumble of disapproval, she scraped the chair along the floor while muttering something about '*young people today.*'

This was her fault.

If she'd left Ari alone yesterday, then—*then what*—I wouldn't have gone out of my way to protect her?

The old woman made a show of settling into her seat, radiating with excitement despite the grave look on her face. The sudden change was either the result of a new medication, or Helen had finally found a way to sue *True North* for not living up to her high expectations.

With the way she was leaning across the table, I wouldn't have to wait to find out. "I'm sure, by now, you've seen my face and have some questions."

I narrowed my eyes, seeing the exact same wrinkles and fine lines as the last time I'd been forced to interact with her. "Do you mean now, or was it off wandering the building alone?"

Helen slapped her palm against the table and cackled before becoming solemn again. "Yes, well, you're very kind not to draw attention to it. If you must know—" She paused dramatically. "I was attacked this morning by another patient. It seemed only fitting you should be told."

"What happened?" Despite my every attempt to remain indifferent, the old bat had piqued my curiosity. I took another glance, still seeing no visible evidence that she'd been injured or maimed in any way.

She paused to sniffle into her tissue before palpating her cheek with a sharp wince. "Well, I was sitting in the gardens, just enjoying the sun when she came out of nowhere—"

"Who came out of nowhere?"

"That girl, of course," Helen snapped as if there could be no other culprit.

"Ari?"

It didn't make sense.

She lifted her shoulder before spearing a piece of chicken. "Is that what people call her? I swear, she's more hellhound than human. I told the staff that she is a danger to everyone here, but it seems they're not making my injury their top priority. So, I've taken it upon myself to warn as many people as possible. If enough of us speak out, they'll be forced to transfer the little demon to another facility."

I scratched at my jaw, watching Helen shovel food into her

mouth, and growing more confused by the second. Ari might have been a little different, but she wasn't a violent person.

Not even remotely.

Violent people didn't brush their lips against your jaw or smile up at you in admiration. They didn't look at you like maybe you deserved a life without caveats.

Christ, what was I doing?

The old woman startled at my sudden grunt before going back to her chicken.

I shook my head, fighting to clear my head. "Wait. You're telling me that Ari, the woman you had lunch with yesterday, attacked you?"

"Yep." She nodded emphatically. "I'm telling you, there was evil in that girl's eyes."

"Ari, the woman who is usually in a wheelchair with a nurse present, came at you, unprovoked?" I drummed my fingers against the table, suddenly keyed up.

Given the way Helen had treated her, Ari would have been well within her rights to lay the old woman out.

But it didn't fit with the girl I knew.

"I don't know what you're not understanding here, young man." Helen's voice grew louder. "She attacked me and that—that oriental nurse of hers practically encouraged it! And do you know the worst part? That mulatto director says I can't claim it was racially motivated, even though it's obvious the cow worshipper has it out for me."

Jesus Christ.

I didn't even know where to begin in tackling half the things she'd just said. "Uh, Tsega is Ethiopian, Helen. You'd know that if you'd taken the time to read the staff bios in the hallway. And I'm like one-hundred percent sure that every term you just used is politically incorrect, not to mention, offensive to—well, to basically everybody."

Her lips curled up in a sneer. "Are you calling me a liar? Look, I'm just telling you to stay away from that girl because she's a menace. And after everything I did for her—"

"What exactly did you do for her?" I instantly regretted asking.

"Um..." Helen cleared her throat and lowered her chin to her chest, suddenly finding her half-eaten chicken riveting. "Nothing, really."

The old woman was more crooked than the Brazos.

"I'm sorry I didn't quite understand your mumbling. Did you say nothing?" I pushed.

"Well, I..." She danced around it for several more seconds before admitting, "I guess, in hindsight, I did it for you. Saved you from being manipulated by that snake."

"How in the hell do you figure that?"

So, I was a little defensive.

For whatever reason, the mention of manipulation had triggered some very detailed fantasies involving the aggressor in question and a pair of handcuffs.

Helen mashed her lips together firmly, glaring across the table. "I will not be spoken to like that, young man. I don't give a hoot who you think you are!"

Clearly, if I wanted the old woman to admit to anything, it was going to require me to stop fixating on a certain redhead.

"Look," I sighed. "I just want to know what you did, so I can thank you properly. It really sounds like you put yourself out there."

Helen nodded along to every word, the hard line of her jaw softening. "I did. I most certainly did. The way she was watching you during our lunch yesterday was downright deplorable."

"Mmm-hmmm..." I mashed my lips together, fighting to remain serious.

"People like that need to be taught a lesson in manners. Someone failed her along the way, so naturally, it fell to me. I was certain she was after you because of who you are, so I might have gone a bit overboard." She snorted. "That girl read over my notes like she was going to be tested on them later!"

"That's—"

Impossible.

If what Helen was saying was true, then Ari had dressed up

because she liked me enough that she was willing to take someone else's advice no matter how crazy it seemed. She could have thrown the old woman under the bus when I came to her room, but that wasn't who she was.

And Helen was a woman in dire need of a few tread marks.

Confused irritation grew into a simmering rage when Helen began cackling again. "That's not even the best part! Turns out, the little monster didn't even know who you were until this morning. She saw a newspaper article—oh, you should've seen her face! Like someone just ran over her dog!"

Well, she was absolutely correct on one point. There was a psychopath in this facility, and she just happened to be sitting directly across from me.

"Wait—" I released a pained breath, unable to decide which was worse—the fact that Ari had gotten hurt by this hateful and entirely racist bitch of a woman, or that I'd been the cause of it.

I'd finally found a girl who liked me, and I'd let her down—thrown her to the wolves.

Clearly, I deserved every one of the caveats in my life.

I forced a hand through my hair and stared down at the white tablecloth. If I'd done more to put a stop to the condescending way Helen had treated Ari over lunch, none of this would have happened.

"—she was gardening and saw the paper," the old woman droned. "Then, it was like something took over her body, and she flew into a rage. I was lucky enough to escape with my life. The next patient might not fare as—"

Enough. I held up a finger, silencing her. "Thank you for coming to me with this."

"Absolutely, we have to stick together in here. Especially you, now that she knows who you are. No one is safe anymore. We can't even lock our doors at night!"

My control slipped as I got to my feet, briefly unmasking the fury underneath. "I meant, thank you for showing me exactly the kind of person you are. It'll make my request to have you removed from the facility much easier."

The fork slipped from Helen's fingers, clattering loudly against her plate. "You wouldn't"—

"Oh, you bet your ass I would, and will. My only regret is not doing it yesterday before you had a chance to humiliate Ari. Now, if you'll excuse me, it seems I have an appointment I just can't miss."

I got several feet from the table before turning back, unable to resist one last dig. "Remind me again what you called the director? You know what—never mind. I'm sure it'll come to me by the time I get to her office."

As I took the elevator down to the first floor, I couldn't help but feel that by not giving Ari the benefit of the doubt, I'd earned my final strike.

I couldn't change what happened, but I could damn well ensure that everyone here knew I wasn't fucking around when it came to her.

———

I was empty-handed when I knocked on Ari's door a little later that afternoon. There were no carefully rehearsed speeches tucked away in my pocket. No words would fix what had already been done.

Kinda like trying to put the toothpaste back into the tube once it was out, it would just make a bigger mess.

Apologies only worked when there was a marked change in behavior. Otherwise, they were just pretty words that meant nothing. It was time to suck it up and let the chips fall where they may.

Granted, I wasn't physically opposed to groveling on my knees if needed. Theoretically, of course, as I was still non-weight-bearing.

Strange, I never thought I'd live to see the day I'd be willing to sacrifice anything for a woman—*but Ari wasn't just some woman.*

Not that there was a chance in hell of me ever admitting it, but Bailey had called it.

My teammate had seen in one evening what I'd missed in weeks. I might have been good at reading people in baseball but hadn't even cracked the spine on her. She wasn't like the rest of them. And maybe if I hadn't been so damn cynical, I would have realized it sooner.

Tsega gave me a cursory glance when she opened the door before shaking her head. She was like a guard dog, which I appreciated. Ari needed someone who did the right thing for her. "Now's not really a good time—"

"I won't stay long," I interjected, catching the closing door with my right foot. "Look, I heard what happened. I came to see how she was doing."

"You want to know how she's doing?" she hissed. "See for yourself."

The cryptic response came out sounding more like a warning rather than an invitation to enter, but I was just desperate enough to overlook it.

Ari lay with her back to me, facing the window. Her arms were tucked beneath her chin, making her appear much smaller than she was. I assumed she was sleeping until she sucked in a ragged breath.

Hearing her cry demolished the last of my control, and I didn't think. *I couldn't.* By the time I stopped to consider how it might look, the crutches were already forgotten on the floor, and she was wrapped up in my arms.

"I've got you," I murmured into her hair. "I've got you."

She hiccuped against my chest, gripping handfuls of my t-shirt before releasing another anguished sob. The raw sound shredded barriers I hadn't even known existed. I felt the depths of her pain as keenly as my own.

The truth was like a fastball between the eyes. I might have had feelings for this woman, but I would never deserve someone like her in this lifetime.

Maybe not even in a million lifetimes.

"I spoke to the director. They're transferring Helen to Oak Lake. She won't hurt you ever again—"

Ari lifted her chin to meet my eyes. "Why?" The word came out like a strangled gasp, and she touched her throat before repeating, "Why would you do that?"

This was no whisper, either. I heard Ari loud and clear, in a voice almost as familiar to me as her face. Even Tsega seemed to be fighting surprise, although she quickly channeled it into a stoic expression.

"She speaks," I chuckled, keeping one hand tangled up in her loose hair and the other firmly around her shoulder as if afraid she was going to disappear on me.

"Why did you do it, Killian?" Her chest heaved, but she held the sob back, pressing her cheek to my chest. "I'm not Terry, and you're not Nickie! I'm not a good person, don't you see that?"

Who?

Tsega cracked a rare grin. "It's a movie with Cary Grant—you know what, it's not important."

"You were given bad advice, Ari. It doesn't make you a bad person." I remarked as I stroked her shoulder blade with my thumb. "Nothing could be farther from the truth."

"What, um, what exactly prompted your little visit with the director?" Tsega asked in a tight voice.

If I wasn't mistaken, the aide seemed a little nervous.

I placed my hand on Ari's cheek and lifted her face to mine. "I did it for you. You don't deserve a quarter of the bullshit that woman put you through. And pretending to be an expert on relationships? Please, I doubt the old bat would know what do with a man if one came right up and kissed her."

Any rational thinking on my part ceased when she released an audible breath, her swollen eyes intently focused on my mouth. I wondered if she was thinking about last night. Did she know how many times I'd relived that almost kiss?

"I thought—" I paused and took a deep breath before swinging for the fences. "I thought that last night was you, but it's not. And I know I haven't exactly gone out of my way to make you feel welcome, but I want to change that. I want to get to know you—the real you, I mean. All I'm asking is for a chance."

Ari burrowed her face into my neck, letting her fingers move lightly along my back. It felt right, holding her like this.

I just hoped she felt the same.

"What do you say, slugger?" I leaned down to whisper in her ear.

"Slugger?"

"Yeah, figured with your fighting skills, girl just wasn't gonna cut it anymore. So, wanna team up? See who else we can get thrown out of this joint?"

She brought her gaze back up to mine, a smile tugging at the side of her mouth. "Okay."

Tsega cracked another grin before catching herself. "He's going to have to do the training."

"Deal." I released the breath I'd been holding and grinned like a damn fool, almost hearing the roar of the crowd as the ball left the stadium.

CHAPTER THIRTEEN
ARIANA

"Forget them Wendy. Forget them all. Come with me where you'll never, never have to worry about grown up things again."

-J.M. Barrie, *Peter Pan*

"HEY, ARIANA," Bess sang out as she pushed the door to my room open with her hip. "You ready for your meds?"

I nodded and stuffed the magazine beneath the covers, but not before the head nurse saw what I'd been reading.

The corners of her eyes crinkled as she hooted, "Don't hide that gorgeous man on my account! If I was thirty years younger, you can bet I'd be leaving my phone number all over this building for him to find."

A wave of heat crept up my neck, but Bess didn't seem to notice as she began mixing my medication into a container of applesauce.

The night tech shared a chuckle as she retrieved her purse from the small wardrobe. "I'll be right back, Bess."

"Sure thing. Take your time," the nurse responded, before wheeling the table over to the bed. "Alright, Miss Ariana, eat this while I find something for you to watch on TV."

My lips puckered with the first bite, the tartness sending shivers down my spine. I'd never particularly cared for applesauce and liked it even less with the medicine added in.

I'd just choked down the last bitter spoonful when something in the air shifted. I didn't need to turn my head toward the door to know what that something was, either. I could see his reflection in the window just fine.

Killian.

The hat on his head was backward, but I imagined the logo matched the one on his shirt. In his sweatpants and house shoes, it was almost easy to believe he was a regular guy and not a 'major-league superstar' as the magazine had called him.

I was officially in uncharted waters. By accepting Killian's offer, I'd essentially rejected any notion of a life of obscurity. And without a blue-eyed savior to smuggle me out of the city, I was back to square one with no real plan of escape. But I had time.

And I wasn't capable of walking away from Killian. Seeing him incited a strange physical reaction within me, one that sent goosebumps racing across my skin and a flush across my cheeks.

"Hey, girl. You up for some company?" He asked, meeting my reflected gaze with a smirk. "I brought snacks."

Bess dropped the remote back onto my bed and whirled around with a startled squeak. "You about gave me a heart attack, sugar! I'd love a snack. Come on in here!"

Killian cocked his head to the side in confusion. I turned away before he saw the smile tugging at my lips. I had a sneaking suspicion *snack* meant something entirely different for the nurse.

"Uh, well, I was actually here for Ari."

She let out a booming laugh as she gathered up the empty applesauce container and spoon. "And here I thought it was my lucky day. Miss Ariana has just had her meds, so she's gonna be drifting off to dreamland here shortly, but if you'd like, you can sit with her until then."

I straightened against the pillows and gave a soft, wordless nod.

Please.

Killian caught my reaction, and the corner of his mouth quirked up. "I guess it's settled then. Oh, Tsega said to mention that I did the training."

"Did you now?" Bess asked with a cryptic smile. "Well, will wonders never cease? Alright, well, I'll slip out and leave you two alone then. Just dial the extension on the board when you're ready to leave. I'll send someone in."

She gathered up her things and headed for the door, but not before wagging her eyebrows at me, or Killian's backside. It was hard to tell.

He leaned his crutches against the wall and handed me a plastic bag with another crooked grin. "I heard these were your favorite."

I opened it up to find one of the giant frosted brownies from the cafeteria. The plastic container was warm to the touch, too. It was almost as if it had just been pulled from the oven, seemingly impossible as the cafeteria had closed over an hour ago.

"Thank you," I said, my voice hoarse and grating. "But how did you—"

"Oh, a good magician never reveals his secrets." Killian waved his fingers mystically, his body tilted at an awkward angle to keep the weight off his knee.

"Sit," I offered, ignoring the nervous flutters in my belly as I scooted toward the window. It was the first time we'd been alone together. Technically, it was my first time in my life I'd been alone with a man I cared about, period.

"Want me to get the lights?" Killian asked, watching me with a steady gaze. "I don't want to keep you up—"

"No," I begged, taking a deep breath to calm my racing heart and thaw my insides. "I mean, will you lay here with me—just until I fall asleep?"

"Are you okay? Would it be better if I left?"

I patted the empty spot with a shaking hand. "Stay."

He rolled the table over and sat down, almost immediately shifting as if he was uncomfortable. "What the hell?"

When he stood up and pulled the blankets back, I winced, belatedly remembering what I'd tucked away before his arrival.

"Well, well, well... what do we have here?" He dangled the magazine in front of me with a smirk. "Doing some light reading?"

"Nothing—it's nothing." I snatched it from his hand and pushed it beneath my pillow before reaching for the brownie container.

"Nothing," Killian echoed with a lifted brow. "Right."

He couldn't expect me to talk if my mouth was full. With that flawless logic, I lifted the warm dessert to my lips. I'd never had one right out of the oven but decided with the first bite that I'd never be able to eat it any other way.

"How long does it take before the medicine kicks in?"

I swallowed before answering, "Um, it depends. Sometimes, a half-hour, maybe less. I've never actually timed it."

"Do you want to watch TV?"

I shrugged and took another bite, closing my eyes with a small sigh of pleasure. Chocolate was my weakness.

When I reopened them, Killian was watching me through hooded eyes. "Good?" he murmured.

"So good," I whispered, fighting the urge to moan as the decadent flavors melted on my tongue. "Do you want some?"

"Yeah," he responded in a gruff tone. Instead of taking the container from my hand, he slid the pad of his thumb along the side of my mouth before popping it into his. "Mmm... you're right. That's fucking delicious."

My eyes went round, and I made a noise that sounded a little like a whimper. The chill I'd felt only moments before heated, sending soft ripples of warmth to my extremities.

"Don't look at me like that," he whispered, running his tongue over his bottom lip.

"Why?"

My heart frolicked around my chest as Killian bent his head to mine. "Because I don't want to rush this."

His response was simple, but I couldn't resist looking up at him from under my lashes. The spark burning in his blue eyes left me dazed. Disoriented. Mindless.

For a moment, he just stared at me before cupping my jaw in his right hand and tipping my face up. I wanted to beg him to keep touching me, but I didn't have the words. His proximity left me excited and achy, but in a way that felt good.

Really good.

Killian's eyes moved over my face, narrowing slightly when he got to my lips. Just as I became convinced he was going to kiss me, my voice returned. But instead of telling him all the things I wanted him to do, I blurted out the first thing that popped in my head.

"Did you always know you wanted to play baseball?" I asked in a tight voice, overcome by the strongest sense of loss when his hand fell away from my face.

He settled back against the pillows and reached for the remote, flipping aimlessly through the channels as he considered my question. "Yeah...well, I take that back. As a kid, I told anyone who would listen that I was going to be a ballplayer when I grew up. Then, I hit my teens, and those doubts crept in. I just didn't see it being a lifelong career. What about you?"

"Oh no, I never saw myself playing baseball," I deadpanned. "I don't even know the first thing about it."

Killian playfully pushed my shoulder with a grin. "No, I mean, tell me about yourself. What's your passion?"

"Music," I answered easily. "My passion is music."

His brows pulled together as he scratched his jaw. "Really? Why music?"

"It's an escape," I whispered, lifting my eyes to the netting above my bed. I wondered if it was the medicine making my tongue loose, or just a deep-seated need to connect with someone. "I can get lost in the lyrics, and for those three or four minutes, it's like nothing else exists."

Killian stayed silent, but I could tell he was thinking. "I feel like that, too," he finally admitted. "With the game. When I'm out on the field, I can shut the world out until it's just me and the ball. It's a powerful feeling."

I agreed with a nod. It was when the song ended that my power was stripped away from me again.

"So," he murmured, tilting his head toward me. "Do you play an instrument or sing?"

"I'm a singer/songwriter."

Killian's eyebrow raised. "Really? Well, color me impressed. Anything I might have heard?"

He was fishing for information. Given that I knew who he was, it only made sense he'd want the same in return. Still, I needed to tread carefully to avoid giving too much away. The less he knew about the church and my father, the better.

"I don't know. I doubt it," I answered quietly. It was an honest answer, as Killian didn't strike me as the type of person who spent a lot of time listening to Christian radio stations.

"Don't want me to know about your platinum rap album, do you?" He joked, running his tongue over his teeth.

The idea of it made me laugh. I shook my head, gazing up at his face. "Well, now that you've solved that mystery, could we maybe pick one channel to watch, instead of all of them?"

"What? You don't like this?"

I wrinkled my nose and joked, "You're giving me motion sickness —wait. Go back to that last one."

"What, this one?" He flipped the channel. "*Haunted Places*? You want to watch this?"

I nodded, refusing to make eye contact with the foot of the bed, halfway convinced I'd see the lingering images from the car wreck. It was terrible enough to relive it in my nightmares almost every night.

When I didn't answer, Killian's gaze shifted to me, and I barely resisted the urge to burrow into his side. "Do you—" My voice cracked, and I cleared my throat before trying again. "Do you believe in ghosts?"

He was quiet for several seconds before shaking his head. "No, I don't. I mean, I don't doubt that there are people who think they've seen ghosts, but it seems a little out there for me. Why—you believe in ghosts, girl?"

I chewed at the corner of my bottom lip with a small nod, lost to my memories. "I think that maybe I might. I've been having recurring nightmares since my car accident." I shuddered, hugging myself as another chill descended over me. "There's something wrong with the car, almost like it's not under my control anymore, and I hear people talking. Sometimes, I don't recognize the voices, but every now and then, I do—which is impossible, because that person is dead."

"Christ, Ari," Killian said softly, before pulling my body closer. His hand moved over my back in gentle circles, and I relaxed, feeling the drowsiness settling in. "It sounds like your brain just took two traumatic events and combined them into one, but I can understand why you might believe there was a supernatural explanation."

I stayed silent with my cheek resting against his chest, watching as the paranormal team investigated a haunted movie theater. My pulse had just evened out when he spoke again.

"When I was sixteen, I was in an accident. Well, I don't know that it was much of an accident. Another kid and I got into a fight and I cracked my head on the dock, falling into the lake—"

"What?" I asked, my voice strangled.

"Crazy, right? I remember falling and then coming to on the beach. I swore there was a girl there with me, but she was gone before I was fully conscious. My mama was convinced it was an angel."

My body tensed as I lifted my head to study his features, suddenly seeing a very different sort of ghost altogether.

The brownie in my lap began slipping, but I couldn't look away. Killian managed to catch the container before it landed on the bed and rolled over to place it on the small table. When he turned back, my breath caught. I wondered how I hadn't seen it before now.

Long dark lashes and blue eyes that seemed almost gray against the sky...

My inability to stay away—to suppress my feelings—it was as if all the puzzle pieces had finally aligned. Killian was the boy from the lake. I blinked against the fog settling over my brain, struggling to fight the effects of the medicine meant to help me sleep.

I didn't want to sleep.

I wanted answers. It was no longer coincidence that when I needed a sanctuary the most, I'd run right into the arms of a man whose name meant church. The very man whose life I saved ten years prior.

He'd never been a stranger or a means to an end.

He was *my* beginning and end.

"Hey—" Killian frowned as he brushed the hair back off my face. "You okay?"

Was I?

"I—" I yawned, my eyes falling shut on their own. "I need—"

"You need to get some sleep," he responded dryly, the corner of his mouth lifting. "Come here."

My tongue felt heavy in my mouth, weighed down by the magnitude of what Killian had just revealed. And probably the drugs. But mostly, the revelation.

Tears pricked my eyes as he cradled my head against his chest, feeling the steady rise and fall like the waves that day on the lake.

The silence stretched from seconds into minutes. The paranormal team had already moved on to their next haunted place —a long-abandoned amusement park with a sinister history. Meanwhile, I was still reeling from the bombshell, trying to decide what my next step should be.

"Sometimes, I think, what if she was real?" Killian murmured as he stroked my hair. I didn't answer. I couldn't. My heart was lodged somewhere in the base of my throat, anxiously waiting for him to connect the dots as I had.

"What if she was my one chance at salvation?" He exhaled a breathless laugh. "Hell, maybe my mama was right. Maybe she was just a guardian angel sent to watch over my dumb ass."

I was being suffocated under a blanket of drugs, but managed to stay conscious long enough to mumble, "I'm no angel."

It was the last thing I remembered before drifting off. Later, I'd swear I was already dreaming when I felt Killian's lips brush against the inside of my wrist.

That was the thing about falling asleep with the medication. It could conjure up any number of hallucinations, including a whispered, "No, Ari. You're as real as they come."

CHAPTER FOURTEEN
KILLIAN

"He couldn't. Never again, not with anyone else. Nothing would ever, after that moment, compare. Not with her cry, not with her reaction, not with her kiss. A woman shouldn't be created in such heartbreakingly beautiful combinations. A woman shouldn't, in fifteen minutes, have the ability to ruin him for life."

—Alessandra Torre, *Moonshot*

"YOU GONNA TELL ME, girl, or should I just keep guessing?"

Ari sat cross-legged on the bed, studiously poring over a travel magazine with a distracted smile. Thanks to a tip from Tsega, her worn house shoes had been replaced with a pair almost identical to mine. After delivering them, my mama had pushed to meet my mystery girl, but I'd declined.

This was new to me. I wanted to shield it, and Ari, from the world for as long as possible.

"What about Argentina? There's this fort—the Pucará de Tilcara —where they've found human traces dating back over ten thousand years."

I didn't give two shits about touring ancient ruins in South America, but there was something to be said about watching Ari in her element. She'd mispronounced or completely butchered most of the names of the places in the magazine but had grinned up at me so earnestly that I hadn't dared to correct her.

Because when Ari smiled—a real, genuine smile—it was like someone flipping on a light switch, making you aware that you'd spent your whole life living in the dark.

Her hair fell messily over one eye, and she paused to push it off her forehead. The movement revealed the scar underneath, the only visible wound from her car accident. As if sensing my stare, Ari used her fingers to hurriedly cover it up before going back to her research. I hated that she felt she had to hide from me but kept the thought to myself.

"That's, uh, that's pretty cool. Now, remind me again why we're planning Georgia's vacation for her? Aren't there travel agents for that?" I adjusted the pillow beneath my knee before stretching out on the leather chair across from her.

"Georgia asked me to..." Ari's words faded out, and she cleared her throat until she no longer sounded like a boy going through puberty. "Besides, it gives me something to do in the evenings."

Sanchez and his crew grinned up at me from the *Sports Illustrated* on my lap, and I flipped it over before returning my attention to her. "You could—oh, I don't know—tell me what you did to Helen. That would be a fun way to pass the time, don't you think?"

"Not gonna happen," she chuckled and wrote down a note before turning the page.

"C'mon," I pleaded. I'd been trying to get it out of her for days now. "Did you run her over with your wheelchair?"

"You guessed that one already."

"Wait, I got it. You, uh, you..." I was floundering, and we both knew it, but as long as it kept her amused, I could go all night. "Poisoned her food?"

"Killian," she sighed in mock exasperation. "It's like you're not even trying. How would poisoning cause her great facial harm?"

"You're right." I grinned. "Alright, go back to your little magazine, but just so you're aware, I'm gonna figure you out, girl."

"Are we up for a visitor?" Someone asked as they knocked on the open door.

"Uh, just a second." I looked at my watch with a frown. The nurses weren't due to give Ari her nightly meds for another hour.

And I selfishly wanted every one of those sixty minutes alone with her. I'd grown addicted to our little routine over the past two weeks and the feel of having her fall asleep on my shoulder. Outside this room, I was distant and cold—painfully aware of what it would mean if people spotted us together.

Proving once again that she wasn't like the rest, the whole thing had been Ari's idea. It was a request I'd been only too willing to accept, though.

Maybe once we were both out of here, we could go public. In the meantime, I fully respected her desire to stay out of the spotlight. Getting rid of one old woman had been easy enough, but I couldn't go after the press every time they posted something derogatory about my girl.

My girl.

I couldn't explain when it had happened, but lately, I'd become consumed with the idea of having her by my side, having someone to share my ups and downs with.

A partner.

When I looked at her, I saw us walking hand in hand down the block to my favorite coffee shop and takeout on the couch when neither one of us felt like cooking. I pictured her thighs, gripping me as I took her on the kitchen table. My bed. The floor...

Ari met my gaze with a soft frown before pointing toward the door.

Right.

I was getting ahead of myself again.

First things first, get rid of the unwanted guest.

"Yep." I swallowed and sat the leather chair up before retrieving my crutches from the wall. "I'll take care of it."

The woman at the door gave a small wave before gesturing to a little wagon beside her. "I was wondering if you might be—"

"Absolutely. Come in."

I couldn't help the small pang of jealousy as I watched Ari's confusion give way to pure, unadulterated happiness. I wanted to be the reason her smile lit up the whole damn room.

Baby steps, Killian.

I didn't want to rush this, but my days at *True North* were numbered. Rocky had confirmed it this morning. And, as much as I wanted full use of my legs and therapy in the comfort of my own gym, I'd imagined us leaving together.

One of the puppies yipped out an excited bark when the woman placed it on the bed, before scurrying up to frantically lick Ari on the nose.

"Now the golden retriever here is Kyrie. She's still in training and needs a bit of correcting." She grabbed another one. "And the little black lab is Milo."

The puppies were introduced one by one before joining Ari on the bed. They scrambled over each other, as eager to be near her as I was.

I just hadn't resorted to licking her nose... yet.

"I'll give y'all a few minutes to get acquainted. Pups, settle."

At the stern warning, they immediately flopped down, as still as could be. Only Kyrie checked to see if the woman was watching before playfully tugging at Ari's cat shirt with her teeth.

Once we were alone again, Ari looked up with a wide grin. "Come pet them, Killian. They're so happy."

Yes. Yes, I was.

I shifted two of the puppies over and joined her on the bed. "Hey, I have a question—it's not about Helen, I swear—but I was wondering, why don't you talk more?"

She stroked Milo under the chin. "I'm talking now, aren't I?"

One of the puppies got too close to the edge. I snaked out a hand, returning it to Ari's lap. "No, I mean, with anyone but me. Well, and I guess Tsega."

Ari cleared her throat again, choosing to focus on the puppies again. "I don't know."

I softened my voice, resisting the urge to touch her skin. "Hey, you don't have to tell me if it makes you uncomfortable, I was just curious. If someone said or did something, you give me a name. I'll take care of it."

"It's not that. I—I just..." She was silent for a few moments, before admitting, "Before my car accident, I had a stutter, so I got used to being quiet, I guess. Now, I have the memories, but seem to have lost my stammer."

I scratched one of the puppies behind the ear, earning his undying devotion in the form of licks. "So, Mrs. Peacock, did you attack Helen in the library with a candlestick?"

Her brow furrowed. "Is that—did you just reference the game of *Clue*?"

"Answer the question, madam."

She released an exaggerated sigh and extended her wrists toward me. "You got me, and here I thought I was so clever."

Unable to resist temptation, I latched onto her wrists, tugging her body closer to mine. "I knew it. Only an amateur would have chosen the candlestick over the revolver."

The grin returned. "And who attacks someone in the library when there's a perfectly good cellar nearby?"

I held my grip, running my thumb over her skin before teasing, "Rookie mistake, slugger."

Her gaze settled on my mouth, a furious blush creeping up her throat. "I'll try to plan my attacks better in the future."

This time, when her voice moved between octaves, I suspected it was due to my proximity and not a result of her injury. Four inches stood in the way of our mouths.

Four. Inches.

If I pulled her wrists toward me just a little more, gravity would take care of the rest. Unfortunately, my plan hadn't accounted for one of the puppies getting there first. Kyrie stood on her hind legs and began licking Ari's mouth and chin, whipping my arm with her little golden tail until I shifted away.

Alright, maybe I had that coming.

Couldn't slide into home without getting a little scuffed up on the way.

"Do you think this is what heaven is like?" Ari giggled, letting the puppy feast on her face like I'd wanted to only moments before.

Knowing there was no sense in getting jealous of an animal, especially one as cute as Kyrie, I shifted my focus over to her question. "If, uh, if I believed in that, then sure. I'd imagine this was pretty damn close."

She lowered the pup back down to her lap. Her eyes lingered on the tattoos on my arms before coming up to rest on my face. "But you believe in angels."

I shook my head. "No, I said my mama believes in angels. Religion is right up there with ghosts, as far as I'm concerned. I've seen too many people use it as a way to lessen their guilt. Like, 'Oh, you can't be mad at me for acting like an asshole because Jesus forgave me for my sins.' It's so hypocritical. I've yet to meet someone who wasn't putting on an act to appease some deity. I'll take something real over that crap any day."

I'll take you.

I looked away before I could finish the thought. Because while I didn't buy into the supernatural, I couldn't deny what I was starting to feel for Ari and it scared me to death.

Her eyebrows pulled together again, creating two small lines in the center of her forehead. She didn't seem like an overly religious person, but it appeared my response had left her perplexed. "Well, who do you think that girl was?"

Ari had been hung up on my mystery savior since the night I told her, even going as far as talking about it in her sleep. While I found her need to reassure me she wasn't an angel endearing, I preferred to focus on my future and not my past.

I wasn't that guy anymore.

"A hallucination? Maybe some Good Samaritan who didn't want to stick around to give a witness statement? I don't know. Does it bother you that I don't believe?"

"I guess it's just ironic, that's all," she said, giggling as one of the puppies burrowed under her arm. At my blank expression, she elaborated. "Because your name means *church*. I take it your family's religious?"

"Is yours?" I turned the question back on her, unhappy with the sudden turn of events.

We were supposed to be kissing, dammit. We'd been dancing around it for the better part of the last two weeks with our heated stares, yet neither one of us had made a move.

Ari exhaled a sigh and reached out to stroke Kyrie's head. "Yes."

"You don't sound very happy about that."

She put all of her efforts into the petting. The pup flopped down in her lap with a drowsy groan. "I think that in the wrong hands, religion becomes a weapon instead of a tool."

"Growing up, my mom dragged me to every Sunday service. My father—" I took a deep breath. "Well, for the longest time, I think he was attending the church of Jack and Jim."

"Jack and Jim?"

"Whiskey, Ari. My dad was an alcoholic." The words were just as bitter as they had been when I was a kid. "He'd go off on these benders, disappearing for days at a time. I begged my mama to leave. I thought we'd be better off just the two of us, you know?"

"Did he hurt y'all?" she asked quietly, her green eyes wide with worry.

I clenched my jaw and shook my head. "Physically, no. He just wasn't there when we needed him to be. But my mama, she took her vows seriously and stuck by him, for better or worse. When he found Jesus, he expected everyone to just forget about the things he'd done while drunk. Becoming a Christian was his get out of jail free card."

Ari placed a hand on my forearm, quietly encouraging me to continue.

"There were no apologies. Nothing. And it just kinda soured me on the whole idea of religion." The back of my neck grew warm under the weight of my confession. I'd just admitted something to her that even Bailey didn't know about.

Reed men weren't exactly known for their vulnerability. If I was honest, I wasn't sure I wanted to take it up as a hobby.

Milo stretched until his paws dangled over my hand and gave me the side-eye, before going to town on one of my fingers like it was a teething ring. It was enough to zap me out of my funk. "Anyway, I don't necessarily have the best judgment, so take from that what you will."

"You don't think you're a good judge of character?" Ari asked, observing me with a small frown.

"It's not a matter of what I think. My track record proves that I shouldn't trust myself." I forced a brittle laugh, wishing I could go back to discussing my ridiculous theories on how Helen had sustained her life-altering injury.

"To me, it seems you trust your own judgment just fine. It's other people's you seem to have trouble with."

"How do you figure?"

"Well, take your injury, for example. You were so confident in your own judgment that you didn't trust the call to stay on first."

"Bit of an expert on baseball now, are we?" I teased, remembering how red she'd gotten when I found the magazine in her bed.

She shrugged and held a finger out to Milo. He released me from the grip of his razor-sharp teeth to happily tackle his new target. "Well, I mean, I watched the footage and read the articles, so I'm thinking ESPN is going to come knocking any day now."

"You're screwing with me—you watched that? Why?" I mashed

my lips together, struggling to keep up the appearance of being annoyed.

Ari shook her head, giggling at my expense. "What? I do have interests beyond Georgia's travel magazines. Is it so surprising that I might want to know more about you? A girl has gotta learn sometime."

"Let me guess, you thought asking me directly would be too forward?" I asked with mock concern. "Better to keep it tucked away under your pillow, yeah?"

"Please. You would have had me thinking you were the best thing since—quick, name a great baseball player—" She squirmed away with a yelp when I squeezed her thigh, earning us dirty looks from the puppies that had been dozing nearby.

"Stop! I'm kidding," she panted, struggling to escape the blanket of dogs on her legs. "You never bring it up. When I do, you change the subject. I didn't think it was up for discussion, so I did my own research, okay?"

"Oh yeah?" My mouth tipped up in a smirk. "What else did you learn during your little fact-finding mission?"

Ari rolled her eyes and lifted her index finger. "Let's see—one, Killian Reed is extremely conceited. It's a wonder his shirts manage to fit over his big head"—

"Conceited?" I struck her side this time, tickling along her ribs, and reveling in the sound of her laughter.

"Please," she begged through heavy-lidded eyes, grabbing hold of my wrist. Something passed between us. She moved closer, no longer smiling.

I wanted to reach out to grasp her shirt in my fist, tugging at the material until her body was flush with mine. Instead, I pulled back just as she lifted her chin. It wasn't that I didn't feel the significance of the moment.

It was just too soon.

Baby steps.

Ari released my wrist and tucked her fingers into my palm. A sudden jolt passed through me when she tipped her face up to mine, looking at me like maybe she believed I could save the world.

"You didn't let me finish. Killian Reed is cocky and—"

"Pretty sure you covered that one," I murmured, unable to take my eyes off her mouth. So damn beautiful. An electric current of lust coursed through my body, weakening my resolve. She was wrong. I didn't trust my judgment at all when it came to her.

"Did I?" She looked up at me from under her lashes. "Well, here's one hot off the press. I'm starting to think he just might be my best friend."

True North was going to discharge me sometime in the next week, but at the rate I was moving, I wouldn't get around to telling her how I felt until sometime next century. Screw baby steps. It was bottom of the ninth, with the bases loaded and two outs.

Go big or go home time.

I lifted our joined hands up to my mouth, planting a soft kiss against her knuckles. "Is that right? Okay, picture this. My first ever at-bat was a little league game when I was seven. Got my first home run, sending the ball flying over the chain-link fence." My voice turned wistful as I remembered it, the innocence of youth.

"I couldn't tell you if my feet even touched the ground as I ran, it was like I was flying. Only, the other kids wouldn't play like I did. It used to make me so mad until, one day, my mama sat me down. She told me a player could have all the talent in the world, but that a game won with heart would always be more fun to watch. But that's just it. I've never had to work for anything, Ari. It's always come easy to me. Until you."

Green eyes moved over my face in confusion. "What does that— what are you saying?"

"I'm saying that you're so goddamned perfect and good, and I'm not." I blew out a frustrated breath. "Got a newsflash of my own—I don't want to be your friend, Ari. I've been holding back because it feels like we just met, but I can't keep doing it. I can't pretend that this doesn't mean anything. And I know I'm probably messing it all up by admitting this, but I want to be with you."

Ari's lips mashed together, her breaths coming a little closer together as she freed her hand from mine.

It was too soon.

I'd known that, but like an idiot, had gone ahead and said it anyway. "Look—"

"I've never—" Her voice faded. She placed her small hand in the center of my chest with wide eyes, silently begging me to understand.

She'd never—what?

The answer came to me in the form of trembling fingers and a flushed face.

Ari had never been kissed.

Any man with an ounce of decency would have taken that knowledge and locked it away, before pulling back to let things progress at their own pace.

But then Ari did something completely unexpected. She moved closer, brushing her lips lightly over mine before exhaling softly, "Just be gentle with me, please."

And I was a goner.

Fully aware of her intense gaze, I cupped her jaw in my hand, tilting her face up toward mine. Just like I had the first night I went to her room. Only this time, I wasn't going to hold back. "Trust me?"

She swallowed with a jerky nod, her eyelids already fluttering to a close as I guided my mouth over hers. I'd had the rough, sloppy kisses that came after one too many drinks and perfunctory pecks given out of obligation, but those were minor leagues compared to this.

There was no overthinking it. Kissing Ari felt right as if I was acting on some instinct that had always known it was going to be her.

Mine.

My tongue swept across her pink lips. She parted them with a shiver, subtly inviting me in. One of her hands was still tangled up in the front of my shirt while the other moved up and down my jaw in furious strokes, encouraging me to continue.

The woman was a fucking natural, responding to me in ways I hadn't expected, given her lack of experience. I devoured the sweetness from her lips, tilting her head to gain better access to everything she was offering me.

Maybe this was heaven.

I wasn't a pious man, so if this was as close as I got—sitting in a pile of therapy puppies, kissing the hell out of this woman—I'd take it.

A life well-lived.

Ari moaned when I sucked her bottom lip between my teeth like a man starved. Instead of slowing down, the sound left me painfully hard and beyond reason.

First, I'd gather up all the puppies and shuttle them to the bathroom, keeping their innocence intact. Then I had plans of laying Ari back on the bed, so I could run my hands over every inch of her skin.

Wait—no.

Step two would be stripping her down while she looked up at me in silent excitement. Step three involved my hands taking a field trip over her curves before we progressed to step four.

Ari shifted restlessly against me, her hands frantically raking against my neck and shoulders before her tongue darted out to meet mine.

The puppies were just going to have to keep their eyes closed because I wasn't stopping for anything.

I growled and progressed to step four, imagining the sounds she'd make as her body clenched and pulsed around my fingers. I'd pull my hand free just long enough to coat my tongue in the taste of her before doing it all over again. I wouldn't stop until her body was drenched with sweat, and my name was the only word she knew.

"Knock, knock," the puppy lady called from the doorway. "How are we doing in here?"

I wrenched my mouth from Ari's with a confused pant, before

dropping my hand down to hide the baseball bat in my sweatpants. "F-fine."

It was not fine. I'd been seconds away from slipping my hands into the pants of a woman who, up until three minutes ago, had never been kissed.

The puppy lady entered and I reached for my crutches, stumbling from the bed like a drunk. "Just remembered—late night, uh, icing. With Rocky—he's my therapist. Guy's a little different, but nice enough, you know?"

I was rambling.

Ari tore her gaze away from my erection and reached up to touch her lips, a strange expression passing over her face. "Okay?"

Grief.

I felt it too.

The loss of something too complicated to put into words. It left me aching over the distance I'd put between us. I wanted to be close enough to breathe the same air that Ari was, but I couldn't stay, at least not in my current state.

And now I remembered why I'd been holding myself back. My past was filled with mistakes. I wouldn't let her become one of them by rushing things. If she'd never been kissed before now, I could only assume she was still a virgin. I wasn't willing to take anything she wasn't ready to give.

Ari deserved the best version of Killian Reed, and that was what she was going to get.

Just as soon as I dealt with my dick.

Somehow, I managed to make it back to my room without exploding and leaned against the door frame, fighting to catch my breath.

Her first.

Mine.

I stumbled toward the bed, blaming my limited vocabulary on the lack of blood flowing to my brain and not some sort of regression into a knuckle-dragging caveman.

There were times Ari looked up at me, and I saw a woman with only one thing on her mind. Just as quickly as it was there, it was gone again, replaced with wide-eyed innocence.

I closed my eyes, seeing the briefest flash of a face backlit by the setting sun. The angel who'd saved me. But, instead of a blurred face hovering over me, it was Ari. The rays of light caught her hair, illuminating every strand of red until it appeared to be glowing. Waves lapped against the shore, but I was focused solely on her.

Ignoring a brief twinge of protest from my knee, I shoved my hand into the front of my sweats before diving headfirst into my fantasy.

Need slammed into me. I stroked my cock, envisioning the feel of Ari's long hair brushing against the tops of my thighs while she rode me. How she'd cover her mouth to stifle her moans, her hips bucking forward involuntarily, seeking me out.

It was too much. I quickly lost control with a shuddered growl, dampening my hand and stomach. The sounds of my ragged breathing filtered into my semi-conscious state, delivering a healthy dose of reality.

I was fucked.

Not physically, no. Physically, I was spent and ready for sleep. Emotionally, however, I wasn't faring quite as well. Kissing Ari tonight had only made me want her more, and deep down, I knew that no fantasy would come close to alleviating the ache in my chest.

Did people cherish her back home? Did they feel the emptiness without her there?

I did, and she was just across the hall.

CHAPTER FIFTEEN
KILLIAN

"There are no whys in a person's life, and very few hows. In the end, in search of useful wisdom, you could only come back to the most hackneyed concepts, like kindness, forbearance, infinite patience. Solomon and Lincoln: This too shall pass. Damn right it will. Or Chekhov: Nothing passes. Equally true."

-Chad Harbach, *The Art of Fielding*

"EH, did I call it, or did I call it?" Theo tapped the stack of papers with a self-satisfied smirk. "Philly, Chicago, Anaheim, Tampa, DC, Boston—take your pick. You want sun or snow? Me, personally, I'd go with sun."

I laughed. I couldn't help myself. Six weeks ago, I was being carted off the field, convinced my career was over. Now, I had multiple offers to play damn near anywhere in the country. Life might have thrown me a curveball, but I'd still managed to crush it.

They still wanted me.

She wanted me.

I was on cloud nine.

Theo fidgeted with his eighteen karat gold baseball cufflinks; no doubt worn just for the occasion. "Tick tock, Reed. Let's accept one of these, put some ink to paper, and get you the hell back in a uniform."

"Now, wait a minute. Correct me if I'm wrong, but did you not say I'd have an offer before the end of the season? Hate to break it to you, but you missed your deadline." I bit down on the inside of my cheek to keep a straight face.

His grin shifted from confident to irritated as he retrieved the papers from the table. "While you've been rehabbing, I've been guaranteeing your future on the field. You wanted offers. You've got offers. You don't want offers, then don't fucking call me to say you do."

I dropped my hand onto the stack, sliding it back toward me. "Oh, I want all the offers."

And then it hit me. There was one franchise missing from the list —*Houston*. Frankly, no one in their right mind had expected the team to make another offer after I'd rejected their first.

Well, no one except me.

Crazy: party of one.

Houston was my home. I'd built a life around cobalt blue and white—colors I'd hoped to be wearing until I took my last run around the bases. How was I supposed to make a choice when it would mean leaving the city I loved behind?

Not to mention Ari.

Christ, Ari.

I couldn't ask her to uproot her entire life after just one kiss. Granted, it had been the best kiss of my life, but moving across the country together was not taking it slow. It was a recipe for disaster.

So, maybe we'd live in different cities, but with my parents and Bailey still around, it wasn't as if I was leaving Houston forever. And whatever this was between us, it was still in the early stages.

Delicate.

I'd committed to doing right by Ari. Asking her to give up her life to follow me to a new city went against that. She had her own dreams

—maybe even a musical career here in Houston. If I wanted it to last, then I was going to have to play the long game and take things slow.

We were living in an age of technology—I could video chat her every day if I wanted to—and when I was in town, we'd be together. Plus, if I kept my condo, we wouldn't have to worry about roommates either.

This was a good thing.

Only, I couldn't stand leaving her room at night. How in the hell was I supposed to manage living in another state?

"Is there a problem, Killian?" Theo broke into my thoughts. "You haven't looked at a single one of those pages."

"Sorry, got lost there for a second," I mumbled distractedly before flipping through the stack.

As far as offers went, they were about what I expected, given my injury. They all came with an unspoken caveat in the form of options—optional assignment down in the minors, option to be placed on waivers, option to be released.

Clubs just weren't willing to take a risk on a long-term, high salary contract without knowing how I was going to return next spring.

Philly and Anaheim were both offering a three-year contract at two hundred seventy-five million. Boston and DC had come in with a seven-year contract at three hundred while Tampa and Chicago had gone with an underwhelming three years at one hundred fifty.

Frankly, I wasn't surprised.

Under normal circumstances, the two clubs wouldn't have approached me at all, but my injury had leveled the playing field. Now, they were all banking on me being desperate enough to agree to their bargain-basement pricing. If I came back better than before, then it was a steal. On the off chance I didn't—well, the cost wouldn't sink their franchise.

It seemed I'd been stripped of my crown, my achievements and records reduced to a mere byline in the history of the game.

I wasn't baseball royalty anymore.

I was a liability.

"You know," Theo began casually, scrolling through his phone. "If you're unhappy with the offers—"

"It's not that." I fought to keep the bitterness out of my tone, even though I was basically restarting my career from scratch. "I'm grateful. Really. Just a lot to think about, you know?"

He nodded and slid his phone across the table. "I was actually going to say I've got one more I'd like you to take a look at—kind of a 'best for last' type thing."

Houston Hurricanes-
13-year, $425m

I released a strangled breath, no longer able to feel my face. My eyes moved from the name down to the numbers, and then back again, convinced it was a typo.

"That's—" I choked on the word. "But that's more than their initial offer!"

He sat back with a grin. "You play to win, Killian. So do I. Now, it's less than the sixty million you would have gotten per year with the first offer, but the longer contract means—"

"I can retire wearing cobalt blue and white," I said, more to myself than him.

Sure—in the grand scheme of things—four hundred twenty-five million over the next thirteen years worked out to less money overall. It also meant I wouldn't be competing against rookies for a contract at thirty-two-years-old either, though.

You couldn't put a price tag on that.

Most major-league players peaked before the age of thirty while the all-stars and hall-of-famers typically didn't hang up the cleats until their mid-thirties, or even early-forties.

In thirteen years, I'd be thirty-nine.

Barring future injuries, I'd get to go out on my own terms.

"I'll let them know we accept—" Theo raised a brow. "That is unless you've suddenly grown fond of the idea of digging your goddamn car out every time there's a blizzard."

I shook my head, still in shock. "No, I'm a Hurricane."

"Alright then." He returned the papers to a leather messenger bag that was just pretentious enough to have his initials engraved in the middle. "Once their lawyers draft the contract, I'll have yours look it over. If everything's in order, I don't see any reason that you wouldn't be signed by the end of the week. Perfect timing, right?"

"What do you mean?" I asked.

Theo looked up with a frown. "You're being discharged tomorrow, Killian. This gives you a chance to get home and get settled before doing the media circuit."

"I thought I still had another week or two—"

His eyes narrowed. "Your physical therapist said you'd done remarkably well and recommended you for home therapy in his last report. I thought you'd be thrilled to be rid of this place."

"I am," I quickly added. *True North*, maybe. But not her. "I guess I was under the impression that I'd be the first to know."

Rocky had said I was close but hadn't given me an exact date. Then again, it wasn't as if we'd ever really warmed up to each other.

Theo cracked another grin. "What do you expect? You're a product, man. It's not your job to know, it's your job to perform."

I nodded, chewing on my bottom lip.

He stood up and buttoned his suit jacket. "If you're trying to decide what to get me, I'm partial to those Cuban cigars you had at the All-Star game a couple of years ago. Maybe a box—hell, make it two boxes."

I nodded again, making a mental note to get Theo whatever he wanted. I had more pressing matters to attend to—like how I was going to tell Ari I was leaving. Once news of my record-breaking contract broke, I was going to be swarmed for interviews. It was impossible to know when—or if—I'd be able to make it back.

"By the way," he added. "You're welcome."

Ari might have been under the impression I had a big head, but that was only because she hadn't been introduced to one Theodore Heyman, Jr.

It was part of what made him a great agent. Well, that and his ability to capitalize on just about any situation, spinning it into something the masses would readily consume.

If only he could help me find a way to satisfy one passion without losing the other.

────────

We'd agreed not to acknowledge each other outside of her room. I knew that, but it didn't stop me from chasing her down in the hallway later that afternoon.

After Theo left, I'd called my mama and told her the news. It wasn't long after that my father began blowing up my phone to congratulate me on my contract before asking if he could take me to dinner. His calls and texts would go unanswered until he got the hint that we were never going to be buddies.

From there, I'd spent an hour with Rocky, getting fitted for my new brace. I wasn't cleared to lose the crutches completely, but the smaller brace allowed for more range-of-motion and longer periods of weight-bearing.

I also came away with the distinct impression that physical therapy wasn't going to get any easier once I was out. I didn't mind being pushed, but I'd come to rely on a certain red-haired beauty to distract me from the pain.

Which was why I was currently ambushing Ari on her way to class. The nurse, Tiffani, slowed her steps as I approached.

"Hey," I leaned down, somewhat surprised to see her back in the wheelchair. She'd gotten to where she was walking, with help, almost everywhere she went.

The urge to touch her was overwhelming, but I resisted. People might be willing to overlook a conversation, but any show of affection was going to raise some red flags. "I missed you at lunch."

Ari nodded slowly, staring blankly ahead toward the nurse's station.

Something like panic sparked in my chest, but I quickly snuffed it out, refusing to read too much into the fact that she wasn't smiling. She was probably pissed I'd broken the rules, and rightfully so, but I had news that couldn't wait.

I'd smooth things over—maybe give her the bad news first and then move into the good stuff. She'd make an exception once she saw that I was bending the rules for a reason.

Probably.

"She didn't feel up to eating," Tiffani chimed in helpfully. "I think physical therapy just wore her out this morning, and she needed to rest."

"Late night?" I teased, hoping for a blush or wink—something that indicated I wasn't the only one hung up on our kiss.

Because it had been one hell of a kiss.

Her eyes remained flat as if she was going out of her way to avoid reacting to me. But that was ridiculous. Maybe, like me, she'd just struggled to fall asleep.

"I, uh, I don't have anything going on, so I thought I might go with you to class. It's speech, right?" When she nodded, I whispered, "Maybe after, we'll get you some coffee. I've got some news."

Ari nodded again. I brushed a few stray hairs off her face, noting the ashen tone of her skin. "Are you feeling okay?"

This time, there was no response, which didn't exactly bolster my confidence. Either Ari was agitated that I hadn't held up my end of our agreement, or she was regretting last night.

Dammit, I'd known it was too soon.

It was her first kiss—it was supposed to be special. The puppies were a nice touch, but if I'd known it was going to happen, I could have come prepared with candles and flowers.

Girls liked that romantic movie shit.

"Don't take it personally," Tiffani said. "She's been a little quieter than normal. Usually, she'll write or mouth words, but today I've gotten nothing out of her. I mean, it's to be expected with as much as she's doing. Sometimes, the brain just gets overstimulated. Ari, you want Killian to go to class with you, right?"

Yeah, her brain had just been overworked—by the Neanderthal standing beside her.

Ari blinked in response, her green eyes dull and unfocused. So, it wasn't a ringing endorsement, but as she hadn't asked me to leave, I'd take what I could get.

Last night had been a little too much for her. As much as I wanted to make it better, I had to let her take the lead on this. And me—well, I'd wait patiently nearby, giving her the space to work through it.

That was me, a pillar of strength in my girl's time of need.

Having made my decision, I let the two of them take the lead and followed a few paces behind. It wasn't how I'd pictured spending my last day here, but I'd waited years for a girl like Ari. I could wait a little longer, give her time to see how good we could be together.

And if all else failed, I'd track down those therapy puppies.

The speech therapist met us as we crossed the sky bridge into the other wing, holding his palm up to Ari as if waiting for a high-five. "Hey, Ariana, who'd you bring today?"

When she made no move to introduce me, I extended a hand. "Killian."

"Fynn," he responded warmly before ushering us into his small office. "As you can probably tell, I'm a bit of a fan. I bet you get that a lot, though."

The side of my mouth lifted as I took in the Hurricanes memorabilia lining the wall. The man had just about everything—including a bobblehead of me resting on top of a filing cabinet. "I do, but it's always nice to hear."

He turned back to Tiffani. "Let's get her out of the chair. Otherwise, I'm afraid we'll be a bit overcrowded."

It was almost comical they'd put him in such a small space—the guy was built like an NFL linebacker. Tiffani helped Ari into an empty chair before hesitating in the doorway. "If Killian doesn't mind staying, I could just come back in an hour."

I quickly agreed. "I don't mind at all. In fact, I was thinking of grabbing a coffee from the cafeteria after—maybe you could just meet us there?"

The time would allow me to navigate the murky waters of Ari's emotions. She couldn't shut me out forever, and, who knew? Maybe the news of my departure would make her more amenable to the idea of taking our romance public.

Tiffani agreed to meet us after class, and Fynn closed the door before gesturing toward another chair. "Why don't you take the one beside her? I feel like you'll have more room there. Alright, Ariana, are you ready to get going?"

"Ready to warm up those vocal cords?" I teased, tucking a few loose hairs behind her ear. "Maybe sing us one of your special songs?"

I'd been asking to hear one, just to see if maybe I recognized her voice. The feelings of familiarity had persisted to the point that I began to consider the possibility we'd seen each other before. Maybe in a bar where she was performing.

She nodded almost robotically, seemingly paler than she'd been just a few minutes before.

Fynn studied her with a small frown before retrieving a book from his desk. "Everything okay?"

Another nod.

And I suddenly couldn't remember the name of the puppy lady.

Great.

He cut his eyes over to me. I shrugged, refusing to offer up any information. If the therapist knew I'd kissed her right into a catatonic state, I imagined he wouldn't be much of a fan anymore. I also imagined he would have no trouble breaking me in half.

"Alright," he finally said. "I'll take it easy on you today, but maybe try to get a nap in before you go see Natalie."

Convinced he wasn't about to deck me; I relaxed and shifted my attention back over to Ari.

Fynn opened the book and turned to a list of fictional businesses and their contact information. "Remember this, Ariana? Can you point to the phone number for the hardware store?"

The girl had picked up on my trust issues with no issue but couldn't complete what should have been an insultingly easy task. Her finger bounced from row to row, searching for an answer that wouldn't come. Then, she stopped moving completely.

Sometimes, the brain just gets overstimulated...

I pushed to the edge of my seat, trying to inject my voice with as much calmness as I could muster amid the sound of alarms going off in my head. "Fynn, something's not right. I think she's—"

Ari's hand suddenly flew from the page, shaking like it was in a spasm before contorting into a claw. Her head followed, turning as if she was going to look over her right shoulder. But the stiff, jerking movements made it clear she was no longer calling the shots.

"No, no, no," I pleaded, reciting the word over and over like a prayer as her body went rigid.

Seizure.

The word was amplified in my head, complete with flashing red lights and sirens. She'd been exhibiting all the warning signs, and I'd ignored them.

I'd fucking ignored them.

Her limbs contorted into seemingly impossible positions, but Ari's mouth hung slack, her eyes fixed in a blank stare. When she began sliding down in the chair, I fell back on the training as if on autopilot.

Protect the person having a seizure.

I briefly became aware of Fynn radioing for a doctor as I carefully lowered Ari to the floor, turning her onto her side like I'd been shown in case she began vomiting.

My arms ached with the need to surround her, to squeeze her small body until the tremors stopped, and she came back. But restraining her would have only increased her risk of broken bones. No matter how much I wanted to, I was powerless to stop it.

Fynn pushed the chairs away from us and instructed me to cradle Ari's head in my lap to prevent another injury before calmly directing someone over the radio to call for an ambulance.

No class in the world could have prepared me for the utter helplessness I'd feel watching Ari's body spasm and contract uncontrollably. My heart slammed against my ribs, beating down the bars of its cage to get to her.

To protect her.

Using gentle movements, I brushed her hair back with the tips of my fingers before resorting to something I hadn't done since I was a boy—*prayer.*

Most seizures will end within five minutes.

I had no real concept of time, but it seemed like it should have been over by now. Just as I began to question where the hell the doctor was, the door opened, flooding the small room with people.

"Time of onset?" Someone shouted.

I shook my head, maintaining my hold on Ari.

I didn't know.

"Seven minutes ago," Fynn stated from somewhere nearby, his voice steady despite the situation unfolding in his office.

With the answer, the medical team sprang into action. Ari's dress was lifted, and her panties yanked down before they injected something directly into her body.

I closed my eyes and continued stroking her hair, silently pleading with her to wake up. We should have been drinking coffee while making plans on how to see each other once I was released. When I told Ari about the offers, she would have cracked some joke about me thinking I was a big deal or cheekily asked for an autograph.

It wasn't supposed to be like this.

After stabilizing her, the medical team pulled her from my arms, placing her on a waiting gurney in the hallway.

Then she was gone, and I was left holding nothing.

"I—" I dragged my hands through my hair. "Is she—"

Fynn helped me up, supporting my weight as he led me toward a chair. "She's going to be okay. Unfortunately, with brain injuries, there's always an increased risk of seizures."

"But where are they taking her?" A couple of people walked past the open doorway, discussing some inane topic as if nothing out of the ordinary had just occurred. It was as if the world had been on mute during Ari's seizure. The sudden volume was too much.

"She'll be taken to Methodist—it's the closest hospital. I expect they'll monitor her overnight, make sure there is no swelling or new bleeds before releasing her back to us."

"But she was fine—I saw her last night, and she was fine." I sounded like a broken record, but I couldn't make sense of it. Less than twenty-four hours ago, Ari had been talking and smiling. "How did this happen?"

Fynn dropped into the chair Ari had just been sitting in. I mashed my lips together, reliving the terror all over again.

He leaned in, letting his forearms rest on his thighs. "First of all, it's nothing you did. It could have been any number of things—a change in her medication, lack of sleep, or even stress. We'll know more once they've had a chance to run some tests. In the meantime, I'm here if you just need someone to talk to—"

"No, man. I'm good. Thank you." My words lacked conviction, but Fynn didn't push. He just handed me my crutches and a business card with his cell phone number in case I changed my mind.

My eyes drifted over the staff photos lining the walls on the long walk back to my room, but I couldn't have told you a single name.

Stress.

I'd done it again, taken what I wanted, damn the consequences. But this time was much worse. This time, I'd gone too far by pushing myself on Ari like a caveman.

Are you good?

No, I was beginning to think I might have been the most self-centered bastard who ever lived. I'd gotten caught up in the idea of Ari and how she made me feel, never once stopping to consider the impact her injury might have on her ability to have a relationship.

Then again, if I'd just listened to what Bailey was trying to tell me, I would have known. If Ari wasn't suffering from a brain injury, she never would have considered a man like me.

Just like Tampa and Chicago, I'd fought to exploit her weakness to get what I wanted, because I knew a good thing when I saw one. But Ari deserved more—she deserved that high-dollar, long-term contract with the right person—not damaged goods offered up by a man who'd fucked around with his teammates' wives.

I continued my internal rant on into my room, just shy of the bed when my throat contracted painfully. That first sob was like the sounding of a gong—a deep, reverberating ache that rattled my bones and tore my chest open.

Reed men didn't show emotion—crying was a sign of weakness that got you nowhere. If Joe were here, he'd no doubt have clicked his tongue against his teeth before shaking his head in disapproval.

Maybe he'd never wanted a son, but a dog—something that could have been trained to obey his every command.

For whatever reason, that thought, along with the sight of my shell-shocked expression reflected in the mirror above the sink, made my tears come faster.

I sucked in a ragged breath and mashed my lips together, but it was no use. My grief was not content to go quietly. No, it demanded to be heard as it stripped the flesh off the bone, leaving me to bleed out.

On what should have been the best day of my life, I'd been reduced to a loud, blubbering mess, forced to let go of burdens I'd carried for far too long. With a sharp exhale, I released the anger I'd held toward my father, wishing I could have lived up to his expectations and wondering if it would have made a damn bit of difference.

But Ari—Ari was a wound that would never heal.

I felt the loss of her in each strangled sob, and the gaping hole in my chest grew wider. Eventually, what was left of my heart fell through to the floor.

CHAPTER SIXTEEN
ARIANA

"I looked at the stars, and considered how awful it would be for a man to turn his face up to them as he froze to death, and see no help or pity in all the glittering multitude."

-Charles Dickens, *Great Expectations*

All that running and I'd managed to end up back where I started. Shards of glass from the shattered windshield bit into the skin around my ankles, holding me captive. The headlights flashed on and off like a message being sent in Morse code.

My palms squeaked noisily against the hood of the convertible as I clumsily searched for something to grip—some object that would free me from my glass prison.

But there was no escape.

The motor was still running, heating the metal hood until it burned against my cheek, but I couldn't move. The radio switched stations at random, the volume rising higher and higher. That, coupled with the vicious pounding in my skull, drowned out any hope at a coherent thought.

I was Humpty Dumpty—if he'd tried escaping the wall instead of just sitting atop it. Regardless, the outcome was the same. We'd both ended up cracked open on the pavement below.

And all the king's horses and all the king's men couldn't put Ari together again...

"Ari? Oh, Ari, what have they done to you?"

My skin prickled in fear at the sound. It had been easy to feign bravery with Killian sitting beside me, but I was alone now, and this ghost felt just as real to me as he did.

The leaves began to rustle as if something big was tearing its way through them. I didn't want to be scared, but I knew what was coming through the trees, just like I knew exactly what it wanted.

Me.

"Ariana," it taunted, masked behind the green foliage. I choked back a scream, recognizing that this was no ghost.

This monster was real.

"Those walls were built just for you."

"Ari?" The ghost cried out again, pushing into the clearing. She jerked her head to the left and right, searching for me in the dense smoke of the wreckage. "I can help you, but you have to come back to me!"

The monster mocked her words with a cold laugh. "Ariana, I can help you! Why don't you tell me your sins, and I'll tell you mine!"

I brought my palm down over my ear, trying to block the sound of their voices, but they were too loud. Almost as if the noise was coming from inside my head.

When she saw me, the ghost's mouth fell open in shock, but she didn't come any closer. A twig snapped on the ground from somewhere behind me. Her eyes slowly moved up, taking it in.

It wasn't just me anymore—she could see the monster too.

"Listen to me," she commanded, lowering herself into a crouch. "You're the only one who can end this."

"I can't—"

"It will only get worse unless you can remember who you are and why you left that night. There was a reason, Ari!"

The monster slid around the front of the vehicle faster than I would have imagined, approaching the ghost with a wide grin.

But there was nothing happy in the dark red blood that ran from its teeth, coating its chin and neck. This was a shark in search of a meal. The ghost knew it, but she didn't run. Instead, she straightened and matched its menacing grin with one of her own.

"Ari, you take down a monster by exposing it," the ghost stated before taking a step forward. "Let the world see the truth, and it loses its power."

"Daughter," the monster drawled in Tristan's voice before raising its fist. "Such sin lives within you—"

"Ashlynn!" I screamed, but it was too late. The monster's arm came down on her, and everything went black.

This time, I didn't have to see to know that I was alone again.

A HAND SQUEEZED MINE, pulling me from the nightmare. "I'm here—it's okay."

"Killian," I groaned, before cracking one eyelid open. It felt as though I'd been hit by a truck—or perhaps an entire fleet of trucks. Aching muscles engaged as I stretched and turned toward—*not Killian*.

Tristan's gaze narrowed as he looked me over, making the three deep lines on his forehead more pronounced.

Three meant trouble.

His eyes moved over my face once and then twice before he asked the inevitable. "Who's Killian?"

Shit.

The thought registered, and my lips parted in surprise. I couldn't see myself, but I imagined my eyes were probably as round as saucers too.

My forbidden curses had always been more along the lines of —*shoot, darn it*, or—if the situation called for it—a well-timed *heck*.

They were never spoken aloud but had always given me a little thrill when they popped by for a visit.

Shit wasn't an Ariana word, though. Shit was a Killian word—something that I found strangely comforting. Almost as if the man in question was right here, giving me the strength I needed to face Tristan.

"Killian was the one who helped during Ariana's seizure." Tiffani's voice shook with emotion as she approached the bed with a reverence most people reserved for altar calls.

Seizure?

I frowned my confusion, wondering if Tiffani had been desperate enough to get Tristan here under false pretenses.

*I hadn't had a seizure, I'd been—*I hesitated, my mind still loud with the voices of ghosts and monsters.

Well, I'd been—shit.

So, there were a few holes in my memory. Nothing I couldn't fix. I started with yesterday morning and began working my way forward, trying to grasp where things might have gone wrong.

There were Georgia's travel magazines. Then I was being dog-piled—*literally*— by the sweetest little puppies known to man.

I can't pretend that this doesn't mean anything. I know I'm probably messing it all up by admitting that I want to be with you.

My pulse sped at the memory of his confession, waking the butterflies that had been slumbering in my stomach. He'd kissed me, or perhaps I'd been the kiss initiator. Regardless, our lips had touched in the culmination of a decade-long fantasy.

And, judging by the bulge I'd noticed in his sweatpants afterward, it appeared as if Killian hadn't been bothered by my lack of experience.

He wanted me, maybe just as badly as I found myself wanting him. The lusty little birds still fluttered around every time I saw him, but there was also a deeper sense of longing now—this innate need to be near him always.

Shrouding our friendship in secrecy had been a necessary, but almost unbearable evil. I tried to ignore Killian outside of my room, but there was something in him that called to me. Lately, I'd found myself missing him even when we were together.

And with that came the realization that I couldn't run and hide forever. It was time to confront my monster. I wasn't the obedient daughter who kept her head down and her mouth shut—that girl had died in the car wreck.

I was Killian's, and that made me feel limitless.

Tristan wouldn't agree—in fact, he might go as far as refusing me outright—but I wouldn't back down.

Not this time.

"Where might I find this Killian?" he asked carefully, maybe fooling Tiffani with his concerned tone and disarming blinking. "I'd like to thank him personally."

But I knew better.

Three lines meant trouble.

"He—" The tech swallowed, seemingly wilting under the weight of his stare. "He was released to go home, Pastor James. Like, it was a God thing that he just literally happened to be in the right place at the right time."

Feeling Tristan's eyes shift back to me, I arranged my expression into one of careless indifference, but inside I was reeling.

Gone.

Killian wouldn't have just left without saying goodbye. Not after that kiss. Not before I had a chance to tell him who I was. He wouldn't have left me behind unless there was a good reason—unless something had forced him to run.

The seizure.

I saw it clearly. My brain had finally understood my request and decided to release the memory from the vault. Until now, I thought sleep paralysis was the scariest thing I'd ever experienced, but this was worse.

This was a helplessness I hadn't been able to wake myself from.

Unable to cope with even the smallest sense of freedom, my body had become a cage.

And I was its captive.

My throat burned with rage that any God could be that cruel, leading me back to Killian, only to rip him away all over again.

"That's a shame, isn't it, Ariana?" Tristan's hand tightened around mine. A warning.

"It's a shame," I repeated with a solemn nod, no longer caring whether or not he knew I could speak.

What was the point?

Nothing was ever going to change. My nightmare hadn't just been a fractured memory of my car accident, but a premonition. I could run as hard and fast as I wanted, but I would always end up right back where I started—locked behind the same walls I'd known all my life.

"Brad was sure sorry he couldn't be here when you woke up, but he's handling a few things for me."

I swallowed the bile in my throat and nodded. "Okay."

"Have you given any thought as to when you'd like to set the date?" Tristan's words were a knife stabbing into my flesh as if he needed the reassurance that I was truly dead this time.

I was.

The hope that had been blooming in my chest since finding Killian again shriveled into apathy.

"As soon as I'm well enough," I mumbled, my words surprisingly steady despite the hurricane of emotions sweeping through my body. "No need for a lengthy engagement."

I preferred a quick death.

Tristan's wide eyes told me he hadn't expected my response before he managed to slow-blink his way back onto neutral ground. "I can't tell you how good it is to hear your voice. If I'd known you were talking, I would have—"

"I wasn't."

In saying Killian's name, I'd given myself away. Keeping him safe would mean convincing Tristan that he meant nothing. I brought my hand up to clasp my necklace, needing my talisman like never before. "I feel like maybe—maybe God used the seizure to rewire that part of my brain."

Tristan's eyes flashed with something like pride, and he nodded. "God's still in the miracle business and can use anything to His glory."

"Amen." I cleared my throat against another surge of bile before asking, "Do you think I'll be home in time for Christmas?"

"Maybe—worried you might miss out on presents?" He chuckled, seemingly forgetting the very things he preached against.

Putting Christ Back in Christmas: A Four-Part Series about Leaving Materialism on the Shelf.

"I—" I shook my head, fighting the numbness that seemed to be settling in. God help me, I couldn't bring myself to say it.

Killian. Just think of Killian.

"I just thought it might be nice to have a Christmas wedding," I rushed out on a whisper.

This time, I had him. Tristan made no attempt to disguise his reaction and openly gaped at me for almost a full minute.

Blink. Blink.

"There are women everywhere who would kill to be in my place," I added, sounding infinitely less threatening than Brad had when he'd said it. "I'm just afraid if we wait much longer, someone will steal him right out from under me."

His eyes went distant as he mulled over my offer, probably trying to find time in his busy speaking schedule. And that wasn't even getting into the required appearances and interviews to discuss my upcoming nuptials.

"Alright. Let's do it." *Blink. Blink.*

"Yeah?" I asked, plastering a fake grin on my face.

"Yeah. But that leaves a lot of work to be done." In a rare display of emotion, Tristan lifted my hand to his mouth, pressing a kiss against my knuckle in almost the exact spot Killian had.

Although my palms were damp with sweat, they remained surprisingly steady.

I wasn't afraid anymore.

With that knowledge, I decided to go for broke. "Maybe Morgan could help with some of the planning for me while I'm here."

His smile dimmed, but he jerked his chin in a thoughtful nod. "We'll see, little dove."

"I can help, Pastor James," Tiffani blurted. "I understand you have a busy schedule, but I could literally run out and buy some bridal magazines for Ariana to look over—not like I'd be trying to take over. And, like, you wouldn't even have to pay me or anything like that."

She finally paused to take a breath before adding, "I just want to help."

"How can I say no to that pitch, Tiffani?" He winked at me, and I wondered how different our lives would have turned out had he not been a complete phony.

What would it have been like to be loved unconditionally?

It wasn't the first time I'd considered the alternate version of reality either. Once, I'd caught Mama on a good day and asked something similar. After she stopped laughing, she'd looked at me and said, *"Just because a chicken has wings, don't mean it can fly."*

At the time, I'd taken her response as an indicator that she was slipping back into her delusional state, but it made sense now. We could have remained small enough to fit in the box he'd designated for us, but there was no realm where Tristan became a loving father.

The evil in him went right down to the bone.

"I've got to get back to the church—and you, little dove, need to get some rest so that you're ready to walk down the aisle in just a little over a month."

Tiffani waited until he was gone—going as far as checking to ensure he'd gotten on the elevator—before rounding on me. I braced myself for the onslaught of praise, my cheeks already growing sore from the forced smiles.

I didn't know how much longer I could keep the act up.

"Oh my god—like, Ariana, you can talk! And Pastor James, he was sitting right here!"

She dropped onto the chair with a deep sigh. "I'll literally never forgive myself for leaving you yesterday. When I heard the news, it was like I'd failed you. I should have seen the signs."

"Wait—the seizure was yesterday?" I croaked.

"Yeah, you were taken to the hospital where they ran like some tests before transporting you back here last night. You've literally been sleeping since it happened—not that I blame you—but like it's good to have you back." Tiffani sucked in a rough inhale. "I just have to ask—the man who was here a few weeks ago, was that Brad?"

I gave her a brief nod, waiting for the requisite comment on his good looks or expensive clothes—the same useless drivel I'd overheard women in the church discussing for years.

No one had ever seemed to look beyond the superficial long enough to consider whether or not the man even possessed the qualities necessary for a husband.

Spoiler alert—he didn't.

"But like, he's got to be as old as your father," she hissed. "Oh my god—your sisters! It's not a coincidence that their husbands are so much older, is it?"

It wasn't.

We'd been sold off like livestock.

Brad would bully me into submission before forcing me to bear his children like the prize-winning heifer I was. I'd fake every smile in public, knowing that behind my back, he was seducing any young girl who happened to catch his eye.

Tiffani didn't wait for my response before dropping her face into her hands with a muffled groan. "Oh my God, it's not! Do you even love him?"

"No," I answered truthfully. "If you run, you could catch up and tell my father."

She glanced toward the closed door and lowered her voice. "I won't—like, I know I didn't exactly grow up in the church, but this is not normal stuff. You shouldn't have to marry him—"

"It's out of my hands," I calmly replied, knowing if I said anything more, I'd give myself away. Tiffani needed to think I was weak and helpless.

I reached under the blankets until I felt the comforting weight of Morgan's teddy bear against my fingertips.

This was my only option.

———

Dammit.

One of Killian's curses slipped in during yet another failed attempt at rethreading my sewing needle. With the way this day was going, it wouldn't be my last. My sudden inability to complete even the smallest of tasks had made me miserable company.

Before the seizure, I'd been an excellent cross-stitcher.

Before Killian, I hadn't understood why people made such a fuss over a kiss.

But in the last five days, I'd been reduced to a brittle husk of the woman I was before. I was a woman who'd mastered wallowing in her grief, but not much else.

He hadn't come back.

Each morning I was forced out of bed and into the shower, where either Tiffani or Tsega would hold me through a light round of shoulder-shaking, uncontrollable sobs.

And things had only gotten worse from there, including a regrettable incident involving the miniature Killian figurine in Fynn's office and a surprisingly soft wall.

"Yours is coming along nicely, Ariana," Georgia praised. "Sadly, my eyes just aren't what they used to be."

I leaned in as she held hers up for inspection, only to find her stitching infinitely better than anything I was accomplishing in my current state.

"I think you must have been looking at the wrong weave cloth because this—" I shook the hoop to really drive home my point. "Is completely hopeless. I may as well rip it all out and start over."

Georgia raised her eyebrows in question before turning back toward the small television in the corner of the room. I'd briefly registered it was on when I arrived. Since then, I'd lost myself in the tediousness of French knots and baseball players who disappeared without a trace.

At the amplified crack of gunfire, I flinched and watched in horror as a woman dropped to the beach, bleeding from her wounds. I didn't need to see anymore—I was well aware of how that story would end.

I jerked again when Tsega loudly cleared her throat, but she was looking at something on her phone and didn't seem to notice.

Georgia cut her eyes back over to me and patted my knee. "You know, I don't believe I've told you how wonderful it is to finally hear your voice. Isn't it nice, Tsega?"

"So nice." Tsega agreed with a smile that didn't quite reach her eyes. As she'd been subjected to the sounds of my nonsensical whimpers echoing off the shower tiles, I couldn't say I blamed her.

An odd look passed between the two of them—one that made me think they were up to something. And I had a feeling that something involved me.

Georgia's voice moved up in pitch. "I haven't seen your young man around lately. Why is that, Ariana?"

My stomach tightened at the mention of Killian, but as my last cry had only been an hour ago, I was granted a brief reprieve. "Did you really steal Margaret's boyfriend?" I asked, sounding more defensive than I'd intended.

She let out a loud peal of laughter. "Heavens, Ariana. I imagined that you, of all people, would know you can't believe everything you hear. I haven't looked at another man since I lost Will."

The needlepoint fell forgotten to my lap. "I'm sorry, I didn't mean—"

Georgia waved her hands as if shooing off my apology. "None of that. I'm actually glad you asked because it's why I invited you for a visit." She shared another strange look with Tsega, but neither one of them was smiling anymore.

"Will and I were so young, Ariana, and we fell in love quickly. My mother warned me it wouldn't last, but I knew better—"

I released the breath I'd been holding. "But how did you know?"

It was the very thing I kept coming back to. Despite all the books I'd read and a kiss that would be forever ingrained in my memory, it felt like there was something I was missing.

How could a person willingly hand their heart over to someone else without a guarantee that it wouldn't get broken?

Georgia considered my question. "Well, I can't pinpoint a specific instance where I knew, but it was how he made me feel. When I was with him, I came alive. Most people considered me shy back then, but with Will in the room, it was like flipping a switch. I'd ramble about any and everything."

"What about your fiancé?" Tsega crossed her arms over her chest. "Does he make you feel like that?"

It was apparent the two of them were setting me up to reveal something, but I didn't question it. Instead, I forced myself to think of Brad, trying to determine if he'd ever made me feel alive. I'd been left feeling disgusted plenty of times, but never once had I become a more vibrant version of myself in his presence.

Only with Killian.

It had only ever been with Killian.

Georgia moved her wrinkled hand up to cover mine. "You seem troubled. I hope I haven't upset you."

I shook my head. "It's just that I don't know that I've ever met someone who makes me feel what you're describing."

Another lie.

I'd told so many now that it was becoming a struggle to keep them all straight.

"You know, neither had I until he came along. I'd met men who were nice enough, but they didn't make me feel here."

She released my hand, placing her palm over my chest. "You know that feeling when your heart is pumping violently against your ribs, reminding you that you're alive? That's how it was with Will. I hadn't gone to college or anything like that. But just being around him filled me with a sense of purpose. Like maybe I'd been made to be his."

I closed my eyes, swallowing against the sudden pang of loss. But, if I was honest with myself, Killian had never truly been mine. Maybe the signs were nothing more than the fantasies of an overactive imagination.

But for a brief moment in time, I'd been given a glimpse of what it was like to feel protected and safe. It might have been a mere fraction of what Georgia had with Will, but I was grateful for the experience. I couldn't be selfish enough to demand anything more.

"Ariana," Tsega said softly. "You don't love him—"

They were going to ruin everything.

I pushed Georgia's hand away and stood, glad I'd insisted on leaving the wheelchair back in my room. "Did Tiffani tell you this? Is that what I am to you—some form of gossip at the nurse's station? Did you ever stop to consider that I might have feelings of my own—"

"Oh, for the love of Pete, sit down, Ariana!" Georgia snapped, pointing at the empty chair. "Not one person in this room is a gossip, but we are worried about you."

"You haven't been yourself since the seizure," Tsega added. "We saw the way you were with Killian, Ariana. You love him, and he loves you. I'm just not sure he knows it yet. Life isn't perfect. The stars seldom align, but when they do, you grab on with both hands and don't let go."

"He doesn't love me," I choked, refusing to let the sudden shoot of hope pierce my heart. "If he did, he never would have left. Brad is the man I'm meant to be with, so stop looking for things that aren't there."

Tsega looked to Georgia for back up. The older woman sighed.

"Do you think we haven't heard the rumors about the church's little gated community—the whispers that the pastor's daughters are nothing more than slaves?"

"You're wrong." My voice faded, and I sank down onto the chair, no longer able to stand. People could suspect that things weren't right, but there would never be any proof.

And, even if I were inclined to take a ghost's advice and speak out against the church, my sisters would stick to the narrative they'd been spoon-fed since birth.

I'd be labeled a liar, and then Tristan would ensure that I never left my cage again.

"Just help us understand why you're marrying that man," Tsega pleaded, moving beside me. "Is it because Killian left, and you feel you have no other choice? Was he going to help you?"

No one could help me.

My eyes stung with anger and shame, but I kept the tears at bay long enough to quietly confess, "I only agreed to the marriage so he wouldn't look into Killian. I thought if I gave myself up that he'd back off and I could find a way out of it—find a way to escape. But it's hopeless. He's always going to be one step ahead of me."

"Tsega, be a dear and turn this up real quick, would you?" Georgia stabbed a finger in the direction of the television.

My jaw went slack as Tsega retrieved the remote, wondering if either of them had been listening, or if the pull of on-screen violence was simply too strong to resist.

Just as I was on the verge of standing up to excuse myself for a previously scheduled cry, Georgia began bouncing excitedly in her seat. "This is it! Look at them, Ariana—stuck in no man's land. All around, people are dying or starving. An entire village enslaved. This battalion has been stuck in the trenches for a year, unable to gain any ground. I imagine this is as hopeless as hopeless gets."

I pushed my hurt feelings aside and watched as a couple argued battle strategy, failing to see how the events of World War I related in any way to what I'd been trying to say.

"Diana is a woman in the middle of a man's war," Georgia murmured, no longer watching the screen, but me. "By all rights, she's the weakest among them. Steve tells her that it's not possible to cross—end of story. Except, it's not. Because sometimes, the smallest voices are the loudest. Sometimes, Ariana, the girl gets to be the hero. Watch."

At first, it appeared as if Diana was doing nothing more than unpinning her hair. Then, she stepped up onto the ladder, seemingly ready to sacrifice herself, and I couldn't look away.

"She's taking all the fire!"

Bullets flew all around her, but she managed to deflect every single one. Chills raced across my arms when the hail of gunfire became too much, but Diana just picked up her shield and continued advancing on the German army.

"Ariana," Georgia said softly when the scene ended. I blinked, suddenly aware that my cheeks were damp with tears.

"You might be able to speak, but you haven't ever truly used your voice. You have two choices—keep silent and marry a man you don't love because your father expects it. Or, you can pick up your shield to forge your own path, destroying any man who stands in your way, like a goddess among mortals."

Tsega nodded in agreement and reached for my hand. "You don't have to fight this battle alone."

I'd never seen a woman save the day—either on-screen or off. Growing up, we'd been taught to be respectful and meek, but never brave.

Georgia took my other hand and squeezed. "We'll stand by your side. Oh, and one more thing. If that baseball player doesn't track you down and drop to his knees at your feet, then he's an unworthy fool."

My sex—the very thing that had seemingly held me at a disadvantage was now my greatest weapon. I just didn't know how to hone it into something I could easily wield, something that could expose the monsters.

CHAPTER SEVENTEEN
KILLIAN

"We have two lives... the life we learn with and the life we live after that. Suffering is what brings us towards happiness."

-Bernard Malamud, *The Natural*

I'D BEEN HOME for all of an hour when someone leaked the details of my record-breaking contract to ESPN. From there, news spread like wildfire to every major outlet in the country. My phone had been ringing off the hook ever since.

During the day, the endless interviews and promotional shoots were enough to keep me from fixating on the way I'd left things with Ari. But at night, I wasn't as successful.

It had been seven days since I'd held her. A week spent putting one foot in front of the other, inhaling, exhaling, and dealing with the nagging sense that I'd lost something that couldn't be recovered. Like maybe I hadn't just left her, but a piece of myself back at *True North*.

No matter what I did, the hole in my chest refused to scab over, constantly reopening over the smallest things. Just yesterday, someone had gotten onto the elevator in my condo with a puppy, and

I swore I could feel the blood gushing down my chest and soaking through my shirt.

Clearly, I wasn't going to last much longer and, in desperation, had asked Bailey to meet for a drink. As he was now over twenty minutes late, perhaps I hadn't fully conveyed the severity of my situation.

"Excuse me, are you Killian Reed?" A feminine voice purred in my ear.

I turned toward the blonde with a forced smile, keeping my eyes on her face and not the tits that were dangerously close to falling out of her dress. "Yep."

"Would you sign this for me?" She slid the napkin in front of me with a pout. "Pretty please? It's Marissa."

I scrawled my signature across the napkin and handed it back to her, mustering up enough enthusiasm to drawl, "Here you are, Marissa. Hope to see you at a game."

Her eyes flashed with lust as she dropped another napkin into my lap. "I hope to see much more of you at my place later."

"That's flattering, but I'm good," I said tightly, handing it back to her with another fake smile. I didn't need to see it to know she'd given me her phone number. It made the tenth one in the last five minutes.

"I bet you are." She winked and placed it on the bar in front of me. "If you change your mind, you know where to find me."

Fuck.

My hand was starting to cramp from all the autographs I'd given. I hadn't really considered how my contract was going to impact my ability to enjoy a beer in peace. If I had, I would have had Bailey come to my place.

A blast of cold air from the front door announced someone's arrival. I glanced up at the mirror above the bar, just as Bailey ducked inside.

The weekend crowd parted easily around the third baseman, but it had nothing to do with his size or celebrity. Bailey just had one of those faces. The looks of confusion followed him damn near everywhere he went, with people actively trying to work out how it was they knew him.

A few patrons would assume he was just another regular and go back to their conversations, but others would become convinced they'd seen him in a movie—*you know, the one with that guy who gets the girl.*

Before the end of the night, some brave soul would likely come up to ask if he was in 'that Vikings show' on TV. When it was all said and done, though, only three or four people would leave here tonight, having correctly guessed his identity.

I envied his ability to live in disguise.

"Sorry, I'm late. I didn't want to come," Bailey joked as he slid onto the empty barstool beside me. The humor in his eyes fled when he caught sight of my reflection in the mirror. "Christ, Reed. What the fuck happened to you?"

I raised my pint glass, signaling the bartender for another round. "You were right—about all of it."

He didn't crack another joke or make some reference to me seeing the light. Instead, Bailey ordered a whiskey and demanded I tell him everything.

"Wow," he stated once I'd finished, staring down a bottle of absinthe on the back of the bar. "So, you just bailed?"

"What was I supposed to do—stick around when it was obvious I was taking advantage of her injury?"

"Hey, could we get your autograph?"

"Not right now," I barked at the trio of women lingering behind my bar stool. After offering some very colorful assessments of my anatomy, they stomped back to their table.

Bailey leaned back on his stool with a low whistle, palms raised in surrender. "Easy there, killer. Damn, you're in rare form tonight. As far as your issue, I'm simply trying to understand why you didn't at least have a conversation with the woman before taking off."

"You said yourself, she never would have looked at me had it not been for the brain injury—"

"I said no such thing," he interjected. "Christ, I know I've messed with you over the years, but it was all done in fun. Since when did you start taking me seriously?"

Never.

The bartender slid another beer in front of me. I glared at the glass, trying to remember if it was my fourth or fifth. I knew I wasn't drunk—*not yet*—but I wasn't exactly sober enough to keep my thoughts to myself either.

I paused to sign a couple more autographs before continuing. "Look, I can't help but feel that the seizure was my fault. When I told Ari I wanted a relationship, she got scared. Fuck, I was scared too, but then I went and kissed her anyway—"

"You might be the richest son-of-a-bitch in baseball, but you aren't a god, Reed," he said dryly. "Not everything is about you. So, you kissed—big deal. From the way you described it, sounds like she was a willing participant. Sometimes, bad shit just happens, and if you spend your life trying to find the reason behind it, you'll miss out on everything."

It would have been easy to buy into what he was saying and absolve myself of any guilt, but the persistent ache in my chest begged to differ.

I took a long drink, trying to shake my last memory of Ari. I didn't want to remember her like that. I'd been haunted by the look of nothingness in her eyes, tormented by thoughts of her body thrashing violently in my arms. "Look, it is what it is. Right now, more than anything, I just need some advice on how to get over it."

"How to get over it," Bailey repeated, the side of his mouth tugging up into a smirk. "And what makes you think I have the answer?"

"C'mon, cut the shit," I grumbled, pressing the heel of my hand over the invisible wound on my chest. "You do this all the time—just tell me how to make it stop hurting."

I didn't care if his answer involved a cask of *Macallan* and another night on the old inflatable flamingo, I'd do it if it meant exorcising the ghost of her from my head.

Bailey cocked an eyebrow. "Do what all the time—fall in love? C'mon, Reed. You know me better than that. Feelings are messy—I mean, look at yourself!"

"Love—" I didn't bother hiding the disgust in my voice. "Who the fuck said anything about love? It was just one kiss."

"Observe." Bailey retrieved several limes from a nearby caddy and lined them along the bar before lifting his empty whiskey glass. "This is your brain—"

"I swear to Christ, if your next sentence involves my brain on drugs, I'm knocking the barstool out from under you," I growled.

Bailey rolled his eyes, pressing his thumb and index finger into the okay sign. "Sure you will. You know what? Seems like you've got this all under control. I'll just leave you to it—"

I pinched the bridge of my nose and groaned, "Fine. I'm sorry. Just tell me what to do."

"As I was saying before I was so rudely interrupted, think of this glass as your brain. Now, these limes represent some area of your life. You've got baseball here—"

He began dropping the pieces of fruit, one by one, into the glass. "Your friends, family, and casual sexual encounters—or in your case, an extensive collection of porn. Right now, you're spending time in the friend area. Later, it's definitely going to be the porn one—"

"Is there a point to any of this?" I should have gone to a therapist or priest—someone who didn't know shit about my life.

"My point is that you keep your areas separate. You wouldn't combine your friends and love sections any more than you would, say, the family and porn ones—which is illegal in most states, I might add."

Bailey dumped the limes back out on the bar, along with several drops of whiskey before snagging another lime wedge. "We'll call this one Ari. Here's where it gets interesting. By introducing her into the mix—"

He paused to return the limes back into the glass before squeezing the piece in his hand over them. I wasn't exactly sure why he hadn't just left them in the glass to start with, but as it was one of his rare moments of seriousness, I kept my mouth shut.

"She coats your entire brain. So, you might be in the friend area now, but you're thinking of Ari. Your mom calls up and wants to serve meatloaf at the next family dinner, and you find yourself wondering what Ari's favorite food is—"

"Yeah, now how do I make it stop?"

He dropped the last lime into the glass with a shrug. "You don't? You're in love, Reed. Accept it. Learn it. Live it."

I'd chosen the wrong moment to take a drink and ended up inhaling a mouthful of beer into my lungs. After coughing until my eyes were streaming, I croaked, "But I'm not—we just met a little over a month ago."

A hand tapped my shoulder. "Could I—"

"Yep." I twisted around and scribbled my name across a napkin, grateful for the distraction.

I needed a minute—*who was I kidding?* It was going to take days to break his ludicrous assumption down into something more palatable. Minus the one kiss and a dozen or so dirty fantasies, there was nothing there that would suggest a lifelong commitment and house in the suburbs.

Sure, seeing her in pain had ripped me to shreds, but anyone in my shoes would have reacted the same way. If that Fynn guy had gone down in the middle of class—*well, it was hard to picture as it hadn't happened*—but I was reasonably certain I would have felt the same.

"Reed?"

I blinked to clear my thoughts before shifting my attention back to where Bailey was watching me with an amused grin.

"You're looking a little pale. It's a lot to take in, I get it."

I drained the rest of my pint and turned it around on him. "What I can't wrap my head around is how a man who proclaims to have never been in love is suddenly an expert on the subject."

"Never said I was an expert. No, I'm more of an observer, you might say. I've seen enough to know when a man is fucked in the head over a woman—and you, my friend—are completely fucked."

The longer Bailey watched me with that shit-eating grin of his, the more I found myself wanting to stuff his mouth full of limes—anything to shut him up.

"So, you're telling me the great Conor Bailey has never been wrecked over a woman before? Not even once?"

Bailey's grin faltered. He tapped his phone, where it lay against the bar, checking the time. "Christ, it's getting late."

I pushed. "I take it that's a no. So really, for all you know, I might just be dealing with some residual lust where Ari is concerned. We didn't have sex, so I'm stuck fixating on what might have been, yeah?"

"Residual lust, huh?" Bailey tapped the edge of his phone rhythmically against the bar top. "If you buy that, I've got some ocean-front property in Colorado I'd be willing to sell you. Answering your question—no, I've never been in love. But I am just buzzed enough to admit that there was a girl I was hung up on a few years ago."

Maybe it was the beer and lack of sleep catching up to me, or just a sense of morbid curiosity that prompted me to ask, "Who?"

Bailey resumed his study of the bottles of alcohol lining the back of the bar, his brow tight with concern. "Like I said, it's late. Did you drive here?"

I shook my head. "No, I did the app thing. Didn't know how parking was gonna be and wasn't up for a hike on crutches."

He nodded at my long-winded answer before picking up his phone. "I'll order a sober ride."

"We can talk while we wait. C'mon, don't make me the girl here —" I was poking the bear. I knew it, but I'd long considered Bailey an open book. Anything that would cause him to shut down completely seemed cause for concern.

My teammate was quiet for a long moment, avoiding my question while he ordered our car. I assumed that was the end of the discussion, so I was more than a little surprised when he turned to face me.

"It was about—shit, five years ago? We spent one night together and when I woke up the next morning, she was gone. The end. I need to hit the head. Keep an eye out for our ride, will ya?" Bailey slid off the stool, his usual grin back in place as if the confession had cost him nothing.

I watched as he made his way to the back, regretting ever asking him to open up. Because, if a girl he slept with once was still fucking with his head five years later, then I didn't have a chance in hell of ever getting rid of Ari.

Blasts of cold air hit my back as people came and went, and I watched dispassionately until one man, in particular, caught my eye.

My father.

He seemed to hesitate as he scanned the bar. I shook my head, wondering how often he snuck into the city for a fix. My jaw tightened at the memory of my mother putting on a pot of coffee, prepared to wait up until he made it home safely.

Son-of-a-bitch.

For a minute there, I'd actually considered he was calling because he wanted to rebuild our relationship, but he was always going to be this. The guy who had no trouble jumping my ass over following the rules and not letting people down couldn't take his own advice.

Was my mother waiting up now, trying to convince herself he just had a meeting that ran late? Was she telling herself the same thing she'd often told me—hate the addiction, love the addict?

I wasn't even aware I was pushing off the bar until my feet were on the floor. I grabbed my crutches and began fighting my way through the crowd, gearing up for a showdown.

"Joe!" I roared when I was about ten feet away, hearing the note of hysteria in my voice. When he didn't turn around, the madness gave way to fury. I began elbowing people out of my way to catch up.

"You're Killian Reed!" someone loudly exclaimed, patting my back.

"No shit, Sherlock," I muttered under my breath, before giving the guy a tight nod. Fortunately, my father was still blissfully unaware I was in the room, which worked well for what I was about to do.

Bailey emerged from the bathroom, his eyes narrowing in confusion when they landed on me. I felt the heat in my face, fully aware I probably resembled a tomato, but there was no controlling the fire in my veins. Not now—not when the last twelve years had been a lie meant to placate me into obeying.

I turned away from my friend's pointed stare, coming up behind Joe just as he stepped up to the bar. He leaned forward and out of reach of my hand, loudly calling out, "I'm looking for Conor! Anyone here named Conor?"

My arm dropped, along with my jaw, and I began trying to back away, only to find the crowd had boxed me in, clamoring for me to pose for selfies or quickies—it was hard to differentiate.

Bailey chose that moment to stick his fingers in his mouth, emitting an ear-splitting whistle that could be heard for blocks.

"I'm Conor!" he bellowed, waving his hands.

My father turned at the noise, his jaw flexing when he noticed my presence. "Killian?"

I nodded and jerked a thumb toward Bailey, no longer trusting myself to speak—*or think*. It seemed I didn't know anything anymore.

Bailey stopped to pick up the tab, but I kept my head down and followed my father out of the bar, feeling like a delinquent. My teammate caught up to us and, unaware of the tension, called shotgun. I was perfectly content to sulk in the backseat with my thoughts.

At several points during the drive, my father lifted his eyes to meet my focused stare in the rearview mirror while Bailey poked at random buttons, trying to find music.

When it became clear that alcohol and technology didn't mix, my father took his eyes off me to intervene. "Right there, Conor. You got it. Play whatever you want."

"Thanks, Mr. Joe," he mumbled, sounding infinitely less sober than he had back at the bar. "Reed's got a broken heart, so he needs a song, you know? Just a little pick-me-up."

I winced as Bailey dropped a proverbial bucket of chum where I was swimming, knowing there was no escaping this shark. Reed men didn't get their hearts broken because they never let anyone in.

"Yeah?" My father made brief eye contact with me before shifting his attention back to the road.

"Yeah," Bailey slurred in response. "It's always the quiet ones that get ya."

My father remained unusually silent, even when Bailey managed to sync his phone to the car, blasting hard-core rap through the speakers. I wasn't quite sure how lyrics about putting a Glock in someone's ass and fucking bitches were supposed to make me feel better, but it did save me from having to make conversation.

When we pulled up in front of Bailey's condo, my father parked and turned back to me. "Can I give you a ride home?"

As tempted as I was to avoid any discussion with him, my misplaced anger had fled the moment I realized he wasn't at the bar to drink. Besides, if he wanted to give me a lecture, it was better to get it over with while I was still somewhere between sober and drunk.

I nodded and told Bailey to be safe before taking his seat up front. "So, sober rides—didn't know you did that sort of thing."

He waited until Bailey made it inside before pulling out. "Yeah, going on three years now."

"Oh." I didn't know what else to say. Joe and I didn't usually waste time with small talk. He often started with the laundry list of things I'd done wrong. Then we went our separate ways.

No muss, no fuss.

"Did you get my message?" He cut his eyes over to me. "I called after your mama told me you'd gotten the contract with the Hurricanes. She was really excited, as you should be. It's a huge accomplishment, son."

"Uh, thanks?" I squinted in his direction, no longer sure who was in the driver's seat. It damn sure wasn't my father. Reed men didn't stop to look back at their accomplishments. It was all about pushing on to the next.

At least, it used to be.

Without Bailey around to provide entertainment, we fell back into an uncomfortable silence that neither of us seemed capable of breaking.

The click of the turn signal pulled me from my thoughts. I glanced up to see we'd reached my condo. "Hey, uh, thanks for the ride and—"

"Can I come up?" he asked suddenly, gripping the steering wheel with both hands. "I mean, you've got the crutches. I could help. But if you'd rather I not—"

"No, it's fine," I said automatically, swallowing down my fear. "Just leave the car keys with the valet."

On the elevator ride up, Joe stared down at his sneakers. Meanwhile, I tried to recall the last time I'd seen him in anything other than a suit. If he felt me staring a hole into the side of his head, he didn't let on.

"I just realized I've never even seen your condo," he commented to his shoelaces.

"Really?" It surprised me as his real estate firm had brokered the deal. Thinking back on it, though, I realized he was right. The doors opened, and I straightened before leading the way. "Well, I'll have to give you the grand tour."

He followed me inside, almost immediately zeroing in on the unpacked suitcase lying open in the middle of the living room. I waited for the reprimand, but he walked right past it to inspect the large glass windows overlooking the city.

"Killian, this view—"

I stepped up beside him. "Worth every penny, because you can change the paint—"

He tilted his head to face me, frowning slightly. "But you can't change the view. You remembered."

"Hey," I barked a laugh at his dumbfounded expression. "Give me at least a little credit. I listen... sometimes."

I waited for a chuckle, or at the very least, a smirk, but my father looked like he was on the verge of tears. He slowly backed away from the window and dropped onto the nearby leather sectional with a heavy sigh.

"I've been trying to reach you for weeks now," he said quietly, pulling at the cuff of his long-sleeved Hurricanes t-shirt.

When we were arguing, it had been easy to miss the lines on his face and the gray in his hair. Looking at him now, I was forced to admit he wasn't getting any younger.

It seemed like such a waste that we'd spent years at each other's throats, each of us convinced that we knew better than the other.

"Look, Dad," I began, but he stopped me, patting the cushion beside his.

"Come here. Let's talk."

Typically, those last two words would have sent me spiraling into a state of defensive anger, but this was different. There was something in his voice that told me he was just as tired of fighting as I was, so I leaned my crutches against the wall and joined him.

"When you didn't return my calls or texts, I considered showing up to the rehab facility and forcing you to see me." He grimaced and shook his head. "But that's what got us into this mess—me, forcing you to do things my way."

I shifted my jaw back and forth with a nod. "We never really talked much."

"You're right. We spent most of our time yelling. And I can't say I blame you for ignoring me. Our relationship is what it is because of the way I've treated you."

I gaped, completely blindsided by the admission.

"Tonight, while driving you home, it struck me that you're not a kid anymore, and I don't know anything about your life beyond what your mama tells me." He held up his hand. "Now, don't misunderstand. I'm not saying that to start an argument. You're close to her, and I respect that. She shielded you from so much the first twelve years of your life. But you knew—I saw it in the way you looked at me when she'd let me come home."

"Wasn't enough to stop you from doing it again, though, was it?" I asked, feeling the old bitterness and hurt seeping into my voice.

He stared through the flat screen on the wall, to a past I'd tried to forget. When he finally spoke, his voice was thick with emotion. "I'd swear every time was the last time, but then something would happen, and I couldn't cope. I'd take off and leave your mother and you to fend for yourselves."

I tugged my hands through my hair. "You do remember I was there, right? You can skip the recap, I'm well aware of how it went down."

"Yeah?" He sniffed, mashing his lips into a thin line. "What about your twelfth birthday—you remember that? Because I do. Coming off a three-day bender in the middle of a goddamned tropical storm. I wanted nothing more than to get home to you, but your mama refused—rightfully so, I might add—said I had to get professional help."

"She told me you had a conference out of town that you couldn't get out of," I said softly, picking at the edge of my knee brace with my thumbnail.

His face fell, but he jerked his chin in a nod. "Better than I deserved, but that's your mama. No, I'd hit rock bottom. Woke up on a park bench without a wallet and just wandered the city, trying to sober up. When the storm hit, the streets began to flood. I remembered there was this televangelist with a church nearby—thought for sure they'd take me in."

Something like empathy struck me in the chest as I considered the humiliation he must have felt. "And did they?"

He forced a laugh before shaking his head. "Never even made it past the gate. When they threatened to have me arrested, I left. At that point, the water had risen to my calves, and I just wanted it to be over. And then she appeared—"

"Who?"

"At first glance, I thought she was an angel. The streetlights, they hit her red hair in such a way that it almost looked like a halo. And her eyes were the most vibrant shade of green, but the color wasn't what made them striking, it was the way they seemed to see past my flaws."

He shook his head slowly as if still in disbelief. That made two of us. My mouth had been hanging open for a solid ten seconds, but I was too shocked to speak. The woman sounded just like Ari, which was impossible because she would have been a child back then.

"I told her about you—"

"What—why?"

His gaze softened as it moved over my face. "Because that woman looked at me like maybe she saw someone worth saving and I couldn't help but think of you, spending your birthday without your father. I told her I wanted to get home—to be the kind of dad you deserved." He exhaled a bitter laugh. "Well, can't win 'em all, can you?"

"You weren't a bad father—you were just—" I struggled to find the right word, something that only seemed to make his smile stretch higher.

"An asshole? It's okay, I can take it."

"No," I disagreed with a shake of my head. "It's like, when you were drinking, you loved to make people laugh. And then you sobered up, and you weren't that same person anymore. You were closed-off."

"I thought if I lived by the rules, it'd make up for the time we lost..." His words trailed off as he stared off into the void again.

"But it wasn't just you," I argued, tightening my hands into fists. "You put all that shit on me. Reed men do this, and Reed men don't do that. Hell, even when it came to baseball, there was always some way I could have been better!"

He flinched at my raised voice before taking a deep breath. "I was like you with baseball. It was the one thing that always made sense to me and kept me sane. When I lost it, I spiraled. It was like I didn't know who I was anymore. When I got sober, I thought it fell to me to keep you from making the same mistake. Instead, it just pushed you away."

I studied my father's profile, seeing myself. The similarities ran deeper than physical traits. He and I were like two halves of a coin—forever on opposite sides yet made of the same stuff.

Maybe it wasn't a coincidence the woman he'd described reminded me of Ari.

Maybe it took a certain kind of woman to make men like us want to be better.

Sensing my stare, he glanced over to me with a wry smile. "You've got that look in your eyes—it's the same one you have when you're up at the plate, trying to read the pitcher. Does this have anything to do with that broken heart Conor mentioned? Or are you just trying to decide where to sock your old man?"

I rubbed my eyes as thoughts of Ari took over again. My buzz and what remained of my resolve had worn off sometime during the car ride home, but Bailey's impromptu sermon was like an energy drink, bouncing off the walls of my brain. "He gets a few too many in him and—you know what? Doesn't matter."

He stretched out, placing his feet up on the coffee table and settling against the back of the couch. "I know I'm not your teammate or your mama, but I'm a good listener, and I've got all night."

I shook my head. "Nah, it's not worth getting into again. I just need to sleep it off. In the morning, I'll be good as new."

The side of his mouth tugged up into another grin. "I see. So, what is it that's holding you back from this girl?"

"What makes you think something is holding me back? It didn't work out. Game over." I sounded like Bailey when he'd been describing his one-night stand.

My father laughed to himself. "If there wasn't something standing in your way, you would've been out with her, not Conor."

"It's not like—" My nostrils stung in warning, but I clenched my jaw and shook my head, fighting to keep it together.

"Killian." He cupped the side of my head in his palm. "Let me in —not because I deserve it, but because you do. I bottled up my emotions for too long, afraid you'd see me as weak. But sometimes, the strongest thing we can do is make ourselves vulnerable. So, you wanna cry? Cry. You wanna punch something? I'll grab you a pillow. But, for the love of God, be better than me, son."

With that, the wound in my chest tore open. I didn't fight it, letting the pain and grief strip me down to nothing.

Only this time, I wasn't forced to go through it alone.

My father's arms came around me, holding me through the broken sentences and soul-crushing sobs that made up my story. Eventually, my words and tears tapered off in a rough exhale. We were left with silence. He stayed quiet for so long that I'd started to doze, only to jerk myself awake when he finally spoke.

"What is it you want?"

"I don't know," I admitted as I pulled away.

He nodded. "Yeah, you do. I look at you, and I see a kid who's never settled for anything in his life. Remember those exercises we used to do before your games in high school?"

"Dad, no," I pleaded, running a hand across my eyes. "I'm not visualizing—"

"Close your eyes." His lips pressed into a thin line. I obeyed, but only because I was too tired to argue.

Closing my eyes... playing in the limes—what did a man have to do to get some real advice around here?

"Here it is—five years from now, the Hurricanes have just won game seven of the World Series. You're standing on the field, surrounded by your teammates and reporters, but you're not looking at them. You're looking up into the seats. Who are you waiting for? Who's rushing down to the field to get to you?"

I envisioned it—the deafening roar of the crowd, the stadium lights shining down on me, and a flash of red hair moving through waves of people. The woman who saw the man beneath the player.

"Ari," I whispered as I turned back to him. "It's only ever been Ari."

"You've never wanted something handed to you. Even when you knew it would be harder, you wanted to earn it yourself. Why should this be any different? If you can visualize it, you can make it happen. But first, you need a plan."

CHAPTER EIGHTEEN
ARIANA

*"He's more myself than I am. Whatever our souls are made out of,
his and mine are the same. If all else perished, and he remained, I
should still continue to be; and if all else remained, and he were
annihilated, the universe would turn to a mighty stranger."*

-Emily Brontë, *Wuthering Heights*

"THIS ISN'T GOING TO WORK."

"What do you mean?" I checked my reflection and adjusted the
baseball cap again, avoiding the dark circles and translucent skin that
begged for some attention. "We have a plan. We're sticking to the
plan."

When Tsega had offered her help, it seemed she'd been under the
assumption I needed clothes and some cash—not an accomplice in a
covert operation involving aliases and seedy motel rooms.

Clearly, I was the criminal mastermind of our little group.

I tightened one of my pigtails and, feeling the weight of her glare,
turned with a sigh. "What? Don't tell me you're getting cold feet
now."

On Saturdays, *True North* offered field trips into the city for patients who met specific criteria. Now that I was almost exclusively walking, Natalie had cleared me to attend.

But I had no intention of returning.

I'd wanted someone to save me, but ghost Ashlynn had been right. Only I could save me.

"Do I need to remind you I've been against this plan of yours since day one? Ariana, you're not ready."

Tsega paced the room, listing the cons on her fingers. "One, you won't have access to your medication—medication you absolutely need, I might add. Two, the money won't last forever, and you won't be able to get a job using a fake name. Three—and this is a big one—you can run across the world if you want, but you won't be able to escape your feelings."

Dammit.

My heart sank, but the time for falling apart had passed. So maybe I'd spent the last ten days wallowing in my misery like a pig in the mud—it didn't mean I was broken.

Perhaps I wasn't the embodiment of health and wellness, but I was still breathing, wasn't I?

"Anything else?" I managed not to roll my eyes. Between her and Georgia, I wasn't sure whose lectures were worse. For two women who'd pushed me to take a stand, they'd had a surprisingly negative response to my plan to run.

"Yeah, there is actually," she said, matching my defiant tone. "The aquarium is a lot of fun. I think you might be pleasantly surprised."

"I highly doubt that," I muttered under my breath as we walked down to the bank of elevators.

Tsega tightened her grip on my arm before leaning in to whisper, "I heard that. It'd be a shame if you missed the field trip and had to stay in your room for the rest of the day."

"What are you, my mother?" I hissed. "You're supposed to support me on this—what happened to not fighting alone?"

She faked a smile as someone passed us in the hall, dropping it as soon as they were out of sight. "There's fighting back, and then there's suicide. I'll let you guess which one your plan falls under. Trust me, you'll thank me later."

I tried not to feel sorry for myself on the ride down to the lobby, but it wasn't easy when nothing in my life was going according to plan.

As if it wasn't bad enough that I woke every morning to the memory of his kiss, Killian's ghost refused to vacate the dang building. I was being haunted by the familiar squeak of crutches. When my heart realized the truth, I'd been forced to relive the loss of him all over again.

He wasn't coming back.

It was time to come to terms with the fact that the feelings I'd developed were one-sided. But, as Tsega and Georgia were currently thwarting my every attempt at moving on, I didn't see the harm in allowing myself an extra couple of days to be sad.

No need to rush my grief.

By the time we stepped off the elevator, I was making a mental list on the benefits of using shower wailing as a form of therapy.

Therefore, I didn't immediately respond to my name being spoken. It wasn't until Tsega squeezed my bicep that I shelved the idea of pitching it to the facility's psychologists, and reluctantly returned to reality.

"Aren't you glad you decided to take my advice?" she whispered with a smug grin.

"That's not been officially decided..." My words cut off abruptly as I registered the movement.

Killian was crossing the lobby, his icy blue eyes holding me captive. As he wasn't passing through people, I could only assume that this time, he wasn't a figment of my imagination.

I tried straightening to meet his piercing gaze, only to suck in a strangled breath. The nest of birds had gathered around my heart, poking and prodding it to take a leap right out of my chest. Anything to be near him.

He didn't feel the same way I did, and his sudden reappearance didn't change that. He was probably just here to sign some papers or grab a sandwich because he missed the cafeteria's food.

While I tried rationalizing his presence, my heart was busy working through a slew of new tricks like a well-trained puppy.

Roll over.

Sit up and beg.

Play dead.

This did nothing in the way of calming my nerves. I released a ragged exhale, completely winded just by the sight of him.

Tsega disentangled herself from my grip and pushed me toward him with a decidedly unprofessional snort. "You're welcome."

His grin widened as he came to a stop in front of me.

I channeled every bit of my focus into not jumping into his arms.

Mainly because he still had the one crutch.

But also, because he left with no explanation.

"Did you..." I cleared my throat, struggling to keep the affection out of my voice. "Did you forget something?"

"Yeah." Killian nodded before reaching up to cup my cheek, letting his thumb caress my bottom lip. "This."

His head lowered to mine, and I forgot to breathe—forgot that someone might see—forgot anything that existed beyond the two of us. It was selfish, but I'd missed the feeling of finding my face reflected in his eyes and basking in the glow of his attention.

I watched from under my lashes, wanting to witness the moment Killian claimed my mouth with his. Instead, he held back, letting his forehead rest against mine while his thumb continued tracing a path across my lips.

More.

"I needed this," he murmured, his minty breath warming my skin.

The fluttering in my chest migrated lower, leaving me aching for the unfamiliar. A man shouldn't have had the ability to work me into a frenzy just by breathing on me.

Clearly, my previous heart issues were just indicators of a more serious underlying condition. A condition that left me willing to give up my plans of escape for more of Killian.

The moment ended just as quickly as it began when someone announced the bus' arrival. I pulled away, expecting an audience, but it seemed the massive art installation just off the elevators had kept us hidden from view.

In fact, the only person watching was Killian. His chest rose and fell steadily as he waited for me to say something. His self-control might have remained intact, but I was on the verge of spontaneously combusting and needed a moment to collect myself.

We hadn't seen each other in ten days, and I wasn't ready to walk away again, even if Tsega had insisted that the aquarium was a good time.

I wanted answers—and more kissing, dammit!

"Ari."

I shook my head, still wrestling with my emotions. "Not yet. I'm not ready."

Killian released a pained breath before taking a step back. There was nothing calm in the way he dragged his hands through his hair. "Look, Fynn said seizures could be caused by stress. I felt like—like maybe I was taking advantage of a situation."

In spite of the serious nature of Killian's confession, I burst out laughing. Given that my preliminary plan had involved using him as a means of escape, it seemed like an entirely logical response.

"They tried to wean me off my seizure medication. Turns out, that was a terrible idea," I explained with another chuckle.

Killian, however, did not share my humor. His lovely and decidedly un-caterpillar-like eyebrows pulled together in concern as he took in my reaction. "I just wanted to say I'm sorry—"

My smile faded. I hated that his rejection could crush my spirit as easily as his absence had. "You're sorry—so, you came all this way just to clear your conscience?"

It would have been easier if he'd never come back at all. Because this time, I'd be forced to watch as he walked away from me for the last time.

"I—" His throat bobbed in a swallow. "Is that what you want?"

No.

Yes.

Can we go back to the part where you kiss me, and we never have conversations that feel like goodbye?

After blinking away the conflicting thoughts and sudden tears of frustration that pricked my eyes, I offered up my best fake smile. "Look, I've got to go—the bus is waiting."

I brushed past him, allowing my nostrils the sadistic pleasure of furiously inhaling his cologne, before making my way toward the front doors.

See—progress.

"Ari." I heard the squeak of his crutch behind me and considered breaking into a sprint to avoid hearing anything else. "Ari, wait!"

It only hurts if you let it...

I turned, trying to coerce my wobbling lips into another smile before giving up with a growl. "What? What else is there to say? I'm sorry I had a seizure and made you change your mind? Seriously, you could have saved yourself the trip because I got the message loud and clear the first time."

There was a small part of me that longed to tell him I was the one who'd saved him, just to see his reaction. But I wouldn't trap a man in a cage built of obligation, forcing even the smallest measures of admiration to wither into resentment.

Killian's face paled, and he came to a sudden stop. "Changed my mind? Jesus Christ, Ariana. You really think I'd tell you I wanted to be with you, only to take it back the next day?"

Promises were easily made and easily broken; I knew that as well as anybody.

His eyes narrowed as he took a step toward me. "Answer the question. Do you really think that you mean so little to me—"

"I woke up, and you were gone," I whispered, avoiding his gaze, afraid of what I might find reflected in his eyes. "What was I supposed to think?"

Killian flinched at the cold assessment before jerking his chin in a nod. "You're right. I got scared and ran, thinking nothing could be worse than the seven minutes I held you during that seizure. Turns out, I was wrong. The hardest thing has been living without you for the last ten days."

"Why did you come back, Killian?"

I had to will my feet to stay where they were when he admitted, "I came back for you if you'll have me."

The tingling sensation returned with a vengeance as I watched his teeth come together, flexing the muscle in his jaw. But before I flung myself into his arms and plastered his face with kisses, I had a few questions I needed answered.

"What if it happens again?"

He stilled. "I won't leave if that's what you're asking—not unless you want me to. No amount of apologizing can take away the hurt I caused when I walked away from you, and that will haunt me for the rest of my life. The only thing I can do is keep showing up to prove it to you."

This time, I erased the distance between us to place my hand against his chest, feeling the steady thrumming beneath my palm. "Do you promise you won't look at me differently than you did before —" I bit down on my lip. "I don't want you staying out of some sense of pity."

Killian held my eyes with his. "I feel a lot of things when I look at you, Ari, but pity isn't one of them."

The rumbled tone of his voice reignited the spark of longing in my lower belly, and I gazed up at him in confusion.

What was he doing to me?

He chuckled at my dazed expression before bringing his arms up to encircle my waist, tucking my head beneath his chin. "I missed you, girl."

I didn't care if someone saw us. It felt right—like maybe I'd been made to fit him. So, I stopped holding my breath long enough to whisper, "I missed you too, Killian."

———

"What's wrong? I thought you'd love this place."

I frowned distractedly at the glass, just as puzzled by my reaction as Killian seemed to be. When Tsega first mentioned the aquarium, I'd envisioned a few fish tanks, backlit by fluorescent bulbs. But this was an elaborate theme park, complete with underwater tunnels and a train that passed through the shark tank.

The only real light came from within, casting everything in soft blue light. Sea life surrounded us on both sides, immersing us in an oceanic experience, and making it hard to pinpoint what it was about this place that left me feeling unsettled.

"It's just," I paused as a sea turtle lazily swam up, suddenly overwhelmed with sadness. "They'll be confined within these plexiglass boxes forever."

Killian used his crutch like a cane as he moved to join me at the loggerheads' case. "I don't know, they look pretty happy to me."

A smaller one watched him curiously, using a flipper to drag itself along the front of the case. "Hey, little guy. See? He's damn near smiling." He tapped his fingers lightly against the glass. The loggerhead moved closer, before turning its head toward me.

"Wait a minute, buddy," Killian chuckled, rolling up his sleeves. "You moving in on my girl? I think he's hitting on you, Ari. Hold my crutch, because I'm gonna have to kick this turtle's ass."

I smiled at the possessiveness in his words and turned to study his profile. Not long after his apology, Tsega had appeared from behind the art installation to drag me onto the bus. Once he realized that *True North* had rented out the entire space for the day, Killian decided to tag along.

Separately—as in, he brought his own vehicle.

It hadn't exactly left us with an opportunity to talk or perhaps repeat a particular earth-shattering kiss, just to see if it was as good as I remembered.

After all, I did have a brain injury, so really, it was for purely scientific reasons that I found myself staring at his full lips. I'd been holding my hand down at my side for the last hour, flexing my fingers, practically begging him to touch me.

It was an invitation he'd yet to accept.

"Look at him, just eyeing you like I'm not even standing here," Killian said in mock frustration, the side of his mouth quirking up ever so slightly.

"How can he be happy in a place like this?"

He kept his eyes on the glass when he answered as if he was conversing with his reptilian enemy, and not me. "Well, according to the sign, loggerheads are endangered. In here, he has the perfect habitat and is completely safe from predators. Oh, and he never has to worry about food—sounds like a kick-ass life to me."

My chest tightened when I realized what it was that bothered me.

The turtle was me.

"Maybe he seems happy because he doesn't know anything else. Maybe, to him, the walls have always been there. And sure, he's safe from predators, but only because he's living as a prisoner. He'll never know the world beyond this box—forced to rely on his captors for everything!" Several staff members turned at the sound of my raised voice. I gave a weak wave before turning away in embarrassment.

Killian lifted a brow, blatantly amused by my outburst. "You alright there, slugger? Are we still talking about the turtle?"

Were we?

Even before his return, I'd considered tabling my plans of escape.

Tsega was right, I wasn't in any condition to brave the world on my own. But this place with its pretty glass cages stoked my fears, making me think that maybe I'd never be fully prepared.

"Let's look at something else." My tone was laced with desperation, but I strode ahead, hoping he hadn't seen the terror reflected in my eyes.

The bright colors seemed dull now that I saw them for what they were—*possessions*. Endangered and rare were interchangeable terms here, something that made an object more valuable to its owner.

Why else would they display their shiny, exotic collectibles in glass cases if not to boast of their wealth and power?

If those loggerheads were scarred or damaged in some way, they'd still be in the ocean, blissfully unaware that places like this existed. They wouldn't be worth catching.

Just like Brad hadn't bought me. He'd purchased the one thing that made me valuable, something worth conquering. Once I'd been stripped of it, he'd lock me in a pretty cage, only trotting me out for show.

When Ashlynn had admitted to losing her virginity to Matt, she'd lost her worth in Tristan's eyes. Back then, I was ignorant of just how deep the corruption went, never imagining the uproar it would have caused had the church found out. At the very least, the scandal would have put an end to Tristan's lucrative side business.

I swallowed, suddenly dizzy with the realization that I'd just discovered Tristan's motive for murder. He hadn't just auctioned off his daughters to the wealthy donors within the church. He was a man who was willing to permanently silence anyone or anything to keep his secrets safe.

If Matt had tried to speak out over Ashlynn's death, I never heard it. But by then, he might have been off fighting in a war. Maybe he'd come home and just assumed she'd moved on.

Killian's hand moved to my lower back, sending a small jolt of excitement through my core. The visceral reaction was enough to send my thoughts scurrying off in an entirely new direction—one that involved dark corners and kissing... *lots and lots of kissing.*

"You're making that face again," he noted dryly, his fingers tightening against my skin. "Hate to break it you, slugger, but everything in here is locked behind glass."

I licked my suddenly dry lips before meeting his stare. "Yeah? That doesn't seem right."

"You wanna see it wild and free, maybe you'd better put in a request for a field trip to the ocean next time."

With the exception of an accident I couldn't remember, I'd lived my entire life in *next times* and *maybes*, letting someone else dictate my fate. If I didn't try to chart my own course, then Killian would eventually become just one more thing I missed.

"Promise me we'll go someday," I said in a wobbly voice, extending my pinky finger. "Right here, right now."

Killian took it in his with a grin. "Absolutely, slugger. Once you're released, we'll go down to Galveston for the day. I was also thinking, if it doesn't interfere with your schedule, maybe you'd like to join me in West Palm Beach for spring training. You wouldn't have to stay the whole time—"

What would it be like—to only feel small when wading into the vast waters of the ocean?

"Yes," I breathed, releasing his finger to run my hand along the outside of his arm. He released a sharp breath when I tugged him forward. Closer. "I'd like that."

A visible shudder moved down Killian's body, the muscle in his jaw twitching as he debated with himself.

Disappointment wrapped around my heart like one of the tentacles on my necklace. I needed him to touch me, to erase all the doubts in my mind that told me we could never be together.

He lowered his head to mine, speaking softly through gritted teeth. "Do you know how hard it is for me not to kiss you when you touch me like that? But I don't know if our rule is still in effect.

Christ, Ari. Do you need me to be your friend here—what do you want?"

I lifted my chin, fighting the smile tugging at my lips. "I just want you to treat me like a normal girl."

Killian's eyes flashed as they moved over my body, lingering for a few extra seconds on my breasts before he jerked his chin in a nod.

"There's just one problem with that," he bit out in a taut voice. "You're not a normal girl."

"Oh." I let my arm fall back to my side and put some distance between us, trying to inject cheerfulness in my tone as I stopped in front of another case. "Did you see these? Longnose killifish. That's interesting."

You know what else was interesting? Being told you weren't normal and not knowing whether it was a compliment or an insult.

"Hey," Killian murmured in my ear, his fingertips trailing lightly down my spine. "That didn't come out quite like I'd hoped it would."

He straightened when a couple of patients from our group stopped to read the sign. I took the opportunity to turn around to face him, searching his eyes for some insight into what he was feeling.

"Come here."

With his left hand on my shoulder, Killian led me through the door for the bathrooms and into a deserted hallway. The lighting was harsh compared to the aquarium's, and it took several seconds for my eyes to adjust.

"What are—"

I didn't get a chance to complete the thought before he was pushing me forward. There was an audible thud as his crutch fell to the concrete, and the heavy door slammed shut behind us.

Killian's chest brushed against mine as he guided me back against a wall, before bracing his hands over my head. "I'm sorry." He released a sharp breath. "I suck at saying the right thing—"

"Don't," I warned, letting my hands slowly move up the muscles in his arms before coming to rest against his neck. It seemed like a tragedy that he'd brought me in here just to apologize. He pulled away, and I tightened my grip with a growl of frustration.

Did this man not understand how badly I needed to touch him?

"Ari—" Killian pleaded, the muscle in his jaw twitching in earnest as he inhaled a deep breath. His resolve was close to slipping, he just needed a little push.

"I need to feel you." I reached for his hand, placing it against my hip. "Don't you want that?"

"Does it fucking feel like I don't want that?" He growled, grinding his hard length against the lower part of my belly. "If you'd let me, I'd fuck you up against this wall right now. But you're not a normal girl. Not to me."

There it was again.

Two words that felt like a judgment.

"Why?" I stifled a moan as my hips arched forward, instinctively seeking the friction of him. "Because of my brain injury? The seizure? What is it that makes me so abnormal to you?"

My body's response was foreign but not unwelcome. If sex wasn't meant to be pleasurable, then why did the mere feel of Killian leave me needy with want?

"Christ," he muttered with a ragged breath, tightening his hold on my hip. "I ache for you, Ari, in a way that I've never experienced with anyone else. But our first time together won't be in a dirty hallway—"

It wasn't that dirty.

"Please," I begged, throwing in some very unladylike moans. I didn't want to stop, not when it felt so good. Killian caught my hands as they inched their way down his torso, quickly pinning them above my head with a low growl.

Sensing that I wasn't about to be deterred, he dipped down and let his full lips brush against mine. His tongue moved in all the ways I wished his body would, tangled and twisted around me.

There was something incredibly sensual in the way he held my hands against the wall, guiding our movements using only his mouth.

His stubble roughly scraped along my jaw, his lips devouring my earlier doubts.

Killian was mine—he'd always been meant to be mine.

I hissed out a breath when his teeth connected with my throat, nipping and sucking the sensitive flesh. When his tongue swept over the same area, I was painfully aware of what it meant to be 'turned on.'

Everything felt buzzy and electric. Like I was entirely made of nerves.

I rocked forward and struggled against him, needing to ground myself, but he refused to budge. My nipples peaked against my bra. I was convinced I needed his mouth there too.

My lids fluttered open, and I watched in wonder as his bicep flexed just inches from my face. All that strength, yet he was holding back, his grip on my wrists just enough to keep me still. The blood left my limbs, sending a flood of warmth between my legs.

Killian released my hands and pulled back, his blue-gray eyes drowsy and unfocused as they moved down over my face. "Did I hurt you?" he panted.

"No—why'd you stop?" I whined, which was entirely out of character.

He let out a rough bark of laughter, his chest rising and falling as he fought to catch his breath. "Because you've never done this before."

I snapped my mouth shut, something that only seemed to make him laugh harder. As the nerve endings in my body were still sparking like live wires, I didn't exactly share his amusement.

Killian released another unsteady breath before backing toward the opposite wall. "I'm not gonna lie—I've been rock hard for the better part of the afternoon, seeing you in those leggings and imagining this. But you deserve better than a quick fuck outside of a bathroom. Let me give you that... please."

"Okay," I whispered, feeling frustrated but also slightly pleased that being near me had affected him physically.

His eyes moved to mine as he bent to retrieve his crutch from the floor. "I can tell you're in your head right now, but I promise you, this isn't me changing my mind, girl. I just wanna slow things down and take my time with you."

I pressed my fingers to my swollen lips, fighting against arousal and the sudden urge to take another meandering glance at the notice-able bulge in the front of his sweats—*for scientific reasons.*

Instead, I corralled my wild libido and nodded. "What do you say we go introduce ourselves to those longnose killifish?"

We exited to find Tsega waiting just outside the door with her arms crossed over her chest. Her lips pursed in amusement as she took in our dishevelment. "I didn't realize they had more tanks back there. Anyway, everyone's on the bus. We're just waiting on you."

"Yeah, I've got to head back to my condo," Killian rushed to explain before turning to face me. "Thanks for letting me tag along. I was thinking—if you're up for it—I could maybe have you for dinner. Take you to dinner, I mean! Next Saturday?"

His slip of the tongue set off another explosive chain of sensations within my body, and I ended up blurting, "Why not tomorrow? I'm free tomorrow!"

A flash of something like hunger darkened his expression. Instead of another pleasure-inducing kiss, Killian just brushed his lips over my cheek before pulling back. "Next Saturday, it is."

I observed his hasty retreat with a thoughtful frown, wondering if there would ever be a day when he wasn't running away from me.

Tsega watched him go before shifting her gaze back to me. "Seems like you've made quite the impression on him."

I huffed a laugh. "That man is like a mountain. And I don't know what it's going to take to move him."

"Interesting," she mused with a thoughtful nod. "You know, seeing as to how you're already wearing most of my clothes, what if I loaned you a dress for next weekend?"

"Um..." I scrunched my nose. "I'm not sure that's going to do much. He's seen me in dresses before."

She winked. "Not one of mine."

"That's true," I conceded. "While you're at it, could you get me some underwear too? Not regular underwear, though. Something sexy."

"Oh, Ariana," Tsega laughed, shaking her head in mock exasperation. "What am I going to do with you?"

It wasn't her actions, but Killian's I was most interested in.

What would he be willing to do with me?

CHAPTER NINETEEN
KILLIAN

"It's unbelievable how much you don't know about the game you've been playing all your life."

-Mickey Mantle

"SO, where are you taking her? *The Corner Bistro* is supposed to be good—" Tsega paused to give me a once-over before shaking her head. "No, you're not really dressed nice enough for that. Guess it's ninety-nine cent pitchers of beer and a basket of wings down at the sports bar, huh?"

I'd worn my nicest jeans and button-down shirt too, dammit.

"Thanks for the vote of confidence, pal," I muttered as she playfully socked me in the arm. If the mischievous smirk was any indicator, she was going to continue to play dirty to get what she wanted out of me.

Tsega had been hounding me since I stepped foot in the parking lot. The tiny woman went after information like a terrier with a chew-toy—not that I'd dare voice that thought.

No, I enjoyed my balls right where they were, thank you very much.

She punched the button for Ari's floor as we stepped onto the elevator before lowering her hand to her hip. "As I've been forced to hear about this date no less than a hundred times today, the least you can do is tell me where you're going."

But I wasn't willing to divulge a single detail. It was my first real chance to be alone with Ari, and I wasn't willing to take the chance of anything spoiling our first official date. It was in my nature to be a little superstitious, which was probably why I'd gone ahead and worn my lucky socks too.

Technically, it wasn't our first date, as we'd shared meals several times over the last eight weeks. There was something about being able to touch her without a nurse or staff member nearby that made tonight different.

I couldn't think of getting Ari alone without recalling last weekend at the aquarium—the feel of her body pressed against mine, the taste of her skin, the unapologetically loud moans she'd given me when I used my teeth.

Suffice it to say that I'd enjoyed some very lengthy shower sessions over the past seven days.

But we were taking things slow. I made a show of checking my watch to clear the images from my head while debating whether or not I should have gone with a bigger bouquet of flowers when I was suddenly confronted with all five feet, zero inches of Tsega's attitude.

"You know I could make this date very uncomfortable for you, buddy."

I cocked my head to the side, thoroughly amused. "Did you ask me something, Tsega?"

She calmly leaned back against the railing, her lips twisting to the side. I was more than a little surprised her head hadn't popped off from all that bottled up energy. "I know something you don't."

"Good for you." *Nice try.* I wasn't breaking that easily.

"Yep." Tsega took a step toward me, keeping her chin high as if trying to appear taller. "It involves lace..."

"Okay, and?" I scoffed, trying to hide the fact that my jeans suddenly felt too tight. I should have gone with the joggers, or maybe a nice pair of pajama pants. No one ever considered pajama pants— fashion's most underrated piece of clothing.

Comfort over style, Reed.

"I'm talking skimpy little scraps of lace. Now, what's the purpose of something that's not only see-through but doesn't even cover—"

"*Papi's!*" I snapped, regretting that I hadn't thought to take care of myself beforehand. Nothing was guaranteed to end a first date faster than me showing up with a hard-on. "Christ, I'm taking her to *Papi's.* I know the owner, and it's one of the few places I can go where no one bothers me. After, I thought we'd go next door to *Anchor Lounge.* There, are you happy now, you maniacal little fairy?"

Tsega nodded with a wide grin. "Oh, extremely. I like you, Reed. You're good people."

"Yeah? You have a funny way of showing it," I grumbled, my mouth twitching before I could stop it.

The elevator *dinged.* Tsega waited until the doors opened before adding, "Two words—black lace." With that, she stepped off the elevator, laughing like an evil villain in a children's cartoon.

Fuck.

"What?" I stumbled off behind her, my mouth dry and thoughts somewhere in the basement level of the building. She bounced down the hall excitedly, nearly catching me in the face with her high pony-tail several times. "You can't do that to a man—"

"Oh, I'm sorry. Did you ask me something?"

I shook my head, refusing to play her game any longer. "Nah, I'm good."

"Are you?" She cut her eyes over to me. "You seem a little, I don't know, flushed. And also, why are you still hauling around the crutch? Thought you were cleared."

"Just feel a little more comfortable having it with me."

"So, the crutch has become your crutch. That's really deep, buddy." Tsega tried for serious, lasting all of three seconds.

"How have they not fired you yet?" I shook my head. Truthfully, I was grateful for the distraction. It had given me a chance to get certain parts of my anatomy under my control again.

"Probably because I'm awesome," Tsega responded with a snort. "Although, if I'd been assigned to you—whew, boy—we would have had some trouble!" She suddenly tensed, all traces of amusement gone.

"What?" I followed her glare to a man about my father's age standing near the nurse's station.

"Just—go along with anything I say," Tsega finally said. Her tone made it seem as if things were normal, but it was impossible to miss the way she watched the man—like an animal would a hunter. "Please."

I nodded and reached out, trying to decide whether to go for the side hug or a pat on the back. Tsega didn't seem likely to respond well to either, so I just let my hand hover a few inches above her shoulders. In the elevator, the pretend frustration had been fun to watch, but this Tsega was scary—like capable of ripping someone's throat out with her teeth scary.

The man smiled when he saw her and crooked a finger, signaling her to come.

"Do you want me to handle this?"

She shook her head, refusing to meet my eyes. "Just please don't say anything, okay?"

"Yes, sir?" Tsega asked with a forced smile.

"Yeah, she's having a rough night. I think it'd be best if the nurses gave her medicine early—let her sleep it off, you know?" He reached down to adjust his expensive watch, drawing attention to the fact that he had money. He reminded me of a peacock, or maybe Theo, although my agent didn't seem to have the confidence that this guy did.

"Okay, Mr. Phillips. I'll let them know."

The man turned as if suddenly realizing I was standing there. His annoyed expression quickly turned to scrutiny. "Hey, aren't you that baseball player?"

There was an undercurrent of condescension in his tone. Apparently, being a player was somehow beneath him.

"I am," I said tightly, clenching my fist around the flowers. I wouldn't hit the guy, because Tsega had asked me to let her handle it. And also, because there was a clause in my contract forbidding fights.

"Brad Phillips." He extended his hand with a slight sneer.

Tsega has it under control...

Four hundred twenty-five million...

I reluctantly accepted his hand, feeling as though my bones were going to crack.

For Christ's sake, it was a handshake, not a power-play.

"Killian Reed."

"So, what brings you here?" Brad asked as he released me from his iron grip. His bored expression made it clear he didn't care to hear my answer.

"He's visiting his grandmother," Tsega interjected quickly. "If you don't mind giving me a moment to show him to her room, I can take care of you, Brad."

"Oh, I bet you will," he said, making no attempt to disguise the fact that he was checking out her ass.

No wonder Tsega hated this prick.

He was a grade-A sleazeball.

"Buddy," I bit out through a clenched jaw. "Her eyes are up here."

His smile didn't quite reach his narrowed eyes. "Why don't you stick with the baseball thing, kid? It's what you're good at."

Four-hundred twenty-five million...

Tsega said she had this...

Rage, like I hadn't felt in a long time, turned everything around me to ash. I'd just decided that it was better to ask the Hurricanes for forgiveness rather than permission when I felt a hand on my arm.

"Don't," Tsega warned under her breath, before turning back to Brad. "If that was all you needed, I'll let the nurses know."

"It is. For now." He made a point of letting his eyes roam over her body again before heading toward the elevators, whistling loudly.

"Let's go." Instead of taking me to Ari, Tsega led me to an office. "Sit."

"I don't want—"

Her lips settled into a thin line. "Sit. I told you to let me handle it—"

"Maybe you missed it, but that guy needed to be brought down a notch or two. Who the fuck does that?"

Tsega crossed her arms over her chest and leaned against the door, clearly waiting for me to finish my tantrum. "You finished?"

"No," I grumbled. "You shouldn't have to deal with that kind of shit when you're at work. Who was he even here to see? Maybe we can get that patient thrown out—it worked with Helen."

"Ari."

"Yeah, after what she did to Ari. The director seems like a reasonable woman—"

"No, I meant he was here to see Ari."

"Oh." The chair rolled back as I dropped onto it, confusion clouding my already muddled brain.

"Oh, is right," Tsega agreed with a sigh. "Look, I shouldn't tell you this, but Ari's family is... over-bearing. Brad is a friend of her father's, so we do our best to keep him happy when he shows up."

"Why'd you lie and tell him I was visiting my grandmother, though? If Ari and I are going to be together, eventually, I'm going to have to meet her folks."

Tsega released a bitter laugh before shaking her head. "I don't think you understand. Her family will never allow her to be with you. They don't think like you and I do. If Brad even suspected that you'd looked at Ariana, she'd be gone."

"Then why help me? If her family is never going to approve, what's the point?" The question cut deep, bringing my past behavior to the surface. My track record didn't exactly lend itself to my ability to be in a relationship, but I'd believed that if Ari didn't care, it didn't matter.

I'd never considered what her family would think. With that, the ache in my chest returned, stronger than ever before.

Tsega placed a hand on my shoulder. "Because I see the way she is with you, and I think you just might be the only good thing she has in her life, Killian. Ariana deserves the freedom to make her own choices. As long as she's with me, I'm going to encourage it."

I stared ahead, realizing that even with lucky socks, some curses were impossible to break.

———

"Do you want to order something else?" I asked, pointing to Ari's untouched plate. She'd spent the last half-hour poking at her seared ahi and offering up one-word responses to just about anything I'd asked.

Nothing about tonight had gone like I'd planned. After sulking alone in Tsega's office for a half-hour, she'd returned with Ari, and the sight of her tear-stained face had taken what was left of my battered heart and pounded it into the floor.

At that point, I'd tried to gracefully bow out, but Tsega wouldn't hear of it and had herded us onto a freight elevator like cattle.

Two hours later, and it was apparent we were both miserable. I knew my reasons but hadn't been able to get Ari to admit hers.

She flinched before looking up at me with a watery smile. "No, it's good. I just don't have much of an appetite."

"I don't know that I've seen you take a single bite."

"Here." Ari shoved a forkful into her mouth with a muffled, "Is this better?"

My eyebrows raised. "Sure? I didn't mean you had to eat it, I just thought something might be wrong..." I trailed off. The food wasn't the problem—*it was Brad.*

Something about his visit had caused her to shut down, leaving me regretting my decision not to deck him when I had the chance.

Not that I could tell her that if he was a close friend of her family's. No, the wisest thing to do would be to pretend everything was fine, letting her open up on her own terms.

Once I knew what the bastard had done, we could discuss the logistics of how to maim him. I was leaning towards a baseball bat to his knees—or maybe a fastball to the groin...

Ari lowered the fork to her plate with a sigh. "Listen, I'm really sorry. I just got some bad news earlier, and now I'm taking it out on you."

"Maybe I can help," I offered with a smile. "I'm a pretty good listener."

Ari crossed her arms, dragging my attention down to her breasts. The cut of her dress offered a hint of cleavage, but not enough for me to verify Tsega's black lingerie claim.

Skimpy little scraps of lace...

"I'll be fine. Really."

"I'm serious," I added, sliding my palm across the table. "I used to be able to cheer my mama up when she was sad."

Her forehead furrowed. "And what about you, Killian? Who cheered you up?"

I scratched at my jaw and blinked before bringing my eyes back to hers. It was too warm in here all of a sudden. "Uh, I usually just hit the batting cages when I need to cool down and clear my mind."

Ari's shoulders sagged, and she looked down at her lap. Christ, it was maddening not being able to get inside her head. She seemed to have no trouble reading me while keeping her own emotions locked down.

She was breathtaking but broken in a way even I couldn't fix. Not if she wouldn't let me in. The reality of the situation came up on me like a rogue wave, taking my legs out from under me.

If what Tsega said was true, then we had an expiration date, whether I wanted it or not.

"Hey," I said softly, bringing her eyes back to mine. "Don't lower your head. Don't give anyone that kind of power over you."

"I'm sorry—"

I shook my head with a sympathetic smile. "Christ, slugger, do you always apologize for things you have no control over?"

Ari's lips parted and then snapped together just as quickly. I winced when she covered her face until I heard her throaty laughter.

"I do!" She placed her hand over mine and leaned in, breaking the invisible barrier between us. "Do you ever feel like..."

"Like what?" I asked, giving her fingers a light squeeze.

She sighed. "I don't know if this is the best way to describe it, but like you're an object and not a person? Does that make sense?"

"Perfect sense," I answered with a mirthless chuckle, remembering how my own agent had referred to me as a product.

"Yeah, I guess that's how I feel," Ari admitted, drawing her lower lip between her teeth. "Like my thoughts and opinions are a nonstarter to my father. Just once, I'd like the freedom to be able to choose what I want for myself."

I took a drink of my iced tea, wishing it was something a little stronger. "What would you choose?"

"Hmmm..." she deliberated, her green eyes sizing me up. "Sorry, this is a tough one."

The side of my mouth lifted in a smirk. "You take as much time as you want looking. Sometimes, the answer's right in front of you."

Ari's nose crinkled as she laughed. "Wow, Killian! Hey, look all you want, slugger. I'm the only answer you'll ever need. Did I mention I'm a super famous baseball player?"

I rolled my eyes at her over-the-top impersonation. "That's not what I meant. I don't even sound like that!"

"Ladies, I play—baseball." She snorted suddenly, which only served to make her laugh harder. "I'm Killian Reed."

"Stop," I said, fighting a smile of my own. "That's a terrible impression. Unless you think I sound like Batman, which, I don't."

After dabbing the corners of her eyes with the napkin, she grinned up at me. "I needed that. Thank you."

"Anytime," I deadpanned, but I wasn't lying. If it meant hearing Ari laugh like that, I'd let her make jokes at my expense for the rest of our lives.

Fuck, what happened to baby steps?

I glanced up when I saw Yuri, the owner of *Papi's*, approaching our table. "Hey, hey! You didn't say you were coming by tonight. I would have gotten you a better table, where no one would bother you."

No one ever approached me for autographs here. That, along with the fantastic food, were the two reasons I kept coming back.

"And this is exactly why I don't tell you when I'm stopping by," I joked, before gesturing to Ari. "Yuri, this is my girlfriend, Ari. Ari, this is Yuri. He's the owner of *Papi's*."

He bowed his head, taking her hand in his. "*Cariño*, it's a pleasure to meet you. This guy never brings anyone here. I was beginning to take it personally."

Two bright spots of color lit up Ari's cheeks, and I wondered whether it was due to Yuri's term of endearment, or mine.

"It's nice to meet you," she beamed, before tilting her head toward me. "So, how long have you two known each other?"

Yuri pressed a kiss to her knuckle before returning her hand to mine. "Killian and I met, what was it—five years ago?"

My smile slipped. "Sounds about right. Listen, we need to get going. Could I get the check?"

He let out a booming laugh and shook his head. "It's on the house, you know this."

I opened my mouth to argue, but he'd already turned his attention back to Ari.

"I met Killian when my son was in the hospital—"

"Yuri," I said in a strangled voice. "We don't—"

He held up a finger. "Shhh... let me tell it my way. So, my son was in the hospital, and he decides to write a letter to his favorite rookie baseball player. Now, I didn't think anything would come of it, but then this guy shows up to the hospital the very next weekend bearing gifts."

"Really?" Ari's eyes widened. "Killian, that's so sweet."

"He's exaggerating," I grumbled.

Yuri cocked his head to the side, with another loud chuckle. "You're still hellbent on keeping this a secret, aren't you? Fine. I'll just say this—my son's room was packed with *Houston Hurricanes* gear thanks to someone whose name I can't mention."

"How is your son now?" Ari asked, caressing my skin with her thumb. I took the opportunity to appreciate her beauty. And I wasn't referring to her appearance, although I'd been captivated by that part of her too.

She was perfect.

"Just turned sixteen, doesn't want to do anything but sleep or play video games," Yuri complained to her. "But healthy as a damn horse. Eats like one too!"

After refusing to take my money yet again, claiming my presence alone was good enough for his business, Yuri excused himself back to the kitchen. Being the stubborn individual that I was, I left more than enough cash to cover our tab.

Ari held my gaze. "So, where to next, superstar?"

"You're not ready to call it a night?"

"Hmm... let me think." She tapped a finger against her chin, her mouth curving into a smile. "Nope. Wherever you go, I go. Well, at least until eleven o'clock. I need to be back at *True North* by then."

I pursed my lips in mock deliberation before nodding. "Alright, slugger. There's this band playing next door—"

"Yes," she interjected. "My answer is yes."

Tsega's warning came back to me as I led Ari to the door, but the tightening in my chest as she looked up at me with a hopeful grin made it clear it was too late.

Ari's roots ran deep, and I couldn't lose her without destroying myself.

CHAPTER TWENTY
KILLIAN

"Ninety percent of this game is half mental."

-Yogi Berra

OUTSIDE, the temperature had dropped a good ten degrees. Knowing I needed to get used to doing more without it, I'd left the crutch in the truck. Any doubts I might have had about the decision disappeared when Ari burrowed into my side, linking our hands together.

We made our way down to the *Anchor Lounge,* where a bouncer stood blocking the door. Ari's fingers tightened against mine, but I just tipped my chin up at the guy, and he waved us through without another word.

Once inside, I couldn't resist the opportunity to tease, "Don't you know who I am? I'm Killian Reed. I'm a super famous baseball player."

Ari barked out a relieved laugh as she followed me over to the bar. "Gosh, how could I forget that? I feel so much safer now with Killian Reed to protect me."

"Don't worry, slugger. That's what I'm here for." I ordered a beer before looking down at her. "What's your poison?"

"Just a water, please!" she yelled over the noise, waiting until the bartender had walked away before admitting, "I'm not supposed to drink with my medicine—oh, and also because I'm not old enough."

Wait—what?

I glanced around to make sure no one had heard her confession before calmly asking, "And you are... how old exactly?"

Please don't make me a predator...

"I'm nineteen—" Ari's eyes went wide. "Your face looks really pale. Did you think I was under eighteen?"

"No." *Yes, and I was just imagining how prison was going to work out for me.* "It's probably just the lighting in here."

At the sound of a woman screeching her way through the bridge of Mariah Carey's "We Belong Together," we both turned toward the stage. She'd even added her own choreography. It consisted of tossing her head back and groping her tits at the end of every line, which was impressive as she was almost too drunk to stand.

I leaned in when the old bartender slid our drinks across, raising my voice to be heard over the yowling cat on-stage. "When does Paul Eats the Hurricane go on?"

He shook his head and barked, "Don't you check the social media? Scheduling conflict, so they moved to next week. Tonight's karaoke, otherwise, it'd be standing room only in here."

Goddammit.

"Did you say Paul Eats the Hurricane?" Ari asked. "Is that really the name of the band?"

I nodded, my shoulders slumping in defeat. "Yeah, the name's out there, but you would have liked them. They're a good mix of folk and alternative rock."

"But karaoke sounds fun too."

Holding Ari in my arms while the band played "Storms for Kings" sounded fun. Being forced to spend the evening listening to drunk and off-key renditions of every single one of Mariah Carey's greatest hits sounded like my own personal hell.

"Do you have a list of songs somewhere?" Ari asked the bartender before smiling up at me. "Isn't this great?"

I shook my head. "Ari, admit it. This is fucking awful, and we don't have to stay. Trust me, these are not the people you want to hear singing. They couldn't carry a tune in a bucket."

Her mouth fell open. "But I can sing!"

Shit.

A jolt of something strange passed through my chest, similar to the feeling I got when we lost a game. It wasn't just about the song. Music was her passion, and I'd just crapped all over it.

"Anyone ever told you that you look like an uglier version of that baseball player?" The bartender accused with a scowl. "What's his name—Reeves?"

"Oh, my goodness. He really does," Ari agreed with a laugh, not meeting my gaze. "What a funny coincidence!"

He continued staring me down for a beat before directing her over to the stage. "Sweetheart, Pat's got the binder down there. Just give him your name, and he'll put you on the list."

When she turned back to me, I saw the hurt reflected in her eyes, leaving me feeling no better than Helen or that asshole, Brad. It was apparent she was preparing for me to say no, so I swallowed my pride and squeezed her shoulder.

"Come on. Let's go pick your song!"

Ari's eyes lit up. "Are you serious?"

"Dead serious, slugger."

She was practically bouncing as she dragged me toward a small table near the back before going down to the stage. I kept my head down, hoping no one recognized my face in the dim lighting.

Obscurity didn't last, and I spent the next several minutes half-heartedly scribbling my signature while watching Ari flip through the binder of songs. Her face was a mask of concentration, softening as she leaned in to ask Pat a question.

When he nodded in response, her mouth stretched into a wide grin, and she began clapping. I knew then I'd not only endure more Mariah Carey songs, but I'd also be willing to rip my own heart out if it made her happy.

Ari returned to the table, trying and failing to contain her excitement. She was like Bailey when he was jacked up on energy drinks. Her knees bounced underneath the table, and she kept sneaking glances toward the stage.

"What are you going to sing?" I asked, taking her hand in mine. "I don't think anyone's done 'Fantasy' yet."

"It's not really in my vocal range."

"Christ." I winced as the woman on stage butchered her way through 'Heartbreaker' while her date tried his hand at rapping Jay-Z's lines. "I don't think Mariah Carey's in anyone's vocal range, but it's not stopping these people."

Ari gave a short burst of laughter before shaking her head. "Don't worry, I'll be singing one of my own songs."

"Really?" I gawked.

"Yeah, really." Her whole face lit up as she spoke over the noise. "You cheered me up tonight, maybe more than you even know. This is my way of saying thank you!"

When they announced her name, my heart slammed against my ribs in a staccato rhythm. I studied her as she approached the microphone, no longer seeing the shy girl I'd met, but a woman who looked right at home on stage.

"Hey," she said with a breathless smile. "I'm Ari ,and I'd like to sing y'all a song."

It damn near made my teeth ache with how adorably sweet this girl was.

Just like in a game, everything around me faded into the background as the opening bars began to play. I didn't recognize the song, but it didn't even matter once she opened her mouth.

My jaw hung slack because Ari wasn't just a good singer—she

was a fucking phenomenon. Someone let out a whoop of approval, and I laughed, overcome by a random urge to hug everyone.

There was a strange sense of camaraderie among the audience, a collective energy we all shared, thanks to her. When she reached the chorus, people began clapping, and the hair on the back of my neck stood up. It wasn't just her incredible voice.

She was singing about me.

The song was one you'd expect to hear at church—not an Irish pub—but the lyrics were familiar to me in a way I couldn't explain. It was like Ari had taken what happened to me at the lake and set it to music, which was impossible as I'd only told her the story a little over a month ago.

And even then, I hadn't given her all the details. I thought I was completely crazy until Ari ended the song by repeating the phrase, "You are good."

I didn't believe in signs or messages from above, but those three words hit me like a fastball to the heart, turning everything I thought I knew on its head.

Tears stung my eyes, and I sucked in a breath, before joining the rest of the bar in giving my girl a standing ovation. She pushed her way through the crowd, accepting the compliments with a casual shrug and self-conscious blush.

"Ta-da," Ari exclaimed with a little bow as she reached the table. "What'd you think?"

What did I think?

Part of me was convinced she was the angel who'd saved my life. The other part was harder than granite and in the mood to do some very unreligious things to her. I didn't usually find myself aroused when listening to music, but this song had left me with a sudden need to get her all alone.

I locked a hand around her waist as someone else approached, growling, "Let's go."

Ari shot worried glances my way as I hauled her out of the bar and down the sidewalk, but I didn't trust myself to speak.

Not yet.

Not when my mind was currently traveling to some shocking places. Destinations involving sex up against the side of the building and matching last names. It was madness.

We reached my truck. I unlocked it before opening the back door. "Get in."

Okay, there was a chance I sounded a little like Batman.

Her eyes widened, but she gave me a shaky nod before sliding across the backseat. I joined her and slammed the door behind me, breathing heavily.

"Killian?"

Hearing the fear in her tone, I opened my eyes and lifted my head off the seat. "Do you have any idea how fucking amazing you are?"

She exhaled softly. "Why do you look so mad?"

"I'm not," I said in a strangled voice, before turning away. "I'm fighting to keep from touching you right now."

"Why?" There was an innocence in her question that left me eager to provide a demonstration—to show her the effect she had on my body.

"Because I haven't been with a woman in over a year and I don't —I don't think I'll be able to stop if I touch you. I need to be in control and right now..." I swallowed against the thickness in my throat. "I'm not."

"Oh. So, if I did this," Ari whispered into the dark. The leather squeaked as she moved across the bench seat and settled on my lap, straddling my legs with hers. "Would this not be okay?"

"Fuck." My hands moved to grip her thighs. "Ari, please."

"Is it your knee?" she asked, her dress riding up around her hips as she shifted forward.

"No," I groaned. "But other parts of me are feeling a little... uh, confined at the moment."

Ari's smile didn't seem as innocent when her hands began moving over my chest. "Does it hurt here?"

I shook my head. "Just give me—"

"Maybe here?" She moaned as her hips bucked against my painfully hard dick, her breath warm against my neck as she whispered, "It's okay. That's where I hurt too."

With that, I released my hold on her thighs and tugged her dress up around her waist, giving myself permission to lose control.

"What are you doing?"

I returned her grin. "Consider this my way of saying thank you."

Ari's fingers slipped into my hair, tugging my mouth up to meet hers. There was nothing slow and gentle about this kiss—we were both beyond reason.

For a woman with limited experience, Ari was a quick study and seemed to know exactly what she was doing. She lightly bit down on my lip, before lapping at me with her tongue, just like I'd done with her at the aquarium.

With a ragged pant, she straightened and reached down to where my hands were locked around her hips. "Touch me, Killian. Please."

I was sure there was probably a zipper or buttons on her dress but was too impatient to look for them. Instead, I bunched it into my fists before dragging it up under her arms. "Hold it. I wanna look at you."

Ari complied, biting down on her lip as I leaned back to drink in the sight of her on top of me. There was just enough streetlight for me to see that my girl really was covered by nothing more than scraps of lace.

"Yes," she hissed softly as I cupped her breast in my palm, stroking the material with the pad of my thumb until her nipple strained to break free.

I brought my mouth down over the other, feeling her chest swell with a sharp intake of breath as I greedily sucked her through the lace.

"Please." The word pierced the silence. "Please."

With a low growl, I released her long enough to tug the cups down, letting her breasts spill over into my palms. She lost her grip on the dress when my teeth connected with the sensitive flesh, shuddering violently in my arms.

It wasn't enough. I needed Ari naked, bracing herself on the driver's seat as I filled her body from behind. I wanted her hoarse screams of pleasure to alert the entire fucking parking lot that she was mine.

Ari pulled the dress over her head and tightened her thighs around mine. When she rocked against my erection, the last bit of air was forced from my lungs.

While one hand moved up the inside of her thigh, I used the other to massage her breasts. She jerked when my knuckles brushed over the front of her lace panties before instinctively pushing back against me.

My fingers slipped beneath the band and stroked along the soft curls until Ari's groans turned to incoherent mumbles. We weren't having sex—not tonight—but it didn't mean I couldn't alleviate her ache.

"You want me to touch you here?" I whispered, pushing the curtain of red hair off her face with my free hand until I could see her beautiful green eyes.

Her lips parted with a sigh, and she nodded drowsily, caught up in a haze of lust. I dragged my middle finger through her folds, loving the way her breath caught when I paused to lick her moisture from my skin. "You taste so fucking good."

The words of praise were accepted with a small nod. I didn't need the light to know that Ari was blushing. Her wide eyes gave it away.

I stroked her again. She lifted her hips, trying to direct my speed. When my finger was completely coated in her arousal, I slid it into her body, her inner muscles tightening around me like a vice.

Ari bit down on her lower lip with a whimpered moan and clawed at my shoulders in desperation as I established a rhythm.

I was no longer aware that I was being slowly strangled to death by denim. My entire focus had shifted to finding a way to make her feel good.

So good, she never wanted to leave me.

"Killian, more—I—I need—" Ari threw her head back as I increased my pace, circling her clit with the pad of my thumb. Her breasts bounced with each thrust of my wrist, and I lowered my mouth onto one. She came almost instantly, her body tightening and pulsing around my finger.

Ari squeezed my face against her body, muffling the sounds of her release. Her heart was like a drum, beating a frantic message against my cheek.

Mine. Mine. Mine.

She went lax in my arms, burying her face against the crook of my neck with a contented sigh. I freed my hand from between her legs, overwhelmed by a sudden, unexplainable need to protect her.

My arms came up to circle her back, gripping her hair in my fists. But the furious beating in my own chest didn't slow as it screamed the truth. I'd put Ari's needs above my own, giving up my pleasure for hers.

I thought I'd wanted to possess her, claiming her as mine in front of all the world. It was more than that. Tonight, she'd torn down walls and let me inside her world. I wanted to shield her, sacrificing myself if it meant keeping her safe. Baseball might have been my passion, but she was becoming my life—I felt it in my bones.

Because I—I loved Ari.

And with that, I knew where I wanted to take her next.

CHAPTER TWENTY-ONE
KILLIAN

"A ballpark at night is more like a church than a church."

-W. P. Kinsella, *Shoeless Joe*

I HADN'T SLEPT SOUNDLY in a week.

Without the heat on, the cab of my truck had eventually grown cold, leaving my knee stiff and achy. I'd been forced to wake a half-naked Ari, trailing kisses over the skin beneath her collarbone until she sat up with a sleepy grin.

That had only led to more kissing and touching before I managed to convince her—and myself—that she did indeed want to put her dress on before going back to *True North*.

I'd arrived back at my condo just after midnight, too keyed up to sleep. After tossing and turning for a couple of hours, I'd called Bailey to lay out my plan. He'd been half-asleep and not entirely sober at the time, so I'd ended up repeating the entire thing over a late lunch the following day.

The rest of the week had been filled with physical therapy appointments, radio interviews to discuss my contract, and a meeting with the Hurricanes' GM to make my plan a reality. Every night, I fell into bed exhausted, but wired, as I imagined how Ari was going to react to my surprise.

Incidentally, it was also when I discovered it was possible to miss someone so fiercely that it made your chest flare with pain.

A man in love did not do well on his own.

I needed to see her more than once a week—to hear her voice at the end of the day when I got home. Anything to alleviate the near-constant heartburn I'd been experiencing.

Hopefully, in just a few short minutes, all of the sleepless nights and feelings of reflux were going to be worth it.

The light ahead changed from yellow to red. I slowed to a stop, before cutting my eyes over to the passenger seat, where someone was fidgeting with her blindfold.

I lifted an eyebrow in question. "What are you doing over there, girl?"

"You stopped," Ari protested, one side of her mouth quirking up. "That means we're there, right?"

"So impatient." My hand moved to caress her thigh, and she jerked away with a startled gasp.

"Gah, Killian! Warn me before you do that. I can't see anything, remember?"

I clicked my tongue against my teeth with a low chuckle, finding her stern expression cute. "What—did you think someone else was touching you?"

"No, but I could have hurt you just now—so badly."

"Really? I think I'd enjoy the hell out of that." I smirked as a red flush crept up her throat and flipped on my signal before turning into the lot.

Ari's hands immediately went to the blindfold. "Are we here?"

"Almost." I pulled up to my reserved spot and shifted the truck into park. "But don't take it off yet."

She exhaled an impatient sigh and dropped her trembling hands back to her lap. I studied them with a frown, before leaning across the console.

"It's not a bad surprise," I murmured as I brushed my fingers over her neck, watching as the pulse jumped in her throat. "I promise."

"Okay, can I take the blindfold off now?" she asked, sounding slightly defensive.

"No." With that, I got out and made my way around to her side. Overhead, the sky was gray and gloomy, and the forecast was calling for heavy rain within the next few hours. The air felt different, charged with something. Then again, it might have just been all the caffeine and nervous energy running through my veins.

The impending wave of storms had forced me to tweak my plan at the last minute, but I wasn't going to let it ruin my evening.

Ari looped an arm around my waist when I helped her down, clinging to my side as I led her across the parking lot. Maybe the weather didn't scream romance, but I had no doubt we'd make our own.

Pete, one of the security guys, let us inside and gave me a thumbs-up before disappearing back into his office. Then, it was just the two of us.

I cleared my throat and took a deep breath to calm my nerves before removing her blindfold. "Okay, we're here."

"Killian," Ari breathed in awe, spinning a small circle as she took in the metal and glass that made up the stadium. "This is—this is amazing!"

"Well, this is only the entrance," I said with a laugh, before tugging her hand. "Come on. I've got something I want to show you."

After scanning my badge, we took the elevator down to the clubhouse. Ari lagged behind from the moment we stepped off into the hallway—slowing in front of a sign for the laundry room, before coming to a complete standstill when we reached the Wall of Honor.

Her fingers moved over the plaques, lips moving silently as she read the names of players whose jerseys had been retired and the achievements earned by both individual players and the team as a whole.

I pushed on, dragging her along like a kid at a school open house, eager to unveil my plan. The details were crucial as I'd prepared a speech to coincide with each location. Step one was the locker room where I'd reveal the details behind the day I'd been called up. Step two would take place down on the field.

Shit, I think the field was supposed to be step one.

"Wait." Ari pulled her hand from my grasp. "Just wait a minute. I wasn't done with that."

I nodded distractedly and continued moving forward. Clearly, I should have used my sudden insomnia to prepare notecards in case I panicked and forgot everything.

"Okay, so I take it you're just going to keep going?"

My heart was racing as I tried straightening out the plan in my head. Maybe she wouldn't notice if we turned back and moved to the field. When we got there, I'd tell her—well, it'd probably come to me.

"Killian?" I turned to see find that Ari was still at the Wall of Honor, brows furrowed in confusion and fidgeting with her necklace.

"Come on, slugger. Thought with two good knees, you'd be able to keep up."

She shook her head and planted her feet shoulder-width apart, prepared to stand her ground. "No. You come here."

Locker room... field... stands?

No, that last one definitely wasn't right.

"I will—just as soon as we see this one thing," I coaxed. When Ari didn't budge, I sighed and returned to where she stood. "What's wrong?"

"This is your name, Killian. Right here." She pointed to the American League MVP plaque from last season. "And here—you were the Hurricanes MVP in 2017."

Her fingers moved delicately over the red stitching on the baseball I'd signed after winning an award that hadn't meant anything to me at the time. I lifted my eyes back to hers. "And?"

She shook her head, reaching up to squeeze my bicep. "Maybe to you this is nothing special, but it's my first time in your world, Killian.

Can I just have a minute to soak it all in and celebrate your victories?"

Damn, had she written hers down on notecards?

"I—" I swallowed. The script in my head had vanished somewhere in the parking lot, so I spoke the words on my heart. "I hate karaoke."

The organ in my chest was a terrible speechwriter, something I realized right about the time Ari's hand slipped from my arm and fell back to her side.

"No—wait! Let me start over. I mean, I hate karaoke—"

Ari crossed her arms over her chest with a terse nod. "Yeah, you mentioned that already."

"I do," I admitted with a wince. "Shit—what I'm trying to say is that I've never really enjoyed witnessing drunk people mumble or squeal their way through a song. But getting to watch you do something you love was a priceless moment that I'll keep with me forever. I saw you come alive up on that stage, slugger, showing me a side of you I didn't even know existed. And I wanted to return the favor by bringing you to where I feel most alive."

Her lips curved up in an almost reluctant smile as she reached for my hand. "Baseball is your church, just like music is mine. You wouldn't go tearing through Westminster Abbey or St. Peter's, because holy places deserve respect. And this, Killian? This is a holy place for you."

I nodded once, before taking a minute to regroup. Ari was right—she was always right. I could drag her all over the stadium while rattling off my biography, but she wouldn't know me.

"When I was fourteen, I took the baseball from my very first little-league game and made these." I released her hand to roll my shirt sleeve up. Her attention snagged on my ink before lowering to the two bracelets I wore every single day.

"You made these?"

I took a deep breath and nodded, my voice rough as I admitted, "I made two, thinking I'd give the other to someone special, but there hasn't been anyone... until you."

The old Killian would have been cringing at the display of vulnerability, but I didn't care. I never stopped thinking about Ari, and if I had to make a fool out of myself to convey my feelings, I'd wear the cap and bells with honor.

Her hands came up to cover her mouth as I unknotted one of them from my wrist. I grinned before extending my palm. "Will you wear it for me?"

It sounded like a proposal, and maybe in a way, it was. A reminder that no matter what was going on with her family, she was free to be herself when she was with me. A promise of the life we were going to build together once she was out of rehab.

Ari's chin wobbled, but she managed a small nod and let me tie it around her wrist. I gathered her in my arms but held my desire back for the moment. There was still something left unsaid and only one place in the ballpark that mattered—one place that hadn't made the list.

"Can I show you something?" I whispered into her hair. "I promise, after, we'll go anywhere you want."

She pulled back, gazing up at me with a weary smile. "Okay."

We left the clubhouse, passing through the dugout before reaching the field. I'd wanted the dome open so we could see the stars, but with what I was about to do, it almost seemed right to shut the world out.

The park was completely silent. With the rafters overhead and the lights blazing down on us, it almost felt like we were entering a cathedral. Even the wall of windows set back behind left field let in just enough city light to resemble stained glass.

This time, when Ari slowed, I stepped back and tried seeing it through her eyes. I thought back to the twenty-year-old kid who felt like he'd been handed the world, wondering when I'd started taking it for granted.

When had it become just another day at the office?

"What was it you wanted to show me?" Ari asked, coming back to stand at my side. She hadn't gone starry-eyed over the architecture or wandered off to explore on her own. It was like she understood what this space meant to me and was giving it the quiet reverence it deserved.

There was something sacred within these chalk lines. I wrapped an arm around Ari's shoulders and led her over to stand on first base, clearing my throat against the sudden tightness. "I've made a lot of mistakes—most of them tied to this field in some way."

Ari nodded and pressed her lips together like maybe she was fighting back her own emotions.

"I'm not a saint—far from it actually. The decisions I made off-field hurt a lot of people. While it'd be easy to sweep it all under the rug, you deserve to know the truth."

Confessing my sins had never been part of my plan, and revealing it all now seemed incredibly stupid, but she deserved to hear it from me and not a tabloid.

"You can tell me," Ari said softly, placing her hands over mine to steady them.

I took a deep breath. "I slept with a couple of my teammate's wives—not intentionally—but it doesn't change the fact that it happened. The last one was over a year ago, which is why I haven't been with anyone since—"

Her lips parted in surprise, but I kept going, needing to purge the memories from my system. "You said I don't trust people, but it's me, Ari—I'm the one I don't trust. My injury happened because I made the wrong call—"

"Killian." Tears shimmered in her eyes. "You made a mistake, but it doesn't mean you're a bad person."

I shook my head as she repeated the same advice I'd given her after the Helen debacle. "You don't understand. I've let the fear of getting hurt hold me back. If I didn't excel at it immediately, I walked away. I shut myself off from my dad because I was convinced he'd just let me down again. I thought it was better to live like a monk than to let a woman have any power over my life and career. I even hung onto the damn crutches for longer than they recommended because I was afraid of doing something to damage my knee."

Ari's fingers tightened over mine. "My demons aren't the same, but I know what it's like to be afraid—and it's no way to live."

"Thanks to some people in my life, I'm slowly figuring that out. I brought you here because I wanted you to see me. When the game's over, and the lights are shut out, I want to know I'm going home to you. If I've had a few too many, you're the one I want driving me. If all this goes away tomorrow, I know I could face it with you in my corner."

With the exception of a tear that had spilled over onto her lashes, Ari was a tower of strength, refusing to release her hold on me.

My nostrils flared on a forced exhale, and I nodded down at first base. "You're standing in the exact spot where I thought I lost it all, but it was where I found everything I needed. This was the place that gave me you, Ari. I know I'm not the best, but what I lack in talent, I will make up for in heart. It's yours—all of it."

She hiccuped through another sob before mashing her lips together with a jerky nod. I pulled my hand free, using the pad of my thumb to brush away her tears.

"For most of my life, there have been constant reminders that I'll never measure up. But I've learned there is one thing strong enough to drive out that kind of fear and doubt."

"What's that?" Her tone was gentle as if she couldn't fathom what I was going to say next.

"I'm in love with you, Ari," I admitted softly. "And loving you has silenced everything else, making me think that maybe I could be the man you deserve. You were the first woman who didn't want something from me—the only one who saw me and not the player—"

"I need—" Ari made a choking sound, and then more tears were streaking down her cheeks. "I need—to tell you something."

CHAPTER TWENTY-TWO
ARIANA

"I cannot fix on the hour, or the spot, or the look or the words, which laid the foundation. It is too long ago. I was in the middle before I knew that I had begun."

-Jane Austen, *Pride and Prejudice*

"I'M LEAVING *True North* in two days," I blurted on a sob, revealing what I'd only learned yesterday. I was being discharged on Monday. In two days, I'd be back in my cage, no closer to answers than the day I'd arrived.

"What?" His smile faded. "You're leaving?"

Dammit. Shit. Hell.

"No," I groaned into my hands. "I mean—yes—I mean, I can't—"

Why was I making this difficult? He'd just peeled himself back layer by layer, while I'd nodded along and encouraged him to stop living in fear.

As if I had any idea what that was like. *The bravest thing I'd ever done was throw a clod of dirt at Helen—not exactly the stuff of legends.*

Killian loved me.

It was like breaking the surface to gulp in a lungful of air after a life spent underwater. The moment I'd imagined since I was nine. Only, instead of vomiting up my problems, I just told him I loved him too, and we lived happily ever after. But I could feel Tristan and the church lurking in the depths, waiting to drag me back down.

"Hey." Killian cupped my jaw in his hand, tucking several strands of hair behind my ear. "It's okay, you can tell me. It was a little sudden, right? I know you may not be to that place yet, but it just felt right to tell you here."

If I'd just taken Tsega's advice and come clean last weekend after Brad's delightful little pop-in, we might have been making love in the locker room right now.

And if I was making a list of things to do over, I probably would have reconsidered my decision to leave Killian standing on first base as I fled toward the dugout.

"Ari?" He called out. "Where the hell are you going?"

I heard the confusion in his tone but kept jogging, hugging myself with clammy hands. It didn't matter how hard I tried; I was always going to end up hurting him.

"No, I can't," I muttered to the field. "This place is sacred—I'm sorry—ruined everything."

Pretend like Tristan doesn't exist...

Pretend you're not engaged...

Pretend you were never considering using Killian to escape...

Pretend like tonight isn't the last time you'll see him...

Instead of coming up with a plan, I'd been busy playing a game of make-believe, convinced I had more time. But my clock had officially run out.

"Just wait a damn minute," He grumbled from a few yards behind me. "I can't run!"

I slowed as I reached the dugout and balled my hands into fists, refusing to let myself cry.

You did this to yourself, you stupid, stubborn woman.

"Christ, I'm out of shape," Killian panted as he approached, taking several deep breaths, before adding, "Care to tell me what the hell that was?"

I shook my head, not trusting myself to speak. Instead, I squinted at a bucket in the corner of the dugout and considered throwing up in it.

Without a word, he moved down the stairs. His steady hand landed on the small of my back, leading me through the clubhouse and toward the elevator.

"What are you doing?"

Killian closed his eyes for a brief second before lowering his gaze back to mine. "You need to talk, but you can't do it here. So, I'm going to take you somewhere you can."

I nodded and followed him inside the elevator, not missing the way his jaw flexed and tightened as he scanned his badge. He shoved his hands into his pockets and leaned back against the railing, studying me with a sober expression. "It's your dad, isn't it? He won't let you be with someone like me."

I winced. If a breaking heart had a sound, it would be Killian's voice at this moment. "It's complicated."

You see, it's kind of a funny story, but my father sold me to his best friend so he can expand his ministry. Hilarious, right?

"My dad and I didn't see eye to eye on much of anything for a long time," he admitted quietly. "We're both pretty damn hardheaded, so naturally, we avoided taking any responsibility for the way things were. We wasted years fighting over the same old shit instead of sitting down to hash things out like adults."

"And now?" It surprised me, as his father was typically a subject he tried to avoid at all costs.

Killian tilted his head to the side and cracked his neck, seemingly avoiding making direct eye contact with me. "Well, we finally put our egos aside long enough to talk. Figure we've still a long way to go, but we're both willing to work on it."

"Maybe I could do the same with your father." He cleared his throat and lifted his shoulder in a shrug. "Sit down with him one-on-one, let him get to know me."

I swallowed; my mouth suddenly dry. It would have been perfect had my father been anyone other than Tristan James. As it was, Killian could have been a saint. It wouldn't have mattered. The money had already changed hands.

"What do you think?" His expression was earnest as it searched my face, and I had to look away. It hurt too much.

"Yeah, that could work," I lied, forcing a smile. Inside, though, I was already grieving the loss of Killian. There was no scenario where either of us got what we wanted. With that, a dark cloud settled over me, tainting what should have been the happiest day of my life.

The elevator announced our arrival with a cheerful *ding*, but a storm was brewing in my head. Killian reached out to hold the doors open, and I shook myself from my thoughts long enough to follow him.

"Hey," he murmured against my temple, draping an arm around my shoulders. "We'll get through this. You're not going to lose me, okay?"

My eyes welled up, but I set my jaw, blinking until my vision cleared.

A gray-haired security guard approached with a small wave. "You two kids all finished?"

Killian responded with an enthusiastic nod. "I think she saw it all, Pete. Hey, how's Nat doing?"

"Oh, much better, Mr. Reed," he responded as he unlocked the door. "They're saying she'll be back to a hundred percent soon."

"Glad to hear it." Killian turned his attention to me. "His daughter, Natalie, plays college softball up in Nebraska. During one of their practices, she fractured her non-pitching wrist sliding into home."

"Oh, that's terrible. I'm sorry."

Pete playfully elbowed him. "Don't let this guy fool you. He tracked down a trainer from one of the minor league teams up there—paid for the whole thing himself too—"

"Alright, Pete." Killian clapped him on the shoulder with a strained smile. "You have really gotta stop drinking on the job, man. You're talking complete nonsense."

"What?" The guard shrugged. "I know a good one when I see one, kid."

I did too, which was probably why it felt like there was a vice around my chest. Killian was the man I'd dreamt about since I was a little girl—the standard against which I'd measured everyone else.

The media cared about the uniform, completely unaware of the good and kind heart beating underneath. And I would never deserve him.

"Excuse me," I said flatly, no longer recognizing the sound of my own voice. The glass was cold beneath my palms as I pushed the door open and ran toward the parking lot.

The wind caught my hair, tossing it against my face with stinging slaps, but I just pulled Tsega's jacket tighter around my body and kept going.

I never should have stopped running.

I never should have let myself believe I could be happy. I'd never been anything more than an escaped convict on borrowed time. A prisoner who lacked the courage to fight back. I may have regained my voice, but it was just as small as ever.

Lightning forked through the clouds, closely followed by a booming clap of thunder that seemed to shake the ground.

"Ari!" Killian roared over the impending storm. "Ari—wait!"

I lifted my arms in surrender as I turned to face him, giving myself up. "I'm not the woman you think I am! You were supposed to be a means to escape! Morgan, she had it all planned out—you were my path to freedom!"

He tensed at my words, before taking a step back, eyes blazing with a fierce intensity I'd never seen before.

I shoved the hair out of my eyes and exhaled a bitter laugh. "But I realized during Restaurant Night that I couldn't do it. It's not who I am. I should have told you a long time ago, but I was scared—terrified, actually. I'm not a brave person—I'm just not built for it!"

Another bolt of lightning streaked across the sky, and I glanced up. If it was all going to come crashing down on my head, I'd go to my grave with this, "I think you're wonderful, Killian and tonight—" I gestured toward the stadium. "It was so perfect. No one's ever done anything like this or made me feel even a fraction of what I do when I'm with you."

My eyes filled as I ran the pad of my thumb over my wrist, drawing strength from his bracelet. I took a deep breath and prepared my heart to let him go... again. "But you deserve someone brave and honest—"

When his gaze flickered to mine, my breath caught. The walls had gone up. Only, this time, I was the outsider. I felt the pain I'd caused him under the weight of his glacial stare, as though a stake was being driven into my chest.

"Do you love me?" he asked gruffly.

My mouth opened and closed like a fish's, before settling into a frown. It wasn't what I'd expected. Once I recovered from the shock, I nodded.

"I do," I admitted in a strangled voice. "I'm so in love with you, but I'm not good and you—"

He inched forward, slowly closing the gap between us. "Deserve better? Yeah, you said that already. So, were you planning on telling me you loved me?"

"N-no," I stammered, shrinking back. My teeth began to chatter, and I hugged myself to keep warm. "I mean, yes—I don't know!"

The wind strengthened, picking up dead leaves and scattering them across the parking lot, but Killian didn't take his eyes off mine. "Why, Ari? Why wouldn't you just tell me?"

"Why?" I roared in a voice laced with hysteria. "Because I'm an object, not a person! Don't you see that? I'm never going to be free to make my own decisions because he's never going to let me go! I couldn't even escape when I had the damn key in my hand, Killian! What I feel or want—none of that matters to him!"

"It matters to me," he bit out as he continued stalking toward me, his forehead creased in concern. "Dammit, you matter to me!"

I swallowed hard, entirely baffled by the admission. "But I'm—"

"The woman I'm in love with," he finished for me, a small smile tugging at his lips. "I don't give a damn about the rest, slugger."

"But," I protested, hearing the desperation in my tone.

Killian came to a stop just in front of me, close enough that the toes of my ballet flats were touching his boots. He reached forward to cup my jaw, his blue eyes glowing with affection as he drew me closer.

"I meant what I said. You aren't going to lose me. Now, if keeping my word means going toe to toe with your father, I'll do it. Trust me, I'm stronger than I look." He flexed his bicep in demonstration before lowering his voice. "I know you're afraid, but you're not alone anymore, Ari. You've got me now, and if you trust me enough to give me your heart, just know I'll guard it with my life."

My heart throbbed painfully against my chest with a mounting sense of urgency and an overwhelming need to reveal myself. This man had scaled every wall, seeing me in ways no one ever had. Only a fool could have walked away.

I swallowed my doubts and lifted my face to his, completely vulnerable. "You've had my heart since I was nine. I thought you were the most beautiful thing I'd ever seen. I wanted you for my own, never dreaming in a million years we would meet again."

His forehead furrowed in confusion. "Since you were nine—I don't understand."

He'd been the one constant in my life, the only decision that had ever truly been mine. So, gathering the last bit of courage I still possessed, I whispered, "Are you good?"

"Ari," Killian exhaled my name, pulling me with him as he stumbled back a step. I reached up to grip his shoulders, holding him steady.

There was a second of tense silence. Then his arms were around my waist, and I was being crushed to his chest. "The song, it was you," he murmured into my hair. "Christ, it was always you. You saved my life. You saved—"

I tilted my head back when his voice cut off, needing to see him—to make it okay. He was shaking his head in open-mouthed disbelief, his eyes glossy. My numb fingers smoothed over his stubbled jaw and face, brushing away the tears just like he'd done for me back in the stadium.

The sky chose that moment to open up, drenching us both in an icy shower. I blinked away the drops of rain caught on my lashes and rested my chin against his heaving chest, finding comfort in just being close to him.

Killian huffed a soft laugh and gazed down at me, his misty eyes darkening as they moved over my lips. "All of this—everything I have—it's because of you, Ari."

The ache in my chest migrated lower when his expression heated, my pulse quickening in anticipation. Instead of moving closer, he froze, his eyes filling with tears again. The surrounding squall faded into the background as I pushed myself up onto my tiptoes, pressing my lips to his.

While I took control and explored his mouth, he guided me backward across the parking lot with his hands on my waist. I licked along his bottom lip, and his grip tightened, squeezing as if he was afraid I might disappear.

I jumped when my back connected with something solid, before realizing we'd reached his truck. And then he was kissing me back. I opened up and let him in, my tongue darting out to meet his. The frenzied kisses of lust we'd shared before were just a flash in the pan compared to this. This was a steady shower of sparks, building into an all-consuming desire that coursed through my veins.

Killian's hands moved beneath my soaked shirt, stroking my skin until heat pooled in my lower belly. I slipped my hands into the back pocket of his jeans and pressed my body to his, moaning as I felt him harden against me.

He trailed kisses over my face and jaw before pulling away with a pant. When he reopened his eyes, the distant smile faded from his lips. "Jesus, get in. You're going to freeze to death if you stay out in this any longer."

I mumbled nonsense in protest as he helped me into the passenger seat, using my frozen hands to try to guide his mouth back to mine. He stepped back with a low chuckle, chewing on his lower lip as he surveyed me. "Slugger, there's no sense in either one of us getting hypothermia when my condo is just a few blocks away."

CHAPTER TWENTY-THREE
ARIANA

"So, I love you because the entire universe conspired to help me find you."

-Paolo Coelho, *The Alchemist*

KILLIAN HANDLED the flooding streets with calm finesse, pulling up in front of his condo only minutes later. He tossed the keys to the valet, wearing the same determined expression as the night he'd pulled me into the backseat of his truck.

I dropped my hand into his when he opened my door, letting him lead me through the brightly lit lobby toward a bank of elevators.

It wasn't until we were inside that I caught sight of my reflection in the mirrored doors. Wet hair clung to my face and shoulders, but it was the visible red scar running down the middle of my head that had my heart skipping a beat.

After risking a quick glance in his direction, I discreetly reached up to run my fingers through the dripping strands, fighting to cover the scar.

Maybe he hadn't seen it.

Killian's eyes met mine, his jaw tightening when he realized what I was doing. "Don't," he warned gruffly, tucking me into his side.

I sucked in a breath and lowered my hand to his chest, shivering with the need to press my body against his in ways I didn't fully understand. Maybe it was just the storm, or perhaps our confessions, but something had happened to us back in that parking lot. It was as if a weight had been lifted off both our shoulders.

He kept his focus on my face, watching me with an expression I couldn't quite describe. It reminded me of the way strangers looked at Tristan. Adoration. Worship. It would have been wrong had it been anyone else but him.

By the time we reached his floor, the air between us was crackling with electricity. Killian released his protective hold on my hip just long enough to let us into his condo. I made it as far as toeing off my waterlogged flats when his mouth moved down my neck, not quite touching me, but close enough to cause another involuntary shiver.

"Here we are. Home sweet home." He exhaled a soft laugh at my reaction and nipped my ear lobe, before leading me through the living room and into what I presumed was his bedroom.

Seeing no sense in arguing—*none at all*—I let him.

We didn't stop at the bed, though, continuing on into the roomiest bathroom I'd ever seen. A large mirror backlit with tiny LED lights hung over the floating vanity and dual raised sinks, giving off just enough light to feel romantic.

"I imagine the acoustics in here are fantastic," I mused with a grin, earning myself a wink from Killian.

My eyes lingered on the large freestanding tub in front of a wall of windows overlooking the city below, piquing some voyeuristic curiosity I'd been unaware existed until now.

Killian bypassed it for the large shower spanning the length of the back wall of the bathroom, though, cranking the knobs until water began spraying from multiple showerheads.

"Let's get you warmed up." He returned to my side and began

rubbing my arms, his eyes narrowed in concern. "Do you feel okay? Dizzy? Do you want me to make you some tea?"

My mouth curved into a smile as he fussed over me. I wasn't even cold anymore. In fact, certain areas of my body were quite toasty under the heat of his hands.

"Ari? Baby, I need you to answer me."

I stepped back and grasped the hem of my long-sleeved shirt, lifting it up and over my head. My leggings were next, and I kept a hand on his arm to steady myself as I peeled the damp material from my skin before kicking it aside.

"I'm good," I finally admitted, my chest rising and falling on an unsteady breath.

Killian's nostrils flared as I stood before him in nothing but my bra and panties, the muscle in his jaw flexing as his eyes raked over my body.

"Come here." He took my hand and led me over to stand in front of the large mirror. His chest pressed against my back as he leaned down to nuzzle the side of my neck, whispering, "I want you to see what I see when I look at you. You are so goddamned beautiful, Ari."

I nodded dumbly in response, utterly incapable of stringing together a single thought with his warm breath against my skin.

Killian unclasped my necklace and studied my reflection with another look of reverence before straightening to his full height. He threaded his fingers through my wet hair and pressed his lips to my scar. "Don't ever hide yourself—not from me."

I inhaled sharply and closed my eyes against the sting of tears. Before Killian, I'd never imagined there could be more than one way to say I love you. But under his hands, I let myself absorb the words, both spoken and unspoken until steam from the shower began to fog the mirror.

My skin flushed when his thigh moved between my legs. I instinctively pushed back, seeking him. The corners of his mouth turned up when I reached between our bodies to free the clasp on my bra, before arching wantonly against his chest.

"I love you too," I murmured, letting the straps slip down my arms. Killian kissed my neck as I bent forward to lower my panties, his erection pressing against my skin.

My breasts brushed against the cold marble countertop. Suddenly, every inch of me pulsed with need, like my heart had relocated to the area between my legs. I turned, shivering as his eyes lowered to explore my body. His hands followed, lightly trailing down my spine before latching onto my backside, kneading my flesh.

"Fuck," Killian muttered on a low growl, the word vibrating through me as his mouth found mine. This time, his kisses were ravenous and rough, making it almost impossible to function.

Almost.

I brought my fingers to the front of his wet jeans and gripped the button, overcome with the need to touch him.

He released his hold on me and jerked away with a sharp gasp. "Shower."

I blinked up at him in confusion, my breaths almost as ragged as his. "But—"

"Come on." He kept his arms down at his side as he walked me into the steamy shower, closing the door softly behind me. "I'm just going to throw your things in the dryer."

Six people could have comfortably fit inside, yet he'd left me all alone. Reluctantly, I stepped under one of the shower heads mounted to the ceiling. I'd showered just this morning, but it didn't stop me from washing my hair with Killian's shampoo and lathering his soap into my skin. If I couldn't have him, I'd have his scent.

It wasn't enough. Warm water cascaded over my sizzling skin, but my nipples remained puckered and sensitive to the point of aching.

Why was he not in here with me?

I wiped the condensation from the glass and peered out to find Killian sitting on the edge of the bathtub. If I squinted, I could almost make out the twitching pulse in his neck and the flare of his nostrils.

My heart twisted with longing at the sight of him. I pushed the door open and lowered a hand to my hip before asking, "Aren't you going to join me? In case you hadn't noticed, your clothes are wet too."

The muscle in his jaw clenched, but he refused to look at me. "Ari, I'm trying real hard to be a gentleman with you right now."

"I know," I sighed dramatically, rolling my eyes in mock frustration. "I sure wish you'd stop."

Killian jerked his head toward me with a lifted brow. "You want me in there with you."

A statement.

"I don't really know how much more obvious I could be." I ran a soapy hand over my breasts, fighting a victorious smirk as I watched the last of his control slip away.

He closed his eyes and muttered a curse before kicking off his boots and unbuttoning his shirt. Dark ink climbed up his arms like vines, coiling in a circular pattern around each shoulder.

Bible verses against tattoo markings filtered into my consciousness, but I shoved them aside. I wasn't allowing a two-thousand-year-old book to make my decisions for me.

Not tonight.

I'd known Killian was fit but watching his biceps flex without clothes in the way was an entirely new experience. I drank in the sight of him as he coaxed his jeans down over narrow hips. It was as if the muscles had been carved into his skin.

Boxer briefs clung to his body, highlighting his hard length and leaving me with an overwhelming need to touch—to make him feel as good as he'd made me the last time we were together.

Killian's eyes flashed with determination as he strode toward me, hooking his thumbs into the waistband of his briefs. An involuntary sound escaped my throat when he tugged them down and stepped inside.

"I think she likes what she sees," he murmured with a low chuckle, moving behind me to press a kiss to my shoulder blade.

My breath caught in my throat. I turned, stepping up to press my lips to his while guiding his hand down my belly. "Love me, Killian. Please."

He kept his mouth on mine as his body pushed me back against the tile, grazing my dimple with his teeth. I could have sworn he was speaking, but his voice was too low to hear over the rush of blood in my ears.

The corners of his eyes crinkled as he pulled back to look down at me, tracing my lips with his fingers before moving lower to cup my breasts. His thumb and forefinger kept steady pressure on my tender nipples until my skin erupted in goosebumps.

Shivers of desire coursed through me when he pinched harder, and I squirmed, moaning incoherent demands. I curled my hand around the back of his neck, desperate and greedy for the feel of his mouth.

He exhaled a laugh and trailed kisses down my jaw and neck, before reaching my breasts. A rush of air left my lungs as his mouth closed around one, his teeth scraping over the tip.

I arched my back and forced my heavy eyes open when Killian's mouth left my breast. With one hand on the tile to brace himself, he lowered his head, sliding his tongue over my sternum and down my belly. My hips bucked against his mouth. He pulled back with a growl of frustration, his face contorted in pain.

"I'm sorry," I whispered, pressing my lips to his collarbone. "I didn't mean to hurt you—or is it your knee? Do you want to get out and sit for a minute?"

Killian mashed his lips together and brushed his thumb over my cheek, before exhaling an incredulous laugh. "Baby, you have no idea the things I want to do to you right now."

At my blank expression, he lowered his hand to cup between my legs, keeping his blue eyes on mine as he parted my curls and stroked along my seam. His finger swirled through my wetness once before pushing inside me.

I bit down on my lip and swayed into the palm of his hand with a moan, still not understanding, but no longer caring.

"This," he ground out, freeing his finger and holding it up for display. "But with my tongue. As soon as I'm cleared, you can bet your ass I'll be on my knees in front of you."

He sucked my arousal off the digit with a cocky smirk before returning it to the junction between my thighs. This time, he touched me like I'd often touched myself, rubbing circles around my center until I was pleading for release in broken whimpers.

I opened my legs wider for him, keeping a hand on his shoulder for balance. My body shuddered violently beneath his touch, mindlessly chasing after the same thing he'd given me last weekend in his truck. Just as I began to worry it wouldn't happen again, his finger pushed into me. My body burst into a million fractals of light. I didn't even necessarily know what fractals were, but that was what I'd become.

"Ari, wait," Killian said in a gruff tone, reaching for my hands, trying to still my movements.

I shook my head and traced the line of dark hair down his stomach, whispering, "Can you show me how to touch you? I want to love your body like you love mine."

He nodded and lowered my wrist until his length was pressed against my palm, breathing heavier than he'd been only moments before. My fingers instinctively wrapped around the base. He nodded again, guiding my movements, showing me how he liked to be touched.

I raised a brow when he groaned but continued pumping my fist up and down, loving the way his eyes went hooded. He matched my rhythm with his finger, stroking my inner walls with a gentleness I hadn't expected.

There was something beautiful in the way we gave pleasure, a certain intimacy in an act I'd never share with anyone but him.

"Make love to me," I pleaded breathlessly, rocking my hips against his hand. "Please, Killian."

The muscle in his jaw flexed, and he squeezed his eyes shut before withdrawing from my body. "I want you so badly I ache, Ari."

Taking it as an invitation, I stepped between his legs, sucking in a sharp breath as my sensitive breasts came in contact with solid muscle. When he didn't make a move, I arched upward onto my toes and gripped his shoulders, trying to align my body with his. "Please."

Killian's nostrils flared as he lowered his forehead to mine. "I can't. I don't have a condom." His tone was tinged with regret.

I ignored the pang of disappointment and wrapped my hand around his erection again, feeling wild and reckless.

We were so close.

"I could have your baby," I breathed out, looking up at him from under my lashes, just greedy enough to test his resolve.

The tendons in his neck stood out as he grasped my hair in his fist, gently tugging until there was some distance between us. His other hand covered mine, tightening my grip around his shaft.

My mouth fell open when that very same hand settled between my legs, filling my body with not one, but two fingers. I clenched around them, sending more goosebumps racing over my skin.

"I don't want to run the risk of you getting pregnant our first time together, slugger," Killian ground out through a clenched jaw, his gaze moving over me possessively. "I want to take my time getting to know every inch of your body before we start a family."

The proclamation sent a current of need straight to my core. "You want a family with me?"

He grinned and lowered his mouth to my neck, nipping the skin. "You'll be the woman who carries my babies, slugger. But not for a long time. I want to do this right—make you my wife first."

His wife.

I threaded my fingers through his hair as his thrusts increased, close to coming apart again.

"Keep touching me," he begged, shedding the last of his restraint. "I'm so fucking close."

I tried to mirror his strokes, succeeding in little more than clumsy squeezes when my body tightened around his fingers. I pressed my lips to his jaw as waves of pleasure crashed over me, whispering, "You'll be an amazing husband and father."

Killian thrust his hips forward with a strangled growl, pumping into my fist and coating my breasts and belly with warm liquid. He rubbed it into my skin with his fingertips, before lowering his mouth to mine in a crushing kiss.

Marked.

I was still breathing hard when we finally broke apart, my mind floating lazily somewhere above my body.

Killian's eyes returned to mine. "Move in with me."

"What?" I mumbled, certain I'd misunderstood in my foggy state.

"God, Ari. You are so soft and sweet. No one has ever known how to take care of you; to protect you. No one's ever loved you the way you needed, and it shows. So, don't go back to your father." His lips brushed over my scar. "Stay here—let me take care of you."

I gaped at him, until I realized he wasn't joking. Killian wanted me to live here. With him. No more sneaking around—no more walls.

"Yes," I whispered, quashing the fear in my chest. Tristan and the church couldn't hurt me.

Not anymore.

CHAPTER TWENTY-FOUR
ARIANA

"There are no ambitions noble enough to justify breaking someone's heart."

-Colleen McCullough, *The Thorn Birds*

IT WAS ALMOST midnight when Killian pulled up to *True North*, taking a parking spot near the entrance. He turned to me with a smirk. "You ready?"

"I can't believe we're really doing this." I reached up to tug on my necklace, only to remember I'd left it on the bathroom counter back at Killian's place.

Our place.

"Damn straight we are, slugger." He got out and came around to open my door for me, helping me down. "We'll get your things, your prescriptions, and sign whatever we need to for home therapy. It'll be a piece of cake."

I ignored the churning in my stomach and laced my fingers through his as we walked through the sliding doors. Given the late hour, the lobby was deserted, and I found the silence unsettling.

Something felt off, but I couldn't put my finger on what it was exactly. By all rights, I should have been celebrating my freedom, not tiptoeing around with my guard up.

"Hey." Killian frowned as we stepped inside the elevator, using his index finger to tip my chin up. "It's going to be okay."

"Yeah, I know," I croaked in a hoarse whisper, spinning the baseball bracelet in slow circles around my wrist. It was just nerves and maybe a little bit of fear of the unknown. Once my things were in the condo, the flutters would disappear. I'd be able to relax.

The noise reached us before the doors had even fully opened.

"What the..." Killian began, pulling me closer as we stepped off into a scene of utter chaos. Several police officers milled around the nurse's station, their radios crackling with static.

Blood rushed to my stomach. I kept my arm around his waist, searching for a familiar face. "Tsega was supposed to be—"

"There she is!" Tiffani shrieked, stabbing a finger in my direction. "We found her!"

It took everything in me not to vomit when I realized who she was addressing. Tristan approached us with a clenched jaw, while Brad followed a few steps behind, his face twisted in a sneer.

I briefly considered the possibility that his God had alerted him to my plans of escape before shifting my eyes over to Tiffani. The tech was only on during the week, so the fact that she was here now meant she'd been the one tasked with checking up on me.

Just another one of Tristan's little birds.

Their footsteps moved closer, somehow magnified despite the sheer number of people gathered on the floor. Even Georgia had wandered down the hall in her bathrobe. When she realized what was going on, her hand came up over her mouth.

"I'm not coming back," I forced out through a clenched jaw, taking a step backward toward the elevator. My shaking hands dug into Killian's sides, but I refused to let go.

As long as I held on, we were going to be okay.

Tristan's brows drew together, and he shook his head. "Ariana, sweetheart, you're confused."

"I'm not."

Killian's steps slowed, his muscles tensing under my grip. "Christ."

"Close," Tristan replied dryly, advancing on us. "But most people just call me Pastor James, or Ariana's daddy."

Blink. Blink.

"Where's Tsega?" I punched the button for the elevator and spun around, calculating my options for escape if it didn't arrive soon. There was nothing else.

We were boxed in.

Trapped.

"She's been relieved of her duties here," the director answered. It looked as if she'd been dragged out of her bed. I imagined she probably had once Tristan was made aware of my disappearance.

I tore my eyes from hers as Brad moved in, shaking his head as he gave Killian a once-over. "I knew something was off with this guy. Thank God you're safe. Let's get you out of here."

He caught the collar of my shirt and yanked, sending me stumbling forward. Killian wrested me from his hold, placing his body in front of mine like a shield.

"Don't touch her," he warned in a low voice, his muscles taut with rage. "She said she's not going back. Respect her decision."

Brad rolled his eyes. "I'm allowed to touch my fiancée, kid. How many does this make for you now—four? Five? You seem to have a real knack for taking advantage of unavailable women, but surely even the team has their limits."

Shit. Damn. Hell.

"Fiancée? Okay, buddy. Sure." Killian exhaled a mirthless chuckle before turning to me, his confident expression falling into a look of horrified recognition. "Wait, you're engaged?"

Emotion clogged my throat, but I nodded, forcing the words through stiff lips. "I'm sorry. I wanted to tell you. I swear—I never meant to keep it from you."

Killian raked a hand through his hair with a muttered curse, shaking his head in disbelief. When I placed my palm on his chest, he jerked away, and I was forced to see the coldness in his eyes for the truth it was.

I'd broken his trust. Nothing I said or did now would restore it. Brad's hand came down on my shoulder like a weight, and I closed my eyes, letting it drag me under.

One of the officers stepped forward, almost reluctantly. "Killian Reed, you're under arrest—"

I jerked away from Brad's grip with a cry of anguish before putting myself in the middle. "Please, don't!" I held up my palms, pleading, "He didn't do anything—I'm an adult! I—"

"It's over now, son. I hope you see this as a wakeup call to get the help you need," Tristan stated flatly, shaking his head while remaining a safe distance away.

"Please," I begged again, knowing it was falling on deaf ears. "I wasn't kidnapped or abducted or any of the other bullshit you're charging him with!"

My father's eyes briefly flashed with fury before he managed to *blink, blink* it away.

"You've suffered a traumatic brain injury, little dove," he explained, in a tone so utterly condescending it made me want to scream. "You're not capable of making rational decisions right now. It's obvious he took advantage of your mental state—"

Tristan James was no man. He was a monster who used and discarded people for his own twisted amusement. A villain who preyed on fears and weaknesses, turning those around him into little more than husks.

Chained. Beaten. Sold to the highest bidder.

I would have endured all of it and more if it meant saving Killian. But monsters didn't negotiate, not when they were convinced their way was the only way. Not when he had the opportunity to destroy someone I cared about.

"No," I gasped, my heart clenching painfully in my chest. Tears began sliding down my cheeks, but I refused to move. "I won't let you."

Tristan was silent for a moment. I thought I'd gotten through to him when Killian spoke.

"Just get it over with."

The words were like a punch to my belly, but it was the look of resignation on his face that left me doubled over, fighting to draw a full breath. I barely recognized him as the man who'd promised me forever just a few hours before.

An arm went around my back, and I straightened to see it was only Georgia. "I'm here," she said, lacing her fingers through mine.

Killian stood frozen as they handcuffed him, his eyes dull and distant. There was no greater terror than watching the very thing you loved being ripped from your arms and knowing you were powerless to stop it.

Everything hurt.

I struggled against a sudden wave of dizziness as they forced him onto the elevator, unable to right myself before crumpling against her with a defeated whimper.

"Remember, my dear," she whispered in my ear while rocking my body with hers. "The smallest voices can be the loudest. You have to pick up your shield and fight back."

"I can't," I uttered brokenly.

I knew how it was going to end. I'd always known. I just got caught up in how it all began, almost letting myself believe things could be different for me.

But there were no happily-ever-afters here.

CHAPTER TWENTY-FIVE
ARIANA

"Never laugh at live dragons..."

-J.R.R. Tolkien, *The Hobbit*

I WOKE at the sound of a key turning in the lock of my bedroom door, dragged from one nightmare and into another. One I was all too familiar with.

As soon as the gates had closed, I'd been pulled from Tristan's SUV by two armed guards. They'd marched me upstairs to my room. Just like a prisoner. I didn't know how much time had passed since then, but it couldn't have been long as the sky was still dark.

I shouldn't have slept at all, knowing Killian was in jail, and Tsega had been fired.

All because of me.

I'd been convinced Tristan had his little birds watching in the shadows, but never imagined Tiffani would be the one who'd give me up.

My eyes, hot and swollen from my tears, burned as a sliver of light from the hallway cut across the bedroom. I didn't need to see the figure entering to know who it was.

I felt it, the same way I had as a child. The hairs on the back of my neck prickled while my muscles tensed in warning. There was a primal urge to flee, but nowhere to run. I held myself still, straining to hear him over the sound of my heartbeat thrashing in my ears. My bedroom door closed with a soft *click*.

"Ariana," Brad called softly. The floorboard near the foot of my bed creaked in protest as he bent to switch off my nightlight.

> "Now throw this useless servant into outer darkness, where there will be weeping and gnashing of teeth."

The silence was punctuated by the jangling of his belt buckle as he unfastened it and the groaning of the mattress coils as the bed dipped beneath his weight. "I know you're awake, your breathing always gives you away. Sit up."

I jerked away when his hand connected with my calf and pressed my back to the headboard, pulling my knees to my chest. "Don't touch me," I forced out. "I'll scream."

He snorted. "And here I thought you'd really taken to the idea of being an obedient and submissive wife—"

"You're not my husband yet," I coldly reminded him, clenching my jaw to stop my chin from quivering.

"That's right," he agreed, shifting closer. "But it seems my fiancée has suddenly gotten cold feet and needs to be reminded of who owns her."

I shook my head, stammering, "P-p-people can't own p-p-people."

"Awww... your s-s-s-stutter's back," Brad mocked. "That's good. After your display back at *True North*, I was beginning to think that quiet little girl was gone." His hand moved to my cheek, and I raised my chin before pulling away.

"I won't be quiet," I hissed in defiance. "Not anymore—"

He caught my jaw in his hand, forcing my face back to his. "You'll do as you're told, sweetheart. And if you don't—well, there are other ways of keeping you in line. Just ask your mama. Oh, that's right, you can't."

Mama.

"What did you do to her?"

It was too dark to see his face, but I knew he was smiling as he coldly replied, "Whatever we wanted to, little dove. Now, I'm not necessarily against keeping my wife on her back in bed, but I would prefer it if she had a little bit of spark. Makes it more fun that way, don't you agree?"

I dug my fingernails into the mattress. "Do you really think I'm going to marry you?"

Brad forced a laugh and tightened his grip on my jaw. "Oh, you will. I'll make sure of it. You see, your father already started spending my money, so I thought it was time to collect what I'm owed."

"But we're not married," I choked out, feeling the bile rising in my throat. The church—and Tristan—had preached abstinence before marriage. It was the one message I'd clung to when Brad had begun sneaking into my room.

"What—didn't think your little stunt would have consequences?" He shook my face before dropping his hands down to my leggings. "I'm not in the mood for games anymore. You wanted to humiliate me by running all over the city with the baseball player, and now your father's left cleaning up the mess. Our wedding is on hold until the scandal dies down—"

"There isn't going to be a wedding."

He sighed. "For your sake, I hope you're wrong, Ariana. I really do. It's clear you've picked up some bad habits outside the walls, and it's going to take a little time for you to unlearn them. I think I've been incredibly patient, but I'm ready to start a family and have no issues seeing you walk down the aisle with a swollen belly like some ruined woman. So, you can fight me or learn to submit properly. Either way, your body will remind you with every step what becomes of the wicked."

At the sound of his zipper, I planted my hands into his chest and shoved before scrambling over to cower on the opposite side of the bed. My breaths came in short, panicked bursts as I searched for something—anything—I could use as a weapon.

Think, Ari.

The coils squeaked again as he stood, laughing. I squinted, straining to find his shadow in the darkness before pushing my hand beneath the mattress, feeling. My fingers closed around the jagged piece of glass.

Adrenaline flooded my veins, leaving me with a sudden sense of invincibility. The Hurricanes towel hadn't been the only thing I'd taken from Ashlynn's room. I'd also scavenged a broken mirror from her trash can, slipping the pieces in various spots beneath my mattress.

Just in case.

"Oh, little dove. You amuse me. You always have—" Brad pulled his belt off with a *whoosh*, cracking the leather in his hands as he moved around the foot of the bed. "You can fight me now, but with the right motivation, you'll learn to love being down on your knees soon enough."

"Never," I spat, widening my stance just as I'd seen Ashlynn do in my dream, adjusting my grip on the glass. I would die before I let him touch me.

You're the only one who can end this.

But I didn't get the chance. Brad caught me as I bolted for the door and pushed me against the wall with enough force to knock the air from my lungs. While I was still hunched over, gasping and wheezing, he looped the belt around my neck and tightened it like a leash.

When he yanked me forward, my legs buckled. Then, I was choking. My eyes bulged from the sockets and I let the glass slip through my fingers to claw at my throat, desperate for something I'd taken for granted only seconds before. The leather seemed to grow tighter the more I struggled to get my feet under me, yet I kept flailing and grunting.

It only hurts if you let it...

My vision blurred as the world around me spun like a merry-go-round, faster and faster until it felt like I was floating.

One second.

Two seconds.

Three seconds.

Brad hauled me to my feet and loosened the vice around my neck before tossing me onto the mattress like a piece of trash. I curled into the fetal position and coughed violently before gulping in ragged breaths. Despite my attempts to be brave, I began sobbing.

He hooked his hands under my thighs, jerking my body toward the edge of the bed with a low growl. My muscles spasmed in response and for the first time in my life, I considered the possibility I wouldn't make it out of this alive.

I was going to end up like Ashlynn.

"Now, here's how this is going to go," he snapped as he worked his dress pants down over his hips with one hand, keeping the other flat on my abdomen. "I'm going to ruin your body, and you're not going to move a single muscle. Am I clear?"

My breath caught as I tried to inhale through my swollen nostrils, sounding like a whimper. The belt hung around my throat like a grotesque necklace, a visual reminder of what would happen to me again if I didn't obey.

Brad stepped out of his slacks and kicked them aside before looming over me. "Open your mouth."

I mashed my lips together, praying he couldn't see my disobedience in the darkness. He wrapped a hand around my jaw and squeezed until my lips parted, before spitting into my mouth.

Tears pricked the back of my eyes. It was the most degrading thing I'd ever experienced, and he was only getting started.

"Rule number one- answer me when I ask you a question. Are you going to be a good girl while I fuck the sin out of you?"

I would never give him my consent or my body.

Maybe it was nothing more than self-preservation or a last-ditch attempt by my brain to prevent further pain. Whatever the case, I recalled the aquarium and the living things locked in glass cages like trophies. With that, came another memory, one as vivid now as the day it had happened.

I didn't know why I'd taken Morgan's convertible, but there wasn't a doubt in my mind I'd be risking death if I came into my arranged marriage as anything other than a meek little virgin.

A hymen was a symbol of purity—the only thing that made me valuable. Unfortunately, my horse, Pepper, had taken mine when I was eleven when she threw me from my saddle. My eldest sister, Aubrey, had helped me clean up before making me promise to never tell a soul.

Tristan had no other daughters. Without Brad's money, the entire organization would be crippled.

You take down a monster by exposing it.

Maybe I was the only one who could stop this. And death in battle was still preferable to a life spent in chains.

"You're too late," I croaked hoarsely as his hand moved to the belt around my throat. "Killian."

The lie was bitter against my tongue, but I was no longer asking for forgiveness from any God who would allow this.

Brad recoiled. "What?"

Ignoring the wave of dizziness, I pushed myself up onto my elbows and forced out, "I'm not a virgin. I gave myself to Killian. If you don't believe me, call Sister Helene to check."

He backed away from me and for a split second, I almost believed it was over. But then he lifted the lamp off my nightstand and hurled it at the wall with a guttural roar. "You slut!"

The mattress suddenly tipped, and I tumbled backward, coming down hard on my left hip.

"You were supposed to be mine!" he bellowed. "Mine!"

I couldn't see him, but the sounds of destruction told me he was still on the other side of the room. Something shattered as it hit the floor and I crawled to the nearest wall, tucking my arms and legs to my chest.

The door flew open, and a shaft of light from the hall cut across the room, illuminating Brad—or at least, someone who used to be him. His skin was mottled with rage, the muscles and veins straining against his skin as he trashed my room.

I winced when the overhead light flipped on, blinking until my pupils constricted enough for me to see that my bedroom floor was now littered with glass and splintered wood.

Morgan stood by the switch with her hand pressed to her lips, scanning the room. When her eyes met mine, she nodded and tucked her back to the wall, side-stepping to avoid the half-naked mad man in the center of the room.

Brad let out a harsh breath, and the room fell silent. I ignored Morgan's outstretched hands and jerked my head back toward him, coming face to face with the very thing that had captured his attention.

My treasures.

All the things I'd diligently stowed beneath my bed over the years were now strewn across the floor like discarded toys.

———

Tristan stood in front of the fireplace in his office, his hands clasped behind his back. "You've been keeping things from me, little dove," he said coldly.

"So have you," I bit out from the chair in front of his desk. My treasures had been spread across it like contraband. I balled my hands into fists against the armrests, keeping my eyes on his. Despite the fire burning a few feet away, I couldn't stop shivering.

Maybe because I knew what was to come.

He shook his head, seemingly ignoring my accusation while staring absently into the flames. "Helene says it's true—you united your soul with an unbeliever's."

I tore my eyes from his profile and lowered my head, admitting, "I love Killian. If you'd just give him a chance—get to know him—"

"Know him? What's to know? He's just like the rest of the world!" he roared, pivoting to face me. "Do you realize what you've done?"

"I didn't mean to hurt you," I began, shrinking back when Tristan stalked toward me. "I didn't want to fall in love with him, it just happened."

His nostrils flared as he grabbed my well-loved copy of *Pride and Prejudice* from his desk, waving it in front of the fire. "Your sins will cost you, little dove."

"Please," I whispered, reaching toward him. "It's mine."

Tristan tsked and tossed the book into the fire. "Nothing is yours."

I jumped to my feet with a strangled gasp, only to drop back into my chair when the vein popped out in his neck.

"Why are you doing this?" I squeaked; my voice still rough from being choked. He moved behind my chair, forcing me to crane my neck to keep him in my sights. His large hands came down against my shoulders. I shuddered at the feel of his fingers curling over my collarbones.

Tears blurred my vision as I brokenly whispered, "You've already won."

"How do you figure?" he mused. "I preach abstinence, and my youngest defiles herself with a baseball player. What will people say?"

My shoulders sagged under the weight of his grip. "I won't say a word."

Tristan released his hold on me and walked back to the fireplace, condemning *Wuthering Heights* to the same fate as *Pride and Prejudice*. The cover curled and blackened beneath the flames, but I remained silent.

One by one, I was forced to witness as the things I'd lovingly collected were charred beyond recognition. The only thing missing was Ashlynn's Hurricane towel. I prayed it was because they hadn't found it yet.

After stoking the fire, he leaned against the mantle, watching me with a hardened expression. "It's not you I'm worried about, little dove. How many times did I warn you about people who would try to hurt you to get to me? Men like that live for scandal and would gladly take down everything we've built."

I sucked in a ragged breath. "He wouldn't—"

"You don't even know him," Tristan snapped bitterly, before dropping down into the chair behind his desk. The deep lines etched in his face made him look tired.

Tristan James, the titan, was gone.

This man was frail.

Fragile.

"I used to be a lot like you, Ariana. In fact, it's how I got my start as a pastor. Did you know that?"

I shook my head, having always assumed he'd been born with a Bible in his hand.

He gazed into the fireplace again. "I don't share it with many people. In fact, I think your mama might have been the last person I told. I used to think the world was a broken thing in need of fixing. So, after high school, I climbed into my old Chevy and traveled the country, preaching in any church that would have me. Most turned me away once they realized I hadn't attended seminary, thinking a piece of paper made a difference. Not long after, the money ran out. Things got pretty desperate. I felt like a complete failure and decided to end it."

My jaw went slack, but I said nothing.

"I was living in my truck at the time. One night, I sat there, turning the gun over in my hands, trying to work up the courage to do it when there was a tap on the door. Seeing it was an elderly woman, I cranked the window down and asked if she needed help. Do you know what she said to me?"

"No," I whispered, my heart somewhere in my throat.

The corner of his mouth lifted. "She told me that God had a plan for my life and that I was going to be raised up to lead the flock back to the shepherd. My children would be known among nations, and all who saw would recognize them as a sign of God's strength. I felt hope like I hadn't in years when I came back here. I took out a loan to buy the land we're on and set us apart from the world.

"You see, salvation was meant to be exclusive. Once I figured that out, the flock began arriving in droves, just as the old woman had said. Your sisters were born with dark hair and, for the most part, were quiet babies. Not you, though," he chuckled softly.

The flames in the fireplace flickered, casting eerie orange shadows across his face and making his smile seem sinister. The hairs on the nape of my neck lifted. I hugged myself while my mind scrambled to decode the danger in his words.

His smile faded, and he bit down on his lower lip. "You came into this world with a cry so loud it could be heard beyond the walls of the community. You looked just like your mama with those wild red curls. I thought it was a sign you were special. Instead, you've ripped the prophecy to shreds by sinning against yourself."

"Is that all I am to you?" I asked, fighting back tears. "An unfulfilled prophecy? A threat to your kingdom? All I've ever wanted was for you to love me like you love the church!"

"I do love you, Ariana," Tristan admitted quietly, leaning forward to rest his forearms against the desk. "You know, if I'm honest, Brad isn't the man I imagined you marrying. There's a softness about you that the world's never been able to touch. And you have a heart like your mama's, always seeing the good in everything."

As much as I'd steeled myself for this meeting, I was not prepared for this. I'd tried hardening my heart, but his words had undone everything. I began to weep over the idiocy of it all. He'd taken the people I loved away but left me with the very thing I'd wanted since I was five.

Why were my prayers answered now? And why had it come at Killian's expense?

WAIT FOR IT   323

"If you love me, why'd you sell me to a man who would do this?" I countered with a sob, lifting my chin to expose the marks on my throat. "He started sneaking into my room when I was eleven, wanting to know if I'd bled yet and reciting scriptures at me like they were curses. Maybe I destroyed a prophecy, but you—you let evil into your house!"

I slapped a hand over my mouth and collapsed against the back of the chair, shaking uncontrollably.

I'd done it.

"Brad? I didn't know—" Tristan made a choking noise, the color draining from his face. "You never said a word."

"He said no one would believe me."

"If I'd known it was happening, I would have dealt with it then. Brad is my business partner... my friend." Something like grief clouded his features. He cleared his throat and slow-blinked until the mask of indifference fell back into place.

"You have to understand—the church had been trying to expand for years, but even with new members joining every week, the tithes alone weren't enough to cover the cost of building a larger campus while maintaining our lifestyle."

"But then Brad sold two of his companies," I stated flatly. My mind replayed every agonizing second of the day I learned I'd been bought.

"At the time, I didn't see any other way. There are so many people depending on the church, little dove—on me. I can't do it all on my own anymore." He turned back to the fire and covered his face with his hands, muffling his next words. "I need you, Ariana. I need you to help me make things right."

"I'll help you," I whispered as I approached him, placing my hand on the arm of his chair. My resolve crumbled in the face of his pain and I knelt at his feet, compelled to bridge the gap between us. He'd finally come to his senses. "We'll fix this together, okay?"

And we would too.

First, we'd go to the police station so I could explain that Killian hadn't taken me from *True North* against my will. Then, we'd ensure Tsega got her job back. And when Tristan got up in front of the church and told them how religion had blinded him to the truth, I'd be standing by his side.

"You will?" He asked, lowering his hands to cover mine. I nodded and he let out a breath. "We'll call a press conference."

I squeezed his fingers, trying to find the right words to convey my gratitude. "I think that's a good plan. The church won't turn their backs on your honesty."

"You mean your honesty, Ariana."

I tore my eyes from where our hands were joined, peering up at him in confusion. "Mine?"

Tristan nodded, trapping me against his leg. "You're going to tell the press that Killian Reed raped you."

I choked on the saliva that had pooled in my mouth before spluttering, "No! That never happened—Killian would never!"

I'd knelt in front of a monster, stupidly believing I could appeal to the parts of him that still held some affection for me. But he'd never cared about anyone beyond himself.

"Initially, I was skeptical too. A scandal of this magnitude is almost impossible to cover up, but Brad said he'd be willing to overlook your indiscretion if you admitted you'd been forced. God is already turning your trial into a testimony, little dove."

"I lied!" I hissed, fighting against his ever-tightening grip. "Killian and I never had sex! I just didn't want Brad to hurt me! It was Pepper —I fell off Pepper! Ask Aubrey, she knows!"

He chuckled, shaking his head at me like I was nothing more than a precocious child. "Helene checked you and said it was evident you'd been with a man—"

"No—Helene's not even a real nurse!" I cried, my shoulders slumping forward. "I haven't, I swear it! Please, you have to understand, Killian's a good man—"

"Can a man scoop fire into his lap without his clothes being burned? Can a man walk on hot coals without his feet being scorched? So is he who sleeps with another man's wife; no one who touches her will go unpunished. Your body was never yours to give away, Ariana. It belonged to Brad," Tristan growled, squeezing my wrist.

"You're h-hurting me," I stammered, clawing at the back of his hand to break his hold. I wanted to find Killian and run away. We'd go to Denmark or Finland—someplace where Tristan could never find us.

I could keep him safe.

He rose from his seat and began dragging me toward the fireplace when the string on my baseball bracelet gave with an audible snap. "What's this?"

"It's mine!" I scrambled to my feet. "Give it to me!"

With a smirk, he raised it over his head. "Agree to the press conference, and it's all yours, little dove."

Shit. Damn. Hell.

I moved onto my tiptoes, sweat trickling down my spine as I tried to reach the bracelet. "I won't condemn an innocent man, Tristan. Not even for you."

He cocked his head to the side and exhaled a soft laugh, "If you don't, we'll lose Brad's donation. And if that goes, I may as well admit my entire ministry was a sham."

"I'll go to the police," I vowed over the crackling of the logs in the fireplace. "I'll tell them what you did to Ashlynn and what you're trying to do to Killian."

"Ashlynn?" He drew in a sharp breath, blanching at the mention of her name.

I nodded earnestly, my voice trembling. "You killed her because she wouldn't obey. You'll have to kill me too because I won't stop running. I won't stop fighting."

Blink. Blink.

His lips curled in a slow smile. "Little dove, I'll deny you death even when you're begging for it."

"Listen to me, Tristan. I'm never going to be obedient. Do you know why? Because hungry dogs are loyal to no one, so you may as well end it now."

"Oh, I hear you," he calmly replied, even as his nostrils were flaring. "Now, you hear me. With your brain injury, I was granted guardianship. I control where you go, who you talk to—even who you don't talk to. You'll do what you're told, and then you'll marry Brad as planned. Is that clear?"

"You don't love me," I whispered, my voice almost gone. "If you did, you'd want to protect me from men like Brad."

"That's where you're wrong, little dove," he *tsked*. "Love is sacrifice. Now, if you're willing to die to yourself and step into the role you were created for, you'll find life is much sweeter. Brad is willing to love you, but you've got to put in the work."

I was still trying to wrap my mind around his warped version of a Sunday morning sermon when he tossed my bracelet into the fireplace. I dove forward, wildly grasping at the air. My knees landed against the hardwood with a loud squeal. Flames engulfed the leather almost immediately, but I kept going, fully prepared to climb in after it.

If he wouldn't end this, I would.

Maybe Killian had been right all along. No God was watching over us from above. It was just some lie we told ourselves.

Tristan hauled me up by the neckline of my shirt and returned me to the chair, raising a finger when I jumped to my feet again. "Before you attempt to martyr yourself, Joan of Arc, I've got something I want you to see."

He held up his cell phone, and my mouth fell open. It was a video of Killian, being led out of a building with his father on one side and a man I didn't recognize on the other. It was a media circus. He used his jacket to shield his face, but not before I saw the flash of terror in his eyes.

My God, they were going to crucify him because of me.

Seeing him stripped away my blanket of numbness, bringing me face to face with his pain. I forced myself to take deep breaths, fighting the urge to hyperventilate, or vomit. Maybe both.

"How did you get this?"

"Killian's father bailed him out of jail a couple of hours ago," Tristan explained with a shrug before tucking the phone back into his pocket.

My chin quivered, but I refused to lower my head. "I won't send him back there."

"You're the reason he was arrested, Ariana. Do you really think he's going to want you after all this? If his lawyers are any good, they're telling him to deny everything to make you look like a liar. He's going to hate you."

I touched my wrist, only to be reminded that Tristan had destroyed my source of strength along with everything else I held dear. I took a deep breath and closed my eyes, seeing Killian's face—hearing his words.

Love is the only thing strong enough to drive out fear and doubt.

"It's not about me." I stood and walked around the desk to him, smiling for the first time since I'd left Killian. "Because love is not self-seeking. It's patient, and it's kind. Love does not dishonor others but protects them always. But more than anything, love never fails! You preach the words, but you don't listen! So, do what you want, but I'm not going to move!"

He sized me up with a smirk before clapping slowly. "Very good, little dove. I'm impressed."

"I'm not doing the press conference. You can burn my things and keep me locked away like a prisoner, but I won't do it."

"Yes, you just said that." He walked over to stand in front of the fire, whistling one of my songs. I swallowed hard and glanced down at the large glass cross on his desk, wondering if it was sturdy enough to be used as a weapon. Three deep lines on the forehead meant trouble, while whistling indicated he was close to a blackout rage.

Keeping his back to me, he added, "Last week we held a funeral for a man who was killed while crossing the street. It sounds like a freak accident, but it happens more often than you'd think. People don't always look both ways, or maybe the person behind the wheel is drunk. Driving's not much better. Tires blow, and brakes go out—even the computer systems can be easily hacked. You just can't be too careful nowadays."

I clutched the desk to keep myself upright, panting, "What are you saying—you caused my accident?"

The pedals not working... the radio and lights going on and off— what if it hadn't been a nightmare?

He spun on his heel with a wide grin, swinging the fireplace poker like it was a baseball bat. "Don't be silly, sweetheart. Just thinking out loud. There are a lot of ways to encourage people to change their minds, don't you think?"

I backed up a step, shaking my head. "But I did everything you said! I followed the rules!"

"What makes you think I'm talking about you? You know—" He cracked his neck and swung the poker, the air whistling from the momentum. "I actually wanted to be a baseball player as a kid."

I stumbled over a power cord jutting out from beneath the desk but quickly regained my footing and continued backing toward the door.

"Paul, in his letter to the Corinthians, wrote, 'But when I became a man, I put away childish things.'" Tristan swung again, this time sending a stack of papers sailing over the edge of the desk. "These athletes live like they're gods—free to take whatever they want, whenever they want! But there's a cost—there's always a cost! 'All at once, he followed her, like an ox going to the slaughter; like a deer stepping into a noose til an arrow pierces his liver, like a bird darting into a snare—little knowing it will cost him his life.'"

To him, I'd always been the exotic collectible—the rare find that was worth millions—and Tristan had just discovered the one way to ensure I stayed locked behind glass forever.

Killian.

I stilled as years of bottled-up hurt came to a head, before launching myself at him with a snarl. Tristan's delusions had only grown stronger in my absence. He was committed to his narrative, no matter how far it was from the truth. Ashlynn's death. My car accident. Killian. There was always going to be someone standing in his way. The ground could be littered with bodies, but as long as it furthered his kingdom, he'd gladly rule over a wasteland.

"You goddamned asshole!" I shrieked, connecting with his forearm as he brought it up to deflect my blows. Killian's curses tumbled from lips as I raked my nails over Tristan's skin, drawing blood to the surface. Flames danced in his eyes, making the whites appear to be glowing.

The muscles in his neck stood out like cords as he threw his head back and laughed, before dropping the poker to the floor with a clatter.

He no longer needed it.

Tristan had finally found something I was powerless against. Killian was my greatest weakness, and he knew it.

I staggered back jerkily, bringing my hands up to protect my head, pleading, "I just want to keep him safe. Please, I'll do it, just don't hurt him."

"Attagirl," he praised, stalking toward me. "In the Gospels, John states, 'Greater love has no one than this: to lay down one's life for one's friends.'"

Pretend like you never went back to True North...

Pretend you're safe in Killian's arms...

Pretend you're somewhere else...

Freedom. Safety. They'd never been anything more than illusions.

Pretend it only hurts if you let it...

CHAPTER TWENTY-SIX
ARIANA

"She had not known the weight until she felt the freedom."

-Nathaniel Hawthorne, *The Scarlet Letter*

THE ONE THING I could count on when the world slipped off-axis was being left alone for days, sometimes even weeks afterward. My duties were reassigned, and all of my meals delivered up to my room. Like a mint on a pillow from one of those fancy hotels Tristan stayed in, each tray arrived with a wrapped present.

Sometimes, it was a new cross-stitch pattern or a coloring book. If Tristan had been particularly rough, I could expect a couple of pieces of jewelry. I'd never been able to determine if the gifts were sent in apology, or to buy my silence. Not that I spent much time considering it.

If I wasn't sleeping, I was staring up at the ceiling, watching the shadows cast by both the sun and moon. I stayed in my cocoon of numbness for as long as possible, moving only when it was absolutely necessary.

Which made my current situation all the more confusing. I was on day two of recovery. By all rights, I should have been lying in bed and wallowing in my misery, undisturbed. Instead, I was inexplicably sitting on a small stool inside the ensuite bathroom, letting Morgan braid my hair.

"Hold still," she ordered around the bobby pin between her lips. "I'm almost done."

It was just after midnight when she snuck in and forced me into the shower. My body hadn't even begun to stink. That usually happened around day five, when the sheets stuck to my damp skin and my hair was slick with oils.

The last time I stepped foot in a shower, Killian had been there. His scent had lingered on my skin as I faced Tristan, comforting me— making me believe I wasn't fighting alone.

Now, he was completely gone. I'd watched as the last traces of him swirled around the drain before disappearing completely.

And yet, I still didn't know why Morgan had come.

"I want to go back to bed now," I grumbled hoarsely, trying not to look at my reflection in the mirror. I was no longer *so goddamned beautiful.*

I was nothing more than an empty shell of my former self.

Dark shadows rimmed my lower lashes, almost identical to the necklace of bruising around my throat. My green eyes had a haunted look about them. I didn't remember much of what happened in Tristan's office other than the sharp, metallic tang of blood from biting down on my tongue to keep from screaming.

She went silent for a moment, pursing her lips as she looped the elastic around the end of my hair. "Tristan scheduled a press conference for noon at the church. It's not just the local affiliates, either. From what I understand, the major networks have flown in as well."

"Excuse me," I mumbled, before slipping off the stool to crouch in front of the toilet, expelling what little food and water I'd taken in over the past several days.

Morgan knelt beside me, her hand moving in small circles between my shoulder blades. "Are you?" she asked. "I mean, do you think you might be pregnant?"

You'll be the woman who carries my babies, slugger...

Sweat. Saliva. Tears. They all looked the same as they fell against the toilet seat.

"I'm still a virgin," I admitted, squeezing my eyes shut against the sudden bloom of pain in my chest. I'd been so close to real happiness. To being loved and cherished.

I stood up and rinsed my mouth before turning back to face her. She was still kneeling against the tile, her mouth slack. "But I thought—"

"Brad was going to rape me. I didn't stop to think about the repercussions—I just said it. How could I have been so stupid? I should have let—"

Morgan shook her head. "Don't you dare finish that sentence. This is all my fault, Ari. I pushed you on Killian, thinking it would save you from this, but I only made things worse."

"I love him." I winced and pressed the heel of my hand over my heart. The physical wounds on my body would heal, but the emotional trauma would linger. Every time I looked in the mirror, I'd see the coward who gave up an innocent man.

Her expression sharpened. "Then don't do this—don't go through with it. Killian will go to jail—lose his career—everything!"

I looked down, pleading with my eyes, needing her to understand why I was making this impossible decision. "I know, but Tristan has people watching him. He talked about—" I cleared my throat, determined not to cry.

"He talked about how easy it would be to make someone's death look like an accident. From hacking the car's computer to running someone down as they're crossing the street. You know as well as I do what he's capable of. This was the only way I could save him."

Morgan's forehead creased, pulling her eyebrows together. "What if there was another way?"

"There's not," I said, having spent the last forty-eight hours exhausting every option. "I'm damned either way. Look, I've accepted that I've lost him forever, but at least this way he gets a chance to move on someday."

She glanced down at her watch. "And is that what you want—for him to move on?"

"I just want him to be safe. If I knew of another way—one where he didn't get killed, go to jail, or lose baseball—" I sucked in a ragged breath, squeezing my fists until my fingernails dug into my palms. "I'd do it, but there's nothing."

"We've still got time," Morgan responded cryptically before standing up to lead me back into my room. Instead of letting me climb back into bed, she shut off the lights and dragged me over toward the door.

My breath caught as I stumbled over a shoe lying on the floor. "Morgan—what are you doing?"

After tapping her index finger lightly against the wood three times, she clapped a hand over my mouth, her eyes suddenly glossy. "Do not speak. Do not scream. Nod if you understand."

I shook my head, my nostrils flaring with short bursts of air as I gripped her arms. No one had ever said I couldn't leave my room, but the lock on the outside of the door had implicitly implied I was a prisoner.

"Listen to me," she whispered. "I was supposed to be in the car that night. Tristan set the entire thing up, knowing I was the only one who drove the convertible. You were never the target. I was. And I need you to trust me right now, okay?"

The handle turned, but the hallway was completely dark. A towering figure leaned in and my heart pinged against my ribcage when Morgan pushed me into his waiting arms. I knew it was a man, I could tell by the build, but his identity was a mystery.

I didn't realize I was whimpering until his palm moved over my mouth, where Morgan's had been just moments before. "Fifteen minutes," he hissed.

Her head bobbed in a nod before she leaned in to press a kiss to my temple. "I love you, Ari."

My eyes bulged in response because it sounded like goodbye. I tried looking back as the man hauled me down the hall, but she'd already disappeared into the shadows.

We bypassed the main staircase and slipped through the doorway leading to the staff wing. Blood pumped furiously through my veins, pleading with me to escape.

Morgan wanted me to trust her yet hadn't told me where I was being taken. For all I knew, she'd handed me over to Brad so he could finish what he started. A shiver wracked my body as I considered the possibility, before mentally talking myself down.

She'd asked me to trust her.

The man might have been holding me in a firm grip, but he'd deliberately avoided the bruised areas on my neck and torso, proving he wasn't Brad.

My breaths grew raspy as we moved down a hidden flight of stairs, but he didn't even seem winded. I blinked back the tears and focused on my surroundings. As long as I knew where we were, I was still safe. He took turn after turn with a familiarity that could have only come from living or working here. But if he was acting on Tristan's orders, there'd be no reason to sneak around.

The kitchen was as dark as the rest of the house, yet he navigated the layout without once slowing. When we reached the door leading outside, he leaned down to my ear. "Don't run."

I nodded shakily, exhaling through my nose.

My captor released his hold on my shoulder to enter something into his cell phone. The deadbolt slid back with a low musical tone, and then we were outside.

We crept along the perimeter of the house, avoiding the lights mounted along the top of the wall. I managed to trip over my own two feet, craning my neck to get a better look.

It was Dean, the only member of my father's security team who didn't look like he murdered people on a daily basis. Although, without his signature smile, he seemed just as frightening as the others.

As if reading my panicked thoughts, he shook his head, the corner of his mouth lifting. "I'm not going to hurt you, Ariana."

I wondered if they'd told Ashlynn the same thing.

My lungs suddenly demanded more oxygen, but I inhaled too fast, leaving me feeling sick. I tried again, still unable to draw enough air through the tight band around my chest.

"No one's going to hurt you—not while I've got you, okay?"

I clutched at my chest, seeing black spots as I gasped for my next breath.

Dean removed the hand from my mouth, spinning my body to face his. "Purse your lips—good. Now, breathe in slowly." He gently repeated the words while leading me farther from the house.

We pushed through a clump of Hollywood Juniper shrubs, coming face to face with a hidden door tucked into the back portion of the wall. He stopped to punch another series of numbers into his phone until it opened with a soft click.

Under the streetlights, I could easily see the gun holstered at his side. Even if I put everything into making a break for it, a bullet was faster. Morgan had wanted me to trust her. It was why I'd believed Dean when he lied and told me he wouldn't hurt me.

I was an unnecessary risk—a threat to the lifestyle they'd all grown accustomed to.

My voice was surprisingly steady as I whispered the same words I'd once heard my mama say. "He's going to kill me."

Sadness clouded his features, but he forced a smile. "Not without going through me, he won't. You're mine."

"N-n-no," I stammered with sudden realization, unable to make myself say the words as I began backing away. It was somehow sicker than the thought of being murdered on Tristan's orders. "I won't do that—please!"

I'd been treading water since I got back, fighting to stay alive—to have a say in what happened to my body—only to have it end just steps from the wall.

Dean grimaced and immediately began shaking his head. "No,

no, no. That came out wrong," he rushed out, his tone gentle but firm. "I'm married—happily married, I might add. Besides, my wife could probably kick both our asses, blindfolded."

I swallowed around the knot in my throat. "Then, why bring me out here?"

"Look, Ariana. I know what they did to you. I should have known when he brought you back and dismissed the guards from the house." He shifted his jaw from side to side, avoiding my glare. "And I know what they're going to try to force you to do. I just need you to trust me here, okay?"

My teeth came together in agitation. "Trust you? You'll forgive me if I'm struggling with the concept right now. The last forty-eight hours have proven that no one can be trusted."

"I'm the one who helped you escape the first time—"

"And?" I challenged, trying to make my tone seem indifferent as my heart began to beat wildly in my chest. "Where was I going?"

He lifted a shoulder. "I don't know that—"

Of course not.

"What kind of a security guard are you?" I interrupted with a sigh, unable to hide my frustration. "And you want me to trust you? You work for Tristan. For all I know, you were the one responsible for my 'accident.'"

He watched my tirade with a lifted brow before admitting, "I was tasked with keeping you safe, and I've failed twice now. I don't intend to fail again."

"By whom?" I argued, my chin raised. "Tristan? Nice try, but the good pastor doesn't care about my safety, as evidenced by... well, I guess my entire life."

Dean cut his eyes over to me in a quick glance before crossing the street, effectively ending our conversation.

"Seriously?" I complained as I reluctantly followed, my mind weighed down with more questions than answers. If he wasn't operating under Tristan's orders, then who was he working for? Where was he taking me? Was any of it going to save Killian?

Until he was willing to talk, I could only speculate.

A twig snapped beneath my shoe, and I realized we were following the same path I'd taken the day I saved Killian.

We reached the clearing, and I brought a hand up over my mouth, tensing against the memories washing up along the shore. I'd spent the first couple of years with my nose pressed to the window in the library, searching for his face among the colorful blurs dotting the water. After a while, it became too painful to look, a dark reminder of a life I'd never have.

"Ten minutes, and then we have to go."

I lifted my eyes with a frown. "But you still haven't told me why we're out here."

"Ariana." Dean pointed behind me, his dark eyes sparkling with amusement. "Ten minutes. I'll be right over there, waiting for you."

Someone had fixed up the old dock, adding lights and a railing on either side. I sucked in a breath when I saw the man looking out over the water, and my mind fell silent for the first time in days.

Killian.

Less than ten feet away from me.

I wanted to run to him, but something in the hard set of his jaw told me I couldn't. Instead, I dragged my feet over the sand, every bit the peasant girl who'd fallen in love with a prince.

Two different worlds—I'd known it then, but I felt it now.

He didn't look up when I stepped onto the dock, just continued watching the lazy ripples along the surface of the lake. The hood of his jacket hid his profile, but I'd seen the unshaven dishevelment as I approached. I wondered when he'd last slept or eaten something of substance but kept the questions to myself.

My footsteps faltered when I reached his side. I lifted my hand, aching to touch him, to make him real again. For several seconds, my fingers dangled in the air between us, but then his shoulders rounded, snuffing the dying embers of hope from my chest.

"I can't look at you, Ari," he quietly admitted, his body bristling with tension. "If I do, I'll forget what I came here to say."

Killian wasn't mine—not anymore.

I lowered my hand back to my side, feeling the water close in, pulling my body down into its dark depths. This entire time, I'd been holding my breath. For him. I opened my mouth and exhaled, the swarm of bubbles tickling my nose as they drifted up. I watched them go, racing toward the light shimmering along the surface, but I'd never belonged up there.

It grew colder as I sank, seeping into my bones and bearing down on my heart. Where I expected death, I continued drawing shallow breaths, as if some unseen force beyond explanation was keeping me alive.

Just one more choice that wasn't mine to make.

"I feel stupid, you know?" he mused bitterly to the water. "The fucking fool who'd let himself believe that maybe there really was a God—some higher power who broke me, so I'd find you."

"And now?" I choked on the words, searching for the smallest hint that the man who'd loved me was still in there.

Loved.

Past tense.

Was there anything sadder than the stark reminder that eventually everything ran out?

Time.

Affection.

It seemed the only thing I'd hold onto would be the insurmountable pain of losing him. Maybe that would be the burden I carried in this life.

I'd spent the last ten years wondering if I could ever mean something to him like he had me. I did, just not like I imagined. I would forever be a symbol of destruction, the woman who ripped everything he loved away from him.

The muscle in his jaw ticked as he bit out, "I told you I believed in myself. When you asked me about miracles, I told you it was all bullshit. So, you know what? If there is a God, then I imagine he's probably having a pretty good laugh at my expense right now. I'm getting what I deserve. My biggest sin was pride. I was filled to the fucking brim with it, and now, I've got nothing."

"I know I've hurt you," I said softly, my eyes brimming with tears.

"Hurt?" Killian roared suddenly, squeezing the railing until his arms shook. "Are you fucking serious? Blowing out my knee hurt, Ariana! This is in an entirely new stratosphere!"

I rubbed my eyes but stayed silent. I'd wanted to make him real, but this didn't feel like a victory. His pain was indistinguishable from mine; my heart simply incapable of telling the difference.

The urge to hold him was overwhelming, like the call of a siren. With that in mind, I wrapped my arms around myself and walked farther out onto the dock, giving him my back.

"I broke every one of my goddamned rules for you," he drawled with a bitter chuckle. "Every. Single. One. Then, as I'm being arrested—which, by the way, thank you so very much for that—I find out it was all a lie!"

His footsteps moved closer, but I honored his request and didn't turn around. He deserved the right to purge his rage, to force me to listen to the chaos I'd created in his world. I'd take it, even if his every word felt like a knife sliding under my skin.

"You told me you were scared of your father yet failed to mention he was Tristan fucking James. I should have figured it out when you kept bringing up religion." Killian paused, and I didn't need to turn around to know he was drinking. I could hear the liquid splashing against the inside of the bottle.

"Was it a game to you—making me believe you were afraid?"

"I was afraid. I still am."

"Bullshit," Killian spat, letting the bottle fall to the deck with a thud. "Of what? Growing up in a mansion? Having your entire music career handed to you by your father's church? Tell me, Ariana. What the hell do you know about actual fear?"

My spine stiffened, and I cocked my head to the side, catching him out of the corner of my eye. "Why'd you come? And of all places, why here?"

Killian positioned himself at my back, close enough that I could feel the heat of his body. If I rocked back, my hips would be resting against his thighs. We'd been in an almost identical position just two nights ago in front of his bathroom mirror.

"I thought it was only right that we end where we started," he slurred against my ear, the scent of hard liquor stinging my nostrils.

Killian was drunk.

Broken.

Because of me.

"I want you to have to stand in the spot where you saved me and explain why you lied. I want to ruin this place for you, so you can't come back without remembering tonight. I want to rip you apart like you've done me."

"You're scaring me," I whispered, turning back to the water.

"Good. Now you know what it feels like." The dock creaked as he leaned in to deposit my necklace on the railing, before pulling away again. "I think this is yours."

He could have just as easily launched it into the water but hadn't because he wasn't a bad person.

"I'm sorry," I said quietly, scooping the necklace into my palm and tucking it into my pocket. There was nothing left for me to say because my words meant nothing. I meant nothing.

Little waves splashed against the same wooden pilings that had held his body ten years ago. As I peered down into the lake, I was almost convinced I'd find him there again, but the murky water gave nothing away.

My heart had been racing for the past forty-eight hours, stuck in an endless loop of fight or flight. Now, weakened by hunger and exhaustion, I found myself contemplating suicide. It was a solution I hadn't considered, but the only one that would save us both. Killian would keep his career, and I'd finally be free.

The water was freezing, I doubted I'd be able to last more than fifteen minutes. It'd be fitting, really, to sacrifice myself in the same spot I saved him. Like I was exchanging my life for his, setting things right. Maybe the good parts of me were still down there, caught under the dock, awaiting my return.

Would my body surrender easily, or continue to fight to stay alive because it was all I'd ever known?

I gripped the railing in my hands until my knuckles went white under the bright lights, wondering if there was courage in giving up.

He took a deep breath, close enough that it lifted several strands of hair from my braid. When he spoke again, his voice was low and taunting. "You're sorry? For which part—lying about being engaged or accusing me of rape? I just want to be sure I have it right for my lawyers."

I released a strangled breath, unable to fight the tears coursing down my cheeks. The silent sobs were a depth of pain beyond measure, a frequency of grief humans weren't capable of hearing.

Killian's arms moved on either side of mine, caging me. "Maybe you're sorry for kissing me. Or for not being able to fake it when I made you come. I wonder if Brad will be able to do the same for you," he slurred, letting the short bristles of hair on his jaw scrape over my neck. He was mocking me, not only with his words but his body as well.

I squeezed my eyes shut, trying to block out the nothingness in his voice—the memories of a time when his body against mine wasn't a threat.

Self-preservation pierced the numbness in my chest, and I turned to look back over my shoulder at him. "I think I want to go now."

Neither one of us was leaving here a winner.

He threw his head back with a low growl. "Not until you tell me why you're doing this."

"You've already decided I'm guilty, Killian," I ground out. "What else is there to say?"

"I don't know, Ariana. Maybe start by telling me why you're accusing me of rape!" He slammed his fist against the railing, just inches from my hand. "Christ, how could you? I fucking let you in— told you things I've never told anyone!"

I flinched in response, which only seemed to anger him further.

"Goddammit, answer me!" He grasped my wrist, pulling me to face him. "Just tell me—"

Rule number one- answer me when I ask you a question.

I hissed in pain and brought my other hand up to his chest, pushing him away. "I'm sorry—please be gentle with me!" I sobbed. "Please! I'm so sorry!"

It only hurts if you let it...

Killian released me immediately and stumbled back. I briefly registered the flash of movement from the corner of my eye, and then Dean was in between us.

The security guard held Killian against the railing, breathing normally as if he hadn't just crossed the beach with superhuman speed. He gave me a once-over before asking, "You okay?"

I nodded and tugged the sleeves of my v-neck sweater down over my trembling hands. "C-c-can we just have a m-m-minute?"

"You sure? I don't mind staying—"

I took a deep breath. "I'm okay."

"I'll stay close in case you change your mind."

Killian straightened his shirt, waiting until Dean was a reasonable distance down the dock. When he approached me, his hands were raised in surrender.

My heart sped up, each beat pulsing in my ears as his intense gaze moved down my body. This wasn't lust, though. Killian was cataloging my injuries.

"Don't—please." I ducked my head and turned away, feeling stripped of all dignity.

"Ari, look at me," he pleaded softly. "Please."

I channeled my pain into stubborn determination and shook my head. "Was there anything else you wanted to say, or can I go now?"

"Please."

I slowly turned around to find the fight gone from his eyes. He gazed down at me with a look of anguish I felt in the place my heart used to be.

Killian cupped my chin in his hand. I let him tip my face up, longing for the numbness from before. I didn't want to feel anymore.

"It doesn't hurt," I lied, as he gently traced the bruises around my throat with the pads of his fingers, swearing under his breath.

"Who did this to you?" he asked, his blue eyes wide and frantic.

I sucked in a ragged breath and shook my head, trying my best not to cry. There was a familiarity in rage, a comfort in something I'd dealt with all my life. But Killian's compassion was going to be my undoing.

He lowered his head and brushed his lips over my skin, kissing my wounds as if it might make them better.

"Don't do that," I protested, pulling away to wrap my arms around my belly. "Don't treat me like I'm a bird with a hurt wing or something that deserves pity. I ruined your life. Be mad. Scream. Just don't be nice—not to me."

"I'm sorry," Killian admitted, his nostrils flaring. "For all of it. I didn't—"

"I said it," I suddenly confessed, needing him to hate me. "I told Brad you took my virginity—I'm the reason you're going to lose everything."

"Why would you lie—" Killian paused before lifting his eyes back up to my throat with a low growl. Then, his arms were around me, cradling my broken body against his like it was made of glass.

Instead of fighting his embrace, I sank further into it, breathing him in. I let myself take comfort in the only sanctuary I'd ever known.

Killian's chest heaved in anguish. "It's okay, baby. I'm right here. I've got you."

"I'm sorry," I choked out. "I shouldn't have said it, but I didn't know what else—"

"Don't," he warned in a gravelly tone. "You did what you had to do to survive. Do you feel my heart beating? I want you to focus on that—nothing else."

The guilt I'd been carrying for the past two days fell away as I submitted to the only man who'd ever deserve it, in the only way that had ever felt right.

By being protected.

Submissiveness had never been about degrading or making myself small, but in being strong enough to let him shoulder the weight of my burdens.

"There won't be any need for a press conference because I'm turning myself in."

I lifted my cheek from his chest, swallowing a whimper to whisper, "No, you can't. You'll go to prison—lose everything."

Killian's nostrils flared, and he ground his jaw, fighting to stay in control of his emotions. "I lost you. Nothing else matters."

"But your dream—"

"Was you, girl," he sniffed, his heavy stubble grazing my temple. "It's always been you."

He tipped my face up, brushing his lips over mine like a whisper.

There and gone.

Hello and goodbye.

I instinctively leaned into Killian's body with a soft moan, needing more, demanding an act of atonement. My broken and bloodied fingernails moved up to his neck, guiding him back to me.

Our mouths moved together in repentance, speaking all the words we couldn't say, the whispers of the promises we'd been forced to break. I parted my lips, letting the liquor on his tongue burn away the hurt.

Sister Helene had tried convincing me it was nothing more than young love, but the past two days had aged me a hundred years. I didn't care if it was wrong, I felt more alive in his arms than I ever had inside the church.

Killian was my oxygen.

The only thing that had kept me from drowning years ago.

"Ari," he broke away with a pant, dropping his forehead to mine. "I love you. I don't know that I'll ever be able to stop. So, let me fight for you the only way I can. Let me be your knight in slightly tarnished armor."

I laughed through the tears because I'd never been looking for a knight, just a sword powerful enough to take down a monster.

"What I said before about you being fake—" His eyes welled up. "You are, without a doubt, the most genuine and caring person I've ever met."

I pressed my fist to my lips to hold back my tears, making a sound of protest when I saw Dean approaching. "No. I'm not ready."

"Ariana, we've got a car waiting," he said with an apologetic smile. "Morgan's already been taken to a safe location—"

"No," I repeated, my voice raw. "I won't leave him to face this alone."

"We need to extract you tonight before the shit hits the fan."

Dean said it so matter-of-factly, but every part of my body tensed with the realization that he hadn't brought me here for a nighttime reunion.

He was forcing me to say goodbye.

"Baby," Killian murmured, keeping one hand on my jaw. "He's giving you a way out. Take it. Don't worry about me. I've been through the wringer before. I can handle it as long as I know you're safe—"

"You don't understand—we're not safe! Nobody knows Tristan like I do, and he's not going to stop until he gets what he wants!"

"The case against Killian falls apart without you, Ariana," Dean answered patiently. "It's the only way to keep you from perjuring yourself if it makes it to trial."

Hysterical laughter bubbled up in my throat, and I shook my head. "If I don't go through with the press conference, they'll have him killed." I turned back to Killian. "It was me, or you and I chose—"

Pick up your shield and fight back.

The weight of the words nearly knocked me over, and I suddenly knew what to do.

"Oh, my God." My eyes widened. "Me. I'm the only one who can stop him. Dean, Killian's going to be taking my place."

"Ari, no—"

I silenced his protest with my lips, before pulling away with a victorious smirk. "If I don't make it out of this alive, make sure the world knows I died a hero."

How do you destroy a monster when you have nothing?

By turning yourself into a weapon.

CHAPTER TWENTY-SEVEN
ARIANA

"There is love in me the likes of which you've never seen. There is rage in me the likes of which should never escape. If I am not satisfied in the one, I will indulge the other."

-Mary Shelley, *Frankenstein*

THERE WAS a soft rap at the door. "Fifteen minutes."

A sheen of cold sweat coated my face. I dropped to my knees again, retching violently in the small bathroom attached to the church nursery. I'd prayed for an eleventh-hour rescue, but this wasn't a movie or one of my beloved books.

After promising he'd get Killian to a safe place, Dean had led me back to my room, where I'd spent most of the night hugging the toilet. During the rare moments my eyes had drifted shut in exhaustion, I'd been plagued by disjointed nightmares.

In them, I was back inside the car again. Only, this time, it was sinking. The community pool had decayed into ruins, no longer recognizable as the place where Ashlynn had taught me to swim. Weeds sprouted through the cracked blue tiles, and thick, choking vines had taken over the diving board.

Murky black water swallowed the front of the convertible. I kicked and kicked but couldn't free my legs from the windshield. Something brushed against my arm, and I opened my mouth to scream, inhaling a mouthful of inky sludge before everything went dark.

In another, I saw it. The creature was darkness itself, suspended motionless above me, watching through wide pupils. Its long tentacles unfurled, dancing toward me with an almost mesmerizing grace the likes of which I'd never seen before.

Surprisingly, I hadn't been afraid.

Not at first. It wasn't until I tried bringing my hand up as one brushed across my forehead, only to find I couldn't move. A pale tentacle caressed my cheek before disappearing into one of my nostrils. Two more forced their way past my lips and down my throat, silencing my cries for help, as the car sank deeper.

I wasn't alone.

Mama. Morgan. Ashlynn. Women I'd never even met before. Their bodies were buried in the muck, mouths transfixed in horror. And, at the very bottom—Killian. His eyes, now wholly gray, were fixed on mine. But he was dead. Just like the rest of them.

Needless to say, it hadn't instilled a lot of confidence in what I was about to do.

I got sick again with a low groan before stumbling over to the sink to rinse my mouth and wash my hands. Someone had come and done my makeup and hair, but no beauty product could erase the look of terror from my eyes.

Dean was waiting on the other side of the door with a mint and a lifted brow. "You really don't handle stress very well, do you?"

I took the mint from his hand with a weak smile and rasped, "Apparently not."

He pinned a microphone to the thick cashmere scarf knotted around my neck. It was the only accessory effective in covering the bruises around my throat. Tristan had it delivered to my room just after dawn, along with a Ponte knit dress that fell just past my knees. My wounds were draped in black, completely hidden from view.

With my understated makeup and messy twisted chignon updo, I was the picture of elegant mourning.

"He's ready to see you in his office," Dean murmured, making a final adjustment to the device.

Fear coated my tongue, along with bitter aftertaste of vomit, but I managed a small nod. "And everyone is still safe?"

"Completely," he reassured me. "Just remember what you came here to do."

As if I had the luxury to consider anything else.

I slowly made my way down the hall, my heels clicking loudly against the stained concrete floor with each measured step. When I reached the familiar mahogany door, I stopped and waited for the surge of bravery to flood my veins.

There was nothing but a steady drip of terror.

I swallowed past the lump in my throat and rapped my knuckles against the wood.

"Come in," Tristan said, using his preacher's voice. When he saw it was me, there was a brief flash of venom in his eyes. "Ariana, sit."

Blink. Blink.

I perched on the edge of a chair almost identical to the one in his office at the house. My hands were folded in my lap to mask the shaking.

"Have you spoken to Morgan since you've been home?" he asked, inspecting his manicured fingernails. He'd insisted on separate rooms after their marriage, only allowing her into his bed when he wanted sex.

"I've been locked in my room," I answered sweetly. "Or did you forget?"

"Dammit, Ariana!" Tristan jabbed a finger in my direction. "Don't play games with me—not today! If you know where she is, you need to tell me right now!"

"I have no idea," I answered truthfully. "But if she's smart, she'll never come back."

He smiled coldly. "And why is that, little dove? What makes you so sure she'd want to leave all of this behind?"

My stomach somersaulted in my belly, urging me to keep my mouth shut unless I wanted to coat the surface of his desk in stomach acid.

"The convertible," I gulped, resisting the urge to reach up and touch my necklace. "The night of the accident, I took the convertible."

His expression shifted to one of boredom. "Yes, I'm aware of that, little dove. I fail to see what it has to do with Morgan, though."

Shit. Damn. Hell.

"She was supposed to be in the car that night," I admitted, balling my hands into fists against my skirt. "It was her car, after all."

Tristan shrugged easily and leaned back in his chair with a low chuckle. "So, you took her car and wrecked it. I bought her another. Again, I'm not following how any of this relates to her sudden disappearance."

He wasn't going to admit to a single thing—not without proof, of which I had none. I lightly bit down on the inside of my cheek and glanced up at the clock on the wall.

Ten minutes.

"We'll discuss this later back at the house. For now, let's go over what you're going to say out there," Tristan continued, sliding several papers across the desk. "Here's your speech, along with which reporters you're to take questions from. The answers to what they're going to ask are on the back page."

I skimmed over the pages, almost impressed by the elaborate lie he'd concocted. There was even a doctor's report attached, detailing my internal injuries, as well as a non-existent semen sample that had been taken for further testing.

Clearly, Tristan planned on handling this problem in the same manner he'd dealt with my mama and Ashlynn, by creating a story so airtight no one would dare question or spend much time looking into it. He was willing to condemn a man for no more than having the audacity to love me, a crime in his mind.

"And if I refuse to read this?" I challenged, goading him into an emotional game of chicken. The answer had come to me as I stood on the dock last night.

I'd seen myself as a pawn. In reality, I was the one with all the bargaining power. Tristan had told me as much when he admitted he couldn't do it alone. And unless he wanted to lose Brad's money, he couldn't kill me either.

"You've grown defiant, little dove." His voice held a mixture of pride and anger as he leaned forward to rest his arms on the desk. "I'd advise against making such a hasty decision. Do you happen to know where the baseball player is right now?"

"Do you?" I asked, immediately second-guessing my decision to call his bluff.

Tristan went silent for a moment, his blue eyes taunting me. "Killian's holed up in his condo, waiting to be arrested again. Although, I imagine if you're not going to go through with the press conference, that might change. He might feel safe enough to let his guard down and leave."

He lifted his hands as if to say, *what can you do?* I turned away, resisting the smile tugging at my lips. Killian was nowhere near his condo, but my father didn't know that. It was just another in a long line of empty threats meant to keep me obedient.

"Did you decide?" I studied my broken fingernails, noting the dried blood on the ones that had been torn down to the quick. I'd give myself this, I hadn't gone down without a fight.

"What?"

I looked up, pinning him with my stare. "The night Brad attacked me, you said there were a lot of ways for someone to die and make it look like an accident. I was just wondering, have you decided yet?"

Tristan chuckled at my morbid question. "Why do you ask?"

My gaze drifted back to the clock on the wall.

Five minutes.

We were running out of time.

"No reason." I shrugged. "Just curious."

"As long as you do your part, it won't come to that," he warned, rising to his feet.

"You mean, as long as I lie. We both know Killian didn't rape me—"

"Shut up, Ariana." His face darkened as he rounded the desk, the vein in his forehead pulsing. He came to a stop in front of my chair, forcing me to look up. "You're going to stand in front of the press and do as you're told. Refuse me again, and I'll kill him myself. Understood?"

I nodded and released a sharp breath, suddenly feeling a little claustrophobic. It wouldn't have mattered if Killian was in a different country altogether, there was something in the way Tristan spoke that made me believe he'd do exactly what he said.

Tears blurred my eyes. I quickly brushed them away with the back of my hand before speaking. "I'll do it."

"Good," Tristan responded with a look of resolute calmness as he reached down to stroke my damp cheek.

"This is for our future, little dove. You're my baby girl, and it's my job to take care of you. Now, prove your loyalty to me out there, and Brad won't be allowed in the house unsupervised until the wedding.

"In the meantime, he'll be forced to work on proving himself worthy of you. I'll make it abundantly clear I won't agree to marriage until I'm convinced he can give you the life you deserve—I'm talking trips around the world to places you've only dreamed about. Let me keep you safe."

The words I'd longed to hear since I was a child barreled past my ribs and lodged in my heart, slicing it to ribbons. He was handing me everything I'd ever wanted, freedom and a life without atonement.

All that stood in my way was Killian.

Mama had warned me to run years ago, but I'd stayed like an obedient dog, convinced I could earn my independence. Even now, I found myself devouring his platitudes like any starved and abused animal would, wanting to believe this time would be different.

"Love is sacrifice, little dove," he murmured, pressing a kiss to the top of my head. "And yours will be rewarded."

I pulled away from the fantasy in my mind with a distracted nod. Love was sacrifice, just not in the way he believed. It was a willingness to throw yourself on the sword to save another.

Just like Killian had wanted to do for me.

Just like I was trying to do now.

Love with stipulations wasn't love. It was an acknowledgment between opposing parties, a list of conditions one side was expected to satisfy for the other.

There was a soft knock at the door, and I glanced up to see that it was time. Tristan had just taken my hand when I was struck by a sudden thought.

A stipulation of my own.

"Wait," I whispered, taking a step back.

"Sweetheart, are you okay? Do you need some water?" His concern almost sounded genuine.

I held the speech up with trembling fingers. "Tell me how you did it."

"Excuse me?"

"You heard me," I said, my voice strangled. "You want me to lie for you, the least you can do is give me the truth about my accident. How did you control the car, Tristan?"

"Just give us a minute," he called out to the person on the other side of the door before approaching me with his arms crossed over his chest. "I have no idea what you're—"

"Bullshit," I hissed, ignoring the beads of sweat clinging to the nape of my neck. "The first time the lights flashed, I thought something had crossed in front of the convertible. Then the radio began changing stations, and the volume got louder. When I punched the brakes, the car accelerated. So, tell me the truth—and remember, your sacrifice will be rewarded."

I watched as the color drained from his face, confirming my hunch that my recurring nightmares had been fractured memories from the night of the crash.

Tristan's strength had always come from his ability to strip a person of everything they loved. But in doing so, he'd created a monster. One who would become his greatest horror, because I no longer had anything left to lose.

"And if I refuse?" He loomed over me with a grin, cracking his knuckles in a silent reminder of what he was capable of doing.

"I'd advise you against making such a hasty decision," I stated, repeating the same words he'd used with me. "Considering I've already agreed to tell the press exactly what you want."

His lips pulled back in a snarl, the muscles and veins in his neck straining against the skin as he spat, "Are you threatening me, little dove?"

"This is our future, Tristan. No more secrets. Growing up, I was forced to tell you my sins, it seems only fitting you tell me yours." The ground quaked beneath my feet, but by some miracle, I managed to remain upright.

A slow smirk spread across his face. "There are going to be consequences for this, Ariana."

"I wouldn't expect anything less."

He leaned against a bookshelf casually, but his eyes glinted with barely suppressed rage. We both knew he couldn't hurt me here. There were too many witnesses.

Instead, he wrapped a large hand around my bicep and yanked me forward. "Someone within my own house was conspiring against me, so I did what I had to do to protect my assets," he hissed, sending spittle onto my cheek.

"What are you saying?" I pushed, dread swirling in my belly.

"I'm saying I made the tough choices," he growled, squeezing my arm in a punishing grip. "Now, it's your turn."

"You can't say it." I winced and shifted my weight from one foot to the other, struggling to free myself. "I've given you everything, yet you still won't tell me the truth."

With a condescending sneer, he released my arm and sent me stumbling back in my heels. I caught myself on the edge of his desk and released a shaky exhale, watching him warily.

His face was almost purple, the muscle in his jaw twitching wildly. "'A worthy wife is a crown for her husband, but a disgraceful woman is like cancer in his bones.' You know how you get rid of a tumor, little dove? You cut it out."

CHAPTER TWENTY-EIGHT
ARIANA

"You had the power all along my dear."

-L. Frank Baum, *The Wizard of Oz*

I PEEKED out through the thick velvet curtains to see the rabid faces of the reporters gathered below the stage. There was a blonde woman near the front who caught my attention as she looked like she wanted to be anywhere else but here.

That made two of us.

The press had been salivating like sharks at the scent of fresh blood. They'd fought over space, each one waiting impatiently to see if the rumors were true.

Meanwhile, I'd vomited twice more since leaving Tristan's office when it dawned on me that he wasn't going to be immediately arrested and thrown in jail. In the crime shows on television, when someone wore a wire and got a confession, the bad guy always ended up in handcuffs.

I sat back down and let the stylists touch up my hair and makeup while staring daggers at Dean. He was playing on his cell phone, completely oblivious that I was plotting his murder from five feet away.

Maybe I had more in common with Tristan than I previously realized.

The security guard had wanted me to believe he was looking out for my best interests but forcing me to go through with this press conference was in direct opposition to that plan.

I waited until they finished with me before making my way over to him. "How much longer is this going to take?" I hissed.

He glanced up with a frown. "There are bigger things in play right now. Just be patient and follow my lead, okay?"

My nostrils flared, and I shook my head, hissing, "No. You promised me I wouldn't have to go out there. I was just supposed to go to his office and get the confession. Why can't you arrest him now?"

"Had you listened to me last night and gone to the damn safe house, you wouldn't have to. Now, I suggest you don't read a word of that speech unless you want to be held culpable when the truth comes out."

I squeezed the pendant on my necklace until I could feel each tentacle embedding in my palm. "What am I supposed to do? Stand there?"

"Exactly." Dean nodded. "Just stay silent. They can't prosecute you if you don't speak. Besides, Tristan had you declared mentally incompetent after your accident, so no one's expecting much, if anything, out of you. Trust me."

My skin was drenched in an obscene amount of sweat. There was also a sharp pain in my chest that I was convinced was the beginning of a heart attack.

But sure, why not hop up on stage to play the quiet game?

"Trust you? Why—because you've done such a bang-up job so far? How long do you think Tristan's going to let me stand up there in silence before intervening?" I countered, my voice tinged with hysteria and terror.

Shit. Damn. Hell.

"When this fails, and it will, you do whatever you have to do to keep Killian and Morgan safe."

Dean studied me with a raised brow. "And you—"

"I think we both know it's too late for that," I whispered, running my thumbnail over a tentacle and wishing I could bring the damn thing to life.

Our conversation ended when Tristan's publicist arrived to escort me onto the stage. "Now remember, stick to the script," she clipped out in a brisk tone. "No improvising. Are we clear?"

"Yep," I squeaked out as she nudged me toward the lectern. The stage I'd been on almost every Sunday morning, singing with the worship band, no longer provided the respite it once had.

I squinted against the bright lights and focused on the faces below, coming back to the blonde reporter and her tortoiseshell glasses. A corner of her mouth lifted, and I looked away, bothered by the familiarity.

The microphone boomed loudly as I angled it down toward my mouth, like the sound of someone striking a bass drum. I straightened the papers and licked my cracked lips, my head swimming in warnings.

Stick to the script.

Just stay silent.

Do as you're told.

I'd long associated safety with staying small and quiet when, in reality, it had never been anything more than consent. I had a choice to make—continue to let other people hold my voice or fight through the fear to make myself heard.

Sometimes, the smallest voices are the loudest.

"Hello," I croaked, before clearing my throat. A sharp screech of feedback traveled across the sanctuary, the sound setting my teeth on edge.

"M-my n-name is Ariana James and K-K-Killian R-Reed..." I

stammered halfway through the first line of Tristan's speech, before pausing to gulp a breath.

So far, so terrible.

If I went through with this, there was a good chance I wouldn't be walking out of here alive. But if I stuck to Tristan's script, we were all as good as dead.

Pick up your shield and fight back.

My heart thundered against my breast. The river of sweat running down my spine had become something like a waterfall. I'd imagined bravery like the movie in Georgia's room, with a woman marching across no man's land with her shield held high, but maybe strength came in more than one form.

Maybe bravery could be found in the small things, by doing nothing more than speaking my truth. If there was no one else, then it fell to me.

"I'm Ariana James," I repeated, firmly this time. "And Killian Reed is innocent."

A brief silence descended over the sanctuary, and then questions were being fired at me like bullets from all sides.

"Ariana, why did you lie?"

"Did Killian Reed pay you to say this?"

"Is it true you're carrying his baby?"

My pulse thrashed loudly in my ears, muffling their hateful chatter. I'd sort of imagined Dean bursting onto the stage to whisk me away, not leaving me to deflect the gunfire on my own.

Clearly, I didn't know what I was doing. I nervously jerked my head to the left and right, searching for help, only to find Tristan's silent glare. He brought his hands together in a slow clap, his mouth twisted in a sardonic smirk.

Shit. Damn. Hell.

A bubble of hysterical laughter rose up. I could say whatever the hell I wanted to at this point.

I was already dead.

It was a fact that left me feeling both terrified and invincible. I had no doubt Tristan was going to come on stage within minutes to apologize. He'd pin my outburst on the car wreck or the trauma I'd experienced at the hands of a particular baseball player. Until then, though, the floor was mine.

Let the world see the truth, and the monster loses its power.

See the truth.

My legs had become as useful to me as cooked spaghetti noodles, but a current of strength ran through my veins. There was only one thing left to do.

For my final act, I'll be taking everyone down with me.

I pulled the microphone free and kept my eyes on his as I calmly stated, "To answer your questions, I didn't lie as this is the first time I've spoken publicly, while Tristan James has been insistent on keeping the truth from getting out. Oh, and it would be impossible for me to be carrying Killian's baby as I'm still a virgin!"

Tristan's eyes darkened as he ran a finger across his throat in warning. Deep-set lines appeared on his forehead. Three meant trouble, but I didn't look away. I didn't lower my head. Instead, I blinked back tears and prepared to tell him goodbye in a voice loud enough for him to hear.

Only, this time, I wouldn't be coming back.

This is for you, Killian.

My heart stuttered in my chest as I spoke the words I'd held onto for years, knowing there was no other way. "I've spent my life being physically and emotionally abused by not only Tristan James, but his business partner, Brad Phillips, as well."

With my back to him, Tristan didn't see me loosening the scarf around my neck until the cashmere was already fluttering to the stage.

A collective gasp moved through the sanctuary, but I didn't stop there. With shaking hands, I reached for my zipper and tugged it down. The dress slipped from my shoulders and fell to my waist, exposing the purple and black bruises along my arms and ribs.

Mama once said, '*No one expects an angel to set the world on fire.*'

I hadn't understood it at the time, but as cameras began flashing and the noise in the room became a deafening presence, it suddenly made sense.

"Now, folks," Tristan drawled as he stepped under the spotlights, his voice magnified, courtesy of the microphone pinned to the lapel of his suit jacket. "I think you can see now why I took what happened to my baby girl so seriously. She's been such a fighter these last few months, trying to come back from a brain injury, only to end up battered in violence. That man, who she truly thought cared, brutalized her—"

"No, that's not true," I argued, only to find my mic had been cut off. The urge to scream was overwhelming, but it wouldn't do anything for me now.

I'd been silenced.

The blonde reporter seemed to be the only one not taking notes or shouting questions to Tristan. Instead, she was watching me with a look of unrepressed horror.

Maybe she saw the monster too.

His hand landed against my bare shoulder. I flinched, before trying to step away from the contact. With deft fingers, he tugged the dress back up over my exposed body and spun me around to let him zip it, before pulling me against his side with a punishing grip.

"Ariana fought for her life that night but lost the very thing she'd been saving for marriage," he continued, speaking in a measured tone. "The physical effects are apparent, but it's the emotional scars that have me troubled, folks. My baby girl has regressed in the days since the attack, convinced she's still a virgin as a way of coping with the trauma."

He looked down at me with a patient smile while I continued struggling.

Blink. Blink.

"Now, I'd like to ask y'all for something here today. Right now, Ariana needs to feel your love and support like never before during this time of healing and grief. Please join me in prayer. Dear Heavenly Father, we know that life doesn't always make sense—"

My elbow dug into his ribs, and he exhaled what sounded like a low chuckle, before continuing, "But your plans are not our own, and all we can do is trust that you'll hold us through this pain, leading us to brighter days ahead. In Jesus' name, Amen."

There was no time to stop and consider the ramifications of my actions as Tristan exited stage right with me firmly in tow. Numbness settled into my joints as he marched me off the stage, his fingers compressing the newest bruise blooming along my bicep.

All I could hope for at this point was a quick and merciful death.

I grimaced at the fury reflected in Dean's glare as he met us backstage, getting the distinct sense he'd be open to making me suffer.

He squared his shoulders as we approached. "Do you want me to get her back to the house?"

"Please," Tristan growled through a tight jaw, before dragging his index finger down my cheek. "And I want two guards posted outside her bedroom door—wouldn't want her getting cold feet on her wedding night."

"I'd rather kill myself," I hissed, jutting my chin up in defiance.

Tristan chuckled and leaned down to whisper in my ear. "Not until Brad's done with you, sweetheart. Maybe not even then."

Dean wrapped a hand around my arm and dragged me toward a side door while I gasped and wheezed, feeling like I was on an elevator in free fall. Even with as angry as he was, he still managed to avoid touching my bruises.

We slipped down a hallway lined with empty Sunday-school classrooms before he came to a sudden stop and demanded, "What the fuck happened to not saying a word up there?"

"I—I improvised," I weakly replied, my chin and lips trembling violently.

A condescending smirk lifted the corners of his mouth. "You have no idea what you've done, do you? There was a plan—which you completely steamrolled over—now, we'll be lucky if we ever get anything—"

"He said he was going to kill Killian. What about that, huh?"

"Look at me," he commanded, the muscle in his jaw tightening. "Conspiracy to commit murder is not going to be enough to put him away for life, especially not without proof of a conspiracy!"

"But you have the recording," I argued as he began moving again, trying to match his pace in heels. "He said, 'I'll kill him myself.' How is that not enough proof?"

"Do you know how many people say things like that in anger? Without proof of an actual plan, it's purely conjecture. And, I don't know if you're aware of this or not, but you completely destroyed any credibility as a witness when you took your goddamned clothes off in front of the press!"

I studied the vein throbbing in his neck before asking the obvious. "You're not really a security guard, are you?"

Dean looked at me like I'd suddenly sprouted a second head before sighing, "If you'd just been patient and trusted me—"

"Kinda hard to do when you won't tell me who you really are, though, don't you think?" As Killian would have said, I had zero fucks left to give.

"Since my cover's about to be blown to hell—"

"How? I swear I won't tell anyone."

"Once upon a time, I was an officer in the Army and saw a lot of things I wish I could forget. For the last two years, I've watched you walk the grounds with that same haunted look in your eyes that I used to see in the mirror every day."

We passed another darkened classroom, the window decorated in the Bible verses they were memorizing. I had a feeling it was going to be the last time I saw these halls.

Dean stopped and placed a hand on my shoulder before gruffly admitting, "I know you won't tell anyone because that's the kind of person you are. But you should know I'm not letting you go back to that hell."

"Right," I murmured as we reached an exit that led to the playground, nodding as if his words made all the sense in the world. No one defied Tristan. At least, no one who lived to tell about it afterward.

"I'm serious."

I'd just opened my mouth when the door in front of us burst open, hitting the exterior of the building with a resounding clang.

Dean positioned himself in front of me, only to lower his weapon with a harsh exhale.

"You're late," a female voice stated casually.

"Yeah?" he chuckled. "Maybe you're early."

"We've got a problem—"

I peeked through the small opening between Dean's arm and torso. "Tsega?"

"Hey, Ari," she said, sounding eerily calm for someone who'd lost her entire career.

"I'm so sorry," I blurted, shoving Dean aside to throw my arms around her neck. "You lost your job all because of me—because of my stupidity. If I could fix it for you, I would."

We pulled apart to find Dean scratching at his temple with a smirk. "Ari, this is Agent Simons. She was working undercover to keep you safe at *True North*."

"Oh, you didn't really lose your job then, I guess. Whew!" I swiped a hand across my brow with a forced laugh, feeling my face heat in embarrassment. It took a few seconds more for it to register, and then my eyes went wide. "Wait, you work for the FBI? Are you Dean's boss?"

Tsega cocked her head to the side and squinted up at him with a piercing gaze. "Oh, I absolutely am. Come on, we can talk more in the car. There's been a... development."

With that, she spun on her heel and marched over to a black SUV with tinted windows parked nearby.

"I can't believe she's your boss," I breathed, as I followed behind

Dean. "How lucky are you? So, that must mean you work for the FBI too."

He grumbled something under his breath before opening the back-passenger door for me. "Just get in, Ariana."

"Does she still have it?"

I instinctively took a step back, my legs threatening to buckle beneath me. Dean tried forcing me forward, but I tightened my grip on his suit jacket, suddenly seeing past the blonde wig and tortoise-shell glasses, and into the eyes of a ghost.

"No," I whispered, my pulse hammering in my throat. "It's impossible."

Dean muttered a string of curse words. "Does anybody in this family listen to me? I told you to stay away from here, Ashlynn."

"I told you we had an issue," Tsega noted wryly from the front. "Get in, before we draw an audience."

He deftly maneuvered me into the backseat, before taking the front passenger seat for himself. An uncomfortable silence fell over the vehicle as Tsega pulled out of the parking lot and onto the highway. I tried to come to terms with the fact that my sister had not been killed in a traffic accident.

Or, if she had, she'd recovered from the death quite nicely.

Dean's laptop fired up with a chime and, after stabbing his password in, he shifted his attention to the back seat. "Gonna tell us why you're here this time?"

She took me by surprise when she matter-of-factly answered, "Ari's necklace."

"What?" I wrapped my hand around the pendant protectively and scooted closer to the window. "Not how you've been alive this entire time? Or why you're dressed as a reporter? Just here for the necklace?" My voice rose with each word, leaving me almost shouting toward the end of it.

Ashlynn winced. "I was going to explain everything, but I know what the necklace is, even if you don't."

"It was a gift from Tristan after he tried to kill me in a car accident! But if you want it so badly—" I unclasped the chain with shaking hands and tossed it at her. "Here, take it! Now, you have everything you came for!"

My chest rose and fell with a dull ache. It would have been easier to accept she was dead, but the truth was that she'd left me behind without a second thought.

"Do you know how we all grieved for you?" I mumbled, blinking back the tears. "He might have pretended like you never existed, but we never got over it. It changed everything."

Tsega's sympathetic eyes met mine in the rearview mirror, but I turned away to watch the cars around us.

Ashlynn didn't answer immediately and instead, began rummaging through her purse, probably pocketing her new piece of jewelry.

"Ari," she said softly. "Can I show you something?"

"No," I replied, petulantly adding, "Tsega, would you mind dropping Ashlynn off at the nearest gas station? I'm sure she can find her way to her home, wherever it is."

"Stop! I want to show you what you did—"

"What I did?" I snapped, turning back with a flare of anger. "What about—wait, what are you doing?"

"Watch," she murmured, slipping a silver pin into a small hole hidden in the center of my pendant. It opened with a soft click, revealing a thumb drive.

My mouth fell open. I reached up to pinch my arm as hard as I could, just to ensure I was still awake.

There was a tense moment of silence, during which Dean arched over the console, studying the device like it was a cipher, while my heart flailed helplessly against my ribs.

He carefully lifted it from her palm and asked, "What's on it?"

"Why don't you plug it in and find out? If I'm right, there'll be more than enough evidence to put Tristan away forever," she stated with more than a hint of bitterness. "Something you could have done six months ago had you not dismissed my theory on there being a second laptop somewhere in the house."

"Under his bed," I blurted, before covering my mouth in surprise. Tristan had hidden a laptop in the same place I'd hidden my treasures, but there was no earthly reason for me to have known that.

Unless...

Someone within my own house was conspiring against me.

My stomach knotted, and I licked my dry lips, pushing past the feelings of lightheadedness. Now was not the time to vomit or pass out.

I thought I was running away that night, but I wasn't. I'd been fighting back. And if Ashlynn had the key to my necklace, it meant she hadn't abandoned me.

We'd been working together.

My face scrunched up in confusion, everything in me rejecting the idea that I'd been part of a conspiracy to overthrow my father. I wasn't brave enough.

"I-I don't understand," I stammered. "He told us you were dead. Does Matt know? Does Tristan? Where have you been hiding? How did I get the necklace?"

It was two years' worth of questions in one sentence.

Ashlynn gave me a watery smile and reached for my hand. "If it wasn't for Matt and his family taking me in, I wouldn't have survived. Let's just say they have certain connections that even Tristan couldn't break. Agent Simons tracked me down not long after I left, wanting to know if I had any information that might help the FBI build their case, but I didn't."

"Tsega." I was still having some trouble picturing the woman as a federal agent. To me, she was still a tech from *True North*.

"No, Ari." Ashlynn gestured toward the passenger seat. "That Agent Simons."

I inhaled sharply, and Tsega lifted her eyes to meet mine in the mirror. "How are you doing, Ari?"

"Um," I hedged with a squeak. "I'm feeling a little confused... and nauseated. Mainly confused, I guess."

Her expression softened, and she cut her eyes to the passenger seat, where Dean was hunched over the laptop. "We're married. What else do you want to know? Looks like we've got some time to kill until this traffic clears."

My gaze bounced back to my sister. "And what about you?"

"Yeah, Matt and I got married last year," she explained, her lower lip quivering. "I really wish you could have been there with me."

An erratic burst of laughter slipped free, and I shook my head. "So, was that what made you decide to get me out? Guilt?"

"No," Ashlynn insisted, squeezing my hand. "God, no. I've spent the last two years trying to free everyone. Have you ever wondered why Tristan made all the upgrades to the wall and brought in an outside security firm?"

"Because of the threats against the church?"

"Me, Ari. I was the threat. I broke into the compound once, but he intercepted me before I got anywhere. After bloodying my lip, he had me escorted from the premises by Brother Caleb."

Matt's family must have been pretty powerful if the worst she'd gotten from our father was a fat lip.

Tsega clarified, "We were made aware of the breach and had our plant within the church recommend a specific security firm to Tristan, and he took the bait."

"But it wasn't enough to get me out," I finished for her, ignoring the scratchiness in my throat. The day had been a chaotic and draining storm of revelations that had left me on edge.

I didn't know whether to cry or laugh anymore.

"Matt was the one who came up with the idea of reaching out to you to find the computer. He had the necklace and a letter with detailed instructions smuggled in, using a fake name. Once you had it, you called the number in his letter and made arrangements to meet at the same diner he'd taken me to when we first met."

"Then, I got into an accident."

Ashlynn's voice was gentle as she asked, "Do you remember any of it?"

"No," I whispered, while absently chewing on my bottom lip. "But I've had this recurring dream since the accident. In it, you say, 'Ari, what have they done to you?' Sometimes, you tell me you can help if I come back to you, but the ending is always the same. The monster devours you after you tell me I'm the only one who can stop it. But that doesn't make any sense if the letter came from a fake name, right?"

She cupped her mouth and lowered her head toward her knees with a pained cry. I unbuckled and slid across the seat, struck with the sudden need to comfort, although I had no idea what was wrong.

Tsega cleared her throat, sounding close to tears herself. "She was there, Ari. When you were in a coma in SICU, we brought her in to see you. She sat by your bedside and just talked."

An involuntary sound of anguish escaped my throat as I gathered her in my arms, grieving the time we'd never get back.

"Fuck," Dean muttered in horror, drawing our attention back to the front.

I brushed away my tears and straightened. "You found something?"

Tristan had been willing to kill his own wife to keep the contents of the thumb drive from ever getting out. Whatever it was had to be something truly evil.

"No," he admitted, cutting his eyes over to me. "We found every-thing, Ariana. You did this—"

I laughed hoarsely. "And here I thought I ruined it all."

Dean's jaw hung slack in disbelief. "I think you may have just saved everyone."

CHAPTER TWENTY-NINE
ARIANA

"I had not intended to love him; the reader knows I had wrought hard to extirpate from my soul the germs of love there detected; and now, at the first renewed view of him, they spontaneously revived, great and strong! He made me love him without looking at me."

-Charlotte Brontë, *Jane Eyre*

I TIGHTENED the belt on the fluffy robe I'd found hanging in the hotel bathroom and settled back against the pillows, trying to warm up. My skin had been scrubbed until it was raw in places, but nothing could take away the horror of what had been on that thumb drive.

After being reunited with Killian and Morgan in a five thousand square foot Presidential Suite near Tanglewood, I'd stood under the showerhead for as long as possible, letting the steaming water turn my skin red.

Inside, I was still ice cold.

Murder. Attempted murder. Conspiracy to commit murder. Coercion. Bribery. Fraud. Human Trafficking.

It was worse than anything I could have ever imagined.

The FBI was calling it one of their biggest busts—celebrities, politicians, billionaires—the list of people involved could have filled every seat in Eagle Lake, and probably had at some point. Millions of dollars were siphoned from the church and into *Trident Holdings*, Tristan and Brad's fake company.

My sisters had been auctioned off like property to the highest bidders, but the corruption hadn't ended there. *Urban Mission* and the various other outreach programs meant to aid at-risk youths had been used to identify and exploit potential targets.

Convinced he was above the law and would never be caught, Tristan had kept meticulous records detailing their crimes. Tsega believed they were his trophies, or perhaps an insurance policy should Brad ever decide to turn him in. As it was, the two of them were going to be spending the rest of their lives locked up.

My mama's original autopsy report was among the documents found. There'd never been a brain aneurism. She'd loved him— enough to try to stop what he was doing—and in return, he'd drugged her into permanent silence.

We'd probably never know whether her death was accidental or not, but it didn't change the fact he'd stolen her from us.

Killian slipped into the bedroom, carrying a large plastic bag. "Hey, Dean grabbed dinner. Morgan's still asleep, so I thought we'd eat in here. We've got—" He began pulling out containers and lining them on the credenza near the foot of the bed. "Potstickers, egg rolls, wonton soup, chicken fried rice, and beef and broccoli."

My chest heaved with a sudden sob. I brought the back of my hand up over my mouth, trying to smother the sound. "I'm sorry. I don't know what's wrong with me."

He let the empty bag drop to the floor, before pulling me off the bed and into his arms. "I've got you, girl," he murmured, stroking my damp hair. "You're safe now."

"What if I'm broken?" I buried my head against his chest with a loud hiccup. "I think I might be broken. I can't stop shaking, Killian. Why can't I stop shaking?"

Grief and rage blurred my vision, tinging my voice with hysteria.

"Baby." His hands over my hair and down my back, grounding me. "You've gotta try to eat something. Dean said you hadn't kept anything down since last night. Just tell me what sounds good."

"I'm not hungry."

His eyes blazed with something I couldn't quite identify as he led me back over to the bed. After pressing a kiss to my forehead, he left the room, returning a minute later with a small glass of amber liquid. "Drink this."

"What is it?" I took it from his hand and sniffed, only to recoil immediately. "Alcohol?"

Killian sat down beside me and took one of my feet in his hands, stroking along the arch. "Whiskey. You need it. You're in shock—hell, anyone would be if they'd been through what you have in the past seventy-two hours. C'mon, drink up."

I took a hesitant sip, shuddering as the liquor burned its way down to my belly. My face scrunched up, and I croaked, "How do people drink this stuff?"

That earned me a small smile. "Practice—lots and lots of practice."

I forced a little more past my lips until my limbs flooded with heat, and the world didn't feel like such a dark place. "What do we do now?"

"Whatever we want." He passed me a container and some chopsticks, before reclining against the pillows. "But first, you have to eat something."

After a brief struggle, where I only managed to snag a single grain of rice, I groaned, "How do you use these damn things?"

"Here. Like this." Killian snagged a piece of beef and brought it to my lips. "Open."

A ripple of pleasure spread throughout my body and down to my core, warming me faster than the alcohol had. Before I'd finished chewing the first bite, he was there, offering me another.

"Open," he murmured, his voice gruff.

I obeyed, keeping my eyes on his as I licked the salt from my lips. There was something sensual in being cared for and fed by this man.

The last three days had been shrouded in a fog of adrenaline and self-preservation. But here, in a safe house fit for a king, it all fell away. Killian was right. Love silenced everything else.

And the one thing my starved and broken body needed more than anything right now was to feel loved.

"More," I begged, pouting when he raised the chopsticks to my mouth again. I felt as though I was dying of thirst, and he was giving me mere drops to drink. "Please."

Killian paused, his throat moving in a swallow, before setting the container aside and reaching for my foot. He watched me through hooded eyes before pressing his thumb against the arch of my foot, turning the simmering warmth between my legs to lava.

"Like this?" His hands slid up to caress my calf.

"Higher," I squeaked, closing my eyes against the flush creeping up my throat.

His fingers brushed the inside of my knee. I scooted forward, urging him closer. He didn't move and I blinked to find him staring down at me as if he'd never seen me before.

"Did I do something wrong?"

"No," Killian said softly as he slipped his shirt over his head and lay back against the pillows. "Come here."

I gathered the robe in my fists and lowered myself over the crotch of his jeans, whispering, "Like this?"

He shook his head with a rough exhale. "Higher."

I shifted my hips forward until his naval was resting between my legs before cocking an eyebrow in question. His teeth sank into his bottom lip as he fought a smile, crooking a finger.

I fumbled with the belt on the robe before letting it fall from my shoulders, baring myself to him. Killian groaned a curse as he took in the sight of me, and I couldn't help but feel a sense of power. I'd done that to him.

"Grip the headboard, baby," he growled.

I braced myself against the dark gray upholstery, arched over him shamelessly. Goosebumps spread across my skin, tightening my nipples into hardened points. With anyone else, the position would have left me feeling vulnerable or submissive.

But I wasn't afraid to be on my knees for him.

Keeping his eyes on mine, he trailed his hands down my spine and cupped my bottom. And then, as if needing to prove his muscles weren't just for show, he easily lifted me up and onto his face. The short bristles of his stubble scraped against my sensitive flesh, and I pressed my lips together, fighting back a moan.

Killian lifted his head with a smirk and hooked his arms around my thighs, spreading me wide open. My hips jerked as he exhaled a breathless chuckle against my core, before tightening his grip and pulling me back down. "I've been dying to taste you properly."

A wave of heat crept up my throat when I realized what he was referring to, and then his mouth was there. He kissed me again, higher this time, and my broken fingernails dug into the headboard, holding on for dear life. He guided my body up and down, nipping and sucking my flesh until I was disoriented and dazed with lust.

"W-what are you doing to me?" I panted, dropping my forehead to my arms. It was similar to the way he'd made me feel in the shower, but different, almost like the alcohol had heightened my senses.

But it wasn't the alcohol. It was him, bringing me back to life.

"Worshiping your body, baby," Killian murmured, kissing the inside of my thigh. "Proving you're not broken."

I let out a guttural groan as he pulled me back down, spreading my folds and stroking my center with the flat of his tongue. The ache inside me intensified as he feasted on my flesh with low grunts of approval.

The added stimulation of his mouth had my inner muscles clenching and tightening greedily as I rocked forward to meet him.

"You taste like the ocean," he pulled back to whisper, his wild eyes searching my face.

"Killian," I moaned, my body bathed in sweat. What I needed was just within reach, but I didn't know how to get there.

"I've got you," he said, releasing my leg and lowering his thumb to my center. "Let me take care of you."

I lost myself in the rhythm of his movements, every nerve ending firing as he circled the tight bud. It was almost too much, and I squirmed, chasing my release like my next breath.

"Please. Please."

Killian's tongue thrust up inside my body, stroking my taut muscles. I bore down on him with a muffled scream as he coaxed the orgasm from me.

I gasped his name like a prayer when his tongue flicked in and out of me, prolonging my state of rapture. We were back in the lake—only this time, I was the wave, and he was the shore. I crested and fell over him, again and again, until it felt like nothing existed outside of us.

We were only supposed to stay in the hotel until everyone had been taken into custody. As my lower body twitched with aftershocks of pleasure, I decided I was never leaving. I was going to live in this bed forever.

Killian lifted me up and back onto the bed before standing. I slipped the robe around my shoulders like a cape and gave him a drowsy smile, only to be met with a distant expression.

Without saying a word, he walked over to sit in an armchair near the windows, watching me with a strangely intense expression.

My skin was still buzzing from his mouth, making coherent speech impossible.

His eyes went hooded as they moved down my body, but he shook his head and ran a hand roughly over his face, clearly trying to mask his emotions.

To hide.

A blush rose up my neck. I swallowed, wondering if perhaps I'd done it wrong. The church-funded health class hadn't exactly covered a man kissing a woman there.

Believe me, I would have remembered that.

"Do you want to come back to bed?" I finally asked, my voice uneven. My nerves were frayed. I felt I was dangerously close to another crying spell, but refrained, awaiting his answer.

"I can't."

"Why?" I pushed up onto my knees, facing him with a sigh. "Look, that was a first for me. If you don't tell me what I'm doing wrong, I can't fix my mistakes. I can't be better for you."

The muscle in his jaw tightened. "You think you did it wrong? Christ, Ari. You are so fucking perfect when you come apart. It's taking everything in me not to come over there and fuck you until you're screaming the entire goddamn hotel down."

Killian's words conjured up a variety of erotic images. I shivered, painfully aroused by the thought of him performing any number of them. "Is it because you don't have a condom?"

His deep voice was laced with regret as he quietly admitted, "I don't want to hurt you."

There was a war raging behind those eyes, a hesitancy that left me more than a little confused. The church believed men were created to take and women to endure. Killian had given me pleasure but gotten nothing in return.

"You're afraid because I'm a virgin." I wanted him to have me. Given what little knowledge I possessed on lovemaking, it wouldn't necessarily be pleasurable for me, but I was willing to endure any pain if it made him feel good.

"What?"

His glacial eyes snapped back to mine. "But the bruises—I thought he—"

I resisted the urge to bow my head because I was no longer that girl. I'd taken down one monster armed only with a lie and another, armed only with the truth. Maybe bravery had never been about making myself unafraid, but in standing up to evil with empty hands and a wounded body.

"No. You gave me the courage to fight back, Killian." My heart pounded as I studied his dark expression, trying to read his thoughts. "You—it was always meant to be you."

He got up and moved to stand at the side of the bed, looking almost guilty. "Before I go any further, I want you to know that tonight was about you, and I wasn't planning on this, okay?"

My eyebrow shot up. "Um, okay?"

He produced several foil packets from his back pocket, his voice suddenly strangled as he admitted, "I had Dean get me condoms when he was picking up food, but I swear, I didn't plan on any of this happening tonight. I just wanted to be prepared."

I crawled forward and pressed my lips to the corner of his mouth before shrugging the robe off again. His gaze dropped between us, leaving my body humming in anticipation.

"Make love to me, Killian," I murmured, shivering as his fingers skimmed over my breasts and belly, carefully avoiding the bruises along my torso.

"Come here, girl." He lowered his mouth over mine. His large hands pulled my hips flush to him, kneading the flesh of my bottom.

I raked my fingers through his dark hair, surrendering to his touch and tasting myself on his tongue. He sucked my upper lip between his teeth as he lowered me onto the bed.

My nipples rubbed against his chest, the friction sending jolts of pleasure to my core. When he pulled back to remove his jeans, I made a mewling sound of protest, already reaching for him again.

"Patience," he demanded, his voice rough.

I pushed up onto my elbows, watching him unashamedly stroke himself before tearing the foil square with his teeth. He rolled the condom down his thick length, his hungry gaze never once leaving mine.

He would forever be the most beautiful thing I'd ever seen.

Killian pulled me to the side of the bed and spread my legs before curling a finger through my folds. He dipped in and out of me until I was rocking against him with broken exhales.

"This isn't something I take lightly. It's everything—you are everything," he whispered, staring into my eyes. "Forever, Ari."

I nodded, blinking back the tears.

He spread my wetness along his crown, before lowering his mouth to my breasts, teasing and pulling me against his tongue to the point of coming undone.

When he braced himself on his forearms over me, I tensed involuntarily, fully aware of the erection pressing against my thigh.

I'd known he was massive in the shower, but the close proximity was a reminder that he would have to stretch my body to fit his.

"Relax, baby," Killian murmured, kissing my chin. "Just focus on my face, okay?"

I nodded and took a deep breath, willing my tight muscles to obey. He spread my legs and guided himself forward. The blunt tip pushed past my swollen lips to nudge against my entrance. His blue eyes blazed with desire as he eased his way into me. There was a sharp burn, followed by an uncomfortable fullness.

"It's too much," I winced, bracing my hands on his chest. "Too much—how could anyone ever want to do this more than once?"

"Fuck, Ari," Killian ground out through a clenched jaw, his nostrils flaring. "Just give me a minute, and I'll show you. I'm a little out of practice."

I made the colossal mistake of lifting my head to see where our bodies joined together, only to realize he wasn't even close to being all the way inside me.

My thighs quivered as his lips moved to my ear and then down my jaw, silently willing me to relax. I lay back and clutched his shoulders against the dull ache radiating through my core.

"I've got you." Killian shifted his weight onto his right arm with a low groan and reached between us with his left, stroking my sensitive flesh until the pain became something different. Even now, his focus was entirely on me and what I needed.

Under his skilled touch, my body liquefied, accepting a little more. I hissed a sharp breath and locked my arms behind his neck as he pushed forward, needing him to move.

He was so deep.

Some primitive instinct had my hips jerking reflexively, making my eyes roll back in my head. I didn't know if the accompanying twinge in my core was good or bad, but I wanted to do it again.

"For the love of God, don't move," he groaned against my lips, sweat beading on his forehead from the strain of holding himself still. "I'm trying not to come."

I tried, but it was as if my body was no longer under my control. My lower belly tightened as I rocked forward, the feeling different compared to Killian's fingers or mouth, but not unwelcome.

So, I did it again.

And again.

"I need..."

"Fuck what do you need, slugger?" Killian asked, nipping at my lower lip, his eyes unfocused with lust. "This?"

With one thrust, he filled me entirely. I sucked in a ragged breath, my back arching off the bed toward his warm chest. He pulled back until I was almost empty before driving into me again, somehow deeper than before. I ground my hips against his, desperate to hold on against the rush of lightheadedness.

The push and pull between us increased along with the sensation that the room was spinning. I choked back a sob and tightened my fists in his hair as my inner muscles clamped down around him, pulsing and quivering. If that was an orgasm, I didn't know what the hell I'd been doing before.

Killian's thrusts turned erratic. I wrapped my legs around his waist and pulled his mouth down over mine in a sloppy kiss. His body went rigid as he came, before collapsing against my chest, showering me in praise.

I cradled his cheek against my breasts, the sounds of our heavy breathing filling the air. We held each other like that for several minutes before he pulled out and padded into the bathroom.

He hadn't hurt me—at least, not like I'd expected. I clenched my thighs. There was soreness, but also something else.

Satisfaction.

The bed dipped as he returned, and his strong arms latched around my languid body, pulling me up to his side. I settled in against the crook of his arm and began smoothing his chest hair with my fingertips.

"Can we do that again?" I whispered, tipping my face up to his with a sly grin.

He exhaled a breathless laugh and planted a kiss on my forehead. "Jesus, girl. Give me a minute here. I'm still trying to recover."

"Was it okay for you? I mean, did you, um, did you enjoy yourself?" I whispered, feeling the flush of heat creeping up my throat.

He tilted his head down to stare at me, letting his fingers trace lightly up and down my spine. "Are you serious? Baby, when are you gonna learn that there's not a single part of me that doesn't crave you?"

I didn't speak. I just watched the city lights shimmering in his blue eyes until my body gave in to exhaustion, knowing as I drifted off that I'd been staring into my future.

CHAPTER THIRTY
KILLIAN

"What would he say to her, if he was going to speak truly? He didn't know. Talking was like throwing a baseball. You couldn't plan it out beforehand. You just had to let go and see what happened. You had to throw out words you knew no one would catch. You had to send your words out where they weren't yours anymore. It felt better to talk with a ball in your hand, it felt better to let the ball do the talking. But the world, the non baseball world, the world of love and sex and jobs and friends, was made of words."

-Chad Harbach, *The Art of Fielding*

"DRINK THIS." My father handed me a bottle of water before sitting down beside me on the stiff leather sofa. I'd spent the better part of the afternoon wondering why the FBI hadn't sprung for more comfortable furniture. Given what they must have dropped on the lavish hotel suite, surely, they could have afforded it.

"Thanks," I muttered as I unscrewed the lid and took a sip. One of the elevators chimed. I glanced over, only to see more men in dark suits. They were starting to look identical.

An evergreen garland with red bows was draped across the

archway of the federal building, while brightly lit trees surrounded us in the lobby, giving off a soft golden glow. Everywhere I turned, there were reminders of the upcoming holidays, but I wasn't feeling the Christmas spirit.

Maybe it was because we'd been here every day for the past week. Since the arrests, they'd been interviewing Ari extensively, compiling evidence to build their case against her father.

Or perhaps my lack of seasonal cheer had more to do with the fact that our faces were being broadcast on every goddamned television in the building.

Even the sports networks had gotten in on the action, covering the dropped charges against me and interviewing legal experts on whether or not I had a case to sue for defamation.

I didn't really see the point as I wasn't hurting for cash, and the Hurricane's front office had released an official statement after my exoneration, claiming they stood behind me. Besides, a lawsuit was a drop in the bucket compared to the laundry list of charges Tristan was facing. He was going to be spending the rest of his life locked up. Maybe if God answered his prayers, Brad could be his cellmate.

That wasn't to say I hadn't considered going after the cult leaders, but my way didn't involve lawyers. All I needed was a baseball bat and a soundproof room.

Not for me, but her.

They'd abused Ari for years. I had no qualms breaking their bodies apart for it.

I moved to the edge of the leather sofa and cracked my knuckles, unable to sit through more non-stop coverage of the famous pastor's fall from grace. Because they weren't flooding the screens with that bastard's face.

It was my girlfriend's body—photographed from a million different angles at the press conference. Late-night talk show hosts had wasted no time in using the images as comedic material. One had spent over five minutes discussing Ari's lingerie choices and a possible future career in modeling, while another had photoshopped a badge on her bra strap and captioned it: *Eagle Lake Church: SVU*.

The tabloids had run an image of Tristan approaching her from behind with the headline, *Preacher's Kids Gone Wild*.

As if she was a joke.

A punchline.

The rage brewing inside me was close to bubbling over. I'd thought that discovering Ari's bruises and knowing I hadn't been there to stop it was the most helpless feeling in the world. But it was this. Watching them eviscerate her, instead of focusing on the man responsible for destroying countless lives.

"How are you holding up?"

I tilted my head toward my father. It was a relief to not have to fake a smile or put on an act. "I'm miserable. I just want it to be over so we can move on with our lives."

He gestured toward the televisions with a heavy sigh. "They've made Ari their scapegoat, and with your name attached to hers, it's only going to get worse."

"I don't give a flying fuck if they run a hundred stories about me." I clenched my jaw, trying to muster the will power to keep it together. "I'm not leaving her to do this on her own."

"Despite what Theo thinks, you're right where you need to be." My father picked at the cuff of his shirt before meeting my eyes. "It's just—Christ—have you been online lately, Killian? These so-called followers are some real wack jobs."

I pressed my fingertips to my heated eyelids with a muttered curse. "I've seen it, but they're not going to get anywhere near her. We've got Noah now." I nodded toward the intimidating bodyguard seated across the lobby. "They've beefed up our security. Now, we just wait for another scandal to break so we can go back to normal."

A small part of me considered the possibility that things might never be normal again, but I wouldn't give voice to the fear.

He sighed and shook his head, watching the screens with barely concealed disgust. "I don't think it's that simple. Tristan was involved with the same people who control the media. Have you noticed how they're not reporting on the senators who bought underaged girls or the women still unaccounted for? These are fanatics who just lost their savior and want someone to blame."

My jaw tightened, and I squeezed the water bottle, wanting to launch it at the wall. And yet, I knew it wouldn't change a damn thing.

When I remained silent, he continued, "You think it's bad now, just wait until the trial in a year—"

"A year?" I echoed, my stomach sinking at the thought.

My father lifted the paper coffee cup to his lips and took a sip. "With these charges, they need an ironclad case to ensure he doesn't walk. It's going to take some time—" He suddenly lost his grip on the cup, the color draining from his face.

"Dad?" I snagged it in my hand before it spilled and placed it on a small table nearby before reaching for him. "What's wrong?"

"That woman," he whispered, pointing to one of the televisions with a trembling hand. "That's the woman I saw—the one I told you about—I was drunk, and she was there."

I looked up and studied the photograph of a much younger Tristan on his wedding day with a bride who could have been Ari's twin, before reading the headline from the ticker below.

Officials are reopening a case involving the death of Tristan James' first wife, Colleen James. The mother of the disgraced pastor's six children died suddenly in 2010 of an intracerebral hemorrhage. Authorities claim they have new evidence that indicates the death certificate was altered. An exhumation for further forensic examination is planned.

"Ari's mama?" I asked, my wide eyes bouncing between the screen and him.

His nostrils flared, but he didn't answer. Instead, he stood up and began pacing.

I scratched the stubble on my jaw with my thumbnail, trying to recall our conversation the night he drove me home from the bar. "Wait—you're telling me you went to Tristan James' house?"

His expression hardened. "The one and only. I never got her name —hell, once I sobered up, I barely remembered her face. Never in a million years would I have imagined there was a connection with Ari, but seeing her picture, the resemblance between the two is uncanny."

There were no coincidences in life. Just two women who shared a mother-daughter bond and a fondness for saving the Reed men when we'd needed it the most. The realization left me feeling hollow and desolate because it was a debt I'd never be able to repay.

She'd put everything on the line for me twice now, risking her very life for mine, and I couldn't even keep her name out of the press.

"Her mama saved you, and she saved me." I shook my head. "What the fuck did we ever do to deserve it, though?"

My father stopped moving, his stony exterior softening into a look of reflection. "There's always a purpose for the bullshit, even when it doesn't seem like it. Maybe that purpose is to bring this full circle. If so, then the question becomes, what are we willing to do to keep Colleen's daughter safe?"

It was my job, and mine alone, to care for Ari. I wanted to be the one to protect her and keep her safe.

No one else. Me.

The elevator announced its arrival, pulling me from my thoughts. In the time it took me to turn my head, Noah had already reached Ari's side and was leading her across the lobby toward us.

My father stepped up beside me and squeezed the back of my neck. "Just because she knows how to fight doesn't mean she should have to keep doing it." His eyes lingered on mine before he went to meet her.

He didn't say a word before pulling Ari into his arms for a long hug, although he looked suspiciously close to tears. She met my gaze with pursed lips and a lifted brow, clearly taken aback by the rare emotional display.

"Dad." *No response.* "Dad!"

"Right." He cleared his throat and took a step back. "Let's get you two home. I was thinking your mama and I might cook tonight. How's that sound?"

"Sounds good to me." Ari pressed a quick kiss of greeting against my jaw.

I cupped her cheek, letting my eyes take a field trip down to her lips. The tension she'd been carrying in her shoulders fled, and she relaxed into my body in a beautiful surrender.

The proximity left me painfully hard and aching with the need to get her alone. Unfortunately, polite society frowned upon me stripping my woman down in the lobby of a federal building.

I wanted to tease her with my tongue until she made those guttural moans that seemed to come from the back of her throat. I wanted to go back to this morning. In the minutes before the alarm had gone off, her body had been clenched around mine like a fist.

There was no better way to wake up.

I'd questioned myself initially on whether I might have been rushing things by asking her to move in, but it had felt right. Necessary even. Being with Ari just made sense, making me wonder how I'd functioned twenty-six years without her.

Her eyes grew hazy as if she knew where my thoughts were. When the corner of her mouth lifted in a lopsided grin, I took it as an open invitation to continue my lustful fantasizing.

"So, I was wondering if we could stop somewhere first," she said, her gaze hopeful. "When I was upstairs, I saw this giant Christmas tree from the window. It has lights and everything. Hang on, I think it was—"

Ari scanned the row of elevators, chewing on her bottom lip. "Out the front door and to the right? Maybe?"

I grinned at her, before cocking my head to the side. "You heard the lady, Noah. Can we make a stop?"

He gave me a solemn nod in return. "The car is on its way. We'll lose the press and then circle back around."

The hopeful look spread into a full-blown grin, and she began clapping her hands in excitement. I decided then and there that I didn't want any gifts this year. All I needed was to see her happy. Although, I wouldn't necessarily turn down wrapping her up in ribbons and bows and making love to her under the tree either.

Ari rose onto her tiptoes and slid her arms around my neck to press light kisses along my jaw, her lips parting on a soft sigh. "Thank you. Thank you. Thank you. Now, kiss me."

At that moment, she could have asked for anything. I would have done my damnedest to deliver.

I placed a tender kiss against her nose and the arch of her lips before capturing her mouth fully with mine. My eyes remained open, fixed on her beautiful face, silently telling her she was safe. Loved. Desired. Worshiped.

My brave girl.

We pulled apart just as the car arrived, and I shrugged out of my jacket, draping it around Ari's neck to shield her from the wolves waiting just outside the front doors. I refused to give those assholes any more material.

Keeping one hand on her shoulder and the other around her waist, we followed Noah through the doors and into a sea of reporters. My father positioned himself against Ari's left side, keeping his arm extended to prevent anyone from getting too close.

"Ariana, have you spoken with your father?" A disembodied voice called out.

"Are you still engaged to Brad Phillips?" yelled another.

"Killian, is there any truth to the rumors that you bought girls from Trident Holdings?"

Jesus Christ.

"No comment," I clipped out impatiently, moving faster.

The shutters clicked in tandem, filling the gray sky with blinding flashes of white that left me disoriented. At some point, this had become our routine, dodging photographs and questions that were growing more ridiculous by the day while scurrying toward the safety of hired cars.

I never felt like we were in danger. If anything, the daily trek through Dante's fifth circle of hell just left me annoyed and in need of a shower.

That all changed when I heard the shouts. I lifted my head to find a group of picketers gathered across the street, calling for the death of the mother of prostitutes.

"'You must take them out to the gate of that city and stone them to death—" one man bellowed, holding up a sign depicting Ari as something of a demon, complete with horns and glowing red eyes. "The young woman because she did not cry out in the city, and the man because he has violated his neighbor's wife. You must purge the evil from among you!'"

Stoning.

Brain injury.

"Noah!" I roared, tightening my grip on Ari until my knuckles went white. My heart thundered against my ribs like a bomb counting down to explosion as I scanned their faces, trying to identify the threat.

"I've got eyes on them," he confirmed calmly as if they were a troop of *Girl Scouts* selling cookies.

A woman raised her fist, shrieking, "Whore of Babylon!"

"God hates whores!"

Convinced we were seconds away from an attack, adrenaline spiked through my body and prepared my muscles for battle. I'd throw her over my shoulder and run for the car if I had to, weight limits be damned.

Ari's spine went stiff beneath my hand, her green eyes wide with terror. My father saw it at the same moment I did and leaned down to whisper, "We've got you, Ariana. You're safe."

She gave a jerky nod in response, mashing her lips together to stop them from quivering. Something about seeing her frightened stoked my rage and made my blood pump harder and faster, urging me to eliminate the danger myself.

What are we willing to do to keep Colleen's daughter safe?

I was willing to plow through a line of religious zealots using only my fists.

When we reached the curb, Noah hustled us into the backseat of the waiting SUV and slammed the doors. I slid across the middle seat and clutched Ari to the front of my body, close enough that I could feel her racing heart.

Just as fast as a jackrabbit's.

"Hey. I've got you now," I said, keeping my voice neutral. "I've got you now."

She tipped her chin up and patted my bicep with a weak smile. "I'm fine, really. It only hurts if you let it, and I won't."

"Yeah, well, I might," I grumbled, glaring a hole in the back of Noah's head. "Because, apparently, I'm the only one who sees a problem with what happened back there."

Until now, my biggest concern had been the media attention. I never imagined that Tristan would still be calling the shots from the inside of a cell, and there wasn't a single doubt in my mind his fingerprints were all over this.

"Freedom of assembly," Noah sighed, lifting his eyes to the rearview mirror. "As long as they're not obstructing traffic or attacking—"

"Did you hear them?" I blurted, immediately lowering my voice when Ari flinched in my arms. "They were threatening to stone her, and I don't know about you, but I'm not big on the idea of waiting to see if they follow through. If even one of those assholes thinks about throwing a rock, I'm putting them down. End of story."

My father cleared his throat from behind me. "He's right, son. This is how these groups work. It's going to be hard to prove a threat based on Bible verses and a badly photoshopped poster. Law enforcement can't charge them with anything until they break the law."

A shudder worked its way from the base of my skull down my spine. Every cell in my body was against the idea of waiting until she got hurt to do something.

"I want to go home now," Ari mumbled against my chest. Her eyes were glassy, unfocused.

"Don't you want to go see the tree, baby?" I asked, tucking her hair behind one ear. "You were so excited."

She gave a subtle shake of her head and pulled away to look out the window. "I think I'd rather just go home."

I debated over what to say, wanting to argue with the decision because I'd seen the way her entire face had lit up over that damn tree. In the end, I gave her what I thought she needed the most.

"We'll go wherever you want to go." I kept my voice calm and soothing. Inside, I was anything but.

"Home," she said, covering my hand with hers.

Tristan might have been the one locked inside a cell, but she was the prisoner. My breath hitched with the realization that I'd been wrong before.

This was helplessness.

Just because she knows how to fight doesn't mean she should have to keep doing it.

After exchanging another look with my dad, I was forced to accept that the city I loved had become a war zone. Ari was no longer safe here.

———

I sat in a chair near the bed with my chin resting against my fist, watching Ari sleep. She'd left the closet light on again and a sliver cut across the room, illuminating her relaxed features.

Her fear of the dark had never come from a monster who lived under the bed, but the one who slept down the hall.

My building had a doorman and security cameras. A keycard was required to access my floor. It was why I'd chosen to live here, knowing it would always be the one place I could go to escape the world. Right now, it was easy to believe there was no place safer for her than in my bed, tucked under the blankets.

Ari exhaled a soft sigh in her sleep. I leaned forward, still on high alert, prepared to do whatever necessary to protect my woman.

Maybe that was why my mind was such a mess. Because 'whatever necessary' didn't exactly fit in with my future plans. It didn't take into consideration my feelings and what I needed.

I would have given her anything she wanted, but she'd never ask for this. A woman who'd been brought up inside a cage would never ask for freedom. If I quarantined her to the condo under some guise of love, was I any better than the man who'd raised her? Did I want to be the reason her spark fizzled out? Become her keeper, instead of her lover?

My version of safety would ultimately destroy her.

"You're kinda creepy," Ari said, her voice scratchy with sleep.

I smirked and watched her stretch, the blankets falling away from her body and baring one of her perfect breasts. "Just admiring the view, girl."

With a yawn, she patted the empty spot beside her. "The view's better over here, superstar. Come snuggle me."

As I stood, I was struck with a sudden need to propose. There was this fear that if I didn't, I'd lose her forever. But I refused to pledge the rest of my life to a woman in panic. This was about what was best for her, not me.

Maybe if I repeated it enough, I'd believe it.

I slipped under the sheets and wrapped my body around hers until the noise in my head died away.

She exhaled a soft laugh and ground her hips lightly against mine. "Were you naked the entire time you were watching me sleep?"

"Just got out of the shower," I lied, before pressing my lips to her shoulder blade. Technically, I'd been out of the shower for hours, but found myself too wired to relax. So, I'd kept vigil over her.

Ari craned her neck to peer up at me. "What's wrong?"

I swallowed, resisting the urge to lie and say nothing—fighting against my selfish need to hold on. "I'm worried about you."

She laced her fingers through mine with a frown. "Why? Because of today? Look at me, I'm fine. I mean, clearly, I'm not losing any sleep over it."

"You know, I initially thought I was going to have to move across the country to find a team that would take me. But, as much as I wanted to, I knew I couldn't ask you to uproot your entire life to be with me."

Her gaze softened as she stroked the back of my hand with her thumb. "Hey, I would have gone with you in a heartbeat."

"I know," I admitted. "And that's why I'm getting you out of here —just until the trial's over."

She released my hand and rolled to face me. "What do you mean? Where are we going?"

I brushed the hair away from her forehead with my fingertips, praying for a divine intervention like never before. "Do you remember Georgia's trip around the world? Well, we thought—"

"Who is 'we?'"

"Uh—" I managed weakly. *Shit.* "Tsega and Dean."

She glared up at me, saying nothing.

"Slugger, I was just trying to do the right thing. They were talking about stoning you, and I'm not allowing you to stay here so they can make good on that promise," I hissed, instantly regretting my choice of words.

"You're not going to allow me?" Ari challenged, the sheet sliding down both our bodies as she moved into a sitting position. "And what if I refuse to leave? What will you do then?"

I'll force you.

I shifted my jaw back and forth and swallowed my pride until I felt in control again.

"Ultimately, it's your decision," I responded carefully. "I was just trying to do what I thought was best, but you're right. I should have come to you first with this. I'm sorry."

She leaned down to press a kiss against the corner of my mouth, before sighing, "No, I'm sorry. I thought you were telling me what I could and couldn't do. It annoyed me."

"Jesus, baby," I laughed. "If that's you annoyed, remind me to never piss you off. Look, you don't have to decide tonight, just promise me you'll at least think about it."

"What about you? Are you coming too?"

"Yes," I blurted, before catching myself with a wince. "I mean, no. Fuck!" I massaged my temples and lifted my eyes to the ceiling. "With spring training and my PT appointments, I don't know if I can right away."

"I didn't think about that," she confessed, tucking her body to my side. "But when the season ends?"

"I'm with you, wherever that may be," I whispered gruffly, my throat clogged with emotion. "I know it's not ideal, but I'm afraid if you stay here, this will start to feel like a cage. And I couldn't live with myself if I did that to you."

But please, don't leave me.

Her hand settled on my chest, just over the heart that was in the throes of a complete breakdown. "I'll do it."

No.

A dull ache spread throughout my chest. I clenched my fists in the sheets, forcing the words out. "I just want you safe, but I recognize how much your freedom means to you."

Keeping one hand centered on my chest, Ari climbed across my lap, her body hovering just over my hips. I was rock hard, something she'd be aware of if she moved any lower.

"Thank you for loving me enough to make the hard decisions," she whispered, unaware of her double entendre. "When would I leave?"

I heard the question she couldn't bring herself to ask.

How much time do we have left?

It was like ice in my veins. "Tsega thinks they could have passports and travel arrangements ready by the first of the year. There will also be a security team in place no matter where you are."

"Okay." She nodded to herself before reaching over to the top drawer of the nightstand. The foil wrapper landed on my chest, and she straightened. "Well, if it's alright with you, I'd like to suggest spending the holidays in bed."

I rolled it on and positioned my cock beneath her, watching her lips part on an exhale as she slowly sank down onto me. Her eyes went hazy as I took her breasts in my hands, sitting up for a taste.

The movement forced her all the way down to the root. She groaned out a curse, clutching my hair in her fists. In this room, I wasn't helpless. I was her safe place, taking care of her the only way I knew how.

Her head fell back as she rocked against me, her long hair tickling the tops of my thighs just like in my fantasy. I tried to stay in the present, focusing on the feel of her heat around my cock. I wouldn't think about how hard it was going to be when she was gone.

"Killian," she panted, tightening around me. "I love you. I love you so much."

When my condo was empty.

"I love you too, girl," I murmured, biting her neck and rolling my hips to give her what she needed.

When my life went back to normal.

"Please," she begged, nipping my earlobe with her teeth. "I'm close."

Please don't go.

"I've got you," I growled, guiding her mouth down over mine and circling her clit with the pad of my thumb.

I don't want to come home if you're not here.

Her back bowed as she came apart with a hoarse cry, frantically grabbing at my shoulders as if trying to stop her fall. I locked my arms around her as my thrusts turned rough, resisting some biological urge to strip off the condom.

You are my life.

I drove into Ari's body, broken and in pain, but she didn't push me away. Instead, her hips shifted to accommodate, welcoming every anguished stroke. She bucked against me with soft whimpers, soaking my lap.

With one final thrust, I crushed her to my chest and came, my body shuddering violently. I didn't know how I was going to ever let her go.

Stay.

CHAPTER THIRTY-ONE
ARIANA

"I wanted to see you again, touch you, know who you were, see if I would find you identical with the ideal image of you which had remained with me and perhaps shatter my dream with the aid of reality."

-Victor Hugo, *The Hunchback of Notre Dame*

I'D SPENT the better part of the past two years traveling the world and immersing myself in other religions and cultures. Beliefs varied wildly by region, but all shared some idea of where we went after death.

For Hindus, salvation was found in reincarnation.

For Muslims, souls awaited the Day of Resurrection, where they would be judged accordingly.

Buddhists believed the mind experienced a rebirth, bringing them one step closer to purifying past mistakes and achieving enlightenment.

Jewish tradition dictated that the soul went to heaven, allowing the person to live on in the memories of the ones left behind.

I couldn't tell you which one had it right, but in the last year, I'd discovered that death didn't always bring closure or justice. There were some wounds so deep that only God could heal.

After being convicted on all but one count and facing a minimum of one hundred forty-seven years in prison, Tristan James hung himself in his cell.

Since then, I'd done a lot of soul-searching to work through the grief that had come disguised as anger. Although he never made it to sentencing, there was justice in knowing he'd died in a cage. Maybe someday, I'd find peace. Until then, I took solace in the fact that he would never hurt anyone again.

I'd let Tristan control me in life, but he wouldn't have that hold in death. He'd been blinded by religion, consumed with finding God in laws and rules. That fanatical thirst for power only destroyed him in the end.

It would have been enough to turn even the most devout person into an atheist, but my faith had never been dependent on the church.

And my savior had never lived behind stained glass windows.

He'd been with me all along.

Right on cue, my phone began buzzing from beside me. Killian's name flashed across the screen, along with one of my favorite pictures of the two of us. Georgia had taken it when we were in Mauritius last November during the festival of Diwali. We'd spent most of the day on the beach, our faces sunburned but smiling.

Italy. Thailand. Sri Lanka. Each time, we got lost in each other for as long as possible before the real world crept in and stole him away again.

Living apart eight months out of the year had certainly tested the strength of our relationship. There were even times when I wanted to reach through the phone to flick his forehead in aggravation.

Not anymore.

I swiped my finger across the screen, my stomach giving a gentle flutter as his face came into focus. "Is this the Killian Reed, world-famous baseball player? I can't tell with the giant beard in the way."

His lips curved into a grin, and I felt the tug of missing him all over again. "You know I can't shave until we win it all, girl. What are you up to?"

I lifted my shoulder in a shrug, fighting my own grin. "Oh, you know, just *Eat, Pray, Love*-ing, and all that jazz."

"I gotta say, I'm a little surprised you know what that is, darlin'."

There it was again, this longing to be next to him. Hearing his southern twang come through with certain words left me feeling homesick, not for a place, but for him. I'd been surrounded by a variety of accents over the past two years, but his was my favorite of all.

"Oh, you know Georgia. She reads anything Oprah recommends," I explained with a laugh. "Anyway, what are you doing? Ready for tonight?"

He stretched his arms overhead. "Just woke up and made breakfast. I couldn't unwind last night. I think it was close to three before I finally fell asleep."

"Mmm..." I licked my lips. "Egg white omelets, my favorite."

Sleep hadn't come easily for me either. I might have been just as nervous about game seven of the World Series as he was, but for entirely different reasons.

"Hey, knock it all you want. You're missing out on the best way to start your day—" Killian paused and lifted an eyebrow suggestively. "Correction—the second-best way to start your day. So, are y'all still in Paraty, or were you going to go to São Paulo?"

"We're still here," I lied, heat staining my cheeks. Hopefully, he'd assume my blush was due to his veiled reference to morning sex and not any duplicitousness on my part.

He settled back against the pillows with a relaxed sigh. "I was thinking, if you're going to be sticking around for a while, it might be fun to explore Brazil together. I mean, once we get through tonight. Or..."

"Or," I parroted, biting the inside of my cheek to keep from smiling.

"Or you could come home, slugger. The trial's been over for months now, and after what happened with Tristan—"

"I know," I responded in a tight voice. "Tsega said the followers had disbanded whatever the hell it was they had going on. It's over."

Killian cocked his head to the side with a frown. "You talk to Tsega?"

Shit. Damn. Hell.

"Um, yeah. She calls to give me an update every so often—says Brad's not enjoying prison life all that much." I picked at a loose thread on the comforter and gathered my thoughts before changing the subject. "So, are you going to head down to the field soon? Get geared up for tonight? Atlanta's going to be bringing their best."

He nodded distractedly, scratching his beard. "Yeah. I'll head down there in a couple of hours. Get in some stretching and drill work before everyone else arrives."

I had his routine down to a science. It didn't matter whether it was a regular-season or playoff game, Killian always got to the field an hour before his teammates. It was a time of meditation and mentally gearing himself up.

Then, he'd stretch with the team and get in a quick practice before heading back to the clubhouse for his pre-game meal. After grabbing something quick, usually deli meats and veggies, he'd head down to spend an hour in the batting cages. This was followed by thirty minutes of visualization before suiting up.

During the national anthem, Killian twisted the baseball bracelet on his left wrist, mentally working through the opposing team's pitching lineup and their tendencies on the mound.

After the game, he'd eat the catered meal with the team before showering and heading home, or back to the hotel, if they were traveling. He'd get in another workout before falling asleep watching *SportsCenter*.

"So, what do you say?" The side of his mouth lifted in a barely-there smile. I came back to the conversation, searching the hopeful expression in his blue eyes for a hint as to what I'd missed.

"To what?"

"Am I coming to Brazil, or are you coming home so we can start our lives together?" His gaze softened as he pleaded, "Come home to me, please. The law is insistent you be present in order for me to marry you. Believe me, I checked."

Marry.

I swallowed; my mouth suddenly dry. He knew what that word did to me and enjoyed taunting me with it every chance he got.

I wanted to be his wife. More than anything.

"Tonight's all about you, babe," I said, my heart clenching in protest. "You've worked so hard to get here, and I don't want you worrying about me. This is your moment."

His brows pulled together, the smile slowly fading from his lips. "I need you, slugger. I need to feel you and be able to hold you in my arms. No more living apart for most of the year. Promise me you'll at least consider it?"

I chewed on my lower lip. "Can I give you my answer after the game?"

"On one condition," he stated, lips twitching as he fought to remain serious. "Naked video chat."

A moment passed, in which I squeezed my eyes shut, fighting the flush creeping its way up my throat. "Absolutely."

"And," Killian continued, pulling my attention back to his woolly, yet still gorgeous face. "You have to do that thing where you put the phone at the foot of the bed so I can see everything. I like to pretend you're sitting on my face."

"Got it," I squeaked out, feeling a little out of breath. "Yep. Anything for the celebrity."

He cocked a dark brow and challenged, "For as long as I want?"

"Jesus, Killian. Georgia's going to hear you." I lowered my voice and pushed my lips into a pout, deciding he'd earned a little torment of his own. "Yes, babe. Whatever you want, for as long as you want."

I scrunched my face up when the door opened, and Georgia's winter-white hair came into view. "And, she's here now."

He chuckled, his eyes gleaming with amusement. "Hey, Georgia! You're just in time. I was discussing all the ways I want to defile Ari the next time I see her."

"Oh, good," she crowed, crossing the room to climb onto the bed beside me. "She was looking entirely too pure for my taste, dear. Now, are you ready for tonight?"

"Yes, ma'am. I'm convinced the only thing that would make it better would be if my girl was here."

"Well, the Lord works in mysterious ways," she mused aloud with a wide grin. "Maybe toss up an extra prayer or two before your game."

I discreetly elbowed her side and rushed out, "Oh, do you hear that? Someone's at the door. We have to go now. I love you."

Killian's eyes narrowed, inspecting me. "I love you too—can you call me back? I'd like to continue our conversation."

"I'll try! Okay, I love you. Bye!" I ended the call and turned to the older woman. "What the hell are you doing, Georgia?"

She studied her painted nails with a shrug. "You've been in the same city as that boy for over a month now. You've attended every single post-season game—home and away—why won't you tell him already?"

"Because I don't like the media circus that pops up when the two of us are together," I barked, crossing my arms over my chest. "He's been in a hitting streak for the last thirty-six games, for crying out loud! Do you know how big of a deal this is? I don't want to be the reason that comes to an end. Nothing can jinx tonight for him. Once the game is won, then I'll reveal everything."

"I'm ready!" Morgan entered the room and twirled as if she was wearing a ball gown, not a baseball jersey. "Do you like it? Joe picked it up for me."

I blinked, masking my surprise. My former stepmother had traveled all over the world with us but was back to being afraid of her own shadow now that we were home. "Seriously? You're going tonight?"

"I am. This is important to you, Ari, and if you can go out in public without being recognized, I can too." She looked down at the jersey, color rising on her cheeks. "Although I need to be honest. I don't know a single player, other than Killian."

Her small act of bravery made me smile. "That's okay."

"Not to worry, dear. I've already made a list of potential love interests for you and ranked them," Georgia said, beaming like she'd just solved the world's hunger problem.

I gave her a side-eye. "That's what you've been doing during the games? I thought you were keeping score."

"Oh, I am. Just in my own way. Now, Morgan—" She slipped off the bed and shuffled toward the door. "Do you want the top five now, or would you like to get a feel for all of them first?"

Morgan's wide eyes met mine in a universal signal for help. "Um, maybe I'll, um, just decide when we get there. Is that okay?"

"Perfectly okay, dear. Oh, Ari—" Georgia snapped her fingers as she turned back to me. "I knew I came in here for a reason. I need to know, are you going to be having your usual for brunch—egg white omelet and veggies?"

"Yep. Breakfast of champions." I didn't understand why champions shunned the tastiest part of the egg in favor of white rubber but had somehow forced it down every morning for the past month.

Her lips curved into a patient smile. "Mmm, hmmm... and the jersey hanging up in my laundry room was washed at exactly midnight, I presume?"

I bristled with defensiveness. "Maybe—what are you getting at?"

"Oh, nothing." Georgia waved her hand as if shooing my question away. "Just curious. Those baseball players—so superstitious, you know?"

She began cackling when my mouth fell open before slipping out and closing the bedroom door behind her.

The septuagenarian had some snap in her garters.

So, maybe I'd picked up a few habits from Killian over the past couple of years. We'd overcome so much to get here, and I was willing to do whatever it took to keep their winning streak alive, including following the same meal plan and schedule he was.

No matter how much I hated it.

A little superstition never hurt anyone.

Well, within reason.

I wasn't giving up my razor for anything.

———

"And now, first baseman, number thirty-four—Conor Bailey!"

"Come on," I murmured, clasping my hands under my chin and rocking on the balls of my feet. The current of nervous energy running through my body had made it impossible to sit. We were down by one in the bottom of the ninth with only one out remaining.

Killian stood in the on-deck circle, his eyes on the *Atlanta Thrashers'* closer, Dan Antonelli. Some players worked on swinging or stretching, but not my man.

When I asked his dad about it, he told me Killian viewed it as a free at-bat. He'd study the pitcher, so he knew when to get his front foot off the ground to be on time for the pitch.

It was like watching a choreographed dance, where Killian's body moved in sync with the hitter's. Right now, he and Bailey were like mirror images, finding their rhythm with Antonelli and raising their cleats at the exact same moment.

As much as I wanted to run down the aisle, launching myself over the fence and into his arms, seeing him in element reinforced my decision to keep my return a secret. This was the side of him I never got to see when we were together, a man not concerned with impressing his prodigal girlfriend or keeping the press at bay.

Witnessing the player was sexy as hell.

Besides, there would be plenty of time for trekking through that jungle of a beard to kiss his lips. Plenty of time to breathe in the scent of his body wash.

"He's in the zone," I noted, more to myself than anyone else. Killian's mama, Sheri, agreed. Joe had sequestered himself two seats down and was fidgeting with the bill of his ball cap while watching his son.

"What?" Morgan asked in a thin voice. She'd spent most of the game gnawing her fingernails to the quick and closing her eyes.

I patted her between the shoulder blades. "Are you okay? They're going to come back from this. I feel it. Don't give up."

Georgia hip-checked Morgan with a chuckle. "Oh, I don't think she's giving up, dear. I think she's found the winner." She slid her glasses down her nose and reviewed her notepad, before tapping it with her index finger. "Just as I predicted, Conor Bailey. He was my number one choice too. Lovely job, Morgan. He'll make you very happy."

I pulled my lower lip between my teeth with a shake of my head. There was never a dull moment with Georgia around.

Morgan hesitated before blurting, "It's not that. I, um, I know him!"

"What?" I shouted to be heard over the crowd. "How? You said you didn't know any of the players besides Killian!"

She tucked a strand of dark hair behind her ear, avoiding my penetrating stare. "Conor was my neighbor when I was sixteen."

"Wait! Wait! Wait!" I held up my hands, drawing Georgia and Sheri's attention. "A neighbor, or *the neighbor*?"

"The neighbor," she said with a laugh, her voice full of affection as she watched him.

Morgan's first and only love—the man she'd given her virginity to —was Bailey.

"You have to talk to him!"

Her nose crinkled and she shook her head. "It was a long time ago, Ari. I doubt he even remembers!"

"But he—" I was interrupted by the crack of Bailey's bat and turned just in time to see the ball sail over the second baseman's glove before dropping onto the field.

"Go!" we screamed in unison, waving our arms as if we could make the giant run faster.

Bailey's helmet flew off as he went speeding past the bag, rolling across first just after he did.

He and the helmet were safe.

Joe pumped his fist but otherwise stayed silent. Sheri clung to my hand as Killian's walk-up song began, her fingernails digging into my knuckles.

"And now, your center fielder, number twelve—Killian Reed!"

The noise in the stadium moved to a deafening level. Blue foam fingers waved in the air, as well as several large cutouts of Killian's head.

I drew in a long breath and released it, unable to resist sneaking a peek at Joe. In a ritual that had become just as much a part of the game as the players on the field, Killian's father lowered his head, his mouth moving as if in prayer.

One on, no room for error.

The game rested in Killian's hands.

Morgan linked her fingers through mine before reaching for Georgia's, the four of us forming a human chain.

We stood together in solidarity, drawing strength from one another and praying it was enough to get Killian through the next few pitches.

CHAPTER THIRTY-TWO
KILLIAN

"One of the beautiful things about baseball is that every once in a while you come into a situation where you want to, and where you have to, reach down and prove something."

-Nolan Ryan

THE LAST STRAINS of Andy Grammer's "Good To Be Alive" faded away as I approached the batter's box.

I stopped short and tapped my bat against the dirt when I saw Atlanta's second baseman deep in discussion with Antonelli. The two of them kept cutting their eyes over to me before Antonelli covered his mouth with his glove.

"Fuentes," I said in a falsetto, unable to resist poking fun at the pair to keep my momentum up. "Have you seen Reed's ass in those pants? Why yes. Yes I did, Antonelli. Best ass in the American League for the past eight years. Oh, crap. He caught us looking."

I cracked my neck and bounced on my feet as Fuentes headed back to second base, chuckling to myself when he patted Antonelli's ass on his way.

"Ooh, a love connection?" I mused, approaching the plate.

Their catcher lowered himself into a crouch before peering up at me. "Having a nice conversation with yourself, Reed?"

I smirked. "Sure am, Darcy. Just wondering when Antonelli and Fuentes are gonna take their romance public."

"Heard you tried to do that a couple a years ago and your girl fled the country. Man, that's gotta suck, knowing she won't be here to dry your tears when you blow this game."

My jaw tightened, but I kept my eyes fixed on Antonelli and dug my right cleat into the dirt. "Speaking of sucking and blowing, your wife already volunteered, so I'm good."

Darcy grumbled something in response, but I tuned him out and glanced back at the dugout, getting the sign to take the first pitch.

With a deep exhale, I cleared my mind of everything, until it was just Antonelli and me. Except, it wasn't just us. Just like every at-bat before, Ari was there too.

No matter where in the world she was, a piece of her would forever be standing on first base, gripping my heart in her hands.

"This one's for you, baby," I said under my breath. "It's all for you."

Even before Antonelli's arm came forward, I knew it was a fastball. High and outside.

Ball one.

The organ made a low humming sound just before the opening notes of the "Let's Go Chant" began to play over the speakers, taking the energy of the crowd and amping it up.

I looked to the dugout and got the sign to take the second pitch.

"C'mon, you pussy," I muttered when Antonelli threw another high and outside.

Ball two.

I saw it in his eyes, the next one was going to be on the inside. My eyes darted over to the dugout again, getting yet another sign to take it.

Fuck.

The muscles in my forearms tightened as I adjusted my grip on the bat. I knew what he was about to send my way, convinced myself I could get a piece of it but held back. The last time I'd take my own advice on the third pitch, I ended up writhing on the ground just off first base.

I could be patient—hell, it hadn't failed me in the past thirty-six games.

The slider came across the inside half of the plate, smacking Darcy's glove with a loud pop, like the sound of a whip being cracked.

Strike one.

Shit. I could have gotten a single out of it, advanced Bailey to second...

I stepped out of the box and rolled my shoulders, trying to center myself. The volume in the stadium was like nothing I'd ever heard before—the fans chaotic and wild. One fan had even brought in a cowbell, the incessant clanging of it vibrated through my skull and rattled my brain.

My focus returned to Antonelli, and I took a deep breath, waiting for him to show me what was next. Throwing another pitch inside was too risky. He was going to try to blow one by me again.

"What's it gonna be, Antonelli? Fastball outside because you don't trust me?"

I looked to the dugout and got the signal I wanted.

Swing away.

After taking a practice cut, I stepped back in the box and planted my cleats.

If you can visualize it, you can make it happen.

Forty thousand people, but hers was the only face I wanted to see. In my mind, the entire stadium held its collective breath in silent anticipation. Well, everyone but the mouthy redhead seated behind home plate.

What are you gonna do, superstar? Make a move or just stand there some more?

I exhaled a breathless laugh, hearing Ari's voice as clear as day. Darcy muttered something about my deteriorating mental state, but his insults were garbled.

Her.

I only heard her.

And that was all I needed to face Antonelli. A lot of pitchers sat into the back leg, but not this guy. Atlanta's closer was old-school, using his entire body with every pitch, which was probably why his pitching velocity was unmatched.

A worthy adversary.

He moved into his starting stance, and I aligned my knuckles, keeping a relaxed grip on the handle of the bat.

Like you've done it a million times before, Reed...

Antonelli's arms went over his head as he took a short start-step to the side, before pivoting in front of the rubber, his movements slow and deliberate.

He stepped in, breaking his hands at the exact same time his leg came up off the ground. The announcers, the screaming fans, the cowbell—it all disappeared. I was left with the buzzing stadium lights overhead, and the sound of my exhale as the ball left his hand.

Fastball.

I swung at the offering, the maple bat connecting with my target in a loud crack that sent the ball soaring deep to left field. I turned my face up, wincing when I saw the bright yellow foul pole in its path.

Fuck, I'd been too early on it.

Stay fair. Stay fair.

After tossing my bat to the side, I began jogging to first, keeping an eye on its trajectory. It was gone, or it was foul. I'd made it about a third of the way up the first baseline when it disappeared just inside the foul line.

I stumbled, feeling as if the breath had been knocked from my lungs.

Home run.

There was an immediate seismic shift within the ballpark, a

rumbling magnitude that I felt through the bottoms of my cleats. The sky above me erupted in an explosion of fireworks and cobalt blue streamers as I rounded first, raising my fist in victory.

We'd done it.

I knew I was running faster than ever before, but inside, I was that seven-year-old kid again, flying around the bases like I was weightless. But, unlike most of my career, this game had been won with heart.

It was almost perfect.

The only thing missing was her.

"All for you, baby," I whispered, lifting my eyes to the vibrant bursts of color in the night sky.

The entire team came spilling out of the dugout as Bailey tied it up. I crossed the plate behind him, choking back tears as I remembered the little boy who'd dreamt of this exact moment as he swung a bat in his backyard.

My teammates mobbed me almost immediately, slapping my back while jumping up and down. Bailey pushed through the crowd and lifted me off the ground, knocking my batting helmet to the dirt.

"We did it—we fucking did it!" he bellowed, leaving me deaf in my right ear.

I grinned and punched the air before being tackled to the ground from behind. Network cameras circled around us, capturing the high-fives and handshakes, the water bottles being shaken over my head.

Since the beginning of my hitting streak, I'd avoided looking up into the crowd, convinced I'd jinx myself by letting them in. There was also pressure to perform, knowing my parents and their friends were watching. They'd been buying up tickets left and right since the playoffs began, probably for the kinds of people who didn't care about the game but wanted to be able to brag that they'd been in the seats.

Now that it was over, I couldn't help but glance up to the club level, scanning the crowd for their familiar faces. I found my dad first, seated on the second level behind home plate. His hand was around his mouth, his shoulders rising and falling on a sob. When our eyes met, he nodded and gave me a thumbs up.

My mama was a couple seats down, embracing a woman in a Hurricanes ball cap and jersey. I assumed it was either a friend or someone who'd become one over the course of the game. Mama was the type of person who'd never met a stranger. When two other women joined their hug, I froze, feeling my jaw go slack.

Someone barreled into my side, slapping me wildly between the shoulder blades, but I couldn't move. My eyes were glued on the woman in my mother's arms, willing her to look down at me.

An eternity later, she pulled away, wiping her cheeks with the backs of her thumbs before throwing her head back in a laugh I wished I was close enough to hear. I'd missed her with every fiber of my being, but with one look, the ache in my chest fled, and my mouth curved into a wide grin.

A moment that had been almost perfect was now flawless.

You're standing on the field, surrounded by your teammates and reporters, but you're not looking at them. You're looking up into the seats. Who are you waiting for?

Ari.

After one year, nine months, and twenty-five days, my girl had come home.

For me.

———

"Now, talk to me about that last pitch from Antonelli. What was going through your head?"

I was in the middle of an interview with James Donovan of *Fox Sports* when I felt her presence. I turned and caught a flash of red hair behind the blue barricade set up around the stage. We'd been herded onto it for the trophy presentation. I'd gone through the motions, slipping the championship t-shirt over my jersey and smiling for the cameras.

"Uh," I hedged, loosening the string of my bracelet with shaking hands. "Excuse me for a second. Listen, have you talked to Bailey yet? He's the real star of the show. His single was a game-changer for us."

Bailey looked up at the mention of his name and ambled over, slinging an arm around my shoulders. "You rang?"

"Yeah, Donovan's got some questions for you," I mumbled, closing my fist around a bracelet that suddenly felt heavier before making my way toward the stairs.

Ari lifted her chin with a frown, biting her bottom lip as she scanned the stage, completely unaware that the man she was searching for was making his way toward her. Just like he'd been under the impression she was in a different country.

Turnabout was fair play, after all.

I'd known I wanted her to be my wife since the night I sat by the bed and watched her sleep. The same night I realized that letting her go was the only way to keep her safe. In the time we'd spent apart since, want had developed into need.

Marriage had become a frequent topic of conversation between the two of us for the better part of the last year. I could have proposed any number of times by now, and she'd have said yes. But some part of me had always held back, feeling like the timing wasn't right.

What started as a means of escape had developed into something of a spiritual journey along the way.

Something sacred.

So, I decided to wait until she was ready to come home. When the ring on her finger wouldn't feel like a means of control, but a promise of the life we were going to build together.

I worked my jaw as I took the stairs two at a time, rehearsing the words in my head. I'd always pictured this moment happening in an airport, with me dropping to one knee near the baggage claim.

But I had to hand it to her, this was much better.

Ari's attention was still on the stage when I approached. She tensed, before slowly inclining her head toward me. For a brief second our gazes locked, and then she was shoving people aside to reach me.

When she reached the barrier, my hands wrapped around her waist, easily lifting her up and over. The air around us was suddenly filled with the scent of her skin, and I buried my face against her neck, breathing her in.

We'd spent eight months apart, and not being able to hold her like I needed was pure torture. My way didn't involve clothes. Or the press.

As if reading my thoughts, Ari shied away with a giggle and cupped my jaw in her palm. She raked her fingernails through my beard, stroking and petting, while her green eyes moved over my face. "Hey, wild man. You looked good out there."

Clearly, my mouth and brain were no longer working together, because I didn't return the greeting or launch into the eloquent speech I'd written in my head on the way down the stairs.

No. Proving that I was every bit the wild man, I grunted in response.

Grunted.

Ari's hands fell from my face. She took a step back, probably second-guessing her decision to leave Brazil early. "Are you mad at me? I just wanted it to be a surprise—"

With a low growl, I hooked my finger in the front of her jersey—my jersey—and tugged her to my body, lowering my mouth over hers. She released a startled breath. Then her pink lips were parting in invitation.

The bracelet in my hand brought me back to reality, and after another deep kiss, I reluctantly pulled back to scan the ballpark. There were still people milling about almost everywhere I looked, but this was the right moment. I felt it.

"Ari—"

"Congratulations!" she panted with a grin. "Sorry, I meant to say that first, but I got so tongue-tied when I saw you that I just blurted the first random thing that came into my head."

God, I'd missed her.

"Crap. Now that I think about it, I was actually supposed to lead with I love you, and then—wait, what are you doing?"

I was respecting the hell out of her.

"Be gentle with me, slugger," I said as I took her left wrist in my hands and lowered to my knees.

My girl had never wanted pretty words or a smooth-talking knight. She'd wanted the ability to stand on her own two feet, the freedom to make her own choices. She didn't need my money and had done just fine living off her music royalties for the past couple of years.

So, in the end, I ditched the speech and kept it simple. Not because I forgot the words, but because when I looked into her eyes, I realized I didn't need them.

There was only one thing I hadn't offered yet.

"Ariana, you are the bravest woman I've ever met. With each day that passes, I find myself more in love with you. You already have my heart, my love, and my life. I kneel before you now to ask, will you do me the honor of taking my last name?"

Ari's mouth opened and closed, her eyes flooding with tears as she nodded shakily. "Yes, Killian Reed. I will take your last name and be your wife."

"I know it's not a ring, but—"

"Hush, it's perfect."

My fingers were still trembling as I knotted the bracelet around her wrist, before moving back to my feet. Ignoring the cameras flashing all around us, I lifted her into my arms and took her mouth in a fierce and frantic kiss.

She instinctively wrapped her legs around my waist, her fingers threading through my sweat-dampened hair, fighting to pull me closer.

"I love you," Ari gasped, raining kisses across my face. "And I cannot wait to be your wife. I'm going to make you so happy."

"You already do, girl." I had to adjust my grip on her. My baseball pants, while unrestrictive, weren't exactly hiding the fact that I was painfully hard. "What do you say we skip the after-party, so I can properly demonstrate just how happy you make me?"

"Yes, because I have—"

"Guys! Oh, my God!" Bailey bellowed as he shoved his face between ours, instantly ridding me of my erection. "Now, as your best man, I've got some great ideas for the bachelor party."

I opened my mouth, prepared to disagree when Georgia chimed in from across the barrier.

"Oh, I didn't know we got to pick our role! I'll obviously be filling in as the flower girl, then."

"Georgia, you old so-and-so," Bailey teased, clapping my shoulder roughly as he stalked over to her. "Finally decided to take me up on that date?"

After lowering Ari to the field, we walked over to hug my parents and inexplicably watch my teammate woo a woman who was fifty years his senior.

"You're going to want to see this," Ari said, wearing the smile of someone who was up to no good.

"Mr. Bailey, I do not accept your offer," Georgia exclaimed in a performance worthy of an Oscar, before nudging Morgan forward. "But perhaps she will."

The smirk on his face faded and his body went still. "Morgan?"

She tucked a strand of hair behind her ear, before lifting her eyes to meet his. "Hey, Conor."

"Where in the hell have you been, girl?" He said gruffly, before lifting her up and over the barrier.

I cut my eyes over to Ari with a frown, trying to recall if I'd ever introduced Bailey to Morgan. I was almost positive I hadn't, which left no reasonable explanation as to how the hell they knew each other. "Did I miss something?"

"I'll explain it later." She chuckled and pressed her lips to the corner of my mouth before lowering her voice. "How fast can you knock the rest of these interviews out?"

"Why?" I knew but wanted to hear her say it anyway.

"Because I have a surprise for you too."

I lifted a brow. "Oh, yeah?"

Ari's gaze heated, and she nodded. "Whatever you want, for as long as you want."

CHAPTER THIRTY-THREE
KILLIAN

"I had only one superstition. I made sure to touch all the bases when I hit a home run."

-Babe Ruth

"REMIND me again why you've never worn a suit for me before," Ari murmured in between kisses. One of her hands roamed my torso while the other held my tie in a firm grip.

"I was just wondering why I hadn't seen you in one of my jerseys. Obviously, this is something you should start wearing every day."

Pants optional.

"Oh, this old thing? I've had it for—"

I kicked the door shut behind me and cut her off with another kiss. My hands moved down to her hips, guiding her backward through the living room with only one destination in mind.

She grinned against my lips. "As I was saying, I got this when the Hurricanes made the playoffs. I needed something to wear to the games."

My steps faltered, and I blinked, completely confused. "Wait —what?"

She exhaled a breathless laugh. "Well, I couldn't go in just anything, could I?"

Most of the blood in my body was currently residing in my dick, so I was having a little trouble following. I'd assumed she'd flown in for tonight, but she'd clearly said *games*—as in, more than one—which was crazy. She would have had to have flown in days, maybe even weeks ago, to attend those.

"Hold on," I said slowly. "When did you get into town?"

"Um, right after y'all made the playoffs?" Her voice was high-pitched, making her confession sound more like a question.

I scratched my beard while mentally calculating the dates. "But that was almost a month ago. Why am I just now seeing you?"

A flush crept up her throat. "You were doing so well, and frankly, I didn't know how the press was going to react. I didn't want anything to get into your head."

I'd been wrong before.

Torture wasn't being unable to hold Ari like I'd wanted or trying to give interviews with her hand squeezing my ass. It was discovering she'd been in the same damn city as me for weeks and knowing the only thing that had kept us apart was her reverence for the game.

A man could only take so much.

There was a sudden ferocity in the way I claimed her mouth, the culmination of months of pent-up need. I'd slow down and give her sweet, but right now, I needed to satisfy an itch.

I needed to be inside her.

"Wait," Ari panted against my lips as I slipped my hand under the waistband of her yoga pants. "Just wait—I have a surprise for you."

"I've got one for you too," I murmured, rocking my hips. "Can you guess what it is?"

She freed her mouth from mine, gulping for her next breath. "Just —just sit on the couch. Please."

Completely intrigued, I shrugged out of my jacket and sank down onto the leather with a wink. "The floor's all yours, slugger."

Ari toed off her running shoes and socks, before gripping the waistband of her pants, pulling them down several inches while keeping her eyes on mine.

"Fuck," I whispered, my voice filled with awe. This was the glimpse I'd seen the first time I visited her room, a woman who didn't lower her head for any man.

My brave girl.

"You showered, right?"

I frowned. "Yeah. Why?"

She regarded me silently as she pulled her pants down the rest of the way. The jersey hit her mid-thigh, revealing nothing. It didn't matter, as my imagination had filled in the missing details quite nicely, bringing me dangerously close to losing control.

"Put your arms on the back of the couch and relax," Ari said. She stepped in between the couch and the ottoman in front of me. Using her legs, she parted my thighs and knelt at my feet.

The temporary haze of lust brought on by her striptease dissipated enough for me to recognize her intentions.

"Whoa!" I sat up and placed my hands over hers. "We don't need to do this."

Ari shrugged out of my hold and traced a fingertip down the ridges of my stomach before reaching for my belt. "Why are you the only one allowed to give pleasure in this relationship? Why won't you let me do this?"

"Because," I responded weakly, lifting my eyes to the ceiling. "I don't need it."

"Yes, you do." The belt opened with a click, and she moved to my pants. "Everyone needs to be loved, Killian."

I tensed and caught her hand in mine again. "No. Not like this—"

"Why?"

"Because I'm not an asshole!" I snapped, my chest heaving. "And I'm not degrading you for my pleasure. End of story."

Ari's green eyes widened as she peered up at me in silence. I couldn't tell whether my sudden outburst had left her angry or upset. Her expression was completely unreadable.

Once again, I'd made a mess of what was supposed to be a night of celebrating. I squeezed my eyes shut and let my head fall back against the couch, jumping when I felt her fingers on the button of my trousers. "Ari—"

"Hey," she said quietly. "Look at me."

Reluctantly, I lowered my gaze to hers, still wrestling with my guilt. "I don't want to be the guy I was before."

"You're not." Ari freed the top button and set to work on the other. "And I want to do this—"

"Why?" I was genuinely curious.

"Why?" she repeated, scrunching up her nose as if finding the question silly. "Because I want to."

Ari freed the last button and lowered my zipper, her voice soft. "Because there's nothing degrading about being on your knees in worship. Let me love you this way, Killian. Let me show you how proud I am to be yours."

I exhaled a ragged breath when her touch moved to the front of my boxer briefs, stroking me through the thin material.

"Please."

"Fuck," I groaned through gritted teeth, before nodding. "Okay."

How in the hell was I supposed to argue with that?

"Lean back." She reached into the waistband and freed my cock before continuing her slow and steady strokes. Her eyes glimmered with excitement like I was giving her something, not the other way around.

I couldn't look away from her. When she leaned in to press a gentle kiss to the tip, I had to dig my hands into the back of the couch.

Fuck.

No one had ever handled me with such care. With such love.

Ari slicked her tongue over the same area, before rocking back on her knees to pant, "I'm not going to ask if I'm doing it right. I know I am."

With that, she fisted the base of my cock, wrapping her lips around the crown with a low moan.

"Christ," I ground out, before pulling her off. "What do you mean, 'you know you are?' Were you practicing on someone?"

Her tongue swept over a bead of moisture on the tip. "Not exactly."

"Explain."

"Well..." She slowly worked her fist up and down my shaft. "Let's just say my trip was very educational. There were the sex shows in Amsterdam..."

I opened my mouth, prepared to ask something along the lines of, *what the fuck?* Only, Ari chose that moment to introduce my cock to the back of her throat, and I ended up spouting off a string of nonsense.

She leaned back with a smirk. "Oh, and Kanamara Matsuri in Kawasaki. It's an entire festival centered around a Japanese legend involving a steel phallus."

"What—" I shuddered and lost my train of thought when she took me all the way again. Her nose was pressed against the hairs on my lower abdomen. "Jesus Christ."

Ari lifted off me and casually ran the back of her hand across her mouth. "But, by far, the most intellectual experience we had was in Finland, during the Kutemajrvi Sex Festival. They even had professional lectures."

Struggling with the tattered remains of my impulse control, I held her shoulders back and begged, "Wait—just give me a second to think! Did Georgia know you were sneaking off to do this?"

"Whose idea do you think it was. She said Morgan and I needed to experience sex without the religious stipulations. Plus, we had the security team with us, so we were all safe. Any more questions, or can I continue?"

I didn't remember providing a response, but I must have because she took me in her mouth again, pinning my wrists against the cushion. It was a nonverbal nod as to who was in charge.

Her.

Completely. One hundred percent. Her.

A jolt of desperation shot down my spine when her throat contracted around my cock, pushing me closer to mindlessness.

Not yet.

Ari watched me through shimmering eyes, and my fists shook with the need to touch her, to wipe her tears. Instead, I kept my arms at my sides, finding beauty in the vulnerability.

Mine, not hers.

She was perfect. So damned perfect.

Her grip on my right wrist loosened and she slipped her hand under the jersey. I clenched my jaw, trying to prolong the inevitable, but knowing she was touching herself while I was deep in her mouth was too much.

"Baby," I groaned, fast approaching the point of no return and not wanting to finish in her mouth. "You gotta stop. I'm gonna come."

Instead of pulling back, she took me deeper until it felt as if fireworks might shoot out of my skull. I was convinced I was close to death because no blow job had ever felt like this. When her tongue caressed over the ridge of my cock, I was a goner. I pressed the base of my palms to my eyes and surrendered with a roar.

Ari swallowed every drop before collapsing against the ottoman with a harsh pant. I stood and she blinked up at me through heavy-lidded eyes, her pink lips still swollen.

"You are so beautiful." I lifted her lax body into my arms and carried her into our bedroom. I gently placed her on the bed before grabbing a bottled water from the fridge. When I returned, she was curled into a ball, fast asleep.

I set the water on the dresser and sank down onto the mattress, taking my time undoing her braided pigtails and running my fingers through to separate the waves.

This was the woman I was going to marry.

My throat tightened with emotion, and I shifted my jaw from

side to side until the urge to cry passed, before retrieving a small velvet box from the nightstand.

"What's that?" she asked, suddenly wide awake.

"Your surprise," I admitted gruffly, reaching for her left hand.

"And here I thought you were my surprise," Ari responded, holding still while I slipped the ring over her knuckle.

"Oh, I am, slugger," I chuckled. "But after that blow job, I figured I better make it official before someone else snatches you up."

"Turn on the light. Let me see." She blinked against the brightness when I switched on the lamp, before lifting it up for inspection.

My heart was lodged somewhere in my throat as I watched her admire the ring, wondering if perhaps I should have gone with a flashy diamond instead.

"Killian," she breathed, letting it catch the light. "It's gorgeous. What kind of stone is this?"

"Sea glass. It reminded me of you."

Ari held it against my face, her lips curving up. "It matches your eyes. Now, every time I look at it, I'll be reminded of you."

I wanted to tell her that I'd chosen it because of how we'd first met. Water represented life, and she'd not only saved mine but transformed it completely. The glass in her ring had been rolled and tumbled in the ocean for years, chaotically honed into something desirable. Something worthy.

Just like that boy she'd dragged from the lake.

My throat bobbed in a swallow. I couldn't make the words come out.

But she knew.

"I've been in churches all over the world, but yours—" She placed her left hand over my heart, her chin wobbling. "Yours is my favorite."

There was a peace in being seen, not for my talents, but for the man I strove to be. For her.

"Does this mean you're home to stay?" I brushed her hair back with my fingers, feeling that familiar tug of hope.

"I'm with you, wherever that may be," she whispered, repeating the same words I'd given her the night I let go.

She kissed me, and I savored every moment, every brush of her lips. This was the beginning of the rest of our lives. When our kisses turned frantic, Ari reached for my tie, loosening it before reaching for the buttons on my shirt.

I slid my hand up under her jersey, cupping and squeezing her breasts through the thin lace of her bra before casually asking, "Did you come earlier?"

"It wasn't enough. I need more." She curled her hands against my pecs and dropped a kiss to my sternum, slowly working her way up to my neck and jaw. "Please."

"What do you need?" My fingers dipped under the lace, drawing her nipples out.

Her warm breath fell against my throat as she stroked my cock back to life. "I need you to touch me."

I pulled Ari's hand from my shaft, before sliding off the bed. "Relax. It's my turn."

She rested on her elbows, shamelessly watching as I slipped the tie over my head and let my shirt fall to the floor. My need to touch her soon trumped any desire to get undressed. I left the trousers and briefs hanging from my hips.

My hands moved between her thighs, spreading her like she'd done for me on the couch. I tugged her lace panties to the side and stroked, only to stop at the feel of bare skin.

"Baby, where's your hair?"

Ari smirked. "I think it all went to your face."

"Yeah?" I tugged the panties down and tossed them aside, before playfully nipping the inside of her thigh with my teeth. "Let me see if I can put it back."

I curved two fingers inside her body while using the flat of my tongue to lap at her clit. She gasped and arched her back, forcing my fingers deeper. I took my time sucking and stretching her body, getting high off of every whimper, every groan.

"Killian—wait!" She babbled to the ceiling. "Please."

"What is it, slugger?" I asked, using the pad of my thumb while my fingers stroked her inner walls. "Like this?"

Ari's hips pushed forward in confirmation, using me to get where she needed. With a shattered cry, her body clenched around my fingers before she went completely limp.

"Babe," she panted, her chest rising and falling rapidly. "You can never shave that beard."

I grinned and stripped from the waist down, stopping to help Ari remove her jersey when she didn't move. With a giggle, she raised up just enough to unclasp her bra, exposing nipples that were already hardened into points.

"Do you want me inside you, baby?" I asked, fisting my cock with fingers drenched in her release.

"Please," she begged, looking up at me with drowsy eyes. "Make love to me."

"I hope you're comfortable because I've got eight months to make up for." I felt around in the nightstand and then muttered a curse.

"What?"

Frustration crept into my voice. "I don't have a condom."

Ari shrugged, displaying a hint of a grin. "And?"

"And... I want to make love to you." I pinched the bridge of my nose, cursing myself for not having a sixth sense about her coming home early.

Now, no one would be coming at all.

She sat up and placed a hand on my bicep. "So, make love to me without one."

"I've, uh—" I swallowed, feeling the undeniable need to put her mind at ease. "I just want you to know I've never been with anyone without one."

"Can I be your first?" she asked, pulling her lower lip between her teeth.

I nodded dumbly and positioned myself at her entrance, unable to resist taking a bite from her breasts, thrust up at me in offering.

"Please," she whispered, legs spread and red hair completely untamed. Wild. Mine.

Ari gasped when I entered her, and I lowered my head to capture her mouth. If I thought she felt good before, nothing came close to the feel of sinking into her body bare.

I angled her hips upward and thrust, completely filling her in one stroke. Her tight muscles clamped down, and I shuddered as the first waves of her orgasm broke.

She dug her fingernails into my shoulders with a cry, meeting me stroke for stroke as she rode it out. I wanted it to last, but the sensations of her spasming left me greedy and beyond any form of reasonable restraint.

I drove into her body twice more before pushing deep and flooding her body with my seed. When my arms gave out, I collapsed against her chest, fighting to catch my breath.

Ari stroked my hair, and I drifted off in her arms, our bodies still connected. She was my safe place, and I was hers.

We laid together like that for a long time, before she sleepily asked, "What do you think Bailey and Morgan are doing right now?"

After pressing a kiss to her throat, I rolled onto my side, bringing us face to face. "Well, he offered to drive her to Georgia's. But, if he's got a brain cell in his head, they're back at his place, doing this."

She laughed and snuggled against me. Our legs were tangled together, my hand draped across her hip. It was a nightly routine I'd missed fiercely when we apart. We fell into a comfortable silence again, not quite awake but not yet asleep.

"There's an expression in French, *tu me manques* which, when literally translated means, *you are missing from me*," she whispered.

"I like that," I said softly, turning the phrase over in my head. I'd felt Ari's absence like the loss of a limb or vital organ. She was the piece of me I hadn't known I needed, but one I couldn't live without.

"And I don't know that there's a more accurate description of how I've felt when we're apart. It's why I came home, Killian. Because you were missing from me."

EPILOGUE
ARIANA

"And he took her in his arms and kissed her under the sunlit sky, and he cared not that they stood high upon the walls in the sight of many."

-J.R.R. Tolkien, *The Return of the King*

"HEY, I thought I might find you here." Morgan settled on the beach beside me, watching the waves roll onto the shore.

I closed my notebook and turned to her with a welcoming smile. "Hey, are the guys back yet?"

We'd flown down to Florida a little over a week ago for the start of spring training. Killian and Bailey had rented a four-bedroom house just a short walk from the beach.

The third baseman had tried to play coy, insisting that he'd only invited Morgan along to keep me company during the day. However, it hadn't escaped my notice that her bed hadn't been slept in even once. For a lovable goofball, he was surprisingly tight-lipped when it came to his feelings.

Morgan dug her toes into the sand with a relaxed sigh. "They were just walking in when I left to come find you. Gosh, it's nice here, isn't it?"

The sunset had cast the almost cloudless sky in a brilliant blend of pinks, blues, and oranges that reflected on the water. Night after night, I made my way down to the beach to watch nature's show.

"It really is." I stood and stretched, before dusting the sand off my backside. "You ready to head back, or do you want to stay a little longer?"

Morgan tried and failed to hide a smirk. "We'd probably better get back before they break something." She waited until we'd taken a couple of steps, before gesturing to the notebook. "How's it coming along?"

The sand shifted beneath my bare feet, engaging the muscles in my legs and forcing them to work harder. "These songs just keep coming to me. Killian says it's a sign."

"Well, if the skeptic has become a believer, then it must be something big."

It was. And I had plans of tracking down a guitar in the next few days, so I could put them to music.

"What about you?" I asked. "Have you thought more about what you want to do?"

She shrugged. "I'm not sure. I'm still thinking about going back to school, maybe getting my degree in counseling. I just want to help people who might have gone through something like I did."

"Have you reached out to Ashlynn? She and Matt might have some recommendations for schools."

"I did. She's going to do some research and get back to me. For now, it's just nice having the freedom to consider it, you know?"

I did. In the two years and two months since Tristan's kingdom had fallen, Ashlynn and I had spoken on the phone almost daily. Our combined actions had not only destroyed a monster but saved the sisters who'd been sold as well. Some had fared better than others, but as we worked to piece our family back together, I couldn't help but remember a Bible verse we'd been taught growing up:

'So, I will restore to you the years that the swarming locust has eaten.'

The ocean breeze swept my hair across my eyes as we reached the driveway, bringing the raucous sounds of laughter with it.

We exchanged an amused look and slipped through the side gate around to the back of the house. Killian and Bailey had gotten their hands on a couple of inflatable flamingos. They were perched on them in the middle of the pool, using plastic bats as paddles. Or swords. I couldn't decide if they were attempting to paddleboard or joust.

"Tip over!" Bailey belted, the corner of his mouth quirked up.

"No," Killian tossed back with a breathtaking grin that never failed to leave me weak in the knees. "You tip over!"

I cupped my hands around my mouth and shouted, "Why don't you both tip over?"

Their heads jerked in our direction, smiles stretching from ear to ear. They were like children. Giant children who made me laugh until my sides hurt. I hoped that never went away.

"Ari, go get your suit on. I'll let you ride on mine."

Bailey chuckled and cocked his head to the side. "Yeah? Well, that seems like an unfair advantage, Mr. Reed. Morgan, hop on so we can beat 'em lawfully."

She pressed her lips together, her eyes gleaming with amusement as she crossed to the patio. "No, thank you. I don't have any desire to drown this evening."

"C'mon," Bailey pleaded.

Morgan paused and glanced back over her shoulder at him. "I was actually thinking of grabbing a quick shower to wash the sand off, but y'all have fun."

Bailey grabbed the flamingo by the neck and tipped himself into the water. "Shit, Killian. I almost had you there. Well, better luck next time, right? Morgan, wait up! You might need some help in those hard to reach areas!"

He hauled himself out of the pool and followed her inside, leaving us alone.

Finally.

I felt a little winded, but it was probably just due to my walk on the beach and not the nerves currently gnawing a hole in the pit of my stomach. I frowned at my trembling hands and willed them to obey.

We're fine. Nothing to worry about.

Killian raised a brow, looking almost mischievous. "You coming in, slugger? Water's warm."

My breath came faster, and I spun the engagement ring around my finger before nodding. "Sure, I'll sit and put my feet in."

I placed my notebook on the patio table and rolled up my leggings, mentally tweaking the song lyrics I'd written on the beach.

When Killian abandoned the inflatable flamingo to take a few laps, I made my way over to admire the view. His body glided through the water with ease, muscles rippling with each stroke.

His beauty, inside and out, left me suddenly fighting the urge to cry. If the dampness on my cheeks was any indicator, it was a battle I was clearly already losing.

Stupid hormones.

Finding a spot near the shallow end, I sat down and waited for him to resurface. A couple of seconds later, he swam over to join me. I slowly kicked my legs, letting the bubbles tickle my toes.

Killian reached for one of my feet, gently kneading along the arch. "Morgan said you were down by the beach. Did you write again today?" His gravelly voice pulled me from thoughts of songwriting and directed me toward the bedroom.

He was good at that.

Maybe a little too good.

"I did." I drew my lower lip between my teeth. "It's a little different, though."

"How so?" Killian might have been rubbing my feet, but I knew I had his full attention.

Something wet landed against my cheek as I leaned in to brush the drops of water from his lashes, and I realized I was doing it again.

I lifted my eyes to the darkening sky and blinked to clear my vision before softly admitting, "Well, it's a lullaby."

"A lullaby?"

I sensed he was smiling but didn't dare look. I'd never get my words out if I did. "Yeah, you know, songs for babies."

"Babies," he repeated, definitely grinning. "Well, that is different for you, slugger."

"Right?" I agreed, my face still tipped up to the sky.

Killian lowered my feet back into the water and moved between my legs, sending flutters throughout my lower belly. His hand lifted to my jaw, tucking several strands of windswept hair behind my ear before bringing my eyes down to meet his.

"That's better," he murmured, the corner of his mouth quirked up. "Now then, tell me more about these songs."

I took his free hand in mine. "Well, I just started writing it today. It just kinda came to me this morning. And now I don't know if I want to wait to do a big wedding after the season's over because this, um, song, it might be really big by then."

"Is this song—is it one you want to write?" Killian asked quietly. The pad of his thumb stroked along my cheek while his blue-gray eyes surveyed mine.

"Absolutely," I answered without an ounce of hesitation. "It just changes things a bit."

A smile tugged at his lips. "Alright, so what are you thinking, slugger?"

"We could elope." My voice cracked, and I cleared my throat. "I mean, just so we would have more time to focus on the song together. Do you understand what I'm trying to say?"

Killian ran his tongue over his teeth with a soft chuckle. "Yeah. Seems to me there'd be only one reason a girl like you would wanna elope with a guy like me. You're trying to lock me down before the ladies come knocking this season, aren't you?"

I let my head fall back with a dramatic groan. "Yep, that's it. Back off, ladies. Killian Reed, World Series champion, is mine."

This only made his smile grow wider, but he made a show of cocking his head to the side, as if deep in thought. "Well now, wait a second. There is another possibility. Since the night we got engaged, song, uh, prevention hasn't really been a priority for us, has it?"

I shook my head, trying to keep a straight face at his analogy. I could count on one hand the number of times we'd taken preventative measures in the almost four months we'd been engaged.

"What are you thinking right now?" I asked, feeling the familiar surge of heat moving up my throat.

Killian tugged me off the stone decking and into the water, drenching me from the waist down. Before I could form a protest, he was wrapping me up in arms. "The woman I love is having my baby. I'm fucking ecstatic! When did you find out? How far along are you? Do you feel okay? Do—"

"Babe," I giggled against his chest, tucking my body tighter around his. "One question at a time. I just found out this morning. I'm only a week late, so I can't be too far along. And I feel fine, just weepy at unexpected times. Otherwise, I'm perfect—"

"You are perfect, baby. So perfect," he murmured against my temple. "I'm going to take such good care of both of you—"

"You already do." With that, I tipped my face up to meet his mouth in a gentle kiss, relaxing into his touch. I knew with every fiber of my being that I was safe in his arms.

Happily-ever-after made for a sweet story, but real love wasn't perfect, and things didn't always go according to plan. We were born on the banks of Lake Karankawas, so it seemed only fitting that we'd be together in another body of water when the current sent our lives in a new direction.

My heart skipped when his hand moved down to cradle my flat stomach, already protective of the life we'd made together.

All those years ago, I saved his life, never imagining that one day, he'd save mine too.

When I pulled him from the water, I wasn't just looking into the eyes of another lost soul.

I was looking at the man who'd become my world.

The man who would give me the courage to fight back.

I'd fallen in love with his heart before I ever even knew his name. He was the melody in my head, the song I would never forget the lyrics to—as if some part of me knew it was always meant to be Killian.

When he was just a boy who needed saving, and I was a girl running.

I don't run anymore.

I'm finally free.

The end.

———

Need another fairy tale fix? Keep reading for a sneak peek of *Through The Woods*, book one of the Fairest series.

———

Want to be the first to know when my books go on sale?
Follow me on BookBub!

For new release alerts, follow me on Amazon!

AFTERWORD

"Now I know, that only love can truly save the world. So I stay, I fight, and I give, for the world I know can be."

-Diana Prince, *Wonder Woman*

DREAM CAST

Killian Reed- Kevin Kiermaier
Ariana James- Bryce Dallas Howard
Morgan James- Odette Annable
Conor Bailey- Bryce Harper
Georgia- June Squibb
Tsega Simons- Liya Kebede
Dean Simons- David Annable
Tristan James- Jay Haizlip
Brad Phillips- Eric Rutherford
Ashlynn James- Nina Dobrev
Matt- Aaron Taylor-Johnson

ACKNOWLEDGMENTS

This book would not have been what it is without the following people. It takes a village, y'all.

Beta Readers (Andrea, Lily, Jenni, Nicole, Alicia, Cecilia, Jazmyne, Jodi, Shannon, Lisa, and Karen) - You guys are the real MVPs! Thank you for your feedback and constructive criticism. You gave me clarity when I couldn't see the desert for the trees and I am forever grateful!

Dani- Thank you for keeping me sane and talking me off the ledge when I'm second-guessing my every life choice. You are the absolute best and I am so lucky to have you on my team.

Ellie- You are the rebel to my princess, the peanut butter to my jelly. Thank you for still speaking to me, even when the deadlines become guidelines.

Readers- Thank you for picking up this book. I wanted to give you a standalone, only to realize halfway through that I'd gotten used to writing series. So, enjoy this novel and its added "girth."

Laura- Bunny, you are the apple of my eye. Thank you for getting me out of my writing cave every now and then to socialize with real people. Best wishes!

Wendi- Thank you for being you. You are one of the strongest women I know, and I am honored to call you my friend.

Zach- Well, it's finished. Who thought we'd ever say that? It was a little touch and go there for a while. You're always there as my sounding board, my snack provider, and my coach. Thank you for loving me, especially in the moments when I'm on a deadline and forget to take care of myself. I love you pints and gallons.

ALSO BY SHANNON MYERS

From This Day Forward Duet

(David & Elizabeth's Story)

From This Day Forward

Forsaking All Others

Standalone Novels

(*Travis & Katya's Story*)

You Save Me

Operation Series

(*Dakota & Zane's Story*)

Operation Fit-ish

(*Kate and Nate's Story*)

Operation Annulment

Silent Phoenix MC Series

(*Grey & Celia's Story*)

Deserter (Book One)

Protector (Book Two)

(*Mike & Lauren's Story*)

Renegade (Book Three)

Traitor (Book Four)

(*Full Cast*)

Savior (Book Five)

Fairest Series (Can be read as standalones)

(Charm & Neve's Story)

Through The Woods

(Killian and Ari's Story)

Wait For It

Fictioned Series

(Hayden & Jake's Story)

Protagonized

ABOUT THE AUTHOR

Shannon is a born and raised Texan. She grew up inventing clever stories, usually to get herself out of trouble. Her mother was not amused. In junior high, she began writing fractured fairy tales from the villain's point of view and that was the moment she knew that she was going to use her powers for evil instead of good.

In 2003, she moved to Denver and met the love of her life. After some relentless stalking and a few well-timed sarcastic remarks, the man eventually gave in to her charms and wifed her so hard. They welcomed a son in 2007 that they named after their favorite Marvel superhero, Spiderman.

Sick of seeing beautiful mountains through their window every day, the three escaped back to the desolate landscape of the west Texas desert in 2009. She welcomed her second son not long after and soon realized that being surrounded by three men was nothing at all like she'd imagined in her fantasies.

After an unplanned surgery in 2014 and a long pity party, she decided to pen a novel about the worst thing that could happen to a person in order to cheer herself up. She's twisted like that. Thus, From This Day Forward was born and the rest, as they say, is history. Not only does Shannon enjoy stalking people, she also has a fondness for being stalked.

Find her online at: http://shannonshaemyers.com
Or in her fan group: https://www.facebook.com/
groups/630229377127363/

www.ingramcontent.com/pod-product-compliance
Lightning Source LLC
Chambersburg PA
CBHW060804030726
47503CB00002B/320